Brenda Grace de Jong

My Name is Elpee

~ A Trilogy ~

Book 1
Book 2
Book 3

My Name is Elpee – A Trilogy

Book 1: Cherry Castle by the Sea
Book 2: Return the Snail to the Earth
Book 3: Forsaken Paradise – The Road to Freedom

http://cherrycottagefi.com

Artwork © 2018 by Mike "Sport" Murphy
Graphic design © 2018 by Craig Kempf

ISBN: 978-0-9997506-5-0

TABLE OF CONTENTS

Book 1...7

Preface...15

Introduction...18

The Princess of Bedford Avenue...19

The Castle..21

Elpee, Princess of Cherry Castle by the Sea....................................24

The Other Princesses..26

The Gnomes...29

TV and Dinner...32

The Puppet Show...34

Butter...37

Leaves...42

And Rocks..44

danDay-leon to the Rescue..46

The Birthday Party...49

The Rocks Protest..52

The Dream..55

The Change Begins...57

J. Alpert VII...60

Planting the Seeds..63

The Road 'Home'..65

Banished...68

Devastation..70

The Prizes...74

The Shell..81

Into the Abyss..84

Anna...87

Amazing Grace...91

The Market...95

Eggs, Ham, and Butter...97

Will the Real Butter 99

Planning a Party...103

Having a Party..107

The Potteress..110

The Masks Must Go and Where do the Flowers Grow?................114

The Beach...118

Book 2..121
    Prologue..129
    Confusion Reigns Once Again...130
    Who Took The Letter???????...134
    Meanwhile, Back at the Cottage..139
    Leave the Dog Alone..141
    Pippy Comes and Tea Leaves..143
    "Say Elpee"...146
    Breakfast, Tea, and Bubbles..150
    The Second Coming of J. Alpert VII...154
    Elpee Loses More Than Her Mind...159
    Crazy Witchdoctors..164
    Running on the Beach...168
    Goodbye for Now...172
    Alone Again..174
    Cleaning and Communing...177
    Anna is Back in Town...179
    Powder Puffs Please..182
    My Name is Elpee...184
    An Unwanted Visitor..187
    Euterpe the Queen..190
    HELP!...193
    What, No Hot Dogs?...195
    Dinner and Dresses...197
    Simon Says...199
    The Last Breakfast..202
    Banished Again...206
    Eve of the Apocalypse...209
    The Dawn Breaks on a New Day...211
    High Noon..214
    HOME AGAIN..217
Book 3..223
    Prologue..231
    The New(est) Faraway Land..232
    Who's on First, What's on Second . . . ?..235
    Masks...238
    Preparations and Then Some...244

Just Like Old Times...247
Party Time...250
What to do Next..253
Tea Time at Cherry Cottage.....................................255
Inside..258
And Out...262
Memory Lane...266
Trouble Came for a Visit...269
Who Goes There . . . Under the Sink?.........................272
Reading the Letter...275
SHUT UP!...279
A Whole Lotta Crying Going On................................283
Lullaby and Goodnight...287
Called on the Carpet..290
Reality...292
The Gory Details...295
The World According to the Queen.............................299
In the Wake of the Tornado......................................303
PoliM'aladroit Gets Nosy...305
The Potion is Brewed..308
The Majestic Fern..311
Pray-Embrace?...314
The Letters . . . Number Two....................................317
Wednesday – The Day Before....................................321
Tea and Tissues...325
Feelings Aren't Fact . . . But Tea Leaves Are.................328
Pray and Embrace..331
October Three One...333
And Another Thing...335
Half Past Something..338
Arrested for Being Stupid...342
On the Launch Pad...344
From the Light – To the Dark – To the Light.................347
Up, Up, Up and Inside the Mountain..........................349
They Are Off to See the Wizard – Not..........................351
J. Alpert VII (?)...354
The Terms of Release..356

The Queen 'Rules'...358
Elpee Alone...360
The Trip Home...363
It Is Elpee's Turn..366
On the Dock..369
Elpee and Alpert – The Lessons...371
TTFN (Ta-ta for now)..374

Brenda Grace de Jong

My Name is Elpee
~ A Trilogy ~

Book 1

Cherry Castle by the Sea

This book, singly and as part of the series, is dedicated to the woman who almost half a century ago predicted its buried existence.

"Someday, you will write a book."

She saw and knew something I did not.
She believed in something I could not.
She pressed me to do something I would not.

And so, a lifetime later, I dedicate this book to my mother, Veronica (Pat) de Jong, for having spoken those few words to me when I was a child. With them, she planted a seed that managed to survive long enough for it to eventually produce a bud.

We are, at this moment, on the same page,
and Heaven and Earth are smiling.

Spinning, laughing, dancing to
Her favorite song
A little girl with nothing wrong
Is all alone
Eyes wide open
Always hoping for the sun
And she'll sing her song to anyone
That comes along
Fragile as a leaf in autumn
Just fallin' to the ground
Without a sound
Crooked little smile on her face
Tells a tale of grace
That's all her own . . .

Spinning, laughing, dancing to
Her favorite song
A little girl with nothing wrong
Is all alone

~ Lee Alexander

PREFACE

Magick was afoot when these words were set on paper, where together, they joined forces and conjured up this hauntingly enchanted tale. Although I own the circumstances, confusion, delusions, heartache, and freedom, which are at the core of this set of books, I cannot lay entire claim to having written the 100,000 plus words contained within them. This story very much invented itself, and I sense that I was merely the wordsmith used as the vehicle to do so.

I penned this whimsical and quirky trilogy not quite a decade ago; however, it has remained in two dusty binders and several fragmented flash drives since that time. It is only now that I find myself able to share the dark account of my coming of age. While the words were written by the adult, they are expressed through the eyes of the child.

Its inception coincided with the demise of my long-term marriage and the subsequent exchange of my half of everything we jointly owned for the cottage by the sea and its sizeable mortgage. Although not employed, I somehow knew I needed that house to anchor me, as I felt alone and adrift in a sea of unpredictable storms I was ill-equipped to handle. She sheltered me as I undertook the painful and seemingly bottomless process of confronting the ghosts that had owned and ruled my life for half a century.

While it may have been evident to nearly everyone else, I could not see the lost, fragile, and broken person they saw. Those close to me were concerned for my welfare and questioned my choices. They did not understand I had no choice—that I could not live one more day in a world I did neither create nor belong. Some supported me, others did not, but most doubted my rationality and ability to survive the road on which I was traveling, which included my obsessive need to put pen to paper and author this story.

I wrote the first two books between April and July 2009 when I had just begun attending college – an opportunity not afforded to me in my youth. During that time, I bore the weight of a full-time curriculum, worked odd jobs as much and as often as possible, and managed the cottage's upkeep and rental to help offset her expenses. I ignored the fact I was simultaneously burning several candles at both ends, as an unseen driving force gave me no alternative but to continue writing—what and why I did not know.

Thoughts were handwritten in notebooks, on napkins, and at times on my hand or arm. I would record these disjointed ideas and sentences during classes, in my car, but mostly late at night while lying in bed. I would fall asleep with pen and paper on my lap and wake the next morning to find words on the page that had not been there before I had dozed off the previous evening. Initially, this phenomenon was unnerving to me, but I grew to look forward to reading the verses I had subliminally scripted while sleeping.

I admittedly do not fully comprehend it myself, nor do I grasp the broad range of symbolic allegory used as the means to unearth and resolve the issues necessary to move forward with this story and my life. I am entirely unaware of why words and phrases would enter my mind and instruct me to inscribe them in the back of the still-unwritten book for later use, but I complied, and they became integral components of this anthology.

The third book was written several years later when I had obtained my degrees, was established in a career that fed me in all ways, and had at last exorcised most of my demons. It tells a much different story than the first two books, and the characters express themselves in tones quite unlike the ones spoken in the preceding volumes. It is where I, like the main character, had visited the past, viewed it for what it was – and was not – and acquired the ability to choose personal realities and futures – what and wherever they may be. We also discovered that if our current reality no longer served us, we were free to craft new ones.

The writing of this accounting was relatively easy because, as stated earlier, it was surreally scripted for me. However, reviewing and publishing the books caused me great angst. I hesitated to release the story and the books, which had been a deep-rooted and central part of me seemingly forever. Conversely, I also knew that they could not live inside me any longer and needed to find another home.

Something, perhaps the same force that gave me the ideas and words, nudged me one day and provided me with the awareness that in their publishing I would be discharging that which no longer served me while also honoring the circumstances that made this all happen. I inwardly recognized that in doing so, I would find genuine freedom.

Introduction

"Hello, and thank you for being here. I would like to introduce myself and invite you to accompany me on my deliciously deep and whimsical journey. Hmmm, is it even possible to be delicious, deep, and whimsical all at the same time? In any event, it is a magickal trip that will transport us to both times and places as yet unknown, to people and not-people still unmet, and to adventures unlived and lessons unlearned.

"For a multitude of reasons, you see, I had to leave the place in which I began my life – the most obvious one being that I am a princess and I needed a more 'princessly' place in which to live. So, off I went in search of the perfect land in which to reside, and indeed I did find that princessdom . . . Until that is, the day it was no longer perfectly perfect. No bother! Off again I would go to search out another one!

"Together, if you choose to, we can explore the deep crevasses that exist within our minds and the matters that lurk hidden inside those crevasses. Always and perfectly hidden. Oh, never mind! Explore or not, we shall journey, here and there, far and near, outside or inside (the crevasses) – your choice – until we find that special station where we can park our caboose and travel no more. We will have found the terminal in which our carriage is new and bright, with clean and shiny windows, and where all the passengers are safe.

"Now, in search we go! Let us begin with the castle.

"Oh, by the way, My Name is Elpee . . ."

The Princess of Bedford Avenue

Once upon a time, a princess was delivered to a distant land called Brooklyn, New York. Out of the baby princess sprouted a girl who had milky-white skin, emerald-green eyes, big, fat, chubby cheeks, and long, brown braids. Despite her adorable nature and keen intellect, she was doomed to a life intolerably dreadful in its landscape. Having no power to change that, which encircled her; she would eventually split by altering her own world – the one within her mind.

As she grew older, her mostly absent father escorted her daily through the hoodlum streets to a school in which the wardens ridiculed, punished, and instilled the fear of God in the children under their care. When the school day ended, she would return home to the fortress on Bedford Avenue and remain there until the next morning when this desolate and ritualistic practice repeated itself as it did five times a week for what she suspected would last an eternity.

The adults within warned her not to venture outside alone, as there were monsters out there. Every day of this bleak existence, the little princess would peer out the gray and cloudy windows of her bedroom and wonder on which side of the glass the danger lived.

The **Little Princess**, or Elpee as she will be referred to from this sentence on, lived in a realm that existed only to her. It was a land that was more suited to a princess than the one in which the grown-ups lived. Their world was built on a foundation of fear – at home, at school, and in the streets. It was a place where the walls were painted with threats and the floors tiled with dread. Ghosts lived in the attic while a fire roared in the cellar. Elpee accepted this as the world in which the others lived, but it was not a place in which she chose to reside unremittingly.

At some point in her very early life, Elpee left their world and entered a dimension of her personal design; a place she could temporarily visit whenever she chose to. She would come and go, back and forth between these two lands for some time until one day Elpee concluded that it did not fit someone of her stature – a princess – to live in Brooklyn any longer. And so, she permanently departed the bonds of home and hood, moved to her princess palace of pink petals and bluebonnets, and never traveled between the two worlds again. She deserved a home crafted by faeries and angels where all children were wanted, loved, and always felt safe.

And so it was!

THE CASTLE

Elpee's castle was uniquely her; it was all she was and all she loved. It was whimsical yet serene, and it created a much-needed sense of safety and security for the princess. Although its location was by the sea, patches of trees and plantings surrounded her home. Inside her side garden was a meandering boardwalk, which led to the rear, where a smaller guest cottage stood. Hostas, ferns, hydrangeas, and potted impatiens bordered the wooden walkway, while birdbaths and feeders dappled the lush greenery of the landscape on all sides of the castle. A white picket fence outlined the perimeter of the yard and graced the entry to the castle grounds. Originally, Sweet Williams and catmint overflowed the window boxes that rested beneath each of the lower level's front windows.

Most of the walls inside Elpee's new home were adorned with plaques or framed artwork inscribed with sayings, adages, and affirmations. Some were silly and others profound, but it was undeniable Elpee needed them all.

The front porch of the castle was brimming with sunshine, which cast dancing designs on its cloud-white walls. One half of the room housed rocking chairs that looked out onto the front and side yards. The other side of the porch contained a small eating area, which allowed Elpee to view the beautiful gardens as she dined. Weather permitting, she would eat all her meals there, and it was unquestionably her favorite place to entertain guests when serving a light menu.

Greeting visitors as they entered the central part of the dwelling was the living room with its white brick fireplace and magickal mirror that hung above the mantle. Nothing ever reflected poorly from the silvered glass, for if it shed an ill reflection, the mirror might have lost its place of honor and been banished to a more unremarkable location in the house. A massive brick chimney backed the fireplace and rose through all the stories of the castle before exiting the middle of its striking green gabled roof. On the far left side of the living room, an oaken staircase led to the upper floors. Directly across from it, under and around a five-window bay, was built a deeply cushioned bench. Beyond the living room lay the dining room with two built-in cupboards, each having drawers that held the traditional household items of flatware, napkins, tablecloths, and placemats. The top portion of these cabinets stored Elpee's best china, glassware, and silver, as well as the most magnificent teacups in the land. Within the bottom section, she hid her prized collection of games, puzzles, and candles, along with a few coloring books, and a box of crayons for an emergency.

Adjacent to the dining room was the kitchen. Its floor was tiled in a black and white ceramic checkerboard pattern on which Elpee could play hopscotch, tiddlywinks, or jacks. This room included an abundance of cabinetry and a cupboard dedicated solely to the storage of snacks, soda, and all varieties of goodies. Over the table hung a sign whose message held only two words – 'Say Grace'.

The most unique and amusing parts of the downstairs level of the castle were the bathroom and the shower, both of which were located outside. Anyone desiring to use these facilities needed to leave the house proper and turn right onto the deck until they were stationed directly beneath the ancient holly tree which loomed over these two separate rooms. These al fresco accommodations allowed Elpee to remain outside all day if she desired to, without having to enter the castle.

The solid wooden staircase in the living room gave access to the bedrooms located on the second level. After ascending fifty-three steps to a landing, another magickal mirror hung on the wall above an ornate antique table. On its marble top sat an ever-present vase of fresh flowers and on the floor beside it stood a large, potted fern. Following the landing was a turn to the right and an additional twenty-seven-step climb to a hallway at the end of which lay the guest bedrooms.

The first room on the left was Elpee's bedroom, which included among other stately pieces of furniture a mahogany four-poster bed festooned in a peach chenille bedspread. Atop the coverlet and strewn about the bed were more than several books and the princess's collection of stuffed toy animals.

The guest rooms were purposely named for their settings and characters. At the end of the hallway on the south side of the house was the 'Rose Room'. It was in this room that the afternoon's brightest sun shone through the windows from which the fragrance of roses entered and wafted throughout the entire second floor. The princess's most out-standing collection of hats, garlanded with rosettes in all shades of pink and yellow, decorated the walls.

The 'Green Room' was precisely that – green. With its northern expo-sure, dark wooden furniture, and exclusively green decor, it presented a denser mood than that of the other rooms.

Inside the pink, white, and blue 'Children's Room' were two built-in captain's beds designed specifically for children to sleep and jump on. These beds rested on drawers that served as a foundation while providing plenty of storage space for the wee ones' toys.

The last room on this level of the house revealed the most striking bathroom ever created. It, like the downstairs front porch, was starkly white in its appearance, and in the middle of the oversized room was an enormous, white cast-iron soaking bathtub that sat atop silvered claw feet. Carved within the room's solid walls were several double-hung windows clad in white shutters on their lower halves and sheer curtains of various-sized polka dots on the upper halves. The pastel-shaded polka dots and several aquamarine mermaid and seahorse decorations were the only con-trast to the room's severe pallor.

Under the eaves of the roof and the staircases were great hiding places. There were a significant number of miniature doors whose access was lim-ited by a person's size and dexterity.

There were thirty-six windows in total, and they all were ornamented with either polka dots, lace, or tartan curtains. They looked out upon green meadows with countless wildflowers where Elpee could run barefoot at any time because she did not need permission from anyone nor did she require accompaniment.

Her world was one of laughter and games, of hugs and happiness, of light and warmth, but most of all it was a world in which no fear existed and where security and freedom prevailed. This dwelling was her home, and it was perfect just as its distinctive monikers were – 'Cherry Castle' for the main dwelling and the 'Cherry Pit' for the small guest cottage.

ELPEE,
PRINCESS OF
CHERRY CASTLE BY THE SEA

When Elpee first arrived at Cherry Castle by the Sea, beautifying the castle was the primary focus, and so she was busy designing and fixing up the house and the gardens to her perfect liking. These tasks took longer than she had expected they would, leaving little time for the newly crowned princess to concentrate on her appearance. Since there was no measure of time in her land, she was unaware of actually how long she took to reach a satisfactory state of castledom before turning the attention to herself and how she presented.

At last, she gazed into the mirror that hung in her bedroom to evaluate what, if anything, needed to be altered about her appearance. Elpee jumped back in surprise, for although she did not see a ghastly image staring back at her, neither did she see a princess. Thinking the mirror was weeping its silver and therefore not portraying an accurate view of her, Elpee descended the twenty-seven steps to the mirror on the landing, which sadly told the same tale. Entirely befuddled, the princess, who appeared to be in grave need of a makeover, went down the next fifty-three steps and into the living room to gaze into the mirror of all mirrors, which hung above the fireplace. With all the regality she could muster up, Elpee approached the looking glass and confidently looked into it. The reflection she espied was identical to the two she had previously been shown. As much as the mirror on the wall wanted to change the image it presented to the princess, it could not. It began to violently quake and shake on the wall, anticipating that it would immediately be banished to some unknown but distant destination – or worse. Elpee, seeing the poor thing in such a state of distress, walked closer to it and uttered only one word.

"Thanks," she said.

Hanging below the bottom frame of the mirror was a sign that bore the inscription, 'Always Truthful'. Elpee knew it had vowed to be honest, and she had no reason to disbelieve its integrity or loyalty.

What Elpee had seen was the reflection of a very dull, tired, and ordinary child. Nothing at all like a princess. She realized that no one would take her seriously if she did not immediately, if not sooner, doll herself up. She contemplated having long braids like princesses of old, but it reminded her too much of what she looked like in that other world – the world of the grown-ups. Instead, Elpee dyed her hair emerald green, and when she was satisfied it was the exact color of leprechauns, she then painted streaks of sapphire blue onto it.

"No bother about those stupid old braids anyway," she thought aloud. "I shall have a crown in their stead."

Elpee closed her eyes tightly and fashioned up a diamond and ruby tiara, which dramatically complemented her new hair colors and was much more suitable for a girl who ruled her own empire.

With her hair and its adornments in order, Elpee shifted her attention to her wardrobe. She went into her bedroom and opened the wee door to her closet that was located under an eave in the roof. Inside were brand new sundresses with big, brilliant blossoms painted on them, cotton overalls, tie-dyed shirts, and some linen jackets. There were knit sweaters and scarves in every imaginable color and design, raincoats and hats with matching umbrellas, and pajamas that were warm, fuzzy, and seersucker. Whatever Elpee's ensemble of the day was, it did not include shoes. Absolutely no shoes, no matter what, never – ever – ever. Ever!

Now that the castle was in perfect order and Elpee was a picture-perfect princess, it was time to have an excellent meeting with some of the other royalty in the surrounding dominions. Elpee decided she would first take a rest in the hammock outside before framing an invitation for her much-desired and long-awaited meeting of the princesses.

THE OTHER PRINCESSES

The Honour of Your Presence is Requested
For High Tea at High Noon
On the First Blue Moon of the Next Month
Of the Present Year
In Which You Receive this Invitation
By the Current Princess of
Cherry Castle by the Sea
"Elpee"

Having fashioned and dispatched the invitations, Elpee had nothing else to do but excitedly wait for the appointed day. Although she amused herself well enough with a gallery of books, music, and television, she wished to become acquainted and make friends with other people of her royal stature. She was deliriously eager for this to take place, and she frequently reminded herself that the day would be here before she knew it.

And so it was!

As the princesses arrived one by one, Elpee felt somewhat puzzled because she had assumed that all princesses were like her, but these people were not, and they varied considerably from each other as well. The first to arrive was danDay-leon of Teacup Manor, who landed in a helicopter on the lawn across the street from Cherry Castle. Elpee's first impression of this princess was that she seemed to be a bit peculiar and walked rather oddly, as if weighed down by her oversized coat and suitcase. After relieving danDay-leon of her frock and bag, Elpee realized that she was indeed weighed down because her satchel held a collection of teacups and teapots. The interior of the princess's coat had numerous pockets stitched into it where she had packed a plethora of teas and tea leaves. Elpee found The Princess of Teacup Manor to be warm, friendly, and maternal; however, she was not at all regal as Elpee had expected a princess to be. Although surprised by her plain peculiarities, Elpee immediately sensed danDay-leon's caring and gentle nature. She hoped that they would become friends and call on each other regularly.

Shortly after Elpee and danDay-leon settled in, a sports car came screeching up to the castle and out stepped the next princess. It was Hortense of Grouse Hollow. She donned dark shades, a hooded sweatshirt, and green and black skull sneakers with no shoelaces. She appeared slightly dark and punkish, but Elpee soon recognized that Hortense was generous and much tamer than she would have people believe. As a welcome gift for Elpee, Hortense brought with her a number of plant specimens, which she directly went into the side garden to plant, flat-leaving the other two princesses.

Nice, but another cuckoo, thought Elpee about the Princess of Grouse Hollow.

As Hortense tilled the garden and dug the holes for the plants, up rode PoliM'aladroit of ShinyShores. She was traveling on a multi-speed bicycle with her full head of unbound, dark hair whooshing behind her. With her was a dog-like pet, a scruffy little creature not known to man but loved by all. As she attempted to dismount, she stumbled and landed bottom first on the ground. Out of her mouth in a very subdued voice came the most eloquent cacophony of swearwords Elpee had ever heard. When she was finished with the diatribe, PoliM'aladroit rose, sauntered over to Elpee, and most politely introduced herself. Sans the minor tirade, Elpee found her to be the most princessly of them all, but still quite odd.

Sauntering up the same road PoliM'aladroit had taken just moments earlier came Euterpe, the outlandish self-proclaimed *Queen*. Euterpe was a poetry-spouting, pink-haired princess who elevated herself to the title of *Queen* because she wanted to. It did not seem to Elpee that this *Queen* could speak properly at all without the use of rhyme or the adoption of iambic pentameter. Euterpe, with her flowing clothes and abundance of jewelry, did, however, appear to be what Elpee believed royalty should look like. Unfortunately, despite these trappings, she like the others, was a bit off her rocker.

No matter what Elpee's first impressions of these women were, she was determined that they would become her friends for the rest of time. They would each teach her things about life and friendship, and she hoped that they would help her to forget what her life was like before she met them. She never wanted to imagine what it would be like to be without them and alone again.

THE GNOMES

One morning Elpee got up early – around eleven o'clock – and munched on a jelly donut rolled in cinnamon sugar while she contemplated what she felt like doing that day. She decided she wanted to get her hands dirty and so she would leave the tiara at home, don some old clothes, and plant a garden. With one more jelly donut in her belly, Elpee ventured outside to begin her self-appointed task. After much walking and searching, and searching and walking, she found the perfect location for her new garden. The ground was pleasant and flat and received just the right amount of sunlight to keep the flowers and vegetables happy and help them grow. She began by clearing out the extra four-leaf clovers that interfered with her plan.

"One can definitely have too many of these," she muttered to herself as she tossed the little green flora into the pail that sat on the ground beside her.

With only a few minutes of clearing done, Elpee became distracted by a cluster of dragonflies floating about on the nearby meadow flowers. She hopped on the old green bicycle she'd brought with her from the other world and peddled over to watch them dance in the sunbeams. How she admired their grace, for even though Elpee was royalty, she was a bit heavy-footed and tended to make her presence known, unlike these elongated butterflies that glided effortlessly through the Universe. Watching their dancing to the serenade of the bees made the princess extraordinarily sleepy, and so she lay down on the meadow and promptly fell asleep under the early afternoon sun.

Sometime later Elpee was awakened by the clamor of laughter and singing. She hopped on the green hornet of a bike and sped off in search of the source of the gaiety. What she found amazed even her. Within the confines of the patch she had begun clearing for her garden was an army of gnomes digging, planting, and throwing dirt at each other. They romped, and they stomped, and had the best time she had ever seen people, or rather gnomes, have. Off in the distance, Elpee spotted Hortense of Grouse Hollow clearing more brush and ordering the slackers to shake a leg. They must have heeded her, because at the end of the day, despite all their frolicking, the little people had created the most beautiful garden in the entire world. There were flowers representing every color of the rainbow along with a border of rocks complete with polka dots and cherries painted in a myriad of shades. Elpee introduced herself to the gnomes and thanked them for all their hard work and the beautiful flowers and vegetables that their labors had produced. She turned to thank Hortense but found that she had again vanished, as was her custom. Hortense's ability to slip in and out of places unnoticed was incomparable and appeared somewhat supernatural.

With all their work and play completed, one by one, the gnomes began to reintroduce themselves to Elpee. The tired and thirsty tree people invited Elpee to retire into their village located under the vegetation. Although she was too tall to fit through their passageway, Elpee used her royal powers and voila, in she went. The rooms were painted orange and purple, and the mushrooms that were growing out of the floor served as their tables and chairs. Bowls of nuts and berries sat on every available flat surface. The gnomes boiled water for tea by using a pot that they hoisted up to the sun. It was attached to their dwellings by a string which allowed the gnomes to effortlessly retrieve it once it was sufficiently heated. The hosts brewed tea that was made from local herbs to which they added several pounds of sugar before serving it in their most outstanding acorn cups to their new best friend, Princess Elpee. Before drinking the tea, they each said a blessing for all they had, and especially for each other.

As the day grew shorter and the tea was drunk, Elpee thanked everyone for the refreshments, their hospitality, and for all their help. She promised she would visit again and invited them to come back to the garden whenever they wanted. The little princess became even littler, squeezed out the door hidden within the tree, and returned to her above-ground dwelling. She was so grateful to have met the gnomes and for the incredible job they had done in engineering her garden. They were a delightfully funny crew both in looks and in attitude, and she was sorry she had not met them sooner.

Suddenly she asked herself aloud, "Why haven't I met them sooner?"

No answer was forthcoming.

"Why? Why didn't they come out of their village and introduce themselves earlier?" she continued asking of herself.

No matter how long or hard she pondered those questions, she could not figure out any reasons. Lacking an answer and too tired to think any longer, she mumbled, "No bother!" and continued on her way home.

TV and Dinner

Weary from all the excitement, Elpee spread a blanket on the meadow close to the giant cypress trees that held her swing and rested there for a while before going back to the castle. Her now life was joyful, and she seldom reflected on her previous life.

The sun was low in the sky, and Elpee wanted to sit and ponder all that she had to be grateful for, but unfortunately, the afternoon was growing to a close and evening was rapidly approaching. When the air became overly moist and she began to feel a chill, Elpee picked up her blanket and headed the short distance home.

Once inside her castle, she turned on the music machine and listened to some heavy metal while preparing her dinner, which consisted of a bologna sandwich on white bread, a handful of cheese doodles, and a root beer soda. She decided that head-banging music, although good for inspiring and preparing a meal, was not especially conducive to eating or digesting it, and so Elpee switched to some Celtic strings to serenade herself while she dined.

The princess said grace, began eating her meal, and when done, she retired to the living room to enjoy her dessert of another jelly donut and raspberry iced tea. Although a new magazine arrived earlier in the day, Elpee decided instead to snuggle up on the sofa with a very broken-in copy of her favorite book, *The Canterbury Tales*, while enjoying dessert.

How she loved her books and longed for them to have a room of their own dedicated just to them. Of course, she could make that a reality if she genuinely wished it to be, but that was not necessarily the truth. She wanted her books around her rather than having them tucked away and hidden from view as if they weren't alive, which of course they were. The cottage, or more precisely the castle, was getting a little messy and cluttered with the overabundance of them, but no bother to Elpee because the elves would be there as always on Wednesday to tidy up.

"Oh my goodness," declared Elpee as she gently put the book down next to her.

It was time for *Lost in Space* – the best show in the entire world. She thought, were she not a princess, she might like to be Penny Robinson, but not Dr. Smith. They all wore fabulous clothes and had so many accessories, but Elpee reminded herself that she too owned beautiful gowns and sundresses, and a more than adequate amount of baubles.

The Princess of Cherry Castle decided that during the commercial she would get herself a bowl of ice cream to eat while she watched the remainder of the program. Oh no, she remembered there were no commercials in this one-girl monarchy, but then Elpee also realized that she had no ice cream before remembering that she didn't like the sweet treat even if she did have it. Relieved, she just sat back down and continued enjoying her favorite show. How fantastic and perfect her world was, and wasn't she the luckiest princess in all of the worlds?

THE PUPPET SHOW

Finally, with the episode over, it was time for Elpee's bubble bath and puppet show. The giant bathtub was filled with suds the size of apples and the color of pearls; its contents emitted the musky fragrances of frankincense and clove. Montovani string orchestra music played in the background as Elpee entered the cast iron water cave.

"Lights! Camera! Action! And here once again by popular command are Clancy and Puggo, those amazingly talented kewpie dolls," announced MC LP.

Lifting both her hands out of the foamy water, Elpee began the dialogue with the quiet and meek, right-handed Clancy, followed by the quick-tongued, left-handed Puggo.

"Hi, Clancy."

"Hi, to you, Puggo."

"Isn't it a beautiful night, Clancy?"

"I don't know, Puggo, there are no stars out, and the moon is hidden. I feel kinda scared."

"Oh, Clancy, don't be such a gop. There's nothing to feel afraid of."

"I can't help it, Puggo."

"Yes, you can."

"No, I can't!"

"Well, try."

"I am!"

"No, you're nah-aht."

"Yes, I am, so shut up, Puggo!"

"I don't have to. You're not the boss of me, scaredy pants Clanceeeee."

"SHUT UP!"

"I hate when you get all goppy."

"SHUT UP AGAIN!"

"See ya layta, pah-tay-ta, wah, wah, baby, baby stick your head in gravy. Bye-bye goppy head."

Wow, thought Elpee, her one-girl puppet shows were getting very sophisticated and so much fun too. Well, at least to her they were.

As was her custom after withdrawing from the bath and drying herself off, Elpee powder- puffed her body with gardenia-scented talc until she sneezed precisely three times. That was always her indicator she had applied just the correct amount of talcum powder without having overdone it. After slipping into her pajamas, Elpee grabbed a handful of chocolates and retired to her bed with a stack of comic books.

Her bedroom, also painted snow-white, had windows dominating two of the walls while a never-used pair of slippers hung on yet another of them. The ceiling was emblazoned with fire-engine-red paint and fluorescent stars that shone when lying directly under them in the dark of night. The windows looked out onto the rolling hills that adjoined the large body of water that lay just to the south.

There was hardly enough room on the peach bedspread for Elpee to place the comic books, as it was barely visible beneath all the stuffed toy animals and books that were already present. Somewhere below those items, Elpee slept on an eiderdown-filled mattress with pillows and a comforter made from the same materials. Although Elpee was comfortable everywhere in this, her mind-made castle, her bedroom was by far her most favorite room to relax and reflect in. It was a fantasy place to her, if that were possible. It was a dream within a dream.

Oddly, though, there were times when it seemed that this room was bizarrely summoning her and inviting her in. Because she did not create this specific atmosphere, she could not understand it, nor could she begin to explain to herself why there was what seemed to be a request being made of her. Often, the level of the appeal rose to that of a command ordering her to do something that needed to be done. Those occurrences reminded Elpee of the many tales written by the great author, Edgar Allan Poe in which he detailed some of the same unexplainable events.

At times, she could hear the voice of what she thought of as the 'dark one' and referred to as It. It produced in her an unexplainable mixture of heaviness and discomfort. Elpee got so angry when It came to visit, which fortunately was not so often that it completely ruined the warmth and light of her beloved room. She was baffled as to whom the voice belonged and why its calling was always generated only from within this place, calling her inside it. But for tonight, it was no bother!

She soon fell asleep without ever reading a page.

"To sleep, perchance to dream," was Elpee's credo, or at least one of them, borrowed from The Bard of Avon.

And so she did!

She dreamt of cartoons, comic books, and funny movies.

BUTTER

Before Elpee knew it, the rooster was crowing, the sun was up, and she was hungry. Because several large trees canopied her bedroom, it was always slightly dark and chilly in the morning when she woke. Her routine was to take her clothing with her downstairs where she would then turn on the oven to heat up the kitchen and get dressed while standing in front of it. This morning she chose to wear her red madras shirt with a pair of faded blue dungarees, while suffering the the cold of the tiles beneath her feet.

When she and the kitchen were toasty enough, she sat down in a chair and looked out the window while she ate her breakfast of tomato soup. As the warm soup filled her belly, she contemplated what she had to do that day. Nothing. Perfect! She thought of embroidering a heart on her pink pocketbook or perhaps a skunk on her green coveralls.

"Too many choices," she said aloud, and with that declaration, Elpee decided to go for a walk in the woods.

While walking through the thickets and singing one of her favorite tunes, Elpee found a dog quietly and calmly sitting in a hole. It had a blue satin bow tied around its neck to which a packet was attached. As Elpee approached, the animal smiled up at her, ripped the item off its neck, and handed it to the stunned princess. Smiling back at the dog, Elpee took the dispatch, opened it, and read it.

High Princess! My name is Butter, and I am lost. Please take me home, so I don't have to stay here in this hole for the rest of my life and maybe for all eternity too. That is until there is nothing more than a pile of bones and a mound of fur left here for others to find after I am gone, (whimper, whimper)

Please and thank you,

Butter!

As she was reading this pitiful plea, Elpee wondered where this cute little creature lived and how she could return it to its home when she noticed something else was written at the bottom left-hand corner of the note.

over please,

My home is:

Cherry Castle by the Sea
I think you know the way (smile)

Elpee was confused yet also very excited to have the pet she never had, but how did this happen, she wondered? Oh no bother, she had a new friend. The name 'Butter', however, would have to go, of that she was sure.

She lifted the little black dog out of the hole and together they walked side by side to its new home. As they approached the castle, the dog, although not straying too far ahead of Elpee, took the lead and entered the house. It immediately took up residence in the kitchen by sitting sentinel at the refrigerator while moaning from pangs of hunger until its new owner deciphered the message and complied with its wishes for nourishment.

"Oh," said Elpee to herself, "I wonder if it would like . . ."

But before she could complete the sentence, the animal was nodding its head vigorously in an affirming manner.

"Steak," Elpee finished her sentence in an attempt to ignore what had just happened.

Because there had never been a pet at the castle, the princess found it necessary to go over to one of the built-in cupboards and extract two china bowls in which to give the dog food and water. Unsure of how much to feed the animal, Elpee cut more steak than she thought was prudent for a dog its size, filled the bowl, and placed it down on the black-and-white checkerboard floor alongside a bowl of water. In what seemed to be a microsecond, the food was gone – entirely devoured by the new addition.

When Elpee and the dog went outside for a walk, she found out that it was a 'he' when along the way he began to relieve himself on the trunk of a tree. He faithfully stayed right next to his new mistress the entire walk while matching her paw for foot. Oh, the princess felt so loved by this little black dog who adopted her and her home as his own.

"Sit, Scamp," Elpee commanded in an attempt to see how smart her new charge was.

His response to her command was to leave her side, turn around, and give his butt to her.

"How rude, you fresh little dog," replied Elpee, at which the dog approached her again and began licking her leg.

"Oh, you do love me," she said as she bent down to give him a hug, "and I love you too."

They returned to the castle in the same manner in which they left it – side by side.

Just as she felt a deep attachment to the princesses, Elpee could not imagine living life without this little creature in it. They went everywhere together, especially the kitchen, which was apparently the dog's favorite room in the entire castle. It seemed that no matter what or how much Elpee fed the little guy, he was always begging and waiting for more. She even sent a message to PoliM'aladroit seeking advice on this matter, as the Princess of ShinyShores had a little dog-like creature of her own. While waiting for a response, Elpee maintained the feeding schedule of five or sixteen times a day. It varied.

When finally the answer Elpee was waiting for arrived, it puzzled her and left her with no firmer grip on what to do than she had before. The note simply read:

Why don't you ask him?

PoliM'aladroit

"Okay, Rascal, let's go for a walk while I ponder the meaning of PoliM'aladroit's note," Elpee said, believing it had to have some profound inner message that was just not obvious to her yet.

"Rascal," she cried out again, but the little dog did not come.

The search began upstairs and downstairs and inside and outside, all the while Elpee yelling his name. Finally, she found him in their bedroom, and when she exclaimed, "There you are, Rascal," the dog responded by turning around and again showing Elpee his rear end. Exasperated at his incessant acts of indiscriminate defiance, the princess did what she thought was best. She turned around, gave him her butt, and walked out of the room.

They carried on like this for many days, or weeks, or whatever amount of time, with the animal camping out in front of the refrigerator howling for food or having a power struggle in which Elpee was never the victor. Conversely, when they were not at odds with one another; they were inseparable and repeatedly displayed their affection by the dog lovingly licking random parts of her body and Elpee scooping the little pooch up to cuddle him. The final showdown came on a sunny afternoon when they were playing ball together.

As Elpee threw the ball, she yelled to her furry companion, "Get it, Shadow," to which the dog stopped in his tracks, looked into Elpee's eyes, turned around, and showed her his behind. They saw no more of each other for the rest of the day, which pleased Elpee, for as much as she loved him, she was exhausted from continuously feeding him and tired of having to look at his derriere.

When the princess went upstairs to retire for the night, she heard the dog crying. She went from room to room looking for the location of the weeping until she found him in the big bathtub. Alarmed, she went right over to him and tried to coax him out of the tub, but he would not move no matter what she did. She pleaded, threatened, and bribed, but the dog would not budge. Then, without cause or warning, a horrendous odor permeated the bathroom, causing both Elpee and the dog to gasp for air. Quickly, she realized that the stench was coming from him, and she rapidly turned on the water to bathe the stinky mutt. With water and shampoo in hand, Elpee jumped into the washing process. She lathered him up and began washing, but this chore, like everything else concerning her little friend, seemed out of proportion to reality in that it was much harder than she would have thought it to be. Tired of scrubbing, she began to rinse the suds off the pooch. As the water washed away the shampoo, it also removed his color and added some fifty pounds to her little black dog. Standing there sopping wet in the bathtub was a seventy-pound, butter-yellow dog.

"I don't get it, but I get it," Elpee said through her laughter as she entered the tub.

"I am not sure how the shampoo made you grow and turned you yellow, but now I understand the reasons why you are constantly hungry and always get so angry with me for trying to change your name."

As he shook off with Elpee still in the bathtub with him, they both began to laugh and hug each other.

"Come on, Butter, let's go to bed."

LEAVES

Sometimes, following an afternoon snack, Elpee would venture outside to play a little jump rope. She desperately wanted to skate, but no matter how hard she tried, Elpee could not get the knack of it, neither roller nor ice, and even though she thought about using her princessly powers, she decided that was not a fair thing to do, so she stuck to jumping rope. She had learned how to do this a long time ago in a schoolyard in that other world where at recess all the girls would take turns jumping and turning the rope. Sometimes they would want to play Double Dutch, but Elpee, being awful at it, would have to turn the two ropes for them, hoping they would soon resume playing single jump rope.

Her days were chock-full of delightful and exciting things to do and see. She had books to read and cookies to eat. From morning until night Elpee was busy playing, planning, resting, sleeping, reading, writing, baking, gardening, or bubble bathing. Singing and dancing were on her current list of preferred things to do as Elpee always boogied around the castle and its gardens, randomly imitating the goddess's other creatures. On occasion, she added vocals to her dances and would sing with all her heart, but windows would rattle, Butter would howl, and the gnomes would implore her to cease and desist, for their tree homes were shuddering from the noise.

Elpee, at some point in time, found a new favorite hobby that consisted of going into the forest to collect leaves and rocks. She would choose only the most special of leaves that had fallen to the ground, which she would then take home to dry and display or give them as gifts. While walking through the cover of leaves on the ground, Elpee recalled one of the visits by PoliM'aladroit. The Princess of ShinyShores was in awe of the sights her eyes beheld, as it was always summer in her princessdom and the leaves were permanently green. She had never seen anything such as the brilliant colors that Mother Nature had bestowed upon the giant oaks, maples, elms, and birches.

"Oh, what a majestic combination of oranges, reds, browns, yellows, and deep greens," PoliM'aladroit proclaimed as Elpee observed the look of astonishment and gratitude on her face for having the opportunity to view such beauty.

"Although it is quite a distance from my land, especially by bicycle, I would be willing to travel the distance to see this spectacular sight again. That is if you will have my boy and me here," she added while pointing to her pet that was rolling around in the fallen leaves. With approval and encouragement from Elpee, PoliM'aladroit did visit for many more autumns to come.

On those seasonal visits, they would venture into the woods and spread a blanket among the leaves. The pet cousins would run and play with each other all day while Elpee and PoliM'aladroit observed the beauty surrounding them, taking in the pungent, earthy scents and the sounds of the creatures' conversations. They would nibble on cheese and fruit and discuss the merits of one of their new favorite authors or books between bites.

Even though Elpee loved all her sisters, she especially enjoyed visits from PoliM'aladroit because they were always stimulating, and sometimes quite challenging. Each of the princesses had their own uniqueness: Hortense did not talk much, Euterpe talked too much, and danDay-leon made tea – very much tea.

Elpee hoped that since it was currently autumn in her land, she would soon see PoliM'aladroit for her annual visit.

While still reflecting on those occasions, Elpee began collecting leaves to send to her friend in case for some reason she did not come. When she was done, Elpee had gathered a whole bag of leaves, which was enough for PoliM'aladroit to share with her subjects, if she chose to do so, or to keep them for herself. But because Elpee did not believe that her friend would not share, she decided to increase the size of the bag to ensure PoliM'aladroit would have a plentiful supply of nature's autumnal artwork.

It took her many days to do this, and of course, there was always the need to stop for a liverwurst sandwich and black cherry soda followed by a rest in the hammock to help her digest and regain her energy. No bother. The task would be completed in its own perfect time and then Elpee would send the parcel to her sister princess at ShinyShores.

AND ROCKS

As Elpee wandered the woods, she would watch the sun dance on the tree-tops and sometimes weave its way through a narrow pathway to pirouette on the ground. Then she would sit on a log and absorb this beautiful sight while inhaling those delicious earthy fragrances that could be discovered only in the furthest depths of the forest. She favored the scents found in the early evening after a late summer rain when the air was laden with a woodsy bouquet. It brought back memories of a time and place from long, long ago before she came here. And although they were melancholy memories, they produced a warm presence that resurrected a yearning not overly familiar, but not alien either.

On these days, she would randomly stop and pick up particular rocks without a specific method or pattern to her selections. She retrieved the ones who called to her and signaled they wanted to be chosen. Big, small, flat, round, white, gray, brown, orange, black, purple, and marbled, they were all equal in beauty and design and would each find their very own unique place back at the castle.

Several were placed in the gardens, some lined the paths, while still others were too frail for outside duty and were, therefore, assigned to enhance the decorative foliage that grew inside the castle. Elpee did her best at placing them appropriately, but they each had the final say on the matter. Their arranging was usually completed in short order with only a few protestations by some of the more contrary rocks. Not much rearranging was necessary, at least not initially, but every few days some adjustments were needed due to transfer requests. The reasons for the appeals included the possibility an inside stone felt stronger and wanted to be promoted to outside duty, or conversely, an outdoor rock may be feeling under the weather and needed to rest inside in a more stable environment. Sometimes, the heftier boulders complained that entirely too much was being asked of them by having to stand guard on the perimeter of the gardens both day and night in the event that any delinquent creatures tried to breach the security. Although Elpee listened to and attempted to honor most requests, at times, she would have to employ diplomacy and flattery to quash the complaints of those unhappy ones she was not able to accommodate. Eventually, they would all settle down and adjust to their place on the planet – at least temporarily. Peace would reign until Elpee would again venture into the woods and return with more rocks, which would reignite the competition.

"How could these docile stones who gently whispered to me and implored me to adopt them become so cantankerous when they join the others?" she asked herself.

No bother. Elpee enjoyed their spunk and was amused by their grumbling, for she knew they were all genuinely happy to be a part of her princessdom.

DanDay-leon to the Rescue

Despite there being nothing but deliriously, perfect conditions in Elpee's world, on one rare occasion she did, however, develop a cold that coincided with an unusually severe period of rain and dampness. Elpee, although unwell, felt fortunate that her ill health and the dreadful weather coincided, as she thought it gave her permission to lounge around and indulge herself without feeling that she may be missing some significant event in the outdoors. While wearing polka dot and cherry pajamas and reclining on the couch whining about her current state of unwellness, the under-the-weather monarch heard a flapping noise. She thought it was produced by Butter's ears as he shook his head, but quickly realized that that was not possible, as Butterball had no ears, or at least not the flappable kind, thereby making the assumption not feasible.

Too tired to lift her achy body from the couch, Elpee remained in the prone position, and eventually, the flapping noise ceased, allowing her to relax and concentrate on the dozing necessary for her to heal. Just as her eyes closed and her body relaxed, the sound of clanging and banging jarred Elpee awake and upright – right off the couch.

BANG!!! SLAM!!! CRASH!!! "What in the name of all that's holy?" rasped the ill voice of the castle's inhabitant. The noise grew louder as Elpee approached the front door, at which time she realized that the thundering was emanating from the other side of it. She was afraid to open the door for fear of what was out there until a familiar but muffled screech was audible, prompting her to at last open it.

The vision that greeted her should not have surprised Elpee, but somehow it did. Standing sideways and wedged between the wooden entry walls was danDay-leon with her hat on the ground, her coat askew, and her suitcase opened with tea leaves ready to spill about everywhere. Although ill, Elpee felt sorrier for the princess of Teacup Manor than she did for herself, and so she bent down, gathered the unopened jars of tea, and returned them to their respective places inside the suitcase. Having done that, the two princesses joined forces in getting danDay-leon in a vertical position and into the castle. Once inside and out of the blustery outdoor elements, danDay-leon gave Elpee a proper greeting.

"Hello, my sister princess. I heard you were ill, so I came to Cherry Castle to nurse you back to health. Now, go upstairs and run a hot bath while I light a fire in the fireplace, and when you come down, we will share a pot of tea."

"Thank you so much," replied Elpee. "It is comforting to have someone who cares, and you came all the way from your castle across the street in this abominable weather to help me. You are a true friend, danDay."

"Scoot, Missy, upstairs and into the tub while I prepare for us down here," danDay-leon replied while feeling slightly embarrassed by the compliment. Off to the tub went Elpee, and while it was filling, she gathered a fresh pair of footed PJs and her new robe to place over them. Soon she was soaking in the hot water laced with some vapor salts danDay-leon provided, and before long, the ailing princess heard the tea kettle on the stove downstairs beginning to whistle. As one princess relaxed upstairs, another busied herself down below.

In the living room, danDay-leon put out the tea set and a platter of cucumber and ham-salad sandwiches for them to enjoy when Elpee returned downstairs. As if planned, which it most likely was, both Elpee and danDay-leon arrived in the living room simultaneously. They each sat on a wing chair at the drop leaf table that was piled high with food and beverage.

"What a special afternoon this has turned into," mumbled Elpee as she munched on one of each kind of sandwich while intermittently sipping on the orange-cinnamon tea. danDay-leon drank her standard brew of English breakfast tea. Although Elpee enjoyed the different flavors of tea that Teacup Manor's proprietor exposed her to, she always had to sneak the extraordinarily copious amounts of sugar she liked into her teacup so as not to upset the tea princess by what she referred to as 'polluting the potion'.

Speaking of potions, when all the sandwiches were eaten, and all the tea was drunk, danDay-leon, who fashioned herself to be somewhat of a mystic, offered to read the tea leaves left in Elpee's cup, to which Elpee immediately agreed. With the wisdom of the ages pressed into her face, danDay-leon turned the cup from side to side, swirling its remnants about while focusing on the leaves. She did this again and again until finally she felt confident enough with her discovery to share it with Elpee.

"What I see, Elpee, is only one object over and over," stated dan-Day-leon.

"What is it? What is it?" cried Elpee, who by now could not contain her curiosity a single second longer.

Confused, but confident in what she saw in the leaves, danDay-leon matter-of-factly blurted out, "A kaleidoscope."

"A kaleidoscope? You see a kaleidoscope in my future? That's it? Come on danDay, you have got to do better than that. It doesn't even make any sense." Jokingly, Elpee added, "Maybe you need to go back to seer school."

"I am sorry, Elpee, but no matter what I do, that is what appears. I suppose more will be revealed, but that is all for today. Now back up on the couch for you. I will tuck you in, take Butter for a walk, and then I will be on my way."

When danDay-leon and Butter returned from outside, danDay began tidying up the castle. Once she was done, she entered the living room in a noisy tizzy, which made Elpee giggle as she lay there up to her ears in comforters with Butter on top of them all, creating yet another blanket for her. At times like this, the much smaller creature she found in the hole would be a bit more convenient, not to mention comfortable, but no bother. Butter was the best. He licked her cheek as she again fell off to sleep.

THE BIRTHDAY PARTY

The weeks and months – possibly even years – passed, and Elpee grew older, taller, and smarter.

She contracted the elves to build an alcove directly off the castle's living room in which she could store her overly abundant collection of music and unread books. Although Elpee never attended school here, she was well read, possessed a keen intellect, and knew she could have become something outstanding in the world of the grown-ups—at least by their standards. Maybe a lawyer. No bother, she had used her talents to achieve an already exceptional standing here in her magickal monarchy. She taught herself, she raised herself, and she was able to do anything at all by herself.

After acknowledging her accomplishments and patting herself on the back, Elpee set the table for that evening's dinner with the gnomes. Through the years, the princess and the little people maintained a close friendship and visited with each other often. When there were joint dinners, they would typically partake of them at the gnomes' house under the tree because the little people were frightened to be too far away from home, but tonight was a special occasion. It was everyone's birthday, and they were having a grand dinner at the castle in celebration. Nelly was bringing squash soup, Britania and Julius agreed to bake yam pies with apple butter filling, Gwendolyn and Waldo were contributing stuffed mushrooms, and Elpee was making a big, fat, giant meatloaf. The other attendees – or rather celebrants – were providing nuts, berries, and games to play. Although the gnomes ate mostly fruit for dessert, Elpee had introduced them to sweets such as bonbons and brownies, and tonight they would taste the biggest and best pineapple upside-down cake ever made. In celebration of their shared birthday, they would all have a piece of it after dinner.

The table was set with polka-dotted napkins and a checkered tablecloth atop which Elpee placed her loveliest dishes, glasses, and silverware. Before dinner, Elpee went out to the garden to gather flowers for the table. She collected roses, peonies, carnations, astilbe, lilies, and cinnamon ferns to make a festive arrangement for a centerpiece and then hurried inside, as the guests were due to arrive any minute.

Just as Elpee had turned the dial on the music machine to a station that was playing an assortment of soothing flute and violin solos, the first guests began to appear. There were Simon and Veronica, John and Esther, Sadie and Grant, and on, and on. Princess Hortense tried to inconspicuously slide in with them; however, when Elpee discovered her presence, Hortense looked out from underneath her baseball cap and said, "Hi Mama."

Over time, Grouse Hollow's very own princess had become good friends with the gnomes. She would often come over to help them dig and plant or rather to supervise their progress, each time bringing with her some new specimen from her own gardens. Elpee knew that Hortense was kind and generous and that she was a kindred spirit. Even though she liked to maintain her distance and did not readily open her heart to others, she was likable yet troubled, and of all the princesses, Elpee felt the most connected to her, as if they had known each other in another time and place. It was intriguingly odd and often disturbing, but no bother, it was time to celebrate.

When everyone had arrived, they sat down at the infinitely expanding dining table to eat the vast assortment of foods, which also included a tossed salad made from Elpee's garden, mashed potatoes, corn on the cob, fresh bread with home-churned butter, and applesauce. Before proceeding to eat, they all took the hands of their neighbors on either side of them and said grace. They then began to eat, and eat, and then eat some more.

They all dined until they could barely stand, but that did not stop them from going outside to shoot pebbles for the honor of having the first piece of birthday cake. There was no rivalry in this land, but occasionally they pretended to be like the big people and did things the way they thought they did – through competition. In reality, the whole pebble shooting game was for entertainment only. Even though it was also Elpee's birthday, she, being an excellent hostess, declined to vie for first place. Everyone laughed, played, and encouraged each other until no longer able to wait for dessert, they paraded one by one, single file, into Elpee's house. The princess-hostess greeted each guest at the door with a silver cake fork and kept one for herself.

The celebrants orderly gathered around the table where the gooey pineapple and cherry-topped, now right-side up cake, awaited them. At the count of three – one, two, three – they all raised their forks, threw them over their left shoulders, and dove into the cake face first. The sugary delight was gone in short order, and soon afterward the gnomes began to leave to retire to their underground houses for the night. They all congratulated and thanked each other for a delightful party, but most of all for their friendships.

THE ROCKS PROTEST

———

During one unusually hot summer, the rocks in the gardens began to protest their working conditions, stating that the insufferable heat and lack of rain were against the guidelines as outlined in the *Handbook of Quarry Rules,* and they had the official handbook to prove it. The stone protestors recruited the local ants to help move them into a shadier and cooler area — probably back into the woods from whence they had come. The ants' payment for their work came in the form of food, which they unearthed when they moved the rocks. The insects began by forming a team of engineers as well as a moving crew. The engineers drew up plans and designed roads for the efficient and expeditious relocating of the rocks while the moving manager set up squads of workers to ensure a continuous and steady pace of movement.

Elpee had very little influence over this mass exodus by the rocks. Despite her disappointment, she did understand their motive and the need for them to do so. Every day a few more rocks were gone, leaving gaps in the landscape as well as in Elpee's heart. She hoped it was only a temporary measure and that they would return when the temperatures lowered, but as time passed and more rocks left, her hopes were dashed.

Sad and lonely, Elpee dispatched a letter to *Queen* Euterpe, inviting her to visit Cherry Castle by the Sea. The request read:

My Dear Sister Princess,

I am in somewhat of a sad situation, and I would very much appreciate some company, and perhaps help also in moving some slate. You see, Euterpe, my rocks are staging a walkout, and although I understand their complaints, I have no power to remedy the situation, and their leaving saddens me.

Please come!

Fondly,
Elpee

The letter was barely sent when a response arrived on Elpee's doorstep. Excitedly, she picked up the envelope and ripped it open to see Euterpe's reply:

I am on my way,
To your house to stay.
Will be there in a day,
And then we will play . . . Or not.
QUEEN Euterpe

"Oops," cringed Elpee at the salutary faux pas she had made in her address of Euterpe.

Excited beyond the moon, Elpee prepared for her sister's visit, but before she could even begin to do so, up the path glided Euterpe.

"Hello, hello, hello, I'm here.

"I have arrived a bit early, my dear.

"Don't think it odd, don't think it queer,

"it took not long, perhaps a year," greeted Euterpe.

As Elpee ran to hug her, Euterpe raised her arms, indicating that the Princess of Cherry Castle must wait, as Euterpe had not completed her greeting. Euterpe continued,

"I'm tired and hungry,

"as you shall see.

"I could eat a horse.

"Oh, silly me!

"My throat is parched,

"I need some tea.

"Let's go inside,

"so I can . . . "

Knowing she would not win against Euterpe's insistence, Elpee went to the front door and opened it for her. Euterpe, in all her regality, entered and made herself at home. While Euterpe did whatever it was that *Queens* do, Princess Elpee prepared a snack for them before tackling the task of re-placing the errant rocks with slate.

For many days they toiled in the flowerbeds, moving what seemed to be tons of slate to create a mini wall. The finished project was a remark-able sight. Although most of the rocks were gone and Elpee missed them terribly, she was pleased with the replacement's esthetic outcome. The polka dots and cherries painted on their predecessors were fun, but the slate had a much more developed look and was seemingly more suited to her – or so she supposed.

With the project completed, Euterpe decided that in the morning she would leave Cherry Castle to return to her *Queen*dom. Following dinner, Euterpe arose and proclaimed:

"Roses are blue,

"violets are red.

"If I could view,

"what's in my head,

"I'd have a clue,

"of what to do.

"But I don't. . . sooo,

"with all that said,

"I'm off to bed.

"I need some sleep,

"for my schedule to keep,

"'cause in the morn,

"I will leave at dawn."

And off she went!

THE DREAM

─────

Since Euterpe's departure, Elpee sensed a strange climate around the castle. Perhaps it was just the absence of Euterpe's verses or the princess missing the fun they had together when the *Queen* visited, but it seemed solitary and severe. Thinking back even further in time, Elpee realized that the departure of the rocks might have been the onset of the difference she was now feeling. Despite the current flatness of things, Elpee knew it would change. She would make it change.

The princess went about her days as usual – gardening, reading, relaxing in the hammock, and walking with Butter, but she rarely jumped rope or played games at all anymore. Princess Elpee was maturing, and with that maturity came a degree of demureness. Perhaps it was not that things were different as she had thought, but instead, it was she who was changing.

"No bother!" she said aloud.

"No bother!" she said again, this time louder.

"NO BOTHER!" Again, she spoke out, but this time she was yelling.

Despite her desire to ignore her thoughts, Elpee, no matter how she tried, could not release them as she once had been able to. She convinced herself that everything probably was the way it had always been in her land and that her perception was just evolving and maturing. She would merely have to adjust as she had done in the past. She knew how to do that.

Days – weeks – months went by. Time passed, and things remained the same – not good, not bad, just the same. On one of these days, after working for hours in the garden, Elpee came home especially exhausted. It seemed lately there were noticeably fewer gnomes who helped her with the tilling and planting, but she told herself that they must all be away on vacation visiting their gnome families and would soon return.

On one Sunday, after the previous Tuesday of the week before last, Elpee prepared Butter's dinner of leftover beef stew. She heated the meal in a bowl before placing it on the floor and fixing her own food. She decided to have only a plate of cheese and crackers, which she elected to eat on the couch in front of the fire. Almost before finishing the small amount of food that was on her plate, Elpee began to feel her eyes closing. She finished the last of the food, put her feet up and her head down on the couch, and immediately fell asleep.

The princess had dastardly nightmares that evening, with the final one being the worst of all. In it, she envisioned she was sleeping and that when she awoke, Butter was gone. He had utterly vanished, and Elpee could find him nowhere. In the dream, she frantically walked about the castle looking for him and calling his name, stopping only to sob. This scenario continued over and over throughout the night—searching, yelling, and crying. Finally, at the end of one of these cycles within the dream, Elpee distinctly heard a voice announce to her:

"You can keep walking and crying about how much you miss him, but it won't get you anywhere, and it won't ever end. Perhaps, you would be better served by crying about something real, such as the fact that he is gone and is never coming back!"

Elpee awoke, her body drenched in sweat and her face covered in tears. To erase the thought of the cruel dream and not think about it any longer than necessary, she almost immediately and instinctively went about her routine, and as always, called the dog.

"Butter, come here, boy."

No answer.

"Butterball, come here, my handsome fellow."

Still, nothing.

Finally, in desperation and through tears that were streaming down her face, Elpee frantically yelled, "Butter, come," as she shook his jar of cookies pleadingly. He did not come, and it was not a dream. Butter was gone.

THE CHANGE BEGINS

Nothing was the same, yet very little was different since Butter's disappearance. Other than the profound emptiness his leaving created within both Elpee and the castle, things proceeded, albeit slowly. Her heart grew heavier and time slowed so much so that Elpee did not notice the changes that took place in the landscape – either external or internal – until questions began to enter her head. So many questions. She was not accustomed to her brain going in this direction.

When did the gardens go fallow and the birds' songs become flat?

Was it always this cold and damp in June? And wasn't last winter especially bleak?

As she walked around the castle, she saw its appearance was now shabby; the windows were dirty, and the curtains were torn and gray. Her books were strewn about with spines broken and pages ripped.

When were the elves last in the castle to clean and tidy up?

Didn't Richard and Lanie stop by just last week for a visit? Or was it the week before? Or the week before that?

When was the last time I had dinner with any of the gnomes? She could not remember.

How? When? Why?

Oh, no matter how hard she tried to remember, Elpee just could not. Tomorrow she vowed to work on returning the castle to its original pristine appearance, and as soon as she had finished her work in the house, she would focus her attention on the outside. She would tend to the gardens – clearing out all the debris and spent flowers, uprighting the fallen birdbaths, and putting out some additional feeders for the birds, as the air seemed unusually chilly and they may need more food.

Her once favorite chair summoned her. She sat down on it and attempted to formulate a plan of where to start, but quickly she became so overwhelmed and tired that she drifted off to sleep. Elpee remained on that chair for an unknown, but extensive, amount of time, with no thought or energy devoted to changing her surroundings, neither in nor out. She was too tired to do anything, so exhausted that she became paralyzed and was unable to lift herself from the chair. The days turned into nights, and then back into days, unending, for weeks – and months – and perhaps even years. The sun no longer shone either on her or within her.

Elpee had closed the door to her bedroom sometime long ago when the voice coming from within became too loud and incessant. *It* was maddening. *It* would not be silenced. When Elpee could find no peace or quiet from the insistence of the beckoning voice, she gathered all her strength and rose from the chair. She walked to the bedroom door, opened it, and stepped inside.

It had been quite some time since she was last in there – not since *It* began to come more regularly and with more insistence, causing her to avoid and eventually flee her once favorite room altogether. As she opened the door and entered the room, Elpee found it to be in the same condition she remembered it. It was clean, bright, and as inviting as it always had been. Everything in here was in direct conflict with the rest of the house as if up was down, and down was up.

She earnestly began to question her sanity on an even deeper level now. How could the room she had always favored suddenly bring such trepidation to her? And this, her sanctuary, although not used or even entered in more time than Elpee could remember, was the only room in the castle to remain unchanged since she had arrived here. Her bedroom was spotless, with not a speck of dust on the furniture or the dark wood floor. The sun shone through the clean windows only in this room of the castle. Her books and dolls were as she left them, all in place and more vibrant and alive than she recalled them to be.

"How is this possible when the rest of the castle is gray and in such disrepair?" she again asked herself weakly.

She could not understand, and wondered why she had avoided this room for so many years. She did not hear the voice here in the bedroom, as she feared she would. Where was *It*? Where did *It* go? Was she not nearly driven mad by its vocal disturbances day and night? With her mind flooded with questions and her body tired from the confusion, Elpee for the first time in so very long lay upon her bed of feathers and let it envelop her. She immediately felt safe, and now wanted to remain there rather than face the gloom and darkness of the other rooms. Swiftly, sleep overtook her, and she knew peace – at least for a brief moment in time.

Abruptly, in what Elpee believed to be a dream, a man approached her. His presence terrified her and prompted her to run away from him, but she couldn't. Her feet were frozen in a giant block of ice, but they were not cold, and she did not know how they got there. Elpee also did not remember anything of the dream before the man began approaching her. As the gentleman, whoever he was, got closer, her fear grew and her sense of urgency to escape increased. She felt her heart pounding, and it appeared her hands were sweating despite the fact that the lower part of her body was encased in ice. She tried to will herself to wake up or to move or to scream, but she could do nothing but stand there and wait.

For what seemed to be a century, Elpee prepared herself for whatever might be in store for her. Where once she was a princess and was in command of all things great and small she was now trapped and unable to wake from the dream nor flee from the stranger within it. Elpee collected herself, and with all her courage, she stood her ground, although not by choice, and when the stranger finally arrived at the place where she stood, literally frozen, Elpee proceeded to do the ridiculous – she fainted.

J. ALPERT VII

When she came to, the ice had melted, and Elpee was greeted by an out-of-focus person who gave her a simple hello that made her head reel, her vision sharpen, and her pulse race. It was *It* who spoke to her. She shuddered and screamed while at the same time jumping up, flapping her arms, and running in circles until she fell again, this time from a dizzy head. *It* approached her a second time and leaned over her, speaking his greeting once more in an almost feminine voice.

"What are you?" asked Elpee of *It*.

The creature that stood over her in a polka dot suit replete with a poppy on the lapel confused her and set her to swooning as she began to rise.

"'WHAT,' my dear girl?" I am not a 'what,'" he replied as he adjusted his Kelly green tie in a gesture of indignation.

"And where did the ice go?" asked Elpee.

"Did you bump your head? That is all you want to know – the ice and where it went? How do I know? You created that, not me, and for clarity's sake I am J. Alpert the Seventh," he said while doffing his Panama hat. "I am your friendly neighborhood wizard. A simple term and concept of which I am sure you may be familiar with. Now get up and dust yourself off. We have work to do, and you have spent entirely too much time dallying in disarray."

Elpee, still stunned by this creature and its bizarre appearance, began to object but thought better of it. Mostly though she was afraid of the voice and that it would return if she resisted.

"Don't worry, little miss. I just used that tone to get your attention, and it worked, didn't it? That's why I am the wizard and you . . . you are whoever you are."

With a smidgen of protest, the little girl pronounced proudly, "I am Elpee, princess of all these lands you can see."

"Oh poop, Missy! We may have more work to do than I had thought," replied Alpert.

"I AM GOING HOME, AND YOU ARE GOING TO LEAVE. RIGHT NOW!" Elpee commanded as she at last rose and stamped her foot while also shaking herself off.

"ROAR!" thundered the wizard, causing Elpee to return to the ground butt first with her lower lip in a sonic quiver.

In the soft voice, he said, "I was trying to be nice, but no, you have to have a fit and act like a baby. It is very immature and seriously unflattering on your part. Now, get up *again*, dust yourself off *again*, and no more tantrums, okay? Or I will have to get your attention *again*, and you will be on the ground *again*, only to have to pick yourself up *again* and dust yourself off *again*. I don't know about you, but I am very tired of your *agains*. Do you see what I am saying and what problems you are causing? And all because of your bad behavior," he continued as he shook his head at Elpee and walked off in the opposite direction.

As she got up, shaking and brushing herself off, she watched the man walk into the woods and sit on a log. He was very tall and relatively slim, with brown hair that was much too short for a proper wizard. His clothes were un-wizardly also; they were quite outrageous if one were to ask Elpee for her opinion. He was reasonably handsome and seemed kind enough, but she still did not understand so many things. When she regained her senses entirely, Elpee would demand answers from him. She deserved them – after all, she was the princess of this princessdom, wasn't she? Well, wasn't she?

Elpee coolly ambled over to the downed tree where J. Alpert VII was waiting for her.

"I have some questions for you to answer, and not in that voice either," she informed him, somewhat demandingly.

"Say please," Alpert retorted, imitating her tone.

"Uh hum . . . PLEase."

"What?" he questioned in a voice that deepened an octave below his previous one, but not to its original level, which had frightened Elpee so.

"Ppp-lease, I said."

"NO."

"Excuse me?"

"I told you that the voice you don't like is meant to get your attention – no different than what you intend to do with your fits in trying to get mine. I become who I need to be to suit my needs, much as you do. My method is just far more effective than yours is, so if you stop, maybe I will too. Maybe," Alpert informed her.

"I am a princess."

"My point exactly," he responded.

"I don't get it," she spoke softly to him as her head sunk lower.

"Precisely again," he stated, proudly making his point.

"I don't understand. When can I go home?" Elpee pleaded.

"Where?" asked Alpert.

Fighting back the tears, she struggled to get the words out before erupting into irrepressible emotion, "Please, when can I go home?"

Gently, Alpert touched her hand in an attempt to assure her that all her worries would eventually end, but he knew that she would not believe him for a long time – if ever she did. It was forever since she trusted anyone – if ever she had.

PLANTING THE SEEDS

"Oh, mister, I don't know where I am or who you are and why you are here. I just want to go back to my castle where everything is safe, and I am not afraid," spoke Elpee in a soft and desperate tone.

The wizard pulled some seeds from his pocket and gave them to her, saying, "When these seeds sprout and grow, you will be home, at peace with yourself and all that you love. I don't know what they are, what they will bear, or when this will happen, but I promise you it will, but first, you must agree to this and then help me to plant them."

"Oh," cried Elpee, "I'm so tired and scared, and what you are telling me to do sounds so stupid, but I don't know what else to do."

"Excellent, my little friend, this is precisely the environment we need in order to plant these seeds. Let's go," ordered Alpert.

Up she got and off they went out of the woods and up the hill, higher and higher until Elpee could go no more, but with Alpert's prodding and promises of 'just over the hill,' they made it to the exact spot. Reaching deep into his jacket pocket, the wizard extracted what he called the most magickal of all shovels, which he handed to Elpee, instructing her that she needed to dig the hole and plant the seeds. She begrudgingly took the tool from his hand and began to dig. With every wave of exhaustion and hesitation Elpee exhibited, Alpert encouraged the bedraggled girl.

"Just a little more," Alpert instructed her. "You're almost there," he proclaimed.

Finally, it was time. The hole was big enough, and Elpee gently placed each of the three seeds into it and then began to cover them loosely with dirt. Alpert looked up at the sky and a rain shower developed directly over the soil that blanketed the newly planted seeds.

"I thought you said I had to 'help you,' but I did all the work," protested the little princess.

"Nonsense," replied Alpert defensively. "I watered them, which is the hardest job, so therefore, because I had the hardest job, you simply 'helped me,' my dear."

Elpee, being too tired and scared, said no more to Alpert on the matter. It took all the strength she had to hold back her tears. She had no power left over to argue. Alpert, sensing her exhaustion, did not push her to go on just yet. He created a cup of tea for her and added the required pound of sugar to it before handing it to the damaged person standing before him.

"When your tea is finished, we will continue on our journey.

ALL ABOARD. NEXT STOP, CHERRY CASTLE BY THE SEA," J. Alpert VII announced.

THE ROAD 'HOME'

A confused Elpee turned to him and asked sheepishly, "Where?"

"You need to go to visit where you came from before you can go home," explained the wizard.

"I don't understand. Cherry Castle *is* my home," replied Elpee between sniffles.

"My dear," J. Alpert continued in a rather paternal manner, "I am gentle with you now because that is what you require, just as I spoke to you in that stern voice when I needed for you to listen. If you at all trust me, but even if you do not, my little friend, you must believe me and follow my directions."

"I don't care, I just want you to go away and let me go home," she whimpered in a weak voice.

"I have spoken, and it is done by your hand with the seeds being planted. We must go now," pronounced Alpert as he rose from another log and began the decline from the hill they had climbed earlier. They walked and walked until they reached the meadow, where the wizard spread a blanket in the grass for Elpee to gather her strength before proceeding any further.

"Rest, my dear, while I tell you some truths that are about to happen. First, I must tell you that I am not a 'wizard'. I don't even know what a wizard is, but I needed to use a term you were acquainted with so that it may possibly ease your fears. There is so much for you to know and find, but you will, it just depends on when you bloom. For you see, it has been ordained by you, but much is contingent upon how you tend those seeds," Alpert continued.

Elpee lay down on the blanket and rested her head on a giant toad-stool. She gave up fighting for just a minute and saw Alpert differently than she had before. He was a very kind and handsome man with dark green eyes, and he was much taller than he appeared earlier. It was correct that he got her attention just by his demeanor, be it kind or mean. The wizard, or non-wizard, whoever he was, was now asking Elpee to close her eyes and listen carefully to all he had to say. He also warned her not to fall asleep, or he would be forced to pinch her into paying attention. This statement made Elpee reconsider her new assessment of Alpert, but she thought better of commenting on his use of corporal punishment and bit her tongue instead. She lay there as attentive as any uprooted and kid-napped princess could possibly be.

Squatting down next to the princess-hostage, Alpert began what Elpee hoped would be instructions on how to wake up from this dream and go home. After all, he did tell her she must return to Cherry Castle.

"Yes, yes, I did say that, and you will go there, but please do not get ahead of me. It is my turn now, so shush!" Alpert replied to her thoughts with a sigh of exasperation.

How does he know what I am thinking? thought Elpee.

"Because I am brilliant, or clairvoyant, or both, whichever you prefer," he declared as he began to explain yet again. "After you rest for a bit, we will proceed to your Cherry Castle, and you will find there everything you need to continue on your journey. There is no sense in my telling you all about it now, for you will see for yourself when we get there. Please, my dear, as I asked you to do before – trust me. You will not understand, agree with, or like some things I will be telling you, but if you can believe in me and trust that I came here to help you, things will be easier."

Elpee tried to relax as Alpert handed her a hot cup of chamomile tea to drink. As she sipped the warm beverage, Elpee strained with all of her might to calm down and believe what this stranger was telling her about trusting him and going home, but nothing made sense to her, and what she did know only served to jangle her nerves.

"Drink your tea, my dear, it will calm those jangled nerves of yours," suggested the wizard as he prepared to do his wizardly works. "You re-member the voice and now you know it was me, correct?' he continued.

"Yes," replied Elpee, wincing at even the hint of the voice.

"And you remember how you felt something was, as you say, 'beck-oning you' into your bedroom?"

"Yes," again replied Elpee, still wincing.

"Me! And how your bedroom was so clean and bright and everything was in its place?" questioned Alpert.

"Yes," this time she replied a bit more confidently.

"Me again."

Now, more sure of herself, Elpee excitedly stated, "And the gloom in the rest of the castle – you again, right?"

"NO!" Alpert countered, but seeing the disappointment on her face, he moved closer to her and began his explanation. "That, young miss, was you."

Elpee's eyes began to fill with tears as her confusion and frustration grew, but she said nothing. She merely sat there forlorn and beaten. She knew that she was no longer in control of her life or destiny and this odd man somehow held all the answers to the myriad of unanswered questions scuttling around in her head. Elpee surrendered to that fact and began to listen in earnest.

BANISHED

"Thank you, my dear, things may go easier from here on," he continued. "When you finish your tea and feel sufficiently rested, we will travel back to the place you call your castle. Once there, you will gather up four personal things that you may take with you on your journey."

"What do you mean, *journey*? Won't you leave me when we get there, and can't I stay in my castle?" she questioned the wizard with a slight hint of indignation.

Gently, but firmly, Alpert informed Elpee of the facts that she must accept.

"It is true that I will leave you once we arrive at our destination, but you will leave also. I have told you to gather four personal items, as they will be all you will have to remind you of there, because, you see, my child, you will not return to your castle once you leave, and leave you must."

The tears flowed from Elpee's eyes and down her cheeks. "But where will I go and how will I get there?" she asked in the most desperate of manners.

"You are going home," the wizard replied. "I am not sure where that is or when that will be, or how many stops you will make along the way, but you do, and you will be guided throughout your journey."

"You said you were leaving. Are you coming with me now? Will you help me?" the girl timidly asked.

"Yes and no. I will go with you to our destination, but once there, I cannot go with you any further, but someone else will be there to escort you. You see, you need to have faith in this being that will guide you and pick you up when you stumble. And you also need someone who will sternly encourage you to continue on even when you don't want to. So, therefore, you will be accompanied by these two beings in one. You shall have a Faerie goddess-mother. I don't know who she is, but you will, and when the time is right on your journey, the two of you will formally meet. Therefore, until then, if you can, imagine what you need to believe in and how she could help you. Create her. She will be essential to you on your trip, so it would serve you well to take time to contemplate this and come up with a description of her for yourself."

Alpert continued, "Make sure that this description comes from your heart, not your head. Your mind has served you well, but it is time to give it a rest and let your heart show you the way, because it knows exactly who you are and what needs must be met for you to face your challenges."

"Challenges?" Elpee asked Alpert once again with a sharp edge to her voice. "And why must I face challenges? And why can't I stay here at home where every day is good, and there are no challenges?"

"When, my friend, was the last good day that you had? Last week? Last month? Last year? Or was it two years ago?" he asked more sternly. "You know fun with and in your head, but you don't know joy within your heart. Yes, you must go," he continued. "And a part of you knows that. Now, it appears you have rested enough, so let us go and continue back to retrieve your items before your trip."

With no more questions to ask the wizard, Elpee gave up, rose from the blanket, and started walking toward what she believed to be her home no matter what Alpert said. Somehow, she found the energy to continue; maybe it was that Faerie goddess-mother he spoke of, she thought cynically.

"You had better make friends with the idea and not mock it, my dear. You will need her on your journey, but of course, the choice, as always, is yours."

DEVASTATION

They were soon approaching the castle, and Elpee could not wait because she was sure that when they arrived there, she would awaken from this dream, Alpert would be gone, and she could then resume her princessly life. As emotionally and physically spent as she was, Elpee picked up her pace in anticipation of that becoming a reality. This discernible increase in Elpee's gait did not go unnoticed by Alpert, and it concerned him. But once again, he knew he had little control over the situation, as he was merely a visitor here.

Alpert kept up with her, not allowing too much of a distance to develop between them. He knew the sight that awaited Elpee was just a few hundred yards ahead and he wanted to be near her when she witnessed it. It was becoming more evident how genuinely excited Elpee was at the thought of returning to what she referred to as home. With only a short distance left to go, Elpee broke into a run that caused the wizard to fall behind and, therefore, he was not with her when it happened. All Alpert could see from his position behind her was her back, and how erect she stood for a few seconds before falling to her knees sobbing.

When he finally reached her, and they were side-by-side, Alpert witnessed the scene that crippled Elpee and sent her into such a state of hysteria and despair. Nothing. The sight that lay before them filled even Alpert with emotion, as it overwhelmed Elpee entirely. There was an abandoned old shack that had not seen inhabitants for a considerable time. What once were windows were now holes in the side of the hut. There were no doors on the outside nor furniture inside. The roof and the floor were partially collapsed, and there were no steps that would allow entry even if it were possible. The garden she and the gnomes had created all those many years ago was gone and looked like another overgrown piece of land in the vast expanse of a forgotten world. The hammock and swing that the elves once pushed Elpee in were gone. As she lay on the ground, immobilized by fear, confusion, and an inner sickness she had never known before, a mist came in and blanketed the entire area. It was so thick that she could not even see Alpert, who was standing right next to her. The fog lasted only a minute, and when it lifted, an even more mysterious sight appeared before her. Where just a few moments earlier a dilapidated rendering of Elpee's cherished Cherry Castle stood, there was now a blank canvas. Although no garden, hammock, or swing was visible before, the dilapidated shack that was once Elpee's home was now also absent. There was no trace of it. No roof tiles or windowpanes, no rafters or walls. Nothing — as if it had never existed. Gone.

Alpert, knowing her state of mind, tried to calm her by saying, "All is well, my dear. All is well," to which there was no response.

Elpee just stayed in that same position until Alpert, fearing they may lose daylight before this broken girl would respond in some manner, reached down and pinched her. Elpee flinched but nothing more. Another pinch and the same reaction. Still another one, this time inflicted with fifty zips of pinchpower behind it. Elpee began yelping, flailing her arms, and hitting him. Her gesture was a reaction created more out of fear than in response to pain at his tinge of torture. Alpert grabbed Elpee in a bear hug and did not let her go until she finally went limp in his arms. He knew the questions she was asking within her mind, and he began answering them for her.

"The house disappeared after the initial shock was somewhat absorbed. You are an intelligent girl. You knew how to soften the blow. Well played, but then again, you are sadly familiar with all manner of survival techniques. It would have served no purpose to have it missing initially, other than to shock your psyche into catatonia. Viewing the ramshackle building first was an excellent idea for your psychic survival. I must say I was a bit confused. First, there was a shack, and then there was none, but now I see. It makes perfect sense the way you did it."

Still holding Elpee loosely, Alpert continued, "My dear girl, all that you had is gone, but you knew it had to happen, and you will be fine, especially if you use your guide. You have a long way to go, but no longer than it took to get here and no longer than necessary to get there. You must trust the Universe with all your heart. It is guiding you – taking you for the ride of your life. Let it. It is time. It is your time, and you must seize it now, or it will be forever lost. It will never come again. So now, my dear, come and let us go forward so that you can retrieve the four items you will be taking with you on your journey."

Shaking and pale, Elpee looked up at the wizard and asked, "How can I do that? There is nothing left to take. Everything is gone. It's all gone."

"Come, my child, I will help you to look," Alpert said to her as he released her and gently took her hand in his, leading her to where the earlier apparition had appeared.

"There is nothing, you see. I told you," stated the beaten princess.

"There must be, so let us look," he said encouragingly as he prodded her along. As they approached the scene of what was, it appeared that Elpee was correct. There was nothing left. How, he wondered, could he help her to find what seemed to be not there? Sometimes he was not fond of his job, especially at times such as these when he was almost as confused as the person he was trying to help. Details were often omitted, leaving him without the advance information needed. It is not as if they gave wizards a handbook or anything. Well, actually, they did, but not all cases were covered in it, and in this case, the little princess was so intense and complicated that the story was ever changing and evolving. Not to mention the most obvious reason of all why he did not have a Wizard's Handbook: because he was not actually a wizard.

"Stop here for a moment, Miss," Alpert stated inconsequentially, as Elpee was already stationary and it appeared that she would not be moving any time soon.

Suddenly and without warning, Alpert vaporized, and an ethereal clone of him shot forward to their future destination while his more substantial form remained motionless with Elpee. There they stood, absent of life, like wooden figures positioned in place. Elpee could do nothing even if it were possible. It was all gone. At the same moment that she realized the wizard was gone, leaving only a shell of himself behind, a vapor trail shot back, arrived next to her, and Alpert returned to animation.

"Away we must go, Missy, to retrieve your tokens so that you may be on your extremely overdue way," Alpert proclaimed confidently.

Afraid to go any further, Elpee was encouraged by the wizard, who took her arm and supported her as she moved forward. Slowly they proceeded at what appeared to be a snail's pace, but eventually, they made it. They arrived at the area in which the castle, gardens, and meadow once were. Elpee began to cry, as she did not know how to proceed or in what direction to head. Her whole world had disappeared, leaving her without a trace of where it went and where she was to go. But most of all she missed Butter and wished he was here to accompany her to wherever it was she was going.

"Thinking about that scruffy canine will not help you right now, Miss," said Alpert, "But looking for your four possessions will."

"I don't know what to do or where to start. I don't even know what I am looking for," sniffled Elpee.

"Well, I do," replied Alpert, "so focus on me and my energy."

And off they went!

THE PRIZES

As they approached the area where the princess once lived, Elpee again froze in place and refused to move, forcing Alpert to use his tried and true method of body moving. He reached over and pinched the once-princess's arm, to which she immediately responded by moving her limbs and eyes. She was afraid that if she lingered in that stationary state, he would continue pinching her as he had done the last time. To avoid this, she merely marched forward and stood amid the vacant rubble. With no other viable options – or any options at all – Elpee focused on Alpert and trusted that he would help her find what she needed to.

"Think of an Easter egg hunt. Do you remember when you were a little girl and your mother would hide the hollow, plastic eggs with the money inside and you would have to use your imagination to locate them? Well, it is the same premise here. Apply it," said Alpert.

Slipping back into her head again, Elpee wondered how he knew about the Easter egg hunts.

"I am a wizard . . . Or not, you know. And besides, prior to coming here, I was briefed on your childhood history and what you had and had not," Alpert responded.

"Thank you," Elpee sheepishly proclaimed.

Taking a deep breath, she opened her eyes wide and focused her mind's energy on Alpert so that she could find and recognize the things she needed to find and recognize. Within a minute or so amid the stark silence, Elpee heard the song of a bird in the distance. She followed the sound to the edge of a barren forest where she found hanging on a branch of a brown, but stately tree a single, spectacularly colored autumn leaf. It was so stark and bold that it appeared out of place against the bleak landscape of the dead forest. With some hesitation on her part and encouragement from Alpert, Elpee reached for the leaf and was surprised by its texture. It felt almost silk-like, as if it could be folded or rolled. She attempted to do just that until she detected writing on the underside. As Elpee turned it over, she read:

Oh, Elpee, I am so happy for you! You have worked very hard to be where you are, and look how things are changing for you. How wonderful! I will miss you and so will my little companion, but . . . Oh well, never mind. I love you.

PoliM'aladroit

The once princess began to cry, for she remembered how much the Princess of ShinyShores loved to visit in the autumn when the trees were ablaze with color, and how they would gather leaves to save as a reminder of Mother Nature's glory. She thought of how the little gray creature and Butter would play with each other and roll around in the fallen leaves. Elpee missed PoliM'aladroit and the delightful visits they had together. She could not indulge herself in reminiscing because she knew there was work to be done, even if she did not know what it was or where it would lead.

Elpee walked back to the wizard to show him what she had found in the brown forest.

"Interesting. So beautiful, and profound also," the wizard replied after examining it.

Tired and confused, Elpee mechanically gave a slight nod of her head as an acknowledgment of his statement. Unsure of where to go and what to do next, the girl stumbled around, kicking stones randomly for no particular reason. Alpert stood in the shadows, letting her find her own way. He accepted that it was her journey and she would have to experience what was necessary for her to proceed. It was an encouraging sight to see her tossing rocks around almost light-heartedly. It seemed as if in response to Alpert's thoughts, and perhaps it was, that Elpee picked up her pace and began to prance. As the girl brought her right leg back and gave a kick to a perfectly round rock, she watched it sail through the air and land somewhere in what was once the gnomes' garden. Elpee, not knowing why, maintained her pace and direction, following the rock into the abandoned patch. Once there and finding nothing, she assumed that her search was fruitless and the rock was lost. As she turned to leave, she stumbled over a garden tool with the initials *H. of G.H.* engraved on its handle. Just to the left of this tool was a large brown paper scroll tied in the middle with a piece of pampas grass. Tucked inside the scroll was a single long-stem yellow rose. Elpee loosened the pampas grass, removed the flower, and unrolled the paper. A message in block letters read:

Hey Sunshine,

I guess you gotta suck it up and do what ya gotta do, mama. I just want to tell you that I'm sorry I never stick around. I don't think you ever knew how much I cared for you and what I learned from you.

I'll talk to you later. No, really.

Hortense

A brief smile appeared on Elpee's face, but quickly disappeared as a look of sorrow replaced it. Her heart hurt at the thought of not seeing the Princess of Grouse Hollow again and out of regret for not having gotten to know her better as she had done with the other princesses. That thought prompted tears to begin flowing down Elpee's cheeks for what she believed may become an eternity. And her earlier brief smile would not appear again for perhaps as long.

Her mood grew even graver as she left the garden patch and approached the area that had previously housed the castle. There was total devastation there also. Elpee's mind began to wander back in time to the vision of what was once her beautiful home, but she quickly brought herself back to the present moment. As her mind returned there, her eyes spotted a fractured piece of pottery on the ground. Elpee bent down and picked up a section of a broken teapot with an object tucked inside its spout. When she removed it, Elpee could see that it was a bonded fiber material, much the same as was used for containing tea leaves. Written inside the unfolded parcel was the message:

Dear Elpee,

I will miss you and our tea parties. I wish so much
you could take some tea along with you, especially that
maple-vanilla you are so fond of. Maybe you will find some
when you arrive there. I miss you already.

Goddess speed,
danDay-leon

All the while Alpert watched the young woman from a distance as she
stumbled around unsure of herself, but deliberate in her actions. He
caught a glimpse of the person that was emerging from her, and a hint of
optimism surfaced from within him. Elpee stopped telling herself how
confused she was, as it seemed to serve no purpose in clarifying the issues.
However, she did not stop asking herself questions.

"Hmm, why have the princesses left me letters? They each left them in
a very personal way and place, and are the only signs of aliveness that are
left here. Are these letters the things I can take with me? Surely, I would
not take a garden tool or broken teapot. It *must* be the letters themselves,
but . . ." Elpee said, thinking aloud.

Alpert was still standing off to the side, waiting for Elpee to approach
him rather than he being the one to initiate answering the questions. It was
time she began to do that on her own. As he waited, she walked right past
him, without saying a word, in the direction of the once flowerbed area.

"I have gotten three letters from three princesses so far. There is one
letter from one princess missing, and that would be Euterpe. If the other
princesses left their letters in the areas closest to their hearts, like PoliM'aladroit in the woods, Hortense in the garden, and danDay-leon in a teapot,
then Euterpe must have left hers in the slate-enclosed flowerbeds," Elpee
stated confidently out loud.

With that possibility in mind, she stood by the flowerbeds and looked
for something that resembled a letter. At first glance, Elpee saw nothing.
Nor did she see anything on her second, third, or fourth attempts to spy
something. In this most fragile state, Elpee as always of late was on the
verge of tears, and this lack of discovery coupled with the disproval of her
theory sent Elpee into a mass of crying humanity. For just an instant,

Elpee had felt a small degree of sanity amid the madness of her present life, but it appeared she was deceived. She turned to Alpert and humbly asked him to help her find the missing letter that she hoped existed. As the last word was spoken, a hot-pink lacey parchment vision flew before Elpee's eyes at what seemed to be mach 2 speed and landed on a piece of slate that Euterpe helped Elpee place there. As Elpee reached down to pick up the pink parcel, it jumped up and began to fly around her just out of reach. The parchment at times stopped and floated in front of the ex-princess, baiting her, but it would resume its flight maneuvers each time Elpee attempted to capture it.

And the games began!

The parchment flew, and Elpee chased it around the flowerbeds and beyond. She laughed and played, and ran and shouted, all the while ignoring the bleakness of her surroundings. Alpert acted as host and served Elpee a chilled glass of peach iced tea with the maximum amount of sugar. Always polite, the girl thanked him despite her distraction and preoccupation with her flying friend. It had been so long since Elpee enjoyed herself as she was now doing, and the wizard wanted this to last uninterrupted for as long as possible. He knew, however, that it must, and would, end soon, as the day was coming to a close and evening would soon be upon them.

The laughter and games continued until Elpee was exhausted but re-energized at the same time. Finally, the lace-trimmed pink parchment floated down and settled on a piece of slate, where it stayed until Elpee reached for and opened it. It read:

To the Mistress of Cherry Castle by the Sea
Oh, how much I will truly miss thee
It is now 'I' instead of 'WE'
I hope you will remember me

When the moon is on the rise
It will be time for all who are wise
To abandon this world and reach for the skies
To ride a star to the grandest prize

It is time, my friend, to drop the disguise
And let the tears flow from your eyes
Let go of all this, and all of the lies
And you will see that everything survives

So, if you look beneath the willow tree
Within a special shell, you will see
A velvet satchel that holds the key
To the place and person, you need to be

Peace out, Sista,
Euterpe the *Queen*

A look of puzzlement mixed with resignation came over Elpee's face as she handed the letter to Alpert. He read it only briefly, as it was of no importance to him. He was with Elpee merely to help her complete this part of her journey, and at this point, his purpose was more one of support than guidance. As Alpert handed the letter back to the girl, he reached for her hand, and together they walked the short distance to the willow tree. No longer strangers, they walked in silence while holding each other's hands.

When they arrived at the willow tree, there was a weathered conch shell sitting beneath it. Elpee did not remember ever having seen it there before; then again, nothing about her present was reminiscent of her past. She parked herself on the ground, leaned against the tree, picked up the shell, and just held it before choosing to look inside. Alpert also sat alongside the tree and waited for Elpee to make a move. They reclined together in quiet for some time before Elpee sought direction from the wizard.

"What do you think I should do?" she asked Alpert.

"Look inside," he replied.

She looked at him, amazed at the simplicity and accuracy of his answer.

"You surprise me, my dear. The most complex of questions and problems you manage, but the clearly obvious ones you stumble over. Many people with enough fortitude can be a survivor, but it takes a special person to live truly, and to simply live. You have the gift of both, Missy. You lack only one thing—the most important thing—the ability to trust yourself and your instincts," Alpert advised her.

The wizard slipped back into his old ways one last time and responded to Elpee's confused thoughts.

"I know you can't even begin to comprehend what I am saying, and certainly not this concept, so for right now just tuck it away in your mind, and it will be there when you are ready, and when you need it."

Together they sat under the darkening sky and remained still until it was time. Alpert reached over and once again touched her hand.

"I must leave you now, my dear. The time has come. I suggest you reread your final letter when I am gone. It has a message in it for you. Don't dally either, my dear, the day is growing old." He continued, "Read the letter."

As Alpert began to rise, Elpee touched his arm and said, "Alpert, I need to ask you one question before you leave. I have wanted to ask you this for what seems to be a long time," asserted Elpee.

"Well, why haven't you ever asked me, Missy?" responded the wizard quizzically.

With a look of defeat on her face, Elpee replied, "Because I was afraid of the answer."

Alpert stood there patiently waiting for the question to be posed to him. Finally, Elpee asked, "Why have you never called me by my name? Elpee. Not even once."

Alpert paused before answering. "Because that is not who you are yet, my dear. You must earn your identity."

"I know," the girl replied with a lilt of resignation in her unsteady voice.

"As did I know, so you knew also," the wizard said, both with a hint of humor as well as compassion as he walked away into the light of the rising moon.

THE SHELL

Elpee sat there and watched as Alpert left her side and her life. She felt emptier than she could remember ever having felt before, and could not have imagined that she would feel this way about a man who entered her life such a short time ago. Initially, she would have done anything she could have to make him disappear, but now it was quite the opposite. If only he could have stayed. Elpee believed that by herself she had no answers; she did not even know the questions.

"Why did he come into my life so suddenly and leave the same way?" Elpee asked herself. "I feel so all alone and afraid. First, the rocks left, then Butter disappeared, and now Alpert has gone. All I have are these farewell letters. What am I supposed to do?" she continued.

"Read the letter," a voice that was distinctively Alpert's resonated in her head. Alpert's interruption served as confirmation as to why Elpee at times was annoyed by him.

"NOW!" *It* more forcefully continued.

Elpee, despite her annoyance, had come to have faith rather than fear in the wizard. And so she heeded his command and reread Euterpe's letter.

To the Mistress of Cherry Castle by the Sea
Oh, how much I will truly miss thee
It is now 'I' instead of 'WE'
I hope you will remember me

When the moon is on the rise
It will be time for all who are wise
To abandon this world and reach for the skies
To ride a star to the grandest prize

It is time, my friend, to drop the disguise
And let the tears flow from your eyes
Let go of all this, and all of the lies
And you will see that everything survives

So, if you look beneath the willow tree
Within a special shell, you will see
A velvet satchel that holds the key
To the place and person, you need to be

Peace out, Sista,
Euterpe the *Queen*

"When the moon is on the rise? That would be now," muttered Elpee.

"Abandon this world and reach for the skies? Drop the disguise and let go of this and all the lies?" she continued, asking aloud.

"Within a special shell . . . Velvet satchel . . . Key?"

Before Elpee could finish reading the letter, she once again heard Alpert's voice, "Look inside."

It was as good an answer as any, so Elpee picked up the conch shell and looked inside where a blue, velvet pouch sat tucked away. She removed the packet and spontaneously opened it before she changed her mind.

What awaited her eyes caused her to gasp in surprise and disbelief. Within the satchel was a kaleidoscope—the most beautiful kaleidoscope she could ever imagine. It was dressed in iridescent mother of pearl and was belted on either end with brass rings. Mesmerized by its beauty and wondering about its meaning, Elpee could not look away but instead began turning the brass eye ring around and around.

She reflected on that afternoon a long time ago when danDay-leon read her tea leaves, and the only thing that she could predict in Elpee's future was a kaleidoscope. The confused and despairing princess felt as if her life was a giant jigsaw puzzle in which all the pieces were there; some fit together while others did not, but there was no total picture to be seen, just fragments of a whole.

"The picture is as vague as you are, my dear," spoke the voice of the absent wizard. "For too many years you have been undefined. Now it is time to find that definition, but you are the only one who can identify you," Alpert concluded.

Elpee sat there with her thoughts and her memories playing in her mind for what someone apparently viewed as too long. Suddenly, she felt a sharp pinch bringing her back to the present and the task at hand.

"Stupid dope, Alpert," she hollered, reverting to her less mature days.

The night was growing old, all she knew was gone, and with nothing else to do, Elpee checked her pockets for the four notes from her sisters, picked up the kaleidoscope, and brought it to her eye.

INTO THE ABYSS

As Elpee gazed into the kaleidoscope, her eye was met with a blinding, white light that enveloped not only her vision but also her entire being. In response to the overwhelming sight, Elpee inadvertently turned the ring on the kaleidoscope and instantaneously become one with it. Now, it was no longer all that she had known that was gone, but also Elpee herself who had left everything that once was.

And so it began!

The girl was tossed and tumbled round and round. The white light became one with all the other colors of the spectrum with Elpee at its core. It was like a rollercoaster ride of prisms and crystals, and although at times it felt too much to bear, the battered girl was powerless against its forces. She did not know how she got in there, how and when it would end, nor where it would take her. Maybe she would never get out, she thought. Maybe this was death.

At times, it would speed up, throwing her against the sides of the tube like a rag doll. There seemed to be no air or life inside this tunnel, just movement and colored crystals in which Elpee was at the center. When she finally surrendered to its colossal speed and might, the rate at which she was traveling decreased slowly, moving her toward what she perceived would be an unidentified final destination. Thinking the ride was over, the girl inside the tube felt relieved, although in actuality it was just beginning.

The next level of this whirlwind travel was in stark contrast to its predecessor. The lighting – or lack of – was so black that it appeared purple, and the prisms, although far less in number, were sharp and stinging, piercing Elpee's skin as she was pushed against them. She tried to cry out, but it was not possible in this vacuum. The only option available to her was to withstand the cutting pain and accept it as it was.

Elpee soon realized that there were different segments of this place she was in and that as soon as she accepted this level of darkness and pain, a new one washed over her and propelled her body into one that alternated between the first two. The ride would take her from speed and light to pain and darkness, back and forth, time and again, until she seemed to lose consciousness.

What Elpee experienced when she came to did not resemble anything from any of the previous levels of this tunnel travel. The section she was in now was bathed in neutral colors and was absent of both the blackness and the colorful stinging prisms. She traveled steadily and forward as if she were on a conveyor belt. This stage was neither safe nor frightening compared to the other regions she had just tumbled through. It just was. Elpee welcomed this neutral place, believing that she could rest for a minute and let herself sluggishly glide.

Once again, just as soon as Elpee was accustomed to where she was, a change occurred and so did the landscape. Although it remained indeterminate in all ways, it took on the flavor of the land from which Elpee had originated – the location she had left all that time ago. As she was thrust forward, images from her past appeared on either side of the tube. Unable to avoid viewing them, Elpee for the first time in her life came face to face with her origins. All the pictures and feelings she had run away from were here again. This time, however, there was no running. She was in a place from which there was no escape. The only thing she could do was to see, to feel, and to keep moving through them because there was no way out.

At times, feeling as if she would break in two, Elpee continued in this phantasmagoria for miles and miles. She had spent her entire life running and avoiding only to end up in a place where she could do neither. At times, she found herself wailing in pain as the memories of the past projected themselves before her. Any connection to her life at Cherry Castle was broken in the miles she was currently traveling. And with the help of all that was holy, she prayed that soon any link to that former existence she was now revisiting would also be destroyed.

As Elpee got on her knees, half-praying and mostly sobbing, all motion stopped. When she looked up, she once again was in the midst of the blinding white light that had begun this time travel. The tattered waif could see nothing, but she heard a soft voice calling to her.

"Hello. Hello in there. Come out, my dear. I won't hurt you. I am here to help you. My name is Anna, and I was sent here by Alpert."

Elpee believed and trusted nothing anymore, but the voice was so kind and gentle, she felt compelled to listen to it. That, combined with the mention of Alpert's name, caused her to relax enough that the kaleidoscope spit her out into the land of Now, causing Elpee to give birth to herself.

ANNA

————

As Elpee sat on the ground of some unknown and nondescript area, Anna approached her. She was a woman of average height and weight with golden blonde hair that was styled in a short, trendy bob. This woman wore tailored clothing with a neatly tied neck scarf and modest jewelry. She sported modish eyeglasses and a light spirit. Elpee liked her.

"I am Anna, your . . ." she began.

"Faerie goddess-mother," finished Elpee. "Alpert told me about you, and that I should be nice to you because I will need your help."

"Being nice to me would be good, and you most certainly will need my help, dear. If you allow me to be honest with you right off, perhaps we can begin with your appearance. I certainly do not mean to embarrass you, but you are a sight, and it seems that you have rather neglected yourself of late. What I am trying to say is that you are such a beautiful young woman, and your beauty should be recognized, not disguised."

"I thought I was taking good care of myself," said Elpee, a bit embarrassed.

"And you did take good care of yourself, dear, to the best of your ability for where you were, but I am here to help you adjust to the present, and we may want to change some things about your current appearance. Let us make this fun!" Anna stated, trying to encourage Elpee.

"Where are we going? Please tell me," asked Elpee, anxious for some answers.

"I have a limited time here. I will begin your journey with you, and then you must find your own specific way. I will always be listening for you should you need me. Make yourself a necklace with a shell hanging from it that you can whistle into when you need me, and I will hear you and come," Anna instructed.

"Right now, let us leave here and go to your home where we can get to work. Is that all right with you?" the Faerie goddess-mother asked.

"Okay," was all Elpee could say.

They walked along a wooden road for a short distance until they came upon a small cottage with a green roof, white picket fence, window boxes, and an overall appearance that produced a feeling of home in Elpee's heart. It had a front porch with an eating table on one end that looked out on a side garden replete with birdbaths and feeders. There was a living room with a fireplace and mirror hanging over it, a dining room with its built-ins, and a kitchen with her favorite tiled floor in a black and white checkerboard pattern. Upstairs, the bedrooms were small, but the master bedroom had a four-poster bed with a peach chenille bedspread atop it. At the end of the hall was a large bathroom with white wainscoting and a clawfoot bathtub. All the windows in the cottage were decorated with the most delicate lace curtains, which wafted gently in the warm summer breeze.

"This is my house?" Elpee asked Anna.

"Yes, it is. It is one of my favorites," replied the Faerie goddess-mother.

"Perhaps, my dear, while I am preparing lunch, you could go upstairs and have a bath. I am sure that after your long journey you will find it soothing," suggested Anna, trying not to offend this newly reclaimed life.

What Anna saw was a neglected and fragile young woman who needed some immediate attention and grooming followed by some long-term care in the way of loving. Most of her hair would need to be cut off, as it was too tangled and damaged to be saved. Anna, knowing that she would have to be gentle in her approach to Elpee, hoped that the new wardrobe along with the necessary primping would not prove too traumatic to this waif.

As Elpee bathed, she scrubbed her body and attempted to wash her hair, but it was much too tangled to be able to do so. She began to cry, and as she breathed in, she made a whistling noise that brought Anna immediately to the bathroom door.

"Did you call me, dear?" Anna asked.

"I don't think so," replied Elpee curiously, "but I think I would like to cut my hair off when I get out. Do you think we could?"

"I think that is an excellent idea, and it would be delightful and much more stylish and mature," Anna answered.

Elpee continued to bathe while Anna went downstairs and prepared for her charge's arrival there. When she was finally done bathing, Elpee dried herself off and chose a pair of linen pants and a silk blouse to wear. She descended the staircase clad in an entirely new and clean outfit with the exception of one item – shoes. Anna commented on her stunning appearance and did not feel the need to address the absence of footwear at that point in time.

"Shall we give your hair a trim now?" asked Anna.

"I think so, but I would like more than a trim. I want it all cut off. Very short, please," responded Elpee.

"As you wish. I think short is very fun and stylish," encouraged Anna. "Why don't you sit at the table and we shall begin?"

Anna cut, and cut, and cut some more until Elpee was pleased, and when the haircut was completed, she looked stunning. It was carved into a short, spiky style that was mature and fashionable, making Elpee feel light and new without her straggly long hair. When she looked in the mirror on the landing at the top of the stairs, the appearance of a sophisticated woman stared back at her. It would be some time before Elpee saw herself in the same way instead of only as the image that stared back at her, but that is all that she had in this world—time. With both women happy with the results of the mini makeover, they sat together and ate the lunch Anna had prepared earlier.

Anna spent the next few days building Elpee's confidence. Self-esteem, however, she would have to find herself. The two women discussed the need for Elpee to move forward and begin integrating into her new community. Because she had lost so many years and was now emerging anew, Elpee felt bewildered and still afraid. She had left the fanciful girl behind and at present appeared to be a mere shadow of her former self. The new Elpee was somber, pensive, wary, unsteady, and very unsure of how to proceed, all the while lugging around the woman she was becoming.

"What are you afraid of, Elpee?" Anna asked.

"I just don't know how to act or what to say or do," Elpee responded.

"Remember Alpert's simplicity?" Anna continued. "He would say, 'Just walk outside and say something!' It really is that simple."

"I feel so out of place, not only here, but within myself. Who am I, and where did all my polka dots go?" asked Elpee with concern.

"You are still very much the same you, only now you are also the person you were born to be. The polka dots grew up and connected with each other. They are just not as visible as they once were," Anna explained.

"Well, I miss the polka dots sometimes, and don't know how to act now that I can't see them," Elpee continued with her concern.

"You are just maturing, Elpee, and you're not comfortable with that prospect. The girl has grown up, and a young woman now exists in her place. With maturity comes a depth of character that overshadows the childlike qualities. It is all normal – even your discomfort," Anna reassuringly told Elpee.

That did not make Elpee particularly happy, but it did satisfy her in that she trusted Anna, therefore putting some credence into what she said. Before he left, Alpert strongly advised Elpee to do this, and so she did.

As Anna's time with Elpee drew short, Elpee asked her to come to the beach to help find a shell by which she could summon Anna if she needed to. They walked there together, and in short order, Elpee found an abandoned snail shell that she thought was perfect because it was a reminder of her slow progress through this life. Now, if only it worked. She made Anna stand at various distances to test it out, and to both their surprises, each time was a success.

When Elpee was confident that the whistle would work and Anna was sure that Elpee would be all right, they were ready to say their goodbyes. Elpee promised to use the whistle that she had fashioned into a necklace, and Anna, in turn, promised to come whenever she heard it. Although she was afraid of being alone in a strange land and of what was in store for her, Elpee believed, probably for the first time in her life, that she actually would be okay.

Anna poured the tea that she had insisted on personally making, and both women sat at the kitchen table to share one last cup before she departed. Elpee did not question why Anna was so adamant about making the tea, but rather enjoyed the fact that someone else prepared it much like danDay-leon had done.

After a few sips, Elpee could sense the spellbinding effect the tea was having on her. As they sat there, Anna picked up her teacup and asked, "I have a question for you now. What is your name, dear? I don't believe you have ever told me your real name?" Feeling the hypnotic influence of Anna's tea potion, Elpee looked up at the sign hanging on the kitchen wall that hung over the table and replied, "Grace. My name is Grace."

Amazing Grace

The days that followed seemed very similar to, yet altogether different, from the days of old—the ones before Grace arrived here and before the wizard came to her. She cooked, read, tended the garden, and performed all other chores, except now she did all these things alone with no gnomes, or elves, or sister princesses to depend on or interact with. The former princess would need to learn everything unknown and unfamiliar on her own, and in many cases, the process had already begun. Mostly, she lived her life by trial and error.

Although all her lessons were hard, Grace believed the most difficult task she had to master was the ability to visit her past without reliving it or trying to escape from it – to just be and accept it. When she landed here in the land of Now, she was no longer little nor was she a girl. She was a woman who had spent almost half her life in a made-up world, with make-believe people, and manufactured stories. In this world things were real – frequently too real for Grace. It would take time for her to untangle what was right and what was not, as she often felt overly confused and unable to decipher the difference at all. Grace depended on the letters she brought with her from the other princesses to help her navigate this new journey.

PoliM'aladroit's letter was suspended on the front porch wall facing the path that welcomed visitors. To find the wisdom and faith to carry on, Grace would read the words within the dispatch penned by the Princess of ShinyShores.

When in need of nurturing, Grace visited the kitchen, made herself a cup of tea, and read danDay-leon's letter which was located there and would, in turn, lift her spirit and help her to feel less lonely.

It was beneath the outdoor overhang which sheltered the two wicker rockers from the elements and overlooked the gardens that Grace, by reading Hortense's letter, could obtain the necessary courage to do what she felt was undoable.

At times when the little girl in Grace emerged and wanted to play, she would close her eyes and imagine *Queen* Euterpe's letter flying about as it once had, and laugh as she did that day so long ago. She was eternally grateful for these four letters and the memories attached to them.

In the beginning, Grace walked around holding the small shell in her hand, poised to use it if a necessary and immediate emergency arose. That was not the case, however, and on the many occasions Grace did use the whistle, it was more out of a want than a need. The unconfident woman would signal Anna, who would come, and together they would explore options or strategies for Grace and her future.

On her visits, Anna would walk with Grace throughout her community and engage in conversations with Grace's neighbors, in essence breaking the ice for her and showing her how it was done. The most recent time Anna came to visit, Grace was feeling more self-assured in her everyday existence but sensed the need to have one final conversation with Anna in the event they, for whatever reason, should not meet again. As they sat on the front porch, Grace broached the subject.

"Anna, even though I am neither happy nor sad, I think I am beginning to settle into this new life I have here. I know it will take time to grow into my new skin and that I already am, but I have some questions I hope you can help me with," Grace began.

"Of course I will. That's what I am here for, aside from the fact that you make a wonderful cup of tea," Anna jokingly added. "What is it, Grace?"

"I am confused and scared. I don't know what is real and what isn't and it makes me feel frightened. My life now is so very different from the way it was before when it was light and fun with no concept of time or distance or the season. My friends lived under trees, and I had a dog that changed colors and grew. I lived in a castle with a magickal looking glass and a giant staircase. There were no adults and no rules. And now, as you know, I live in a cottage with mirrors that have no special powers, I can tell you exactly the amount of time I have lived here, I don't own a dog of any kind, and I have no friends that live under trees. I want to know if that was real, and if it was, what does that make this?"

"Reality is relative. Therefore, you must answer these questions yourself, Grace, but I must say that I don't know anyone who has a garden with talking rocks that protest and stage a walkout, nor am I aware of a person having a dog that simply vanishes while she is sleeping. So, what do you think?" the woman asked, turning the question back on Grace.

With Anna seemingly talking in riddles and having no answers of her own, Grace began to grow more frustrated until her frustration turned to anger, which she directed at Anna.

"You're supposed to be helping me, so why aren't you? You can see how confused I am and you are dancing around answers sounding philosophical while I feel like . . . Like . . . I don't know," spewed Grace.

"Breathe, Grace," instructed Anna. "I am here to *help* you, but some things you must do for yourself. I can only support you. And reality is relative to the person – not absolute or objective. My reality is very different than yours is, and I have no right to impose my subjective views on you. My role is to assist you in finding your truths and supporting you when you do find them. Do you understand that?" Anna asked.

"I'm sorry," began Grace.

"No apology is necessary, I assure you, but do you understand what I am trying to explain to you?" Anna asked again.

"Yes, and I don't like it! You're saying there is no definitive answer, which is exactly what I am looking for," Grace retorted.

"I know, Grace. We all want that, but *that*, my dear, is not reality. Let me give you an example. Do you see this flower?" Anna asked as she pointed to a wild violet on the side of the road. "Well, it wasn't here yesterday, and it may not be here tomorrow, so, is it real? To you and me it is, but what about to the person who walked here yesterday, or the person who passes it and does not see it at all? The flower is still there and is real to us, but it does not exist to those people. Therefore, it is not real to them. Same flower, but different realities," concluded Anna.

"I know! I understand what you are saying," Grace hesitantly admitted. "I still want you to give me the answers, though."

Both women laughed at Grace's declaration.

"Don't we all want the answers given to us? If only it were that easy."

As Anna was preparing to leave Grace's home, she suggested that Grace give herself some time to adjust and integrate into this new society before taxing her emotional state any more than was necessary. There would be time and opportunity to find the answers without forcing the issues, Anna explained.

"If we never meet again, I want to thank you and let you know that I definitely could not be doing this without your wisdom and guidance," Grace told Anna while holding her hand.

"We will meet again, that is for sure, but thank you for the kind words. I know you are on the right road and will continue to be just fine, but remember to whistle if you need," Anna instructed.

They hugged each other goodbye, and with that, Anna departed, and Grace returned home.

Grace spent the next several months adjusting to the real world, viewing it through reality-based glasses, and integrating into it. She met her neighbors, who, unlike the ones of old, did not live under trees or travel distances by bicycle or helicopter. They lived in houses, went to work every day, and came home every evening. Although many of these people welcomed her when she arrived in this land, Grace sometimes needed to push herself into making their acquaintances. Any difficulties she experienced with them were within her and her nagging insecurities.

Alpert, the wizard, advised her a long time ago that she had spent her life undefined, and that it was time she needed to remedy that. Grace could no longer live by others' definitions of who she was. It was her choice, her life, and her right to make decisions necessary for self-definition. Grace was still very much Elpee in so many ways and was merely presenting a more mature and authentic version of who she once was. Cakes and candy were replaced by a more balanced diet. She now wore skirts and trousers rather than sundresses and overalls. The cottage no longer sported cherries and polka dots but rather linen and lace. As the months passed, Grace settled in more and more and began to develop routines that would, in turn, create her.

THE MARKET

Every few days when Grace needed to purchase supplies from the market, rather than walking, she would ride her bicycle to carry her purchases home in the basket. On this day, however, a flat tire necessitated that Grace push her bicycle to the hardware store for its repair before proceeding to the market. When she delivered the bike to Norbert, the store's owner, she removed the wicker basket from the handlebars and continued on her mission to purchase supplies.

Unaccustomed to hiking to the market, she challenged her routine even further by taking an unfamiliar path. She found the experience entirely different than riding her bike because it gave her the opportunity to use all her senses and the quiet road allowed her to have a visual experience she would not have had had she been riding.

Grace's pace was unhurried, allowing her to view the green landscape that stretched out before her. She occasionally slowed down even more or stopped altogether to smell and feel the needles on the pines and evergreens. Some were soft and tickly, and others were hard and pointy, making it easy to hurt oneself.

Further along the trail, Grace noted a sweet fragrance and followed it to a patch of honeysuckle and wild berry bushes. Because of her meandering ambulation, the trip to the market took far longer than she had anticipated, and she found herself somewhat hungry. The wild berries were sweet and juicy and provided an excellent solution to this problem. Not satisfied with just a few nibbles, Grace picked a handful of them and sat on the side of the road under the berry-laden bushes.

When the edge was taken off her hunger, Grace knew she needed to get up and move on even though her body was content and comfortable and she wanted to linger in the sultry summer heat just a while longer. After a short mental debate with herself, Grace reached a compromise and decided to continue to the market to do her shopping but to allow herself to rest here on her return trip.

Grace rose, picked up her basket, and continued to the store. It was a short walk from where she was resting, and within a few minutes, she was in the shop greeting her neighbors as she placed items into her basket. Because Grace had to walk back to the hardware store to retrieve her bicycle, she kept her purchases to a minimum.

At the counter, Grace spoke to Janie and asked her for some items.

"Good morning, Grace. How are you on this beautiful lazy summer day?" the market owner asked.

"Lazy," she giggled, "but good, thank you, Janie, and how are you?"

"I am doing well also, and thankfully so is the rest of my family. Nothing is new. Business is good. I have nothing to complain about. How about you, Grace?"

"As I said, I am good. I stopped for a rest on my way here today and realized that it had been a year since I moved to this town. It went so fast. At least, now it seems that way. At times during the year that surely was not the case, though," answered Grace.

"I know, dear," Janie said compassionately. "It was a big adjustment for you, and I'm sure it was challenging at times, but you've done so well and come so far. All of us in the village are very proud of you."

"Thank you, Janie. You and everyone else here have helped me so much. I couldn't have done it without you guys."

"All right, Gracie, before we get all teary-eyed, what can I get for you today?" Jane asked.

"You are right," agreed Grace. "I just need a dozen eggs and some ham, please."

As Janie went to get the supplies, Grace took a deep breath and said a silent thank you for the reception she received when she arrived in this village. These people – her friends now – gave Grace, who was then so broken and afraid, the time, space, and support she so desperately needed.

Janie returned with the groceries, gave them to Grace, and after they exchanged hugs, Grace began her trek back to the berries.

Eggs, Ham, and Butter

With her supplies in her basket, Grace sauntered back to the spot she had visited earlier. It was now more visually pleasing than it had been at that time because the sun was lower in the sky, and its beams were dancing through the woods. After picking a handful of berries, Grace again took a seat under the bushes and smelled the pungent, earthy aroma of her surroundings while feeling and tasting the sweetness and texture of the fruit.

A sense of peace came over Grace, and she leaned back against a tree to bask in it and the sunshine. While in this state of serenity and gratitude, she began to doze and indulged herself by allowing it to happen.

Unsure how long she was napping, Grace was gently awakened by a rustling noise. So at peace, she ignored it and continued to relax in the tranquility of the moment and her surroundings. She maintained a meditative state, going in and out of sleep while the white noise continued in the background.

Eventually, Grace, having sufficiently rested, awoke on her own. The rustling noise had stopped, and although she was unaware of the exact time, Grace knew she needed to retrieve her bicycle and head home for dinner. She rose, stretched, and grabbed a few more berries before reaching for her basket. Having done that, Grace found the basket half empty. Still a bit dazed, Grace scratched her head and once again looked inside the basket, seeing only the eggs. The ham had vanished. For some unexplainable reason, Grace elected to search the area for the source of the robbery, unsure what she would do if she found the culprit. She mulled about for a minute or so before coming to her senses and abandoning her search. On her way out of the woods, Grace stumbled upon and came face to face with a pair of giant brown eyes that belonged to a furry little creature that was staring at her from behind a tree.

Startled, Grace jumped back, and so did the creature in response to her response.

She screamed.

It screamed.

She sat.

It sat.

She stayed.

It stayed.

It seemed to be a stalemate. A war of the wills. Who would blink first? In the end, it was the creature that succumbed to the ocular pressure. It came out from behind the tree, walked toward Grace, smiled at her, and then turned around and gave her his butt.

She walked over to the little black creature she could now recognize as a dog, and after a second or two of shock, Grace believed it was Butter, the small black dog she found in a hole all those years ago, or at least a replica of him. It did not much matter to Grace who he was, his name was Butter.

They hugged each other and rolled around on the ground, getting berry juice all over themselves. They were so happy to see each other (again?).

"How? Where? Oh, never mind. I don't care. I don't even care that you ate all my ham, you big dummy. I am so glad to see you again." Grace hugged her lost – now found again – friend and cried all over him as she said, "I missed you so much."

'Butter' cried too.

WILL THE REAL BUTTER . . .

The dog and the woman walked to the hardware store to retrieve Grace's bicycle.

"Stay, Butter," Grace told the dog as she opened the screen door to enter, but as she went in, the dog followed directly behind her, ignoring what he perceived to be more of a request than a command. Grace did not realize Butter had slipped in until the proprietor of the hardware store came from behind the counter to shoo the dog outside.

"Scat, you little mongrel," Norbert scolded the wayward animal.

"Butter, what are you doing in here? Didn't I tell you to stay?"

"Whose dog is this?" questioned Norbert curiously.

"He's mine," responded Grace, "the bad boy that he is."

"When did you get a dog and from where? You were here a few hours ago, and you didn't have him then."

As Grace and Norbert engaged in a game of verbal ping-pong, Butter sat between them, moving his head from side to side as each responded to the other.

"This little guy ate all the ham out of my basket while I was resting and dozed off in the woods on my way here. He scared me, but I think I scared him as well. He was so cute, I couldn't get angry, and besides he reminds me of a dog I also found a long time ago. He too was small and black—that is until I bathed him and he grew and turned yellow," Grace told Norbert.

Norbert looked at Grace quizzically, and she quickly realized that she had slipped back into the past and that what she said to him was nonsensical. She wished she had checked her thinking before saying what she did rather than having to explain it away now.

"I mean, the dog I found then was so dirty that when I bathed him, he turned many shades lighter and filled out from eating so much," Grace said in an attempt to undo her earlier statement.

Norbert's face relaxed with Grace's explanation. Contented that she had redeemed herself, Grace thanked Norbert, got her bicycle, and she and Butter walked the short distance back to her cottage.

The little black dog pranced next to his new master, appearing happy to at last have a home. Grace was angry with herself for having slipped back into the fantasy, partially for saying what she did, but more so because her thinking would still go there. It had been a year since her relocation here, and despite her efforts to be kinder to herself, Grace had no patience for her lapses into the past even though the times she regressed were fewer and fewer and she caught herself sooner. It would just take time, she kept telling herself

When they arrived at the cottage, Grace opened the gate to show Butter the way in. Like Butter #1, he seemed to instinctively know his way around by going inside and making himself comfortable. He went into the kitchen and sat by the sink and refrigerator while Grace vowed to ignore any further similarities to Butter #1. She gave the dog water in a bowl that was in the cottage when she moved in, but no food. He would have to make do by watching Grace eat her lunch, because he would not eat anymore today after all the ham he had stolen from the basket earlier. Grace prepared the tea and scrambled eggs and carried them out to the front porch, where she sat at the small table and ate while watching the world go past.

Butter followed her and lay contentedly without begging, much to Grace's surprise, on the floor next to his new master as she ate. She was used to the incessant begging, whining, and crying for food that she experienced with his predecessor. She finished the last of her lunch and got a piece of paper and a pencil from the drawer in one of the built-ins, with her new housemate following immediately behind her. Grace was going to make a list of similarities and differences between the two dogs to put this issue to rest in her head.

Before giving any commands to the new Butter, she drew columns and categories on the sheet of paper and answered the B1 side and any of B2 she already knew.

	B1	B2
Sit	maybe	yes
Stay	yes	no
Come	no	yes
Begs	yes	no
Always hungry	yes	no
Barks	yes	no
Lays next to me	no	yes
Lays on the furniture	yes	no
Plays by himself	yes	doesn't look good
Crazy	yes	doesn't appear to be
Calm	no	looks good

Well, as she completed this part of her assessment, it appeared that Grace needed to give him several commands as a final test.

"Sit," she commanded, to which the dog obediently complied.

"Okay, Butter on to the last and most important test of all. Upstairs, boy," she told him as she led the way up the wooden staircase. When they reached the top of the stairs, Grace had to coax him down the hall and into the bathroom. He was much timider than his predecessor was; however, he did obey her command and followed her, albeit very reluctantly, down the hall and into the bathroom. The canine sat there with his body shuddering while Grace prepared the bath and tested the water temperature. With everything in place, Grace walked over to Butter, bent down, and while petting him tried to explain that he would be fine and that she would not hurt him.

"Up you go, mister, into the tub," she told him as she lifted him up and gently placed him in the bathtub.

"This is just a little warm water and then some shampoo, and I'll lather you all up, and it will feel good. You may just like it. After that, we rinse you off with some clean water, dry you, and then you will be free to go, okay?" the bather simultaneously asked and advised the drenched puppy. Still trembling, and now also shivering, the wet dog stood there motionless waiting for the torture to end. Grace scrubbed and scrubbed because he was filthy, but mostly because she needed to make sure that this last test was valid and only soap, water, and scrubbing would prove that.

When Grace's arms and the poor dog could stand no more, she turned on the faucet and began to rinse away the soap and grime. At first glance,

Grace gasped, and her heart began to pound because the water rolling off the dog was black. Once again, confusion set in, making her question her sanity. She kept rinsing and rinsing and eventually the liquid began to run clear. It was not until there was no more soap on the dog and the water was thoroughly free of color that Grace felt comfortable enough to terminate the process.

What stood before Grace in the bathtub was a skinny little black dog who had just been very dirty. She was sane. Her mind was just playing tricks on her, making her imagine that this dog was the same one that disappeared all that time ago, but it was not, and now Grace knew that. They merely had similarities to each other, as dogs did, and her mind wanted her to make a connection where none existed, but Grace was recovering and knew better.

She seemed to be pretty well grounded in the present and reality and needed to be gentle with herself when her mind went where it had always gone for so long. It was only natural that there would be situations and times when it would do that, but Grace had to believe that it would merely be temporary and that her rational side would eventually prevail.

PLANNING A PARTY

As Grace settled into her new routine with Butter, she decided that she should venture outside of her comfort zone and have a small gathering in celebration of her one-year anniversary in this village and to thank the people who welcomed and helped her. She had made many acquaintances since she arrived, and had worked side-by-side on projects with some of them, but Grace had never extended herself to the point of friendship. Once again, her wariness and fear stopped her from bridging that gap.

She and Butter walked to the General Store, where Grace tied the dog to a tree on the mall area lest he follow her into the store. He obeyed all her commands except 'stay' because he needed to be wherever she was at all times. Grace just accepted this and adjusted to it.

Pat was at the counter when she entered the store, and after exchanging brief greetings, Grace went directly to the stationary area in search of invitations. She knew in her mind exactly what she wanted and hoped that the store carried a likeness of it. Grace desired the most simple of invites – no balloons or cake – just standard cards, and that is what she found. Awaiting her was a package of ten, off-white, bi-fold note cards and envelopes that contained no graphics. She quickly counted on her fingers the number of requests she would need and found that a single package would be sufficient.

Picking up a beef jerky for Butter on the way out, Grace stopped at the counter to say hello to the store's owner.

"Having a party, Grace?" Pat asked.

Already feeling uncomfortable about the event itself, the questioning made Grace stumble over her words as she tried to respond.

"I am thinking about it. So, do you think I should? Do you think people would come?" Grace babbled, disappointed in herself for her lack of confidence and assertiveness.

"Of course they would. I certainly will if I am invited, not that you should feel obligated to invite me," replied Pat, who was now the one struggling for composure.

"You are the first on the list, my friend," Grace responded. *My friend,* Grace thought, wondering if she had ever used those words before.

"Excellent! I will be there with bells on! Take the invitations as my contribution to the party, Grace, and take the treat for your pup as well."

"Thank you so much, Pat, and thanks from Butter also," she replied as she left the store and untied a wounded-looking Butter who appeared to be suffering terribly for having been left behind. Two scratches behind the ears and the newly adopted canine was back to normal, trotting alongside his master.

When they got home, Grace poured herself a glass of freshly brewed iced tea and retired to the front porch to begin writing and addressing the invitations. One by one she handwrote the notes themselves as well as the individual names on the outside of the envelopes. The front of the card modestly said:

Please and Thank You

Inside was written:

Please attend a small gathering.
I am having at my home,
for you, my new friends,
to say
"Thank you!"

Date: September 13
Time: Sunset

Next came the guest list. There would be Pat and a guest, Norbert and Julie, Jane and Bill, and Alice and Dan. The task took the better part of the afternoon, leaving Grace tired, yet proud, of herself. She and her ever-present companion rested for the remainder of the day, breaking only to take a brief walk, have dinner, and retire shortly thereafter.

The next morning, Grace rose early and made breakfast for herself. She sat outside under the overhang in the wicker rocker, reflecting on the past and planning for the future while eating her oatmeal. As had become the custom, Grace left some grain in the bowl for Butter to lick clean and then they were off.

Because the dinner was only a week away, Grace decided to hand-deliver the invitations instead of posting them. She mapped out her route and began with the Hardware Store, and then she went to the Market, the General Store, and finally the Post Office before looping around and back to her home. Butter tagged along, walking either directly next to or following close behind her. When she returned to the cottage, Grace opened the gate and motioned for the dog to enter, and as he obeyed, Grace crossed the road to deliver the last invitation.

Planting next year's bulbs in her garden was Mrs. Reynolds, a quiet and peaceful woman who lived alone and kept to herself. Grace called to her, asking if she could enter. Mrs. Reynolds turned to Grace and motioned for her to come in, which she did. Once inside, Grace held out a white envelope with Mrs. Reynolds's name written on it and handed it to her. The woman opened it and looked up at Grace with both fear and gratitude in her eyes.

"I came here a year ago, and I don't know anyone – I mean really know – and I thought it would be nice to invite some people over to my home. Just a few people, not too many, and I would like for you to come. I so appreciate your garden and the way you tend it with such patience and love. I admire you. Please come," Grace entreated her neighbor.

"My name is Agness, and I came here a little over a year ago, but I have been too afraid to venture out and be as bold and confident as you are, so I have stayed to myself."

Grace began to snicker at Agness's assessment of her but stopped herself.

"Someone named Anna helped me, so maybe I am here to help you. Please say you will come," pleaded Grace.

"I will . . . If I can," was Agness's only response.

Grace spent the next week cleaning the house and preparing the menu for the party. She decided she would serve:

Mixed greens with fresh apples, walnuts, and crumbled Gorgonzola cheese

Roasted turkey

Oven-baked sweet potatoes

Steamed asparagus

Creamed onions

Homemade cranberry sauce

For dessert, the choices were:

Angel food cake with fresh strawberries and freshly whipped heavy cream

Warm fudge brownies with French vanilla ice cream.

HAVING A PARTY

As the day approached, and then finally arrived, Grace wondered why she would have ever thought of doing such a foolish thing as having this dinner. Her nerves were a jangle even though most of the preparations had been completed. She decided to lie outside on the hammock and relax before setting the table. As she rocked herself back and forth with an old bamboo reed, she pondered the strengths of the princesses of old. PoliM'aladroit had dignity, danDay-leon held warmth, Hortense possessed courage, and Euterpe overflowed with humor. How Grace wished she had a little of each of those qualities, and then she supposed that perhaps she did.

With time growing short, Grace reluctantly left her spot in the hammock and went into the house. She opened the draw-leaf table to accommodate all the guests and then got her lace tablecloth and linen napkins from the left built-in. After dressing the table with the linens, Grace placed ten dinner plates atop it, followed by the equal number of goblets and silverware. Each place setting had individual crystal salt wells with tiny spoons next to them. Grace placed a large crystal bowl filled with punch and fresh fruit on the sideboard.

As Grace positioned the candles on each end of the table, she heard a soft knock on the screen door. Standing there was Agness, holding a bouquet of fresh-cut flowers from her garden. Grace opened the door and invited her in, while at the same time taking the floral spray from her neighbor's trembling hands.

"These are so beautiful. I can't thank you enough because I don't have any in my garden, and their look and scent will certainly dress up the table." Sensing Agness's nervousness, Grace gave her a vase and asked that she arrange the flowers and then place them on the table, hoping that would keep her busy until the other guests arrived. Agness obliged and mindlessly arranged the flowers as Grace quickly changed her clothes.

No sooner had Grace returned downstairs than the guests began arriving. The first to arrive were Norbert and Julie, who came with Pat and her guest, Larry. Alice and Dan, then Jane and Bill followed them. Rather than leave it to chance, Grace made a conscious effort to introduce Agness to the other guests. When everyone was inside, and all the introductions were made, Grace led them into the dining room where, having decided against using the more formal place card arrangement, she asked them to seat themselves. Everyone sat in pairs on either side of the table, which left Grace and Agness to occupy the two ends and put Grace in the perfect location to lead the toast. As she lifted her glass, the others followed suit.

"To my new friends, health and happiness I wish you. Sincere thanks for all your kindness and encouragement this last year. And to my newest friend, Agness, know that you are welcome here and are blessed to also have these wonderful people as your friends. May we meet often for many years to come. Cheers!" When Grace had completed delivering her message, the others echoed her salute before lifting the glasses to their lips.

They all ate and drank while engaging in conversation. Everyone who already knew each other seemed to focus on Agness and her vast knowledge of gardening. She opened up much like her flowers as the conversation centered on her deep interest and love of gardening.

To Grace, it seemed that her role and purpose this evening was nothing more than to stage the event which allowed her to see that these people were already her friends. They knew it, but Grace had to experience it for herself to comprehend that she was more a part of this community than she realized.

When the dinner ended and the evening drew to a close, all the guests wished each other goodbye, thanked Grace, and welcomed Agness, who stayed behind to help Grace clean up. Grace began the conversation, as both women suddenly seemed somewhat uncomfortable with each other.

"Thanks so much for the flowers and for helping me to clean up. I appreciate it, and I'm so glad you came tonight," Grace said sincerely to the other woman.

Agness began to explain her life and feelings to Grace, who quickly cut her off.

"Oh, poop! We all have skeletons in our closets and have felt the way you do. You are a kind woman, Agness, and your presence here tonight and in the community as well are welcome. So please get over yourself," Grace told her as she playfully whacked her on the arm. Agness looked at Grace with a smile of caring appreciation. Grace, in turn, gave her a hug and sent her on her way home after once again thanking her.

Later that night when Grace was alone, she thought about and recognized the source of her earlier discomfort with Agness, as well as her like of and pity for her. Agness reminded Grace of her own mother – a solitary woman who emotionally, and at times physically, abandoned Grace from birth. Grace was glad that she managed to survive and live through the past, including the memories that haunted her most of her life. No bother! This town and house were her home, where her life would be different but thankfully sane. Grace hoped that Agness would fare better than her mother, a woman who was terminally unhappy, had. Grace knew that she and Agness would never be close friends, and she was at peace with that fact. She also knew that they had each helped the other more than they would ever understand.

THE POTTERESS

———

Fall turned into winter, and Grace spent her time designing pottery and making prototypes for her new business. She had opened a studio in the back cottage at the end of October after she and Pat had discussed a potential business arrangement.

The first projects Grace made were clay masks, which were designed to be hung on the wall. These initial attempts were crude and primitive but very much fun to create. Having no idea what she was doing or how to do it, Grace created mess after mess until she was able to figure out the correct mixture of clay and water to cast the masks without having them appear as if the faces were melting.

On cold, snowy days, when she and Butter were especially bored, they would leave the house and go to the back cottage, where Grace would regress back to her days of old and stage a one-person mask show for her canine companion.

"Hi, my name is Olly. What's yours? Chief My Face is Dripping?" asked the mask on the east wall.

"That is just plain mean, cruel, and self-serving, Captain Cauliflower Head," retorted its cottage mate, Beggle, who hung on the west wall and resembled the cruciferous vegetable.

"Oh, nice, drippy drooler," Olly said.

"I hope you fall off the wall and crack your crater head," West came back at East.

"Hey, how about Measles Mug over there? He's a real character," East commented on the polka-dotted mask sitting on the bench waiting to be glazed.

Cleopatra, who hung over the door, intervened by saying, "Please, you two over there. Our hostess did the best she could in making you, so show some respect and gratitude. Besides, the potteress is fairly inexperienced, and it may be reflected in her work. There is no reason to criticize each other for how you look. After all, not everyone can be as beautiful as I am. And what if she heard your mocking? Her feelings would be terribly hurt."

Soon, Grace had every one of the masks talking to each other, which gave her such a sense of satisfaction. As the clay faces argued, she danced around the small cottage singing praises to herself while Butter's head moved from mask to mask as they took turns speaking.

"I am so cool. I am so cool. Look what I have made . . . All these pretty faces. You tell 'em, Cleo. LA LA LA LA LAAAAA. Oh, I am so cool, and I don't care what any of you say! BECAUSE I AM SOOOO COOOOL!"

Grace enjoyed the rest of the winter and spent it mostly making pottery, sometimes even giving classes, despite the critical opinions of her questionable talent that she received from the masks. It was a long and cold winter at the beach, and she and Butter appreciated the diversion the classes gave them. The novice potteress's work improved with practice, and soon she was making earthenware for her gardens as well. The urns and planters were stored under the benches in the studio cottage while she anxiously awaited spring's arrival for her to place them outside. Also, she was running out of room inside.

One day in March, Grace and Butter – or Butter and Grace – walked into town and stopped at all the stores for a visit. There was a pep in her step because she felt spring in the air and knew that soon the days would be warmer and longer, which was more to her liking. When they arrived at the General Store, Pat motioned for them to come in.

"Hi, Pat. What's up?" asked Grace as she entered.

"I was wondering if by any chance you might have decided if you would be willing to place any of your pottery in here on consignment," the owner of the shop replied.

"Willing? Are you kidding, Pat?" replied Grace.

"No, I am serious. I think it could benefit both of us. What do you think?"

"I am so excited at the thought. My studio cottage is becoming overrun with works, and the masks are fighting with each other all the time, complaining of overcrowding and invasions of personal space," the potteress answered.

"Excellent!" Pat replied. "Did you say the masks are fighting? Oh, you're such a nut. I'll start making room, and it will motivate me to clean out some of the old clutter."

"I'd love to stay, but the boy and I have to finish our walk and take stock of our inventory. I'll talk to you. Come on, Butter," Grace said as she opened the door and left without waiting for a reply from Pat.

"How great is this going to be, my little man?" Grace asked the dog as she hurried the walk with Butter, who was struggling to keep up. He could not bear to be far from her, and his little legs were no match for her long strides, so finally he had no choice but to do what for him was the unbearable.

"Arf," Butter pitifully barked out to his master.

Grace suddenly stopped and looked around for the source of the noise.

"Arf," again the tired dog spoke.

His confused master looked in all directions for the animal responsible for such an unkind noise. It seemed that Butter had a rather unmelodic bark, and one that Grace would never think was coming from her sweet little doggie.

"Arf, arf, arf, woof, woof, woof, hooowwwwl," shrieked the dog, forcing Grace to look in the one direction she hadn't. There at her feet, she saw her little companion trying with all his might, but without much success, to produce a doglike tone. He did, however, get her attention.

"Butter? Was that you?" she asked.

He mustered up just enough energy to nod his head in the affirmative before lying down over dramatically.

"I am sorry, Butter, I forgot you have little legs. I think you should get up and out of the road though, buddy."

The dog, more histrionically if that was possible, stretched out even more, and turned over on his back, pathetically simulating his demise.

"Oh, my poor boy! I'll take care of you. Come here and let me pick you up. I will have to carry you home." As Grace picked up the limp animal, he let out another "Hooowwwwl."

"Oh no, my poor, poor boy. Are you dying?" Grace solemnly asked him.

Butter shook his head no. Even though he was tired and decided to play it up a little, he did have a conscience and could not allow his master to think she had killed him.

"Okay, that's good. I'm glad you are not dying, and if it helps, I'll make you a hamburger when we get home. You just go and lie up on the couch while I cook. Okay?" Grace asked as she cradled the ailing creature in her arms. As he smiled and nodded his head in approval, he gazed up at her with those same big brown eyes that had looked out from behind a tree last summer.

After the errands were run and Grace returned home exhausted from carrying Butter the entire way, she was faithful to her promise. She cooked dinner for him as he reclined on the couch and watched reruns of *Lassie* on the television.

THE MASKS MUST GO
AND
WHERE DO THE FLOWERS GROW?

────────

Grace spent the next few weeks gathering and putting into boxes the works that she wanted to display at Pat's. She also made a few extra pieces of pottery to include with the others. Pat had cleaned out an area in the store for the display, but with each trip Grace made to the shop with additional pieces, everything that was already in place had to be rearranged.

Grace had come to love all the masks for their unique characteristics and had a hard time deciding which ones she would elect to sell. She struggled and found herself in the middle of another mask fight, this time one in which they were all in agreement.

"I am not going anywhere," said East Wall.

"Well, neither am I, and it ain't right to send Freckles off either – after all, he is the baby," added West Wall.

"I agree! She will have to settle for asp girl over there," East said definitively.

"I am in total agreement with you. Cleo has to flee-o," replied West, chuckling hardily at his witticism.

"Excuse me, creatures . . ." Cleo interjected.

"We most certainly will excuse you. Right out the door, Cleo," West said as he and East roared with laughter.

No matter what Grace did, the masks continued their little diatribes, each time leaving her sitting with her head in her hands wondering what to do. She tried to reason, plead, bribe, and flatter them, but they continued to harangue her until one day she needed to make a decision and stated, "If you continue to cause me such grief, I will have one choice and only one choice. That choice is TO SMASH ALL OF YOU LITTLE HOODLUMS!"

She never heard even a peep of a complaint from their plaster mugs again, and she allowed them to remain living there while making new masks to sell – this time being sure not to develop a personal relationship with any of them.

As spring came to an end, Grace welcomed the summer by decorating her gardens with her own designed and handmade pottery. Within some of the pots, as well as mingled around the outside of them, were flowers of all different shapes, sizes, and colors, which she desperately hoped that Butter did not decide to roll around on and smush their beautiful blooms.

She was happy, and at peace with the life she had carved out here even though it was not at all by choice at the time it happened. Now, two years later, it was very different. Grace could not imagine living anywhere else or doing anything different. She relaxed on her porch one early summer evening and reflected on the gratitude and the stability she now had. Life was good!

As the days rolled on, Grace found herself busily making pottery and taking orders for particular pieces. It was taking up a great deal of her time, and Butter seemed to feel neglected, so Grace decided that when she finished her current projects, she would spend the day with him in the gardens before beginning anything new. She hurried to complete her tasks because Butter's languishment and unending theatrics were getting to be too much for either of them to bear. Finally, the day came when all of Grace's projects and orders were delivered, and that day went to the dog.

"Come on, Butthead, let's go," Grace announced to him as she opened the garden gate for both of them. He followed her with his tail finally in the upright position and faintly wagging. Grace sat on a bench in the garden to admire the plants while her canine companion rolled around in the grass.

"Hey, mister, doesn't the garden look lovely this year?" she asked Butter, who paid no attention whatsoever to her.

"Even though we – well, rather I – have been here only two years? This is my third summer, and I don't remember the plants ever looking so big and lush," Grace commented. By now Butter was ignoring her entirely and chose instead to play hide and seek with a field mouse. They spent hours out there relaxing and frolicking while Grace was commenting on the beauty of the gardens and Butter was playing dog and mouse.

Thankfully, for whatever reason, the summer seemed to pass slowly despite Grace being busy with her new business project. She did find the time, however, to pay attention to her canine ward and still keep the house in good order. Fortunately, the gardens seemed to sustain themselves, as Grace could not remember the last time she weeded or feeded them. She thought that whoever had previously lived in her cottage had left some extraordinary plant specimens—ones she had never seen before.

Grace hosted many meals for her friends and neighbors and was a guest at a number of dinners herself. She was so happy—happier than she had ever been before. To be accepted and be a part of something was what Grace had always desired, and now she had that precious gift without having to create it in her mind. Gone were the days when she had to do just that. Indeed, life was honest, and she was one with it. So much so, that Grace vowed to go up the incline on the other side of town in the morning to investigate Alpert's prediction. The hill was reminiscent of the one she climbed with Alpert to plant the seeds nearly three years ago. She had visited there several times before, knowing she would find nothing, but was curious nonetheless. This time, however, Grace was sure that the seeds would be in bloom and she would finally discover what flowers they produced.

She and Butter went to their respective beds, Grace excited about her upcoming adventure and hopeful discovery, and Butter excited by his master's excitement. She tossed – he turned. She turned – he tossed. Grace dreamt about that dreadful day when she planted those seeds that Alpert gave her while promising her that she would be in her new home with all she loved when they bloomed, and here it was. The only thing left to do was to find the patch that would satisfy Grace's nosiness regarding the flowers' genus.

Butter woke his sleeping master by bouncing his body against the bed and licking her errant hand that was hanging over the side. She was not happy to have been woken up, but she could not get angry at this little package of black fur and brown eyes. Instead, she tried to get him to nap a bit longer by coaxing him up on the bed and scratching his neck. It would not, and did not, work. The seed was planted – no pun intended – in the dog's head, and he wanted to go on the expedition pronto. Grace was anxious to view the flowers, therefore, she complied with Butter's delightful demands and got up. They went downstairs, where Grace made a quick breakfast for both of them, but the small dog, who was never terribly hungry, sat in full view of her with his big brown eyes saying, 'please hurry, please hurry, please hurry' until she once again succumbed to his charm.

Grace climbed the stairs to her bedroom, dressed quickly, and as she reached the top of the staircase to begin her descent, she was overcome with a desire to slide down the banister. Fortunately, she paused her movement for a second or two, at which time sanity triumphed, and she instead chose to use the steps to reach the main floor where Butter impatiently waited.

"Hold on, mister," Grace informed him. "I want to get some water and fruit to take with us."

She tackled this chore in record time and off they went out the front door and to the left past Grace's south garden. She could not help remarking again on how deliciously beautiful it was, causing Butter to roll his eyes at her.

They followed the road, eventually bearing right at the curve, and proceeded up the steep incline. Up, up, up the duo went, and when Grace felt that they should already be at the spot, she remembered Alpert's prodding of, 'just over the hill' and continued until she and her companion were at the summit with nowhere else to go but back down the hill.

Grace had been to this spot before, so she was familiar enough to know she could not have taken a wrong turn. She did not understand why there were no flowers. She was sure there would be this time. After all, her life was now seamless and real. She had a physical house, a material dog, genuine friends, and a paying job. This place was different, but she knew it was her home and that was all there was to it. So, where were the flowers?

Angry and disappointed after spending hours searching, Grace resigned herself to going home without finding the flowers that should have been there.

"Come on Butter, let's go." The dog just reclined there on the grass, re-enacting his exhaustion routine, waiting for Grace to fawn over him and pick him up. "Forget it, buster!" was all she said as she began the trek down the hill and back home.

Butter picked himself up, shook himself off, and closely followed his master to their cottage.

THE BEACH

For many days, Grace walked around stamping her feet, angry with Alpert for his stupid seed story, but madder at herself for having believed him. She wondered why she did such a foolish thing and trusted such a silly-looking dope like him.

None of that was real, she decided—not even the people. It took Grace two years here to determine what was real and what was fantasy. When she arrived here, she concluded that everything was made up except Alpert, Anna, and the princesses, but now Grace knew that was wrong. They were made up also. Everything was fantasy. None of it was real.

No matter what, Grace would not let go of her grip on reality and allow herself to return to the awful place from where she had come. This was her life, and this was her home; she would not give it up for anything.

She forced herself out of her dark mood with the help of Butter, who insisted she, at last, take him down to the beach. She shook herself off and headed out the door with him. On the way out, Grace noticed the autumn leaf that she had believed PoliM'aladroit wrote the note to her on. Grace reached to remove it from the wall, but felt a sharp pinching feeling in her back, which caused her to stop abruptly. With Butter looking up at her pleadingly and the echo of the pinch still stinging her, Grace decided to wait until they returned home before doing anything. She would then take down and dispose of the letters from the four imaginary princesses that she had taken from some mind-manufactured place. Grace was confident that she produced them, and that they may have at one time served a purpose when she did, but they must go now.

They walked up the road, and as they reached the end, both she and her dog climbed the steps that led to the beach. They stopped at the top and looked out at the ocean as Grace contemplated the unity of the two conflicting faces it reflected. The water could be calm and serene at times, and at others, the same sea could be intense and devastating, yet it was still one.

Both Grace and Butter proceeded on to the sand and down to the water's edge when suddenly Butter took off like a shot running towards another dog further down the beach. It was unusual for him to leave Grace's side, but she thought that perhaps her mood and lack of attention to him lately might have left him with more energy than he could contain.

The two dogs frolicked and ran back and forth chasing each other. It made Grace's heart smile to see the animals having so much fun, and as she got closer, she could see that the other dog was also black, but much more substantial in size than Butter was. Grace also saw a woman who was probably the other dog's master approaching the two dogs from the opposite direction. The frolicking pups continued playing with each other as they and the women neared Grace, and as the canines and the human came into contact with her, the stranger lifted her head up ever so slightly and uttered a muffled, "Hello." She wore a baseball cap and designer sunglasses, causing Grace to flinch at the combination.

"Don't I know you from somewhere?" Grace asked.

"No, I don't think so," replied the woman quietly.

"Really? Are you sure? I could swear I do," continued Grace.

The woman, demonstrably uncomfortable and anxious to escape, replied, "I'm sure.

"Let's go, PippyLou," she called to her dog as she made her exit.

Her canine companion obeyed her command and came running to her side with Butter trailing behind. The big black dog and its owner continued in the direction Grace and Butter had come from, and to where they would be returning. Grace kept her distance from the woman, who apparently did not want to engage in conversation. Both women were uncomfortable for different reasons – Grace for wanting to talk and the other woman for not wanting to join in.

As they neared the steps that led back down to the roadway, Grace approached the woman one last time.

"I am sorry to bother you, really I am, but could I please just ask you one more question?" Grace beseechingly asked the familiar stranger.

The other woman did not answer her, but she did not turn and leave either. Grace took this as a positive sign and seized the opportunity before it was lost.

"I know you say we have never met, but please indulge me and just tell me your name."

"Carol," the woman replied in a friendly enough manner as she put on her green and black skull sneakers with no shoelaces and walked away down the road. Visibly protruding from her back pocket was a garden spade with the engraved initials *H. of G.H.* on its handle.

And so it was!

Brenda Grace de Jong

My Name is Elpee
~ A Trilogy ~

Book 2

Return the Snail to the Earth

To Gracie -

Not a day passes that you are not in my thoughts and in my heart.

Never do any of us get together without your name and/or your antics entering into the conversation.

Thank you for the laughter.

Thank you for your limitless love.

Thank you for giving us Chuck.

You are cherished beyond eternity.

"And the day came
when the risk to remain tight in a bud
was more painful
than the risk it took to blossom."

~ Anaïs Nin

PROLOGUE

Once upon a time, in a faraway land called Brooklyn, New York, a princess was born. She lived in the inner city with urban decay eroding her body and soul as well as her neighborhood. When she could no longer tolerate her environment, the princess – then known as Elpee – moved to another faraway land. This land was filled with forests and oceans, gnomes and elves, cherries and polka dots. Cantankerous rocks that staged a walkout, a camouflaged dog, three princesses, and one queen were just a few things in her princessdom that guarded Elpee's home, known as Cherry Castle by the Sea. Elpee lived there until she did not anymore; that is when J. Alpert VII, the non-wizard, guided her on a journey to yet another faraway place. Her third home was similar to the castle but more mature and absolutely more earthly. There were no creatures or gnomes, no elves of any sort, just plain, old, regular people, living plain, old, regular lives, in plain, old, regular ways, measured in plain, old, regular time. Elpee, now known as Grace, had lived there in that manner for two plus years when she spotted the woman on the beach. Grace knew that she knew her; more importantly, Grace knew the woman knew her right back.

And so it continues!

Confusion Reigns Once Again

———

Grace sat on the stairs that led up from the beach in one direction and down to the road in the other; the same stairs the woman and her black dog had walked down until they were out of sight but admittedly not out of mind. Sitting there with her head in her hands and Butter at her side, Grace had a difficult time believing her own eyes and what they had just witnessed. Long gone were the delusions and visions. Her thoughts were now reality-based and did not include any remnants of the past with all its fiction and fantasy. So then, "Who was that woman?" Grace asked herself, although she was not even remotely ready to begin exploring answers to that question. All she could do was sit as she was with her head in her hands, trying to hold back the tears and gain her composure.

Grace must have remained frozen in that position for longer than she had realized, because the sun had nearly set and a chilly evening was emerging. She began shivering and knew it was time to leave for home despite the trepidation she felt at the thought of doing that. Home, and where it was, were questions this once-again lost waif needed to ask herself. Grace attempted in vain to rise from the step on the overpass, but her mind was in shock, and her body felt as heavy as lead– far too heavy for one human being to propel alone. She supposed that perhaps she would never have risen were it not for the small black dog sitting next to her. He was obedient and faithful, sometimes to a fault, Grace thought, and he would never complain to her, but she knew that he needed to move from the step and go home to have his dinner. Her obligation to him and his needs were the driving force for her to get up and descend the steps that would take them both home.

Unlike her typical practice, Grace did not speak to Butter but instead proceeded solemnly and stoically in the direction of where they both lived. The dog, sensing his master's mood, was not agreeable, and although he walked next to her, it was a step behind his usual position of directly be-side her. She had never been mean to him, but then again he had never felt the negative energy she was now emitting, either. Butter was confused – a feeling unfamiliar to this ordinarily well-adjusted and emotionally se-cure pooch. Grace approached this specific return home nervously as her head replayed pictures of the sight she beheld when she had returned to her castle with Alpert in her time before coming here. As they got closer to the house, Grace could see that it was still standing and appeared to be in good repair.

Was she mistaken about the woman on the beach, she wondered? Grace was so sure it was Hortense. How could it not be with that same elusive manner and attire, especially the green and black skull sneakers? Grace began to doubt herself as she often did when things seemed to be out of the ordinary. No bother! It was what it was, and she told herself to ignore the whole incident and put it aside for right now.

"Just go in the house and feed Butter," Grace instructed herself. "Make yourself a cup of tea and rest on the couch until you can think more ratio-nally, or at least less emotionally."

The woman and the dog walked up to the front path of the cottage and opened the screen door together – she pulling on the handle and he pushing his way through the bottom half. Still unable to shake her hyper-vigilance, Grace automatically scanned the porch as she entered, much as one would do if they were suspicious of the presence of an intruder. She continued into the living room, then through the dining room, and into the kitchen, conducting the same examination in each of those places that she had done on the porch. Nothing had changed. It was just as she left it. Her brain began to wander again to the possibility that she was mistaken, but she quickly reminded herself to let the thought go and to focus on what needed to be done only at that moment.

"Just a minute, boy, let me put the kettle on first, okay?" Grace told Butter in an almost requesting manner. There was some guilt in having not fed him earlier, which caused Grace to feel selfish for tending to her own needs first despite knowing that the dog did not particularly care. She made him the AKC approved diet designed for mongrels, which consisted of leftover meatloaf with cheese along with some raw carrots. Once his bowl was placed in the area of the floor designated as the doggie dining room, Grace felt more comfortable and began brewing her tea. Tonight she chose a mixture of jasmine, chamomile, and hawthorn berries to help comfort and relax her. With the tea steeping in the pot and the dog slowly eating his dinner, Grace began to light some candles throughout the cottage. She chose a variety of her favorite fragrances of citrus and sage, lemongrass, and fig. Lastly, Grace prepared a tray that held the teapot, her teacup and saucer, and a plate containing a slice of peach pie. She wished to savor the warmth of the tea and the sweetness of the pastry, and so she carried the tray into the living room and rested it on her lap as she sat down on the couch.

Grace sipped the tea and then took a bite of the pastry, and although peach was her favorite flavor of pie, she had no appetite for it tonight, so she placed the tray on the table and held the cup and saucer in her hand. Grace gave herself time to drink the tea and relax before forcing herself to relive the events that occurred on the beach. As much as Grace tried to focus on the woman and what she knew in her heart to be true, her mind was determined to minimize her intuition and convince her that she was wrong. No matter how many times Grace's thoughts wandered off course, she was committed to at least not discounting her beliefs and hopefully standing in her truth, whatever that was.

Emotionally drained from the events that were happening faster than she could process them, Grace placed the teacup on the table and put her head back on the pillow that was behind her neck. The pillow read, 'Believe in Yourself With All Your Heart' – a saying that Grace most certainly needed to embrace right now. And, despite the confusion that existed around her, she did believe, at least to some extent. As she had always done when things needed to be sorted out in her mind, Grace closed her eyes and went off to sleep, or if not sleep to some state of altered consciousness that allowed her to process and heal. The tea relaxed the weary woman enough for her to be able to do this, and before long she could feel her breathing slow, her heart rate decrease, and her mind quiet. Having shifted into that state, she thought and felt nothing more.

Images began to invade Grace's head in the form of a dream in which she was in her garden, weeding and trimming the already spent flowers from their plants. In her dream state, Grace felt a pronounced sense of sadness and a desire to abort the chore, but she had an equal sense of duty to her garden and an obligation to continue doing it. The conflicting emotions continued for however long dreams last, and until within it,

Grace could bear the sadness no longer, at which point she fell to the garden's earth and began sobbing. Abruptly, the sleeping woman woke from the dream to find her face wet with genuine tears and an overwhelming feeling of panic consuming her. She was not aware of her surroundings, what time of day or night it was, nor even the day of the week. The only awareness the woman had was that of extreme loss and its accompanying sadness. Hating the feeling, she quickly rose from the couch and physically shook herself off in hopes of shedding the heaviness the dream state had produced in her. 'No more,' she vowed to herself! She had been here too often to accept it any longer unopposed. Despite, or maybe because of, the disturbing dream, Grace got angry.

WHO TOOK THE LETTER???????

As the new day dawned, Grace woke, no longer feeling the profound sadness she had felt the night before, although she did still bear a sense of loss. Grace recognized that her emotions, which seemed to be at a slow simmer, were more manageable, and she needed to keep them at that level until she had a plan. She went downstairs, prepared a pot of coffee, and let the dog out the back door. While the coffee was brewing and Butter was investigating the garden, Grace cooked a breakfast of eggs and ham for both of them. When the cooking was done, and the coffee was finished brewing, she went to the open back door to call Butter. It was uncommon for him to be absent from the kitchen because even though he was not a food hound, he always wanted to be at her side. He did not come immediately, which prompted Grace to call him again, and this time he came to her, albeit skulking and looking as startled as a deer in headlights.

"Butter, what's the matter?" Grace asked as she bent down to his level.

His naturally big brown eyes were now the size of meatballs as he stood there motionless at Grace's feet. His master began petting and comforting him until he lay prone in a state of apoplexy. Finally, she left him to his own devices, made herself a cup of coffee, exited the same back door, and headed for the wicker rockers to drink it. As she went out and turned right facing the chairs, Grace stopped dead in her tracks, causing the coffee cup to fall from her hand and smash on the ground in reaction to what she saw.

There, between the two rocking chairs and behind the white slatted wood table, was a blank wall staring back at Grace. Where once hung a letter written on plain brown paper there was now nothing. When Grace first came here, she placed the notes from the other princesses in her house to inspire her to adopt what she considered their most admirable qualities. PoliM'aladroit's graced the front porch, inspiring faith and wisdom to nurture and lift her spirit. Grace could find danDay-leon's letter in the kitchen along with her tea, both of which Grace depended on for their calming effects, and *Queen* Euterpe's flying around anywhere solely for the fun of it.

Before going to the beach on the day she saw the woman, Grace planned on removing and disposing of these tokens from the past. She had decided that the princesses were figments of her imagination and did not really exist, but she had never gotten the chance to actually complete that task. It was apparent, however, that someone else had at least begun to do it for her. Missing from the wall facing Grace was the letter from the fourth princess – Hortense – the woman she met on the beach.

Grace stared at the blank wall where Hortense's letter once hung while Butter sat in the doorway between the kitchen and where Grace was standing. Time stood still for both of them. Grace's body was rigid as a rage mounted inside of her while simultaneously confusion and fear were building in the canine. She would need answers and a plan of action on how to proceed when time did resume.

"Breathe . . . Breathe . . . Breathe," Grace kept repeating to herself in an attempt to quell the fire she felt burning within her. Butter's clock restarted first, and he scampered off to the garden, leaving his master to do whatever it was she was doing. He hoped she did it soon and got over it and back to her usual self. It took a bit longer for Grace's clock to again begin ticking in real time and for her to return to the present. When it finally did resume, she came back with more composure and focus than she had before. She bent down, picked up the broken pieces of the coffee cup, and then swept up the slivers of glass that remained, all the while being deliberate and controlled.

When she had finished cleaning up the mess, Grace poured a glass of water and carried it out to the wicker rockers as she had done earlier with the coffee. This time, however, she was forewarned of the landscape that awaited her, and therefore she merely sat down. Grace always loved this spot in the morning; it was her quiet place where she could contemplate the events in her life while drinking her coffee and rocking back and forth. This morning was no exception, but her contemplation was very narrow in scope compared to her usual broad spectrum of thoughts.

"Where is the letter? Who took it down? And why only Hortense's? The woman on the beach . . . STOP IT! Stop asking questions and start answering them," Grace told herself.

"Deal with the facts first, draw a conclusion from them, and then you can figure out what to do." She continued on, "I know. How about I make a list?" Grace asked herself before going inside to get a pen and paper. She opened the left drawer of the right built-in cabinet, and while reaching for the necessary materials to make a list, she also grabbed a rubber band and slipped it on her wrist before returning outside.

While rocking in the chair, fragmented and unending thoughts began to fly around Grace's head, so she picked up the pen and began to write the list.

FACT #1
The woman on the beach *was* Hortense
   a. baseball cap
   b. sunglasses
   c. green and black skull sneakers with no shoelaces
   d. elusive manner, not wanting to talk
   e. ***something else I can't put my finger on yet

FACT #2
Her letter is missing – stolen – gone
   a. possibly someone took it – NO
   b. possibly it blew away – NO
   c. possibly it never was – NO
   d. possibly I did it – NO

Grace's mind began wandering and exploring the possibilities of all the above when, suddenly, she grabbed the rubber band and snapped it hard against her wrist while telling her head to shut up. The mind meandering might have helped, or maybe it was the pain of the rubber band's assault that sent her brain into hyper-intuition, because it prompted her to pick up the pen and continue writing the list.

   e. possibly Hortense was here and took it down – YES!

"Butter, where are you?" Grace called to her pet.
Slowly and reluctantly, the dog ascended the three wooden steps that led from the garden and continued walking until he reached Grace's side.

"Where were you, mister?" she asked.

He did not answer her and instead looked up at her lovingly, licked her leg, returned to the steps he had just come up from, and off he went back to the garden. Grace did not understand but was accepting of it because she needed to concentrate on what was happening and finish making the list. She deliberately shook her head and then continued writing.

FACT #3

The . . . often . . . sometimes . . .

"What the heck is fact number three?" Grace asked aloud.

Unable to state it or write it, Grace went to the two cypress trees in the back of her yard, stood between them, and forced her brain to retrieve the information while standing there and channeling the wisdom of the Universe. Soon a pair of cardinals flew into the trees, each landing on a cypress, and began a conversation with each other.

Mrs. C.: "So, what do you think about the diet we've been put on?"

Mr. C.: "I don't like it one bit. And you?"

Mrs. C.: "You know *I* don't like it!"

Mr. C.: "I'm surprised. I didn't think she was like that."

Mrs. C.: "Me either. To just up and leave like that. No warning. No goodbye. It's terrible, I tell you."

Mr. C.: "It's a good thing the family on A Street put out a feeder before she left, and lucky we are to have found it, even if it's not as much food as Mrs. Reynolds used to give us."

"That's it!" stated Grace confidently as she smacked herself on the forehead. She thanked the birds and returned to the rocker where the pen and paper lay.

FACT #3

Agness Reynolds has been absent lately – AWOL, MIA
   a. Agness and Hortense are both elusive and evasive
   b. Agness and Hortense are both master gardeners
   c. both kept to themselves and were kind and caring people
   d. both slipped out without goodbyes
   e. was never able to get to know Agness *or* Hortense
   f. Agness went missing when Hortense came back

That was the absent fact, but Grace had to ask herself one critical question based on that information. Was Agness really Hortense, and did she take Hortense's letter when she left?

A light bulb went off in Grace's head, and she spoke the answer aloud.

"Agness didn't take Hortense's letter when she left. *Hortense* took the letter down when she returned!"

Meanwhile, Back at the Cottage

————

As time went on, three things happened. Days passed, Grace thought, and Butter got fat. Grace expended her nervous energy by cleaning the cottage as she analyzed the facts. Curtains, windows, cabinets – everything got scrubbed, polished, or washed while her psyche sorted out what was going on in her world. Hopefully, when the house was clean and free of dust and cobwebs, so would her mind be. Whenever she stopped to rest, she would call the newly independent canine to visit with her.

"Butterboy, where are you? Come here, handsome boy," Grace summoned the dog as she patted her lap, beckoning him to come.

Lumbering up the steps was a sausage of a dog with a pin-sized head and slanted eyes. He hurdled up, barely making it onto Grace's lap.

"Holy smokes, Butthead." Grace grimaced as his weight fell upon her. "How did you get so fat? You barely eat. In fact, you hardly eat at all anymore."

He told her that he loved her through his barely visible, slanted brown eyes and then hopped off her lap and proceeded to go down the wooden steps back to where he had come from. Grace just shook her head and returned inside the house.

These sanity-seeking labors continued until there was nothing left to clean and still Grace could not figure out what to do with the facts she had garnered. One day, in desperation, Grace took herself outside and again called upon the wisdom of the ancients for guidance. Immediately the sound of screeching filled the air, causing Grace to jump up and follow the direction from which the noise was coming. She ran down the three wooden steps into the garden and found that a squirrel was trapped behind a temporary fence placed over a new planting in the garden. Grace instantly moved the wire and away ran the much grateful critter. Butter just lay there too rotund to move. Grace sat on the bench to catch her breath and rest her racing heart, and while she was sitting there, she had an up-close view of the garden she had not entered in weeks.

"This is unbelievable! I cannot believe how incredibly beautiful the garden is! I haven't been out here to do anything in forever, and yet it's spectacular. All these new plantings too! Hey, wait a minute. Who planted them and who has been tending all of this?" Grace asked herself.

Butter, thinking she was asking him, would have rolled over on his back if he were able to, but instead, lowered his head to the ground. Seeing the lump of dogdom lying there in the garden sparked a memory and created a picture in Grace's mind. She recalled the day she and Butter were on the beach, and he was running around with the black dog. Her mind skipped a few frames and fast-forwarded to the other dog and 'Carol' as they were walking away. Grace's mind's eye then zoomed in further to the woman's back pants pocket and the initialed garden spade that had been peeking out from within it.

"That was the one thing I could not remember the day I made the list! I knew something was missing from my argument about the woman on the beach being Hortense. On the way to the beach, I commented on how this year's garden was better than ever despite the fact I spent much less time tending it because of the pottery business. The woman on the beach had a spade in her back pocket. She – being Hortense and not Carol – was tending the garden then . . . And still is."

LEAVE THE DOG ALONE

"Okay, mister, where is she?" Grace asked Butter.

In keeping with his usual pathetic fashion, the poor and not so little dog looked up at her and burped.

"Nice, Fatboy, but that is not an answer. I know she's here, so you better start singing," she idly threatened the dog.

To Grace's surprise, that is precisely what he did. He began the same unmelodic howl-like noise he produced when he feigned near death some months back. He continued emitting a sound that was akin to that of a humpback whale until a commanding and familiar voice came from behind Grace.

"Stop bullying the dog, would ya?"

Grace turned around sharply to find the woman from the beach standing there. Even though she had it all figured out in her mind, coming face-to-face with this woman again made Grace's knees buckle.

"Hortense, or should I say Carol?" Grace replied sarcastically.

"Whatever you want. You choose," the woman said. "Just leave the dog alone."

"The dog is fine except that he weighs too much, so don't worry about him. I want some answers. Why are you here? How did you get here? Are you Agness, or is it the other way around?" Grace demanded.

The frantically searching for clarity princess went on with a laundry list of questions, to which the other woman stood listening, seemingly unaffected and at times rolling her eyes slightly but saying nothing.

"Are you done?" she asked when Grace finally concluded her soliloquy.

Grace nodded defiantly.

"I got no answers for you, sunshine. You're going to have to ask a higher authority than me if you want to know. Or, of course, you could figure it out yourself," the woman informed Grace.

"Fine! I will!" Grace retorted.

"Good," the woman responded as she opened the gate to leave. "Just leave the dog alone."

"The dog is fine . . . *Hortense*," Grace snidely yelled after her.

"Yeah, well, he likes hamburger ice cream – a lot!" she yelled back at Grace.

"*You* leave the dog alone," Grace said, having to get the last word in.

And so she did!

PIPPY COMES
AND
TEA LEAVES

Days and weeks went by, and although the garden continued to be maintained, Grace did not see Hortense again. Butter began to lose weight and did not visit the side yard quite as often. The masks, feeling entirely abandoned and not privy to what was happening, started fighting – again.

Not being able to handle the bickering any longer, Grace one day decided to take all the masks on a field trip to the garden and leave them there. One by one, she took them outside and hung them on the fence or a tree—all except Cleopatra, who she hung by herself overlooking the birdbath where she could see her own reflection.

"There, are you all happy now? You can see everything that's going on, you nosy holes."

"Thank you," they all replied in unison.

Grace just walked away, shaking her head.

She knew that the woman on the beach, Agness, and Hortense, were one and the same and that one of their alter egos also took the letter. She just did not know why, and no matter how much she contemplated the reason, she could find no solution to that puzzling question—a question that opened the door to a million other queries.

On her way to the market one morning, Grace called Butter to come with her. She thought that because he was finally down from a lumber to a waddle, he could survive the walk. He did not respond to her beckoning, and for a split instant Grace recalled the long-ago event when she had called Butter #1, and he had not come to her because he was gone. Grace shook herself off and yelled for him again.

"Butter, come on, let's go. Get your leash."

She began walking toward the garden and heard the sound of laughter along with what she believed to be the voices of people wagering on something.

"Five bucks on the black one."

"Which one? They're both black?"

"The big one."

"That doesn't help, Crater Cranium, they're both big."

"The big one not the fat one, Drippy."

As she turned the corner, Grace realized that it was the masks who were laughing and betting, and she soon saw the reason why. There, in the middle of her beautiful garden, Butter and PippyLou were playing tug of war with a plant that one of them had apparently ripped out of the ground. Once again, Grace shook her head – a recently acquired and much-used practice of hers – before calling the smaller black dog.

"Come on, Butthead, let's go. We have to go into town," she said to Butter, and then continued by addressing the larger black dog, "and you, mister, or miss, do your thing, enjoy yourself, and have fun. I'm sure your mother is around or will be, or . . . Whatever!"

Grace and Butter returned to the house to get his leash and then walked the short distance into town. When they arrived there, she tied the dog to a fence under a tree in the square while she shopped at the grocery store. Methodically, Grace went up and down the aisles, placing the items she had gone there for in her basket. She went to the aisle where she usually found the jars of loose tea only to discover their absence. Thinking she was mistaken, Grace looked harder and in different corridors until she admitted defeat and went up to the counter to ask Janie about their location.

"Janie, where is the loose tea? I couldn't find it. It's not where you usually keep it."

"Excuse me, dear? The tea bags are in the next aisle where they've always been," answered Janie.

"No, not the tea bags, the loose tea. Where did you move it to?" Grace again asked.

"I'm sorry, Grace, I don't know what you mean. I've never carried loose tea in the store. Too much bother and very expensive to have a good variety in stock. You must be mistaken, or are you kidding me?" Janie responded with a tentative smile.

Without saying goodbye, Grace exited the marketplace, leaving her groceries behind on the counter. She quickly untied the dog and headed home. The anger that Grace worked so hard to contain was once again building. She wanted answers, and she wanted them immediately. Grace and Butter walked at a pace that would accommodate the dog's rather robust physique, because there was no way Grace could carry him home should he have another of his near-death experiences from walking too fast.

Finally, at home, Butter went out to the garden and Grace into the kitchen. She filled the kettle with water and put it on the stove to heat. She would drink a cup of tea made from the small amount of tea she had left in her supply while she decided what to do. Grace looked out the side window into the garden to find Butter lying down, resting, with Pippy nowhere in sight.

What was Janie talking about, saying she never carried loose tea, Grace thought? Of course she did. That is where Grace has purchased all her tea for more than two years.

Grace began to think aloud.

"Imagine her asking me if I was joking. It was more like the joke was on me, as if the Janie I knew had gone away, and someone else took over her body."

With that statement echoing in her mind, Grace turned around to look at the shelf on which the jars of tea were stored and to the area above them where she had hung danDay-leon's letter. The containers were filled to the brims with tea leaves, and an additional number of jars were vying for space on the shelf. Missing was the letter from danDay-leon. Grace moved some of the canisters aside to see if it had fallen behind them, but it had not. It too was gone, just like Hortense's letter.

Grace saw red and could not contain her temper any longer. She took a deep breath, and at the top of her lungs, screamed, "AL-PERT!"

"Say Elpee"

"ALPERT, COME HERE RIGHT NOW!" Grace yelled while staring up at the kitchen ceiling as if she expected him to descend through the rafters from the floor above. With her hands on her hips and her face looking like an overripe tomato that might explode at any moment, Grace continued to command Alpert to appear.

"I am not kidding, Alpert. I really mean it! You need to come here right now! I need to talk to you. NO, YOU NEED TO TALK TO ME and to answer some questions! You have a lot of explaining to do, Mr. Wizard."

Trying to gain her composure, Grace decided to make the cup of tea she had begun moments earlier and drink it while waiting for the funny little man to show himself. She chose a standard English breakfast tea, danDay-leon's favorite, and after pouring the heated water into the cup containing the leaves, Grace began to retire outside to the wicker rockers but thought better of it. She turned around, choosing instead the front porch in which to drink her beverage. There, draping one of the walls in the front room, was the crimson leaf on which PoliM'aladroit wrote her letter to Elpee. Grace was glad to see that it was still present, unlike the letters from two other sister princesses.

While she waited for Alpert's appearance, Grace sat on the couch on the porch, sipping her tea, which she had sweetened with much more sugar than she had used in the recent past. She could not calm herself down, nor could she change the thoughts that were streaming through her mind. Though she found the tea to be soothing, it did little to help her anxious mood, and finally, Grace shakily stood up and began hollering into the air.

"ALPERT . . . NOW! I need you here now."

Butter was resting in the garden just outside the front porch and was awakened abruptly by Grace's banshee-like screams. After shaking himself off from being startled, he skulked into the house to check on his master. He wondered what was wrong with her; she had not been herself lately. The once reserved woman now seemed overly emotional in so many ways and seemed to be persistently off the hook in one form or another. As he entered the house, he experienced a sad feeling for both Grace and himself while wondering where their life together had gone awry. He walked over to her, lay at her feet, and began licking her leg. She bent down and sat on the floor with her canine companion, rubbing his head and trying to ease his fragile psyche. The two troubled souls sat together on the chilly floor, consoling each other. Even in this moment of ire, Grace was so grateful for Butter's presence and all the joy he brought to her. He was the only thing that ever truly loved her, and she loved him right back.

In that split second of peace, Grace heard a barely audible knock on the screen door.

"Hello. Hello?"

The voice matched the quiet of the rapping on the front door. Grace and Butter looked at each other and decided they should get up to see who was there. And so they did. The woman standing at the door surprised them both for very different reasons—Butter because he did not know her and Grace because she did. The woman stood quietly on the top step, waiting for Grace to invite her in or to at least open the door. As was the custom in their home, Grace released the top of the screen door with the handle while Butter pushed the bottom with his body, which presently was rather ample.

"Anna, what are you doing here? I didn't whistle for you," Grace asked the woman who was standing there dressed entirely in white.

"Well, thank you for such a warm welcome," Anna snappily replied.

"I am sorry, and it is pleasant to see you again, Anna, but really, why are you here?" Grace again asked.

"I suppose that is as mannerly as you will be today, so perhaps I should just answer you. I am here because you summoned help. Plain and simple," Anna responded tersely.

"I did not summon your help, and I didn't whistle for you, so please, Anna, tell me why you are here. Oh, never mind. Come inside, and I will refresh my cup of tea and make one for you too, I suppose. You too, Butter, come on," Grace stated as she turned away from Anna and walked toward the kitchen.

Step for step, Butter walked directly next to Grace as they made their way to the back of the house. The confused canine did not know this other woman, but his master seemed somewhat disagreeable towards her. Therefore, he would do likewise. While Grace filled the kettle and placed it on the stove, he sat at her side, looking up at Anna with as much of a sneer on his face as he could muster up.

"I don't think your dog likes me," Anna flatly stated.

Grace looked down and was surprised to see the blatantly surly look on Butter's face to which Anna was probably referring.

"He is just feeling my frustration and is passing it on to you. Be nice, Butter. Please," Grace implored him as she tried to explain away the dog's sneer.

Butter instantaneously complied and gave Anna an enormous grin, to which she responded by giving him a hamburger she took from her purse.

"Sorry, it's not ice cream, but my bag only accommodates warm, not cold, and I understand your current diet does not include ice cream," Anna declared as she gave Butter the treat.

As this interaction was taking place, Grace poured both herself and Anna cups of tea and placed them on the kitchen table along with an oversized bowl of sugar and a pitcher of evaporated milk. The hostess put copious amounts of both into her own teacup, and when Anna was sufficiently assured that she and Butter were bonding nicely, she joined Grace at the table.

"I'm sorry, Anna. I am just totally frazzled by what's going on . . . Letters missing, tea appearing, dogs in my garden, strangers, who are not really strangers . . . Blah, blah, blah . . . blah, blah."

"I understand," replied Anna.

"I'm not sure whether you do or do not understand. However, I still want an answer to my question as to why you are here."

"I told you, dear, because you summoned for help. So here I am to help you."

As she tried to maintain some degree of composure, Grace said to Anna, "I am not in the mood, Anna, for this encoded language you are speaking. I called for Alpert to come. That's it! The next thing I know, you're on my doorstep knocking at my door to come in and now you're spouting something about my having asked you for help."

Without answering Grace's question, Anna, who seemed to be equally as frustrated, told Grace, "I am here in Alpert's stead, so what is it that you wish to discuss?"

"I want to talk to Alpert," maintained Grace.

"There is a chain of command, my dear, and you must respect it . . ."

Grace interrupted Anna by saying, "And you must respect the fact that I am ready to wrap a chain around someone's neck if the *Commander* doesn't come here to talk to me."

Poor Butterball, fearing for his life – his very existence – left his master's side and returned to the garden.

"Well, my dear . . ."

Interrupting Anna once again, Grace began by saying, "And that's another thing! That tea potion you made and had me drink was stupid. It made me say and do stupid things, like I was hypnotized or something. I had a perfectly fine name until I drank that tea, then I looked up at the sign on the wall that says 'Say Grace', and I changed my name to Grace when you asked me what it was. Maybe you think I should change the sign to read, 'Say Elpee'."

Grace, barely coming up for air to take a breath, continued her diatribe, "Grace is a lovely name, but not for me . . . Well, maybe for my middle name, but my name is Elpee, and that's all there is to it. Now if you would please finish your tea and send Alpert here, I would appreciate it. Thank you very much," she concluded.

Sensing that she would not be able to resolve this, Anna pushed her chair away from the table and stood to leave.

"Good luck, my dear," she stated as she left the kitchen and the house.

There was a hollowness in Anna's words that left Elpee with an almost sinister feeling about the nature of Anna and her intentions.

BREAKFAST, TEA, AND BUBBLES

While Elpee cleared away the teacups from the table, Butter made his way back into the cottage and to her side. Master and subject retired to the living room – she to the couch and he to his bed – where Elpee began to read Butter a chapter from a Steinbeck novel. It had been an interminably trying day that left Butter uneasy and Elpee physically and emotionally weary. That being the case, before even a page was read, they were both snoring.

It was morning when Butter, bellowing out his humpback whale imitation at the back door, awakened Elpee. She jumped up at the alarming noise and ran to its point of origin. She opened the door as quickly as possible, and Butter ran out of the house, traveling at a speed his body was incapable of moving. Elpee did not understand his sense of urgency until she saw the newspaper that was sitting on her path. On the first page's banner, the date read, "The Day After Tomorrow."

"How can that be?" she wondered aloud. "How is it possible for the paper to be printed in the future? Or, is it possible that I have slept for a day and a half?"

Butter came into the kitchen looking well rested and full of energy. Elpee secretly hoped that his friend would come to play today so that she would not have to amuse him, which would give her free time to put things in order in her head. Elpee prepared a pot of coffee for herself, and for Butter, his usual breakfast of scrambled eggs and ham – not overcooked, of course. She put his bowl down on the floor in his dining room and watched him. He walked over to it, sniffed it, and walked away.

"What is wrong with you? I know you are not a chowhound, but eggs and ham, Butter? What is up with that? I bet you would eat it if it were a hamburger, especially hamburger ice cream, wouldn't you?" she asked rhetorically. Butter nodded his head, gave her a smile, and squeaked out a diminutive, "Arf."

"Well, forget it, Buster Brown. Take it or leave it. It could be another day and a half before you eat again."

Sluggishly, he moseyed over to the bowl and began eating.

"Good boy. Thank you," Elpee said, acknowledging his compliance.

With that chore completed, Elpee poured herself a cup of intensely strong coffee – a beverage she had recently developed a taste for – and went out to her quiet place on the rocker. While rocking and sipping on her coffee, Elpee tried to make sense of Anna's behavior and the uncomfortable feeling she had regarding it. Elpee remembered using the word *sinister* in her mind to describe the feelings she had concerning Anna's demeanor. *What a harsh word*, she thought to herself. Elpee did not even know that word existed in her vocabulary.

Just when she was on the verge of solving what felt to her to be the riddle of the sphinx, Butter came outside and threw himself at her feet and released a profoundly resonating moan meant to indicate his severe boredom, which he held Elpee responsible for curing.

"What's the matter, your friend didn't come to play with you today? Maybe she or he will be here later," Elpee said, trying to reassure him as she scratched his head.

"In a few minutes, when I have finished my coffee, we'll go for a walk."

While the dog waited patiently at her feet, Elpee continued drinking her coffee and pondering the recent turn of events in her life, and now she had this Anna situation. Finally, she gave up thinking, and much to Butter's pleasure, she rose from the chair and was ready to start the day. She placed the cup in the sink, grabbed an apple from the bowl on the kitchen table, and walked through the house to the front door with Butter in tow. The tag team of human and canine opened the screen door in unison and out they went.

"Let's go, mister. Do you want to go for a walk into town?"

He frowned.

"The beach?" Elpee continued.

He double frowned.

"I'm not giving you a third choice. We're going into town, and that's all there is to it," the pup's mistress advised him. "And furthermore, it's for your own good that I don't give you option number three, because three strikes and you're out, buster, which means we would stay right here and I would . . . Whoa . . . What in the . . . " Elpee was cut off before she could finish her lecture to Butter.

As they were walking past the house across the street where Agness once lived, an escalator-type device scooped up both bodies and transported them into Agness's backyard.

"All right, what's going on here?" Elpee said to the Universe. Butter, thinking she was asking him a question, shrugged his dog shoulders and shook his dog head.

There they stood in the midst of what just weeks earlier had been a garden of spectacular shapes and colors but now was overgrown and mostly dead. It looked as if no one had lived there for years, not for only a matter of weeks. It was really quite frightening.

"Butter? Butter, where are you?" Elpee asked as he came out of the tall weeds that camouflaged his zaftig figure.

"Let's go inside and check it out. Maybe we can find a clue to where Agness went, that is if she left, or if she was ever really here. Oh, I don't know! Come on, let's go inside."

The dog moved forward as best as he could while fighting the weeds, but when they got to the door, he put on the skids and would not go in no matter what.

"Oh, come on, boy," Elpee whimpered in exasperation. "What now? Why won't you come in?"

No answer. Butter stood his ground, and she knew what was to follow. Since she did not want to go in alone, she had no choice but to indulge him.

"Are you afraid of something inside?"

He shook his head no.

"Do you know something I don't?"

No, again.

"Do you want to go home?"

Again a no, this time more adamantly.

"Do you have to make a puddle?"

The dog began huffing, puffing, and rolling his eyes in his head at the ridiculousness of this latest question.

"Is there a ghost in there?"

Butter shrugged his shoulders as if to say, 'Maybe . . . Maybe not'.

"Well, I'm going in; I don't care if you don't. Just know that if I go in there and get arrested for trespassing, you'll need to find a nice new home for yourself," Elpee jokingly advised the poor, black dog as he stood shaking and nodding his head furiously in an affirmative manner.

"Are you kidding me? You are afraid of getting arrested?"

He nodded his head and batted his doggie eyelashes at her.

"You didn't have a problem with stealing my ham out of my basket in broad daylight, did you? Now a simple thing like breaking and entering and you are ready to quit. Well, I never!" Elpee proclaimed.

Having listened to her silly comparison and admonishment, the dog climbed the steps and entered the house with his master. They went in through the kitchen door and took a quick look around. They continued casually exploring the rest of the house before stopping at any one place to investigate further. Everything seemed normal. Things inside the house, unlike the outside, were in order and had a lived-in look. Agness must have left in a hurry, because the house still looked and felt occupied. Elpee was not sure when exactly Agness did depart. She kept to herself, and Elpee respected that by giving her privacy. No one in town knew her very well, but maybe after the party, Elpee – then known as Grace – had given, things began to change, and Agness became more social. She would investigate and ask some questions later if she went to the market. Then there was the question of Janie's strange behavior about the lack of loose tea.

"Oh, never mind! What's the difference? Agness is gone, and it doesn't matter when she left. And so what if Janie doesn't carry tea leaves? It seems I may have an infinite supply of them anyway," Elpee said aloud in an attempt to tell herself to shut up.

As they were leaving the house, they passed the kitchen sink on their way to the back door. Elpee once again encountered something that caused her to stop in her tracks. On the counter was a tin of English breakfast tea, and there in the sink was proof positive of why the house looked and felt inhabited – because it was. Elpee reached into the basin and put her hand into what contained a shallow amount of warm, sudsy water. Sitting smack dab in the middle of that bubble pond was a teacup with some fresh tea leaves floating in its center.

They walked out the door together, Elpee shaking her head in disbelief and Butter shaking his in imitation of her.

THE SECOND COMING OF J. ALPERT VII

As Elpee and Butter crossed the street back to their house, they both saw PippyLou standing in their garden waiting to play.

"Go ahead, Butter. Go play with Pippy," Elpee stated, thereby giving him permission to beat feet.

When she arrived there and went up the path, she was greeted by the big black dog.

"Hey, Pips, where have you been? We missed you. Have you been a good boy? Or are you a girl? I never remember. Sorry! By the way, tell your mother that there is a branch on the side of the house that needs trimming. She'll be thrilled."

As she opened the screen door into the front porch, Elpee, as regularly happened to her, was greeted with a startling sight. There, sitting on the couch in his Kelly green suit and high-top sneakers, was J. Alpert VII, non-wizard. She wanted to admonish him for startling her, but she was glad he was there. After all, she had called him.

"Well, it's about time you arrived," she stated with confidence, or so she thought.

"Hello, Missy. Sorry I scared you. No need to pretend otherwise," he said, reminding her of his powers.

Sheepishly, she continued, "Well I just didn't expect to see you sitting on my couch even though I did summon you," making Alpert grin.

"Summon? You were hollering like a banshee, rattling heaven and earth trying to call me. I got here as quickly as I could. I was on another case and almost had to send a colleague of mine. He's quite a handsome chap, though not as stylish a dresser as I am, but I finished up as soon as I could, and here I am."

"Well, Anna said that there was a chain of command and that was why she came instead of you. I told her no dice, hit the road, and that I only wanted to speak to you, so off she went."

"Anna? Who is Anna?" Alpert asked.

"Anna, the Faerie goddess-mother you told me to look for when I left Cherry Castle," replied Elpee.

"I am not familiar with anyone named Anna, but then again, that is a different department, and we don't usually fraternize outside of our assigned domains."

Wasting no further time, Elpee jumped right in, "What in all the world is going on here, Alpert? I have a gazillion questions, and you had better have a gazillion answers. I tell you that right now, wizard boy!" she proclaimed rather loudly.

Still sitting on the couch in a somewhat relaxed manner, Alpert directly commanded, "Begin."

"I don't even know where to start; it's so confusing. I have been here for a little over two years and have made this my home . . . And by the way, that's another thing, where are the fruits of my labors? The seeds that I planted on the hill that day? I went up there, and there are no plants or flowers sprouted, so why did you make up that stupid story and make me do that work?"

"What do you think?" he responded.

"Not *what*, but rather *why*. Why did you lie to me?" Elpee asked.

"I did not lie. The seeds you planted that day were to sprout when you arrived home and were there together with all that you love. So?" he responded in defense of himself.

"What are you saying, that I am not home? That this isn't it?"

He gave her a slight grin and shrugged his shoulders in a noncommittal manner.

"Listen, mister, and listen well," Elpee asserted, "this is the sequence of events that led up to my calling you here. Number one . . . Out of curiosity and knowing that I was home, I went to check out what the seeds produced. There was nothing there. Stupid! Number two . . . Frustrated and angry that you tricked me, Butter and I went for a walk on the beach, and there was a woman who said her name was Carol, but she was really Hortense, the Princess of Grouse Hollow. I know that because she dressed and acted like her, and when she walked away, I saw a garden tool in her back pocket with her initials on the handle. And by the way, I have a magick garden. It is the best garden I ever had, and I did nothing this year. I was too busy with my pottery. I think it was her! Number two and a half . . . There was a woman, Agness, who lived across the street from me who had an incredible garden but kept very much to herself. There was something about her that I really liked, but for whatever reason, we could never become friends. Mysteriously, Agness disappeared, and Hortense showed up. Number two and three quarters . . . The letter from Hortense that I took with me from the other place was gone when I returned home from the beach that day. Number three . . . I was almost out of tea, and when I went to the market to buy some, there wasn't any. Janie, the market's owner, said she had never carried loose tea, which I know she did 'cause I bought it there all the time. When I got home, my jars were full to their brims, and there were some flavors I hadn't had before. And guess what? danDay-leon's letter was missing."

Alpert was still listening, as were the two canines that were now at the window doing the same. Elpee continued, her voice rising as the story continued. "Number four . . . Somehow I was transported into Agness's backyard, and when I went into her house, it was evident that someone is living there. Someone who drinks English breakfast tea, just like danDay-leon does."

Elpee took a deep breath and concluded her litany of events by saying, "I need a rest! It's your turn."

"What is it you want, my dear? Care for a piece of taffy?" he asked as he pulled a large slab of the sticky candy from his inside pocket and extended it to her. Ignoring the candy offer, Elpee loudly answered him by saying, "Answers. I want answers!"

"Well then go ahead, answer yourself," he said as best as he could with a mouth full of taffy.

"Alpert, if I had the answers, I would not have called you," Elpee stated angrily.

"My dear, this is your world and your life. How you choose to live it and whom you choose to have in it are wholly and entirely up to you," he said, struggling to get the words out while trying to extricate the gooey candy from his dentition.

The two black canines sat outside the window—Butter standing on Pippy's back while watching and listening to the dialogue going on inside.

"ALPERT!" she yelled as she stood up from the rocker she was sitting on. "What are you talking about? It's all because of YOU! YOU made me leave Cherry Castle, and now you are messing with my life here. YOU, ALPERT, NOT ME!"

The wizard calmly replied, "Think about what you are saying. How could I make this happen? I was not there when chaos reigned in your castle."

"I was perfectly happy there, and you plucked me out of that life . . ."

Before she could continue, the wizard interrupted her by saying, "Excuse me, but we had this conversation before, if you remember. You were not happy there for a very long time. Things began to change, so you began to change, and therefore things continued to change, and so on, and so on, and so on. That led you to this place and this life."

"Yes, I remember," she admitted, "but, I am happy here, so why are things changing?"

"I will give you a hint. It is very similar, in fact exactly the same, as the last time when the gardens became fallow, and the gnomes were gone. It happened so gradually, you didn't even notice until it could no longer be ignored. There you go," Alpert concluded, feeling confident enough in his explanation that he placed another piece of taffy in his mouth, hoping to consume it before he was asked to answer a question.

"So what you're saying is that things have been changing here also and I just didn't notice until now when it was impossible to ignore. But I *am* happy here. I made friends, I started a business, and I took care of myself. I was . . . Am a grown-up. Nothing I can think of has changed until recently."

She quieted herself for some time, but in an explosion of emotion, she began hollering again, this time adopting language that made the dogs blush. When she calmed down a little, she took a breath and demurely said, "I need more of a hint."

"Well, this is quite different; quite refreshing, actually. You're yelling rather than crying like 'her majesty, the baby' that you were the last time. The scared little girl who left Cherry Castle has indeed grown up – perhaps too much for her own liking. Maybe she missed some of her childlike innocence and playfulness. Oh no," Alpert said, putting his hand to his mouth in a feigned gesture of astonishment, "I've said too much."

"Really, Alpert, your theatrics are weak at best. I like being an adult, but you are right in that I do miss some parts of being juvenile and creative. What's wrong with that? Can't I have both?" Elpee replied to his speech.

"Of course you can have both, but maybe not here. People here don't understand things such as talking masks, or stories about dogs that change color and grow, just like the gnomes would not understand having to go to the stores to buy things. Which by the way you have a rather large tab down at the market store, as you seem to have carried the belief of hugs for food from your past. You see what I mean? What works here wouldn't have worked there and vice versa. Perhaps you are searching for a blend of these two worlds."

"And perhaps I cannot create that blend here in this world? Is that what you are saying?" Elpee asked.

Once again, Alpert grinned and shrugged his shoulders at her as he put another piece of taffy in his mouth.

And so it went!

ELPEE LOSES MORE THAN HER MIND

While she continued to put the puzzle pieces together, or at least tried to, Elpee prepared lunch for Alpert and her. The meal, which consisted of a liverwurst sandwich, cheese doodles, and black cherry soda, was reminiscent of those that were served at the castle in the days of old.

Alpert carried the tray outside to the wicker chairs where, wanting a change of scenery from the front porch, Elpee chose to eat. He held the tray while Elpee pulled the white wooden, slatted table away from the wall and positioned it between the chairs so he could place their lunch on it. They sat facing each other, Alpert eating voraciously as if it were his first, last, and only meal, while Elpee demurely sipped her soda.

"Let me get this straight. I grew up, or at least out of my life at Cherry Castle, and decided to come here and be mature. I left everything behind except the letters from the princesses. I thought they were reminders of the past . . . Kind of a bridge from there to here, but now it seems to be a bridge from here to somewhere else," Elpee stated, looking for confirmation.

Alpert, whose cheeks were puffed out with food, could only nod in agreement, giving Elpee encouragement to continue.

"Unable to live up to the adult standards I imposed on myself, I began to incorporate some of my less mature traits back into my life, and that opened the door for the girls to return."

Once again, the wizard nodded as he guzzled the soda, his face cheese doodle orange.

"Was Agness really Hortense and Janie really danDay-leon in disguises, waiting for me to figure this out?" she asked.

He shrugged his shoulders and kept eating. As long as she kept figuring things out for herself, he was off the hook.

"Well, what now? Two of the princesses have returned, and if I am correct in my hypothesis, two are soon to be heard from. Hmmm, after seeing the tea at Agness's house, I think that danDay-leon lives there, but then where is Hortense living? Maybe Hortense was the first to return because she was the most elusive and would go unrecognized, unlike the others, until the time was right. But she would have had to adopt a different identity in the community, ergo Agness! She could live as Agness *in* but not *of* the community, and she could make her way back into my life in various capacities depending on my choices. She could tend my garden and live her life unnoticed, that is until my party when everyone met her, and then she had to leave as Agness, but I later stumbled upon her at the beach as Carol.

"IT WAS YOU, ALPERT! You pinched me in the back when I was attempting to remove PoliM'aladroit's letter from the porch wall before Butter and I went to the beach that day. I wanted to take down and dispose of all the letters, having decided they never existed, but you stopped me, which allowed them the opportunity to return. So I was right a little while ago when I said that the letters were, or are, a bridge to another time and place, and if I destroyed them, it would not be possible for the princesses to return, and that is why you pinched me. WOW . . . slick."

Elpee had been thinking aloud for so long and so intensely that she did not notice that it had begun raining.

"You will figure it all out, don't worry, but it has started to rain. Let's go inside," said Alpert, now grateful for the opportunity to finally speak.

"Alpert, please take this stuff inside while I get Butter before he gets all muddy," Elpee said as she got up, motioning to the plates and glasses.

"Butter, Butter, come here boy. Pippy needs to go home . . . Wherever that is," Elpee mumbled the last part under her breath. She waited for a few seconds and then began walking to the garden, calling him again, this time louder.

"Butter," was all she was able to say before she saw the note nailed to the fence.

I got the dog.

I told you not to bully him, didn't I? Well, your screaming today was the final straw. He doesn't need to be exposed to your fits! He's safe with PippyLou and me, and also that scruffy, little gray creature.

Get yourself together, and I'll return him.

Hortense

PS, I trimmed the branch on the side. You're welcome.

"ALPERT," Elpee bloodcurdlingly screamed.

The almost wizard left the kitchen chores he was doing and ran outside to the garden. As soon as Elpee saw him coming in her direction, she began ranting in an unintelligible manner.

"She took the dog. My Butter. I can't do this again. I WON'T do this again. Why did she do that? I want him back right now. We have to find him and strangle her."

"Stop! Calm down!" Alpert said as he reached over to Elpee and pinched her hard. "What is wrong? Speak slowly, please."

"She took the dog!"

"Who?"

"Hortense! Here," Elpee declared, handing Alpert the note for him to read.

"He's in good hands. Don't worry," Alpert assured the nearly maniacal woman standing before him even though he wasn't entirely sure that was a true statement.

"Let's kill her. Yes, let's find her and kill her right now. I want my dog back!"

"My dear," he continued as he again pinched her, "I think the behavior you are now displaying is precisely the reason he was kidnapped in the first place."

". . . Find Hortense, and choke her into a coma," Elpee continued.

"There is a reason, and you will not discover what it is by ranting like this," Alpert implored calmly of the blustering woman.

"Let's burn her at the stake like the witch that she is."

"Please calm down, you are unnerving me, and I don't even have any nerves to be undone," he said, now in a beseeching tone.

"I should cut her up and feed her to the fish."

PINCH

"Cease and desist, or I will call the constable or whatever authority you have here and have you arrested for plotting a murder. Or perhaps the men in the white coats will come instead because you're planning to kill someone who doesn't even exist. What will you answer when they ask you her name? Hortense? Agness? Carol? And how about where she lives? What will you say then? Across the street or somewhere near Cherry Castle by the Sea?"

This time it was Alpert's turn to filibuster.

"All right, I . . ." Elpee began before being cut off by the man, who would not relinquish the floor in his desire to be heard. Indicating that she be quiet, he continued.

"Would you tell them that this person who doesn't exist comes in the night to tend your garden? That this nonexistent person really wants nothing else to do with you, but yet plants and sows your garden? And that this crazy, selfless, invisible person stole your dog?"

"You have made your point, Alpert, I just want Butter back. She had no right to do what she did," Elpee stated as unemotionally as possible.

"I'm sure you are correct, but wrong or right, the woman has your dog, and her chief complaint seems to be that she feels you are mistreating the creature. Let's make some tea and go back to the porch to discuss this further," the wizard suggested.

Elpee took his suggestion, made a pot of orange-cinnamon tea, brought it along with cups, milk, and sugar out to the front porch, and bent down to place them on the table. As she stood up, Elpee noticed something that should have startled her, but she had witnessed the same scene before – two times to be exact – and perhaps she had become immune to being surprised. Missing from the wall behind Alpert was the letter from PoliM'aladroit. Elpee's body stiffened out of anger rather than surprise or fear as she stared at the empty space on the wall.

"What is it, my dear?" Alpert questioned her. "You look ghastly."

"PoliM'aladroit's letter is gone. That makes three of them now," Elpee answered, trying to fight back the tears.

"Why exactly does that make you feel sad?"

"Sad? I'm not sad! Why would you say that? I am furious, that's what I am!"

"Forgive me, but I've had my share of seeing you cry, and I just thought that perhaps you found something emotionally painful," Alpert said, sounding apologetic but in reality was trying to plant a seed in Elpee's mind.

"I'm sorry, Alpert. I shouldn't have been so brusque. I'm just so angry at what is happening. I should have known from Hortense's letter that PoliM'aladroit is here somewhere."

"Why is that?" Alpert asked.

"Because she said Butter was with PippyLou and the scruffy, little gray creature, PoliM'aladroit's animal."

"Oh, I see," replied Alpert. "Come, let's drink our tea and we can talk."

Much like that time long ago, out of exhaustion and desperation, Elpee sat with Alpert, only hoping to relieve some of her confusion.

CRAZY WITCHDOCTORS

———

They sat drinking their tea, each waiting for the other to begin. Alpert won; Elpee spoke first.

"I have never been so mad in my life. Really, Alpert, I haven't."

"Sure you have."

"What are you talking about? I have never been this angry ever in the history of me. How would you know, anyway?"

He just looked at her in a way one would look over their eyeglasses as if to ask with their eyes 'Are you kidding me?'

"Well, maybe . . . Whatever. But, I haven't been," Elpee replied defiantly.

"Would you like for me to replay some of your earlier tirades for you? I can, you know? Such as when you stamped your feet and demanded to return *home*, or . . ."

"All right, but that wasn't really mad, that was more frightened," Elpee said before hesitating and eventually continuing. "And maybe sad too because you were right then. I was sad to be leaving what I thought was my home and scared to venture into the unknown."

"Excellent!"

"What?" she snidely replied.

"Now it appears you are getting it," Alpert told her while clapping his hands together at the thought.

Flatly, she responded, "What is it that I am getting?"

Sighing, he threw his hands up in the air and exclaimed with exasperation, "When are you going to get it that you get it?"

"GET WHAT?" yelled Elpee, her face red and appearing ready to cry as she threw herself back against the chair.

"You just admitted that you were angry back then, but you also said that your underlying feelings were those of fear and sorrow. Why do you say that that was not really anger, but this is?

Do you see what I mean?"

In a gesture of irreverence, Elpee, with her arms crossed and a sneer on her face, answered by saying, "Blah, blah, blah. Blah, blah."

Silence followed. For a very long time, Alpert and Elpee sat, neither looking at nor speaking to each other. Elpee, knowing it was she who must initiate the truce, finally expressed herself in a more mature manner than she had presented in her previous sentence.

"Let me get this straight. There is a parallel between the two situations and they both involve anger, sadness, and fear. I don't know, Alpert. Maybe I do feel all three just like the last time, but I am just not as much a little girl, and the fear and sadness don't feel as overwhelming as they did then. I feel angrier at circumstances being what they are and at having to move again, but you are right, I am sad and afraid also. I thought I had made a home here and that it would be forever, but then, when I couldn't find the sprouted seeds, I began to question that belief. Where am I going, Alpert?" the less hostile and more resigned woman asked of him.

"I don't know yet, my dear," he answered her.

"But I do, right?" the dejected princess asked of Alpert before adding a hint of insolence by again mumbling, "Blah, blah."

Fortunately, the wizard was becoming familiar with Elpee's quirky and irreverent personality traits and merely shrugged his shoulders at her comment to him.

"Before I figure that out, I want to find Grouse Hollow girl, massacre her, and steal my dog back!"

Not knowing how to proceed other than in a murderous fashion, Elpee sought Alpert's advice. Alpert, on the other hand, felt unwilling to collaborate with her and decided to play hard to get.

"I think I'll take a nap," he said as he stretched out on the couch where he was sitting before, placing his Stetson hat over his eyes.

"Are you kidding? Take a nap? Alpert, I asked you for suggestions."

"Nighty-night," was his only response.

"Alpert," Elpee said, louder.

"Excuse me, Missy, but it is not ALL about you, ALL of the time, in ALL ways. Now, if you would, please seek the assistance of another wizard or non-wizard so I may begin my respite in earnest."

"Fine, you big dummy! Who needs you anyway? I am just fine! As a matter of fact, I was perfectly fine until you came into my world and began wreaking havoc on it."

"Ta-ta, Missy," Alpert replied, feigning a deep snore.

Out the front door she went, deliberately slamming it harder than necessary to make a point, which served only to make Alpert softly chuckle. Elpee went out to the garden and sat on the bench that she often employed when viewing her flowers, but this time it was to silently weep. The unnerved woman was more afraid than she cared to admit. The little girl came here to grow up and to feel and act more maturely, but from her recent comportment and conversations with Alpert, she knew she was failing miserably. Her behavior was atrocious, therefore, why would she expect to excel in the business of feelings? Perhaps she did not have all the answers and possibly needed to admit to herself that she wasn't entirely okay in this new world.

Having no choice but to let Alpert sleep off his weak attempt at bullying her, Elpee decided to leave the garden and go to the backyard by the cypress trees, where she stretched out on the grass. Suddenly, she realized the answer to her current problem. Elpee began whistling to summon Anna. Maybe, she thought, she could bypass Alpert and get the information from the Faerie goddess-mother.

Whistle

"Anna . . . Oh, Anna. It's me, Elpee. Where are you?"

Elpee waited a few minutes before repeating the same incantation. More minutes passed and still no answer or appearance from Anna. Dejected, Elpee got up, brushed herself off, and headed toward the house when she heard a noise that made her pause.

"Psst. Psst."

Elpee followed the direction of the sound and found a frightened-looking Anna crouched down next to another tree.

"Anna . . ." Elpee began.

"Shush," the Faerie goddess-mother warned Elpee while holding her index finger up to her lips.

Elpee stooped down, meeting Anna at almost ground level.

"I cannot stay. Get rid of him, and I will come back," Anna whispered.

"Why? Who and what are you talking about, Anna?"

"Shh, please, and get rid of Alpert. I will come back when he leaves," Anna repeated.

"But I need your help. I thought you would help me and come when I whistled," Elpee stated, feeling confused and disappointed.

"I did come when you whistled," Anna replied, "but, I cannot stay. Make him leave, and I will do whatever it is that you want. I must go now." And those were the last words spoken before she disappeared.

Running on the Beach

Elpee stood in the woods for a minute before continuing on to the house. When she arrived there, she peeked in one of the porch windows, found Alpert was still prone on the couch with the Stetson over his face, and so she decided to take a walk rather than to go inside. Almost immediately, Elpee realized it was a mistake to do this. Not since Butter had come to live with her had she ventured out on a walk without him. She felt more alone than she ever had and was not sure if she should continue on her stroll or return home to deal with Alpert. The distraught woman chose to keep walking to the beach in the hope that her head would clear and the jumble of feelings would pass. When at last the steps to the overpass appeared, Elpee felt relieved that she had finally arrived at a destination – any destination – so the focus would be off her walking alone and feeling the very same way.

Elpee's legs felt like lead as she climbed the stairs that led up to the overpass's landing. When she reached the top, she stood on the platform for a moment before descending to the sand below. As she gazed out at the ocean, trying to focus on the strength and consistency of the waves, Elpee caught a glimpse of something off to her left that made her turn her head sharply in that direction, but it was gone. Her focus returned to the waves until this fleeting image again appeared and disappeared. This time, however, Elpee was quick enough to observe the objects of her distraction. She saw briefly, before they vanished, the figures of two black dogs, one large, and one small, running and chasing each other close to the dunes. Elpee ran down the stairs and headed in their direction, but by the time she arrived, the dogs were gone. Their footprints in the sand ended at the dunes, and the high beach grass obscured the direction in which they made their escape.

Forlorn, Elpee turned around and returned to the overpass. She remained on the beach rather than climbing up the stairs in hopes of catching more than a glimpse of the two canines. The remainder of the afternoon passed without any additional sightings of the dogs, which left Elpee feeling even sadder at having thought she had espied her missing and beloved Butter. In the same way that she had lugged herself to the beach in the first place, Elpee, now tired, found herself dragging her heavy legs back to the house to face Alpert. Slowly, she followed the up and down, coming and going ritual of the stairs until she was on the road heading north to her cottage. The walk was short, and within a minute or two, she was standing on the wooden path leading to the screen door, beyond which she hoped she would not find J. Alpert still sleeping.

As Elpee opened the door, she saw Alpert on the couch where she had left him. He was now, however, in a vertical position. He sat there yawning and stretching, delightfully looking, as Elpee thought, well rested and hopefully more sensitive to her needs. She began what she believed was a civil, if not downright pleasant, dialogue with him.

"While you were sleeping the day away on my couch, I experienced another shock to my already shaken mind and weary body. I hope you had a nice nap while this was happening to me. Well, did you? I really need to talk to you because too much is happening too fast and I saw my dog with the other one and tried to chase them, but they ran away into the dunes where I lost sight of them, and the . . ."

"Thank you for your concern. Your selflessness never ceases to amaze me," Alpert interjected in the same sarcastic tone invented by the ex-princess.

"Come on, Alpert," Elpee said in a huff while rolling her eyes. "I asked you if you had a nice nap, didn't I? Why are you getting all snitty about it?"

"Sit down," Alpert commanded as he stood up, and was instantaneously at least a foot taller than when Elpee left him earlier. Obediently, she complied.

"Since I have arrived here, you have done nothing but rant, rave, complain, whine, blather, scream, threaten, cry, moan, gripe, holler, bellyache, etcetera, etcetera. You are no longer a princess living in the 'world according to you.' This is the world you chose to come to when you left the *world according to you* in order to live in a world of, shall I say, *the more mature*. Well, if you want to be more developed, you need to act in that fashion, and of course, if that is not possible or desirable, then move on and find what is. Maybe you need to stop bullying people long enough to figure that out."

Suddenly, Elpee burst into tears. Alpert knew exactly why, but it was her turn to advise him of it rather than the other way around. He stood looking at her and then turned away, biding his time until she finally realized that he would remain doing just that.

"You hurt my feelings," she said softly but with a slight, insolent tone.

"Well, you hurt mine too, so now we are even. So, get over it; that is unless you would prefer not to, at which point I will not either."

"You called me a bully. So did Hortense. That is not nice," Elpee told him.

"What is that saying you people have . . . Something about a shoe fitting?"

Elpee, choosing to ignore this entire conversation until she could sit quietly and contemplate its validity, changed the subject.

"While you were sleeping, I visited with Anna in the backyard. She was acting weird, talking about that chain of command thing again, and then she left. She just confused me, so I walked down to the beach and saw Butter and PippyLou running in the sand, and then they were gone. Just like the princesses, who came, took their letters, and left too. What the heck, Alpert?"

"I still can't recall having met anyone – wizard or non-wizard – by the name of Anna. It seems that people and things are making their presence known to you and then leaving. Why do you think that is?" Alpert replied to her with a question.

"How do I know? After all, I am only an *ex*-princess obviously stripped of my telepathic powers," Elpee said, quickly regretting it as she saw the look of intolerance on Alpert's face.

"ROAR!" the wizard bellowed, as he stood before her unmistakenly taller than he had been before.

His response to her sarcasm elicited a familiar reaction in Elpee. Her lip flew into a sonic quiver just as it had when she first heard the same noise a long time ago. She did not move, and neither did he. Elpee stood there, a bundle of nerves, while Alpert was confident and ready to do battle if necessary. As she tried to gain her composure, her eyes filled with tears, and she ran over to him, threw her arms around his nearly eight-foot frame, and hugged him while she quietly cried.

GOODBYE FOR NOW

"I am really sorry, Alpert. I am just so angry, and sad, and confused that it makes me act stupid. Please forgive me. I would never hurt you, I really wouldn't," Elpee softly spoke as she clung to him. "I thought I wanted to be a grown-up, but maybe I wasn't ready. Maybe I never will be ready. Maybe, I don't even want to be. Maybe, I just thought I had to be – like that was my only alternative after leaving Cherry Castle. I don't know. I just don't want to lose you too, especially if it is because of something I said or did. Please understand, Alpert."

"As you would say, my dear, no bother, and I do understand as best as I can," he reassured the woman-child he was holding as he began to return to his normal height. "I know you are confused by all that has happened and is happening now, but there is only one way to figure it out."

"What is that?"

"Figure it out. There you go, the secret of the Universe in one easy lesson," he lightheartedly stated an absolute truth.

"Wisenheimer! Really, give me some wizardly wisdom, wizard boy. How do I figure it out?" Elpee asked him.

"I wish I could tell you, but I can't. I don't have the answers. You see, the last time I knew that you had to leave, and I knew what you would face, but this time is different. Very different. You have many options, and I don't know which one you will choose. Only you know that, and if you don't, you really *do* need to figure it out. It will all make sense to you . . . Why things are coming and going, why Hortense took Butter, and most of all why you are faced with this situation now just when you thought you were settled. If you look back, you will see that you were not as settled as you thought you were. You carried too much from the old world into this one, but the worst part was that either you tried to ignore those things you brought with you, or you tried to make them fit. Do you understand what I am saying?"

"I do. I know it is all up to me, but I am tired. I just want everything around me to stay just the way it is. To stop changing," Elpee replied.

"Nothing, absolutely nothing, my dear, stays the same. It is just a matter of what we are willing to accept, reject, ignore, adapt to, or change. There is part of your answer, my friend. You always want hints, so there you go. I must leave you now so that you can do your work. I am of no help to you. Unfortunately, this is a solo mission – no copilot on this one, but the good news is that there are clear skies over the horizon. So, put on your flight suit and plot your course. Destiny awaits you," Alpert advisingly proclaimed.

"You have to leave again?" asked Elpee.

"I will be back, I'm sure. I just don't know when," the non-wizard stated with as little emotion as possible. Alpert gave Elpee a quick hug and exited the house just as swiftly before any waterworks began anew. As he left, he yelled back to her, "Figure it out, Elpee!"

ALONE AGAIN

As Alpert left, Elpee walked around the porch, feeling lost and alone. No Butter, no Alpert, no princesses, not even any friends in town. All the people she met here had turned into someone else as if their bodies had been inhabited by other beings, either now or before. Even the masks were quiet. Feeling dreadfully sorry for herself, Elpee decided to put on some old, sappy music and have herself a good cry. At some point in time, Elpee had adopted the philosophy that one is born with a finite amount of tears and that the quicker they could be shed, the sooner happiness and peace could arrive. As she got ready to turn on the music, she felt a sharp pinch underneath her arm.

"OUCH! Alpert, you big dope! I am trying to be sad, can't you see?" Elpee yelled into the vacant air. With the mood ruined, she decided to go for one last walk to the beach, hoping to see her dog before she would take her bath and retire for the night. Elpee grabbed a sweater and began hurriedly walking to the beach, believing that if she could not stay home and have a good cry, she would at least go there and possibly have a good laugh if she spotted the dogs on the sand. Although it was not yet sunset, the path was empty, leaving Elpee by herself. After climbing the stairs to the platform and then descending to the sand below, Elpee sat at the edge of the dunes. She focused her gaze in only one direction, which was down the beach to the east in search of the dogs, but the sand was deserted, and they did not come.

When daylight was mostly gone, so were her hopes of seeing Butter. Elpee rose to leave, and as she stood on the platform looking out toward the ocean one last time, hoping to catch a glimpse of the dogs, Elpee noticed a dim light in the house on the dune. The house had not been occupied recently, and except for the faint light, it still appeared that way. Perhaps someone had bought it and was planning to repair it, Elpee thought. She slowly walked the road leading home, looking for signs of life in any of the houses along the way. They were just average cottages – some in better repair than others, some with prettier gardens, some larger than others were, but mostly nondescript. They neither looked lived in nor abandoned; they just were.

As she approached her more-than-average-looking cottage, Elpee took a deep breath before entering. She did not want to have to do this again in any way, shape, or form. No matter what Alpert said about things not staying the same, she wished with all her heart that he was wrong. Elpee felt that she had faced more changes in her lifetime than the entire population of the planet had in total, and she truly believed that she had found a state of permanence when she had arrived here.

She climbed the several stairs into the house, expecting Butter to be at her side matching her step for step, but instead she felt only emptiness at his absence.

"Damn that Hortense!" she thought aloud. Once inside, she continued grumbling as she climbed the inside stairs to the second-floor bathroom.

"What did I ever do to her to receive such mean treatment? People do not steal other people's dogs. That is just not normal. Even if you don't like the other person, you still don't steal their dog," Elpee huffed and complained aloud while she filled the tub to take a bubble bath.

She thought that the warm water might relax her by quieting her mind and calming her rattled nerves. Despite her good intentions, Elpee continued to mentally and verbally assassinate the Princess of Grouse Hollow, knowing that by doing so, her intent to gain serenity was being undermined.

"I always knew that there was something peculiar about that one. Who does she think she is to judge me and my treatment of my dog? We had a rapport . . . A mutually understood partnership, Butter and I did. One that she wasn't aware of. She doesn't even know Butter, so how could she decide what was good for him? I should have never let her hang out with the gnomes in my garden, and what a dummy I was to befriend Agness or Hortense, or whoever she was," Elpee said, continuing her monologue while adding some clove and myrtle bath salts into the filling bathtub.

She started to speak again but stopped herself and finally surrendered to the error of her ways. Instead of continuing to emit negative energy, Elpee began to create an atmosphere of peace that she desperately needed and now actively sought. She put a match to several candles to illuminate the room and added a dollop of bubble juice to the large, cast-iron vessel. At last, the moment arrived when all systems were a go for Elpee's entry into the body of water that was waiting for human immersion. The contrast of the earthy scent of the salts to the playful appearance of the bubbles made the bathing experience unrivaled.

As she relaxed, submerged in the warm water, Elpee remembered her one-woman puppet shows and the fun she had staging them. At that recollection, Elpee realized how much she missed certain parts of her old life and wondered if she could incorporate them into her existing one. As she posed that question to herself, a realization came over her. making her aware that the 'existing one' would soon no longer exist. She had to come to terms with the fact that she was on her way somewhere else and that her current reality would shortly become her history.

The emotions of the day combined with the heat of the bath made Elpee suddenly very tired, precipitating an early exit from the tub. She automatically reached for the talcum powder on the shelf where she had once kept it, only to find no powder there.

"That's right, I haven't used any powder since I have been here because I thought it was too juvenile. That's another thing I would like to buy – powder, and a big, fat, giant powder puff. Maybe tomorrow I will go to see if Pat has any in the general store. Oh, I am so tired, I can't think anymore. I need some rest," Elpee said aloud as she entered her room. She then pulled down the chenille spread, folded it neatly at the bottom of the bed, and climbed in. The feather bed enveloped her, and the tired ex-princess felt as if she were floating, suspended out in the Universe.

As she drifted off to sleep, she softly whispered, "Goodnight, Butter."

CLEANING AND COMMUNING

As a new day dawned, Elpee began to make plans for her future and how she would live it. If Hortense was honest, then once this task was completed, Butter could come home. Every time Elpee thought about the situation she became livid, cursed, and condemned the Grouse Hollow princess. She felt that it would be much easier to 'figure it out,' as Alpert said, if Butter was at her side. But no, the Universe and Hortense had different plans, and it seemed as though Elpee had no say in how those strategies were developed and decided upon.

Elpee spent the rest of that morning vowing to stop being so angry and to instead use positive thoughts and actions to move her forward, as it appeared she was destined to leave this world, like it or not. She began cleaning the cottage from top to bottom in an attempt to expend some energy and as a kind of meditation. Cleaning was the one thing that Elpee found had the ability to keep her in the absolute present moment with no thoughts other than for what currently existed.

The next few days were filled with washing windows and floors, cleaning out closets, and all matters of a domestic nature. The only time Elpee ventured outside was to commune with her natural surroundings and to ask for guidance. Once or twice, however, she did escape to the beach in search of her beloved pet, but was disappointed each time by his absence. When all was said and done, everything had been cleaned, and nature was communed with, Elpee had no more awareness or answers than she had before she began trying to 'figure it out.'

One night she went to bed feeling thoroughly frustrated at having given up hope of gaining any insight into the situation. The muddled woman was stuck in a state of limbo because of it, knowing she was unable to stay where she was but not knowing how to proceed. Before going to sleep, Elpee reviewed in her mind the sequence of events that had occurred before Butter's abduction and the arrivals of Anna and Alpert.

Three of the princesses, one of which was Hortense, the evil one who stole her dog, had returned and were currently living somewhere nearby. The people in town – her friends – were absent of their previous personas since the princesses came back, so they, in essence, did no longer exist. Anna came but could not stay because Alpert was there and then Alpert left because he could not help her. Elpee fell off to sleep wishing the non-wizard, whom she deemed responsible for the total muddle she was in, would come to revisit her and bring with him a sack of clarity for her.

Elpee's sleep was unusually deep and without dreams, which was in sharp contrast to her usual fantastical nocturnal visualizations. It appeared that she had not moved in her sleep at all during the night, and despite the depth of her sleep, Elpee did not feel rested when she awoke. She actually felt jittery and unsettled, possibly because of the events of late and the toll they were taking on her. The weary, in-between-destinations woman struggled to leave her bed, but she eventually rose and made her way downstairs and into the kitchen to brew the morning coffee. On her way, she saw an ominous scene in her head that caused her to briefly stop to catch her breath. It was a fleeting mental vision that Elpee could not even identify. However, it gave her a feeling of terror and impending doom. She just hoped it was not a premonition of trouble and that it did not pertain to Butter.

Elpee shook herself off and continued on to the kitchen, going through the standard motions, but she still felt petrified on the inside. While trying to calm herself down as she made the coffee, she did a mental inventory of what, where, and with whom she could find support. The townspeople were out, the princesses were gone, and Alpert could not be there. There was only one option left.

"Anna," she reluctantly spoke in a weak tone.

Whistle, whistle.

The Faerie goddess-mother responded with her almost immediate appearance.

ANNA IS BACK IN TOWN

"How did you get here so fast?" Elpee asked.

"My dear, I said I would always be here for you when you called for me . . . Or rather whistled. I see you no longer wear the shell around your neck – the one we selected at the beach. Why is that?" Anna questioned Elpee in return.

"I didn't think I needed it anymore. I figured I was staying here for good and wouldn't need to call you any longer. Kind of settled in, you know?" Elpee replied with a nervous chuckle.

"Perhaps I should put it back on," she continued jokingly.

"You must not ever lose it, or I will be unable to come to you should you need me."

"Really? It's in my top dresser drawer. Without it, you can't find me?"

"Something like that. It ties you and me to each other, and if you lose it or give it away, the bond between us would be broken. I would then become connected to whoever inherited it, and therefore, I would be bonded to the new recipient," Anna explained.

"Well, it looks like I might be needing it again," the dejected former princess proclaimed.

"Why would you say that? This is your home, and you should stay here."

"I should stay here? Why? I thought it was my home too, but clearly, everything that's happened lately says differently. Do you know something I don't?"

"Don't be ridiculous. This is home, and you will stay here. Period!" proclaimed Anna.

Based on the astonished look on Elpee's face, Anna felt the need to expand on her comment in an attempt to soften the message and to keep her centered in thoughts and actions.

"Well, no need to decide that now. You have your whole life ahead of you to move or explore, really to do whatever you want to. Hence, for now, at least, this is your home."

Elpee stood there, wondering if Anna had lost her mind or at least her identity as the others in town had. It seemed to Elpee that Anna had not heard a word that was said to her. Trying not to take out her frustration on and scream at the Faerie goddess-mother, Elpee took a deep breath before speaking.

"Have you lost your mind?" Elpee blurted out, apparently being unsuccessful at containing her ire.

"Well, Miss, I don't believe I have, and I also don't believe your manner of speaking to me is at all appropriate or courteous."

"Anna, you have been here three times in as many days – if days still existed to me – and each time I have expressed my concern about having to leave here, your way of helping me accomplish this upcoming move has been to tell me that I don't have to do exactly that. That sounds crazy to me, Anna, and it appears that you haven't heard anything I've said. How is all this supposed to help me?" Elpee asked while trying to explain how she felt.

"Well, you don't have to go anywhere. That is all in your head. This is your home, and this is where you should stay."

"I can't stay! Everything has changed here, and I must go. I don't belong here anymore . . . If I ever did. Don't you see what's going on, Anna?" Elpee probed. She then paused to think for a moment before continuing, "You are the one who is supposed to be helping me, encouraging me, and supporting me. I don't understand why you aren't doing that. You are almost contradicting what I am saying."

"If you are incorrect, my dear, I cannot support you. If you are about to make a mistake, I will try to stop you from making it. I cannot help or encourage you to do the wrong thing. I am sure you understand and agree with me."

"No, I don't. I really don't. It's my life, and I have the right to make my own choices. Some of those choices will be mistakes, and it would be nice to have someone who would support me in those choices whether they may prove to be right or wrong, good or bad," Elpee stated.

"My dear, you are only serving to upset yourself with too trivial a matter to even discuss. Now, why don't you go for a walk and clear your head?" Anna said as she waved Elpee off. "I think it would be a good idea for you to do so."

"Well, I don't think so, but I don't want to say anything mean, so I will leave the house for a while," Elpee informed Anna as she walked out the door.

POWDER PUFFS PLEASE

"How dare she!" proclaimed Elpee indignantly, but in the next breath, she asked herself, "Or is it me? Am I all mixed up? Maybe she is right, and I do belong here. I think I was happy with my new, grown-up life and world. Oh, I don't know, I just thought she was supposed to help me, not confuse me even more."

Elpee stumbled around the town, kicking rocks in the road along the way as she reflected on her life here. She was happy in the beginning, but over time things began to change. Her old habits slowly crept back into her new life. She had managed to suppress them for a while, but they apparently were such a part of her nature, character, and personality that they could not be silenced indefinitely. That was precisely why she was where she was today. As much as she did not want another upheaval, Elpee knew this was not where she belonged, and finally understood why she was never able to find the seeds that had been planted.

When she arrived at the general store, Elpee went in to purchase the biggest powder puff she could find. She searched the aisles and obtained the same outcome that she had at the market; she was unsuccessful. Despite knowing the fruitlessness of even posing the question, Elpee, to prove that point to herself, asked Pat, "Do you have powder puffs? Big, fat, giant ones?"

"What? Are you serious? Why would I carry such a ridiculous item? No one would ever use them, much less buy them," Pat answered while laughing heartily.

"Just as I thought," replied Elpee, more as an affirmation to herself than as an answer to Pat's questions. This display of Elpee's left Pat wondering about the woman's soundness of mind and her ability to care for herself.

Elpee left the store and started for home, feeling more assured than ever that she did not belong in this world and needed to depart from it. The uncertainty, however, remained in how to accomplish the move and to determine the destination. Elpee chose a different route to take home and continued past where she should would ordinarily turn to get there, and instead decided to go to the beach. On the overpass west of her routinely used one, Elpee looked down the beach to the east. In the distance, she saw three creatures frolicking about, two of which were black and one that was gray. She wished she could see them up close, but knew this faraway glimpse would have to suffice, which made her even more resolute to 'figure it out' if she wanted to get Butter back from Grouse Hollow lady.

Elpee left the beach to return to her cottage, and as she approached the side garden, she saw Anna removing the masks that had been hung on the fence and trees months earlier. They were all griping and yelling at their sudden and unexpected eviction from their homes. Furious, Elpee yelled to Anna, "What are you doing? Leave them exactly where they are! And be gentle, you're hurting them. Can't you hear them?"

"They are silly and ugly, dear, and they destroy the integrity of any proper garden. Those hideous objects are made of clay and have no feelings to hurt, and no, I can't hear them because they are not real, Grace. You need to get your wits about you," Anna replied steadfastly.

"My name is not Grace! You need to put those masks down right now and come in the house. We need to talk!" retorted the irate owner of the house and masks.

As the former princess deliberately walked past her and to the front door, she turned to Anna, who was still in the garden, and said, "My name is Elpee—remember that!"

MY NAME IS ELPEE

When both women were in the house, Elpee began their conversation by saying, "I cannot live this life any longer. It doesn't work for me, and I need to go. I don't know why it doesn't work or where I am to go, but those are the truths. I asked you here to help me find the answer to those unknowns, not to convince me to make peace with the situation as it currently exists. Do you understand what I am telling you, and are you going to help me?"

"I clearly recognize what you have expressed," said Anna. "I am not sure it is the truth, however."

"Well, I am. It is my truth, and that is all that matters in my life and my world. My truth. Do you understand that?"

"Calm down, my dear. There is no need to be so brusque and hostile. Of course, it is your life to live the way you see fit. Now, let us have some tea and forget all this nonsense. We can put it all behind us," Anna said calmly, trying to soothe the savage beast that was alive, well, and growing more substantial in the woman who stood before her.

"I want chocolate milk, and we will continue this discussion later," Elpee told Anna as she went to the fridge to fix herself a giant glass of the sweet drink.

Anna knew it was time to retreat, as Elpee was not in a receptive mood and could not be reasoned with. The woman also realized that she needed to go slower and be gentler with Elpee, because it was definitely going to take much longer than she had initially thought. Anna left the rebellious one alone to drink her chocolate concoction while she enjoyed the savory taste of one of the teas she had selected from on the shelf.

"Poor girl," the woman muttered, "still delusional and still in denial about it. These are the hardest cases to break through and help."

In the backyard, Elpee noisily guzzled rather than drank the chocolate-flavored milk in a futile effort to quench her insatiable thirst for respect. No one, including herself, ever understood her. She wondered whom she should believe and whom she should question. Perhaps a swing in the hammock would help her find some answers. On her way there, she grabbed a long bamboo shoot and climbed into the fabric cradle, knowing she would need to propel herself to and fro, as the elves were no longer living in the backyard. With a few pushes from the reed, Elpee was on her way to somewhere. She lay in the blazing sun, her face on fire, as she endeavored to either 'figure it out' or calm down and relax – either one would do. Unable to stop her racing thoughts, Elpee began counting each time she swung back and forth.

"One . . . Two . . . Three . . . Seven hundred and sixteen."

By the time she reached a six-figure number, Elpee, despite the scorching sun, began to feel a chill – actually, a quite chilling chill. She opened her eyes to find a winter wonderland surrounding her. How could it be snowing when the outside temperature was a bazillion plus degrees? Now Elpee knew without a doubt that she, in fact, was crazy. She could no longer trust herself, and she began to cry at the thought, sure that her life was destined to be in an indeterminate state of insanity for the remaining history of her. As her tears increased and her heart got heavier, Elpee saw that the snow was changing colors in one specific area. It was the most purple of purples, and it prompted her to go toward the spot where it was snowing that color. Struggling to plod through the snow with no shoes on her feet, Elpee witnessed an awe-inspiring sight when she arrived at the place of the purple snow. Engraved into the white background were the colored letters that read:

"You lack only one thing – the most important thing – the ability to trust yourself and your instincts. I know you can't even begin to comprehend what I am saying, and certainly not this concept, so for right now just tuck it away in your mind and it will be there when you are ready and when you need it."

Alpert spoke these words to her before he left her two-plus years ago. He was right, she had no idea what he was trying to tell her then, but she did now because she was ready. Elpee shook the snow off her body and walked back to the house with a new pep in her step and a renewed vim in her vigor. She threw the door open and stormed into the house.

"ANNA," she bellowed.

Silence was the only answer Elpee received.

"ANNA," Elpee yelled again, this time even louder.

At that moment, the Faerie goddess-mother appeared from the porch, seeming to be larger than life to Elpee, who although startled, stood her ground.

"Yes, dear. What is it?" Anna replied in a gentle manner, which was quite in contrast to Elpee's thundering voice that had just summoned her.

"We need to chat. I'm sorry you came all this way for nothing. Please don't think I am ungrateful, but you can leave now. Thank you. Goodbye."

Having said that, Elpee turned to leave, expecting Anna to do the same; however, she did not. Instead, Anna sat on one of the rockers and began reading a book. Confused, Elpee turned back around to face Anna and said, "Well, aren't you going to go? You can leave to help someone else who really does need your services."

"I'm drained, dear. I think I shall stay here and rest for a while," Anna, feigning fatigue, replied, in the hope of not reactivating Elpee's overly active anger and imagination.

Unsure of what to say or do next, Elpee responded by exiting the porch, knowing that when Anna was gone, she could concentrate more on her mission and its destination. In her infinite kindness, Elpee would allow Anna to rest – perhaps several minutes, but no longer – before giving her the boot.

An Unwanted Visitor
and an Unwanted Message

Days turned into weeks – and then into months – and the seasons changed. What did not change, however, was Anna's continued presence at Cherry Cottage. She seemed to have one excuse after another for not leaving, none of them being terribly legitimate or believable to Elpee. Initially, Anna felt too tired to move on, and then she developed a stuffy head and nose, which sent her to bed for a week. When she recovered from her fatigue and the cold, she acquired a migraine that prevented her from leaving her adopted home to its rightful inhabitant, who had requested that she do so long ago. It was delay after delay, and it hindered Elpee's ability to formulate and execute a plan of re-creation for herself. Occasionally, the frustrated ex-princess would secretly go down to the beach, hoping to spot Butter playing in the sand. She hid this from Anna, fearing that if the Faerie goddess-mother knew, she might think it abnormal and use it as another excuse to remain. Finally, when Elpee could stand it no longer, she confronted her unwanted visitor.

"Anna, I have understood about your illnesses and fatigue, but it is really now time for you to go. I'm sure there is someone else who needs your help, and quite frankly, I need to get on with my life, where and however that may take place. I know you are aware of that and will respect my wishes. Once again, thank you and goodbye."

Elpee spun on her heels to leave, but before she could exit the room, Anna said, "Sit down my dear, now it is I who must speak."

Elpee was surprised by this emphatic command and not sure of what to expect the message to be. She obediently complied by sitting on the nearest piece of furniture to accommodate Anna's directive.

"I have been trying to let you find your way, hoping against hope you would realize that everything you say and believe is a delusion. I know this must be very difficult to hear, and I so wish you had been able to come to terms with it on your own, but unfortunately for both of us, that has not been the case. For some reason, you have espoused the notion that this is not your home and that you must find a different place to live. You are incorrect, my dear. This is your home, and this is where you must stay. There is no other place or life waiting for you to find it. To believe that there is is pure folly. Now, having shared that information with you, I hope you will understand my concern and I also hope that you will let me help you accept this as your fate."

Elpee could not believe her ears. What Anna was saying was impossible, and Elpee did not know how to respond. She sat there with a blank expression on her face while her head reeled with questions. When Anna realized that Elpee was not going to answer anytime soon, she continued, "I am sorry to have to tell you how incorrect your thinking is. I thought if I gave you enough time, you would come around and leave your delusional state; that you would finally see what is real rather than the fantasy and delusion that was in your head. I do so hope that you will not be angry with me for making the excuses that I did. They were made so that I could bide some additional time in the hope that your sanity would return."

"I would like to lie down now," Elpee said as she rose from the couch she had been sitting on. She headed upstairs to her bedroom and vaguely heard Anna say, "That is a wonderful idea. Rest. You have so much healing to do."

Elpee went up to her bedroom that day and remained there for an unknown amount of time. Anna, in the meanwhile, brought Elpee's meals to her so that she would not have to venture downstairs and witness firsthand the deconstruction process that was occurring. The Faerie goddess-mother had removed all that was whimsical, silly, or juvenile and anything that would encourage Elpee's belief that having these items around was proof positive she did not belong here in the more serious-minded world. Anna had hoped that when Elpee finally came downstairs, the house would be rid of any objects that could trigger her regression into what was her escalating, freestyle, and delusional beliefs of how life should be.

Anna spent her days merrily singing and removing what Elpee believed to be her most prized possessions—the very things that defined who she was. Meanwhile, the despondent and rightful owner of the cottage remained upstairs, a prisoner in her own home. No matter how much she tried, Elpee could not believe the things Anna had presented to her as truth, and despite knowing that to do so would be the path of least resistance, it was not a path Elpee was able to navigate.

After having seen the message in the snow that day, Elpee knew that she could not go back to distrusting herself and denying her truths, but what was she to do, she wondered? Another question without an answer. She was exhausted and could not manage to overcome the conflict that was raging between her head and her heart. It was easier to just lie in bed rather than to attempt to find the answers. *Maybe Anna was right after all,* she thought as she closed her eyes in sleep.

EUTERPE THE *QUEEN*

Elpee awoke to the sound of the shutters banging against her window. She had neither the strength nor the desire to get up and secure them, so she lay there listening to their rhythmic battering against the building. This unrelenting clamor continued, not until Elpee grew accustomed to the noise, but instead until she collected herself enough to realize that there were no shutters on her house. She forced herself to get out of bed and investigate the source of the pounding noise.

As she approached the window, Elpee saw a piece of pink parchment paper flying about and persistently crashing into the glass. For a fleeting second, she detected a hint of joy and excitement that the last of the four royals was making her presence known. Quickly, however, the dejected and despondent inhabitant of the room disavowed the possibility that it might be *Queen* Euterpe who was outside her window. Instead, Elpee turned around and got back into bed.

The noise continued harder and more furiously, until Elpee sat up in bed and faced the window. Smashed against the glass was the gawking image of Euterpe's face and her hand, which held a note within it.

"Open the window, and hurry it up,

"I haven't all day, it's time for sup(per).

"Get out of bed, you sleepy head,

"I have to rush; we're having mush(rooms).

"I have a message from a faraway land,

"that I must place in your hand(s).

"So, open the window, would you please,

"and hurry up 'cause I have to sneeze."

"Aaaaaaaaa chooooooo," spewed *Queen* Euterpe, who blew herself right off the glass and into what appeared was going to be outer space, giving Elpee an excellent and much-needed laugh.

As she was giggling at Euterpe's orbital disappearance, Elpee got out of bed and opened the window. First, she looked up, and then she looked down for the *Queen*, but when she could not spot her, she thought that perhaps Euterpe had indeed flown into space.

"How silly you are to think such a thought, Miss," Elpee reprimanded herself. "It was just as senseless to believe anyone was ever at the window in the first place, and then to laugh about it is really lunatical. Anna is right, I am off my rocker."

As she pivoted from the window to return to her bed, Elpee was greeted by *Queen* Euterpe, who was reclining in the exact spot Elpee had exited from just moments earlier. With her bubblegum-colored hair flowing across the pillows, Euterpe indeed looked regal except for the few bumps on her head she suffered as a result of her having flown into the glass or perhaps from the atomic sneezing that had launched her out of orbit and back to Earth. Elpee did not know what to do. Should she hug a delusion or ignore a friend? She climbed back into bed but said nothing, having decided that was an excellent compromise. As soon as Elpee got under the covers and closed her eyes, the voice began.

"Say hello, so I will know,
"that you are a friend, not a foe.
"Give me a smile, so I can see,
"the Princess of Cherry Cottage by the Sea."

Elpee did not respond but instead lay there, ignoring her impulse to do otherwise. When the pink-haired princess received no response, she continued.

"My dear sister Elpee, why so cold?
"I came a distance for you to behold,
"a note in my bag with letters bold,
"a warning to you that must be told."

That caught Elpee's attention, and she turned to the other princess and said, "Euterpe?"

"Who else would it be, you silly bee?
"Let's go outside and hug a tree.
"Or maybe run barefoot through the lea,
"and then perhaps you'll see it's me!"

"Oh Euterpe, I am so happy to see you. The others are here, but I don't know where . . . Except for Hortense, that demon seed. She stole my dog!" Elpee began telling Euterpe excitedly.

"Oh my, oh my, oh my, you say,

"your little dog has gone away?

"She must bring him back this very day,

"or there will be a price to pay."

"Thank you, Euterpe. Will you help me get him back?" implored Elpee.

"We shall find the dog,

"and steal him back.

"Then stretch the hog,

"out on a rack."

"I like your style! Let's go," Elpee said while rising from the bed.

"I only kid.

"It was a joke.

"For if we did,

"we'd go to the poke."

Disappointed, Elpee replied, "Rats."

"Let's get off your pet before I forget,

"to give you the note that the author wrote,

"for you to read the message you need."

"Euterpe, give me the stupid note, for Christmas's sake," commanded Elpee.

"Right now, right here,

"there is something to fear.

"Be patient, be calm, I mean no harm,

"by what I say, or for the delay," she paused slightly.

"So, here is the note,

"and that's all she wrote," *Queen* Euterpe spouted as she handed Elpee a Kelly green envelope that was sealed with wax and an impression of the letter 'A'.

Elpee broke the seal and pulled the letter out of the envelope. The note contained only five words.

There is no Anna. Beware!

HELP!

As Euterpe seemed quite comfortable and at ease still lying on the bed, Elpee began to press her for answers.

"Did Alpert give this note to you?"

"The answer is yes, I must confess."

"When?"

"Yesterday, by the way."

"What did he say to you?"

"Deliver the note by plane or by boat."

"I mean about the contents?"

"Not a word did he say, simply be on my way!"

"Euterpe, you have to help me. What does this note mean? No Anna?"

Quizzically, Euterpe looked at Elpee and asked, "Anna, Anna, who is Anna? Don't ask me, but I'd like a banana."

"Thanks, Euterpe, but this is obviously not your area of expertise. Will you bring a note back to Alpert for me?"

"I suppose I could,

"for the better good,

"if you just would,

"do what you should."

"And what is that, Euterpe?" Elpee asked.

"Give me a banana, Hannah!"

"My name is not Hannah, and I don't have any bananas," replied Elpee woefully.

"I'd love to stay, but I must be on my way."

"Fine, Euterpe," interrupted Elpee, "but you have to wait until I write this note for you to bring to him. I mean it, Euterpe! Wait!" Elpee stated with such authority that for whatever reason the *Queen* acknowledged the command and lay back down on the bed while awaiting further instructions.

Elpee walked over to the small desk, which was situated in the corner of her bedroom and where she kept only stationery and a fountain pen. She removed one sheet of paper and one envelope and uncapped the pen, all the while thinking of how to reply to the wizard's warning until she finally came up with it.

'HELP!' was all Elpee wrote before sealing the envelope and holding it out to Euterpe, who now seemed in no hurry to vacate the feather bed on which she was reclining.

"Euterpe, please bring this to Alpert as quickly as you can. Don't stop anywhere to shop or collect shells. Please. This is urgent. I don't know what to beware of, so please give this to him pronto and tell him to come here and help me. Thank you, Euterpe," Elpee said as she gave the *queen* the envelope and a goodbye hug.

Queen Euterpe sang her farewell to Elpee as she left the same way she came in.

"Goodbye, my sister,

"I will give to the mister,

"this envelope and letter.

"Sure hope you feel better."

Elpee's head was swimming with this information, which only added to her already confused state. Unsure of how to proceed, she decided to sit in her rocking chair that faced the window and looked down onto the street below. She could meditate, hoping for some wisdom to be conveyed to her. She rocked, and rocked, and then rocked some more, but she remained absent of any divinely inspirational answers. She decided to, at last, leave the room she had been holed up in for some time, and reinhabit the rest of her house.

Elpee took a deep breath and began the descent into the living room below, and as she slowly stepped on each stair tread, she remembered why and how much she loved her home. It was a reflection of who she was, and despite some confusions, there was a tender comfort in that image. As she reached the last step, that sense of well-being rapidly dissolved because there were no likenesses of Elpee anywhere in the room. She went out to the front porch and then into the dining room and kitchen only to find the same absence of her belongings and in essence her being.

WHAT, NO HOT DOGS?

———

Elpee's first reaction was to scream for, and then at, Anna, but she thought of Alpert's warning and tried to refrain from doing anything that might prove unwise. Instead, she decided to slowly walk through the cottage, taking a mental inventory of what was missing, and would then ask Anna in a calm manner where they were so that they could eventually be returned to their proper places. When Elpee had completed her accounting, she left the house in search of Anna. She found her in the garden digging out the black-eyed Susans and tossing them into a pile.

"Anna, what are you doing?" Elpee instinctively shrieked, immediately forgetting her pledge to use caution.

"Why are you down here? You should be upstairs in bed, resting. Now run along," Anna gruffly directed Elpee.

"I am tired of being upstairs, and I want to know why most of my things inside are missing and where they are," Elpee responded as Anna continued to rip out the yellow and black flowers.

"Stop pulling my flowers out!" Elpee screamed at Anna.

"These are meaningless and unsightly weeds and not worth the room they take up in the garden. A garden should be precise and geometrical, not scattered and filled with this and that kind of weed. Order and greenery is the key to a beautiful and mature garden."

"No . . . I couldn't disagree with you more. Those blossoms are beautiful, and a friend of mine gave them to me, so stop digging and move over. I'm going to try to rescue the ones you have already uprooted," Elpee demanded.

Anna moved out of the way, but in the process of passing Elpee, she deliberately stomped on the flowers that were on the ground, which Elpee was endeavoring to save. Elpee wanted to talk with Anna about the conditions inside the house, but her present anger along with her priority of having to tend to the withering blossoms caused by Anna's wicked weeding made it impossible to do so at that moment. It took Elpee most of the afternoon to replant the flowers that were yanked from their homes, and by the time Elpee was done, she was filthy and exhausted but also thankful that she had managed to return her garden to its proper wild-flower state. The masks were sullen and lifeless from having been tossed in a pile of overgrown weeds in the back of the garden by Anna that day long ago. Elpee would clean and re-hang them tomorrow because she could not do one more thing today. Hopefully, none of them were broken, or cracked, or worse yet.

Elpee entered the house, planning to go directly upstairs to the bath, but smelled something putrid coming from the kitchen, which caused her to detour into that area. Anna was cooking some potion that was not fit for man nor beast, of which neither resided at the cottage, but Elpee was sure that if they had, it would not be fit for either of them.

Anna, looking up from stirring her blend of nasty ingredients, said to Elpee, "Dinner will be ready in twenty minutes. You need to clean yourself up before I bring it up to you."

"It won't be necessary to bring anything up to me, Anna. I will be eating down here, and I am going to have a hot dog," Elpee replied.

"There are no hot dogs; I disposed of them. Such a horrible little food. What person beyond the age of three would intentionally foul their body with such poison?"

"There are no hot dogs? You threw them out? Why would you do that? You may think they are poison – and maybe they are – but you don't have to eat them, so why didn't you just leave them alone? You can't just go around deciding that the world needs to live by your rules. You have no right . . ." Elpee, hearing herself, decided she needed to back off before she said too much too soon. There were a lot of discussions to be had, but she needed to pace herself and her words.

"I will find something for myself to eat, thank you, Anna. You go ahead and have your supper without me while I take a bath," said Elpee calmly as she turned and left the room.

Dinner and Dresses

Elpee drew a tepid bath and added some lemon verbena salts to it. As the tub filled, she laid clean clothes out on the bed, choosing things that would help lighten her somber mood and help her to deal with the tasks at hand, whatever they may be. When her outfit was chosen, Elpee entered the wholly filled tub, breathing deeply and rhythmically, placing herself into a harmonious union with the Universe. After soaking for almost thirty minutes, Elpee exited the container with a greater sense of balance and confidence. Feeling more grounded, she dressed and descended the grand wooden staircase to the lower level of the house.

When Elpee entered the kitchen, she found Anna eating some sort of mixture that was unidentifiable. Choosing not to stop to examine it any closer, Elpee opened the refrigerator and then the freezer in her quest for food to eat, only to find both empty – devoid of all that Elpee had stored in them. Still serene from her bath experience, she calmly checked the cabinets, but there she was met with no better success in her pursuit of nourishment. Anna had bread and butter on the table, and there was a canister of ground cinnamon sugar in the cabinet. With not many options for something to eat, Elpee chose to make several slices of cinnamon sugar toast. In a vain attempt at civility, Elpee decided to sit at the table with Anna to eat her hastily prepared dinner.

"I don't know why you didn't eat what I cooked. What is that you are eating . . . Butter, cinnamon, and sugar on bread? That, along with the outfit you are wearing, is so outrageously adolescent that I cannot help but find them both appalling. Tomorrow, I will go through your clothes to see if there is anything that can be salvaged and the rest I will dispose of, which I venture to say is most, if not all, of your wardrobe. Then you will need to learn how to sew in order to make yourself new, more appropriate clothing," Anna announced.

"I don't want to sew myself new clothing, and I certainly don't want you going through my closets and throwing things out."

"You are right, my dear, your clothes may be perfectly fine. It is how you mix and match, not to mention accessorize them with trifles, that is more of the problem," Anna said.

"What do you mean? And by the way, why do you care?" Elpee asked her in response.

"Because you look bizarre . . . Er . . . Forgive me. That was a harsh word to use. It's just that you got new stylish clothing when you arrived here and yet you coordinate them so poorly."

"I have a closet full of linen and silk; what do you think I should be wearing ermine and pearls?" Elpee retorted.

"Calm down, dear. I am only suggesting that you choose the combinations a bit more carefully. Striped pants, linen or not, do not match a floral blouse, for goodness's sake," said Anna as she snickered disapprovingly.

Elpee in return replied, "Why not?"

Anna chose not to address what she perceived to be Elpee's insolent question and instead began clearing the table.

"Well, why not?" Elpee pressed her for an answer.

"Because you look like a child who has been left to her own devices to dress herself instead of an adult who would naturally choose her ensemble with a sense of taste and decorum."

Elpee was about to antagonize Anna even more, but before she could, Anna announced to her, "I will clean out your closet in the morning and dispose of what is inappropriate. By limiting your choices, I will be eliminating the possibility of your dressing in the silly manner you seem to be so intent on."

"DON'T YOU DARE!" Elpee proclaimed rather loudly.

"Don't *you* dare, Miss. I will not be spoken to in that manner," Anna advised Elpee while standing and waiting for an admission of guilt from her, which did not come. In fact, Elpee did quite the opposite. She walked directly up to Anna, looked her squarely in the eye, and said, "Get out!"

SIMON SAYS

Both women stood their ground, glaring at each other, before Anna finally broke the standoff by speaking first.

"No, I won't, because I can't trust you to do the right thing," Anna responded to Elpee's demand that she leave.

"The right thing? The right thing for who?" Elpee asked.

"For you, of course. You need to learn that you must simply do the things that are in line with society's norms and standards. It is time you learned to function in the world in which you live and as the adult that you are."

"Anna," Elpee stated with authority, "it really is time that you leave. Now. When you first arrived, I was confused and trying to figure out where I was going, but your continued and seriously overextended presence in my home just serves to confuse me even more. So you really do need to go."

"Understand something, my dear. I am staying here just as you are, so you need to accept that fact," Anna told her as she walked out of the kitchen, leaving Elpee and the mess behind.

Feeling frustrated and powerless over Anna's position, Elpee would need to find a solution to both her feelings and her situation. She left the kitchen and went outside to sit on the wicker rocking chair. She sat, swaying back and forth, for what seemed like hours as she looked up at the night sky and the barely visible new moon that decorated it. Knowing that the new moon was a time to draw in that which one wanted in their life, Elpee gazed up at the sky one last time before going into the house. The picture painted on an otherwise black velvet canvas made her resolve to 'figure it out' even stronger. There was a celestial portrait crafted from stars and clouds that depicted the three princesses, one *Queen*, the scruffy, gray creature, PippyLou, and her beloved Butter, all smiling down at her.

Once inside, Elpee went directly up to her bedroom, too exhausted to do anything else but sleep. She knew she should have cleaned up the kitchen, but instead the weary waif got under the covers, vowing to do it tomorrow, and she immediately fell asleep. The next thing Elpee heard was a clanging noise coming from out back somewhere. She ran down the stairs and out into the yard in her polka dot pajamas to find Anna removing the contents of the back cottage that Elpee used for her pottery studio.

"What are you doing *now*, Anna?" Elpee asked of the fallen from grace Faerie goddess-mother.

"What do you think?" Anna replied, inferring that Elpee was somewhat dimwitted to ask a question with such an obvious answer.

Not knowing what was going on with Anna, and having no success in the current way she was handling the situation, Elpee instead appealed to Anna's gentler nature if there was one, which was something she definitely doubted. Elpee began with words that unwittingly flowed from her mouth without first being formed in her brain. In fact, Elpee had no idea from where the words or the idea had originated.

"Anna, please leave the tools and just a little bit of materials . . . *Please*. Before I take your recommended road, I would like to make one last mask . . . Like a symbolic or ceremonial rite of passage. Just one and then I will give everything to Pat. It was her idea in the first place, so I am sure she would be glad to have the materials."

Anna thought for a moment before answering and then asked Elpee, "Are you sure you will make only one more of those hideous things?" Anna paused before continuing. "I will tell you what – you may put aside enough material for one mask, and I will throw the rest away. When you have completed it, we will arrange for your friend to pick up the equipment. I am very proud of you, my dear. Finally, you are coming to your senses."

Elpee was amazed at herself but even more amazed at the ease with which the words exited her mouth, not to mention the positive effect they had on Anna. She was also unaware of the meaning held within her own words and wondered why she would want to make another mask. Not knowing what else to say, Elpee firmly but politely stated, "Thank you, Anna."

"You are welcome, my dear. Now put aside what you need for one more mask and then I will clean the rest out. When you are done, go out into the woods and pick some blueberries for breakfast," Anna commanded.

She showed Anna what materials she needed and then obediently headed beyond the back cottage and into the woods for the fruit. All the while Elpee felt more like a child from Anna's treatment of her than she did from her own behavior, and although she resented Anna's conduct, she was grateful for the opportunity and the distance Anna's order had afforded her. Elpee relished her time among the trees as she strolled slowly along the paths to the patch of berries where she had found Butter those many years ago.

While standing amid the trees and bushes, inhaling the blend of musky and sweet fragrances, Elpee suddenly felt a vise-like tightening on her right ankle. A bear trap, she wondered? No. She looked down, and attached to her lower limb and encircling both feet were her old friends, the gnomes. Immediately and instinctively, Elpee dropped to the ground and began hugging them all—not one at a time but rather as many as her arms could encircle simultaneously. They rolled around on the ground, laughing and hugging, until someone realized the imprudence of their behavior. Simon, seemingly the quintessential elder elf, came forward and spoke to Elpee in friendship and respect.

"Princess Elpee, I have a message for you from Mr. J. Alpert VII. He said you would understand what it means and what you need to do."

"Alpert? What did he say, Simon?"

"He said, 'Return the snail to the earth,'" Simon answered.

"What? What does that mean?"

"You did not let me finish, Princess. The wizard's the message ended with the words, 'Figure it out.'"

THE LAST BREAKFAST

Elpee thanked all of her tree friends for their friendship and for coming to her aid. As much as she wanted to stay with them, she knew she must gather the berries and return home.

As she placed the fruit in her basket, Elpee kept pondering the meaning of Alpert's message—'Return the snail to the earth.'

She did not understand what the words themselves meant, no less the meaning behind them. Time would tell, she knew that, and so she relaxed her grip on the need to 'figure it out' and returned her thoughts to collecting the blueberries. Soon the basket was full, and Elpee was on her way home feeling lighter than she had in a long time. She was delighted at having seen her gnome friends. Her glee, in conjunction with having received a message from Alpert, albeit cryptic, served to reinforce her truth in having to move on regardless of what Anna said.

As Elpee approached the back cottage, she got a knot in her stomach because as much as she loved her house, Anna's presence changed its personality and Elpee's as well. She decided that she would have a heart-to-heart chat with her unwelcome visitor and settle this once and for all. Anna was in the kitchen preparing pancake batter as Elpee returned with the berries.

"Thank you, my dear. Oh, they do look lovely," Anna said as she took the full basket from Elpee. She then placed the fruits in the colander to wash them, and Elpee put the kettle on for tea.

"Shall I make us a pot of tea?" Elpee asked. "I thought vanilla-maple might be nice with the pancakes."

"That would be delightful," Anna responded. "A splendid choice, indeed."

While Anna made the pancakes and the water in the kettle warmed to a boil, Elpee set plates, cups, and silverware on the table along with pure maple syrup, cream, and sugar. She ran into the garden to pick some flowers for the table only to find most of them gone or in shock from Anna's method of natural selection along with Elpee's attempt at trying to breathe life back into the species. They would have to do without the amenities, which disturbed Elpee, but there was nothing she could do about it. There were no flowers that survived Anna's wicked hands.

By the time the table was set, Anna had finished cooking the pancakes and placed them on a platter to take outside. Elpee, having prepared the tea, joined the other woman as they exited the kitchen to the outdoor dining table where they both sat in anticipation of eating the delectable breakfast. They both seemingly gave the meal that awaited them their individual seal of approval. As Anna served the pancakes, Elpee poured the tea, but as she reached for the sugar, a severe look of disapproval came over Anna's face. Elpee was sure she knew why, but she nevertheless continued putting spoonful after spoonful of the sweetener into her teacup until Anna, while shaking her head, finally interrupted the ritual.

"Please, my dear, your adding an overly abundant amount of sugar to your tea causes me to feel ill. There is no need for either sugar or milk if one uses a quality tea and prepares it properly, both of which are true in this case," Anna admonished the determined Elpee.

"Forgive me, Anna, but I have never thought that doing something such as enhancing the flavor of one's beverage was akin to the crime of the century," Elpee flippantly responded.

With that remark spoken, Anna stood up, placed her napkin on the table, and began to leave. Elpee, knowing that what she said would ignite Anna's ire even before she said the words, also stood, ready to apologize.

"Anna, I am sorry. I don't know what got into me, but please sit down. You prepared such a lovely breakfast, and I would hate to think I ruined it. Please," Elpee selfishly implored.

Although somewhat begrudgingly, the other woman sat down, which helped to ease Elpee's state of apprehension over the conversation she would initiate following their meal. When, she thought to herself, would she learn her lesson and just shut up? They ate their breakfast in silence. It was a quiet born out of enjoyment rather than resentment, and when the food was gone, Anna stood to clear the table, but Elpee put her hand on the other woman's arm, gesturing her to stop. Anna, looking surprised, quizzingly asked, "What is it, dear?"

"There is no rush, is there? And it's such a beautiful day. Why don't we take our tea over to the rockers and sit for a while?" Elpee suggested.

Anna was surprisingly receptive to the idea and led the way. They sat, and as Anna began rocking, Elpee filled both their cups with the remaining tea, deliberately and conspicuously leaving her own black. After several minutes, Elpee gathered the courage to initiate saying what she had planned to say – although she had no actual plan at all.

"Anna, can we please have a conversation as we used to without throwing barbs or threats at each other? You saved my life and brought me here when I was lost. You helped me become the woman I am today, and I will always be grateful to you for that. So, can we please talk like we used to?"

"I would most certainly like to. Where would you like to begin?" Anna coolly responded.

"I was so very lost when you brought me here, and with your help, I was able to establish myself in the community and mature into the woman I never was before. But time changes all things, and as time passed, I found myself becoming a bit discontented with some of the things in my life. I don't need to explain what they were – you know – and that is why you are here. I thought you came here to help me move on again, but it seems that you believe I belong here and should remain even if I don't feel the same way. I am totally unsure of where I am going, and that scares me so, so much. I could really use your support and help in getting there."

"I can't help you because I see no need for you to change or to move."

"But Anna, you know all the things that have happened here recently, like the princesses coming back, and the real people becoming like . . . Like vapid ghouls. You see, Anna, I can use grown-up words, and I have learned how to live here, I just don't want to. I want my friends, the princesses and the gnomes back, and most of all, Butter. He won't be returned until I do what it is I need to do. So, will you help me?" Elpee pleaded with Anna.

"My job was and still is to bring you to a world of grace and dignity without ridiculous cherries and polka dots. To teach you to drink tea from china, not dirty acorn cups. To do this, you must see . . . I must make you see . . . That there are no hideous gnomes or elves living in disgusting and dirty trees. I want a world of beauty and palaces with stunning clothes and music. I want to be invited to parties at the most important people's homes. YOU MUST GIVE ME THESE THINGS!"

"Anna, stop! What are you saying? What are you talking about? This is about me and my life and my happiness, not you and yours," declared Elpee. "And by the way, I guess you were absent the day they had the lesson on Faerie goddess-mothers being in the same category as gnomes and elves."

Standing up ominously while shaking her fist, Anna demanded, "YOU WILL GIVE ME THESE THINGS OR YOU WILL DIE!"

Elpee displayed an equal measure of confidence and determination as she also rose from her chair and moved closer to Anna. The rightful inhabitant of Cherry Cottage possessed something the other woman did not; she carried within her an integrity born of strife, struggle, and success.

"Then die I must. I will never live unhappily again, not for you or anyone else. You will have to find another poor wench who is willing to sell her soul to do your bidding."

BANISHED AGAIN

Both women stood there glaring at each other until Anna, seemingly mystified by Elpee's response and equally unsure of how to handle it, briefly stepped aside. This short amount of time was enough to allow Elpee to digest the words of the message she had just delivered to Anna, as well as to view the tea leaves in the bottom of her cup for a possible strategy on how to proceed. The residue did reveal the solution to at least her current and immediate problem.

Encouraged by having some insight into what needed to be done, Elpee stood her ground and confidently waited for Anna to return to her previous position with the deliverance of a surly comment to Elpee's statement. But before Anna could utter a word, Elpee began, "It appears that we are at a crossroads, Anna. Only time will tell how this will conclude, and until that time or such time as one of us chooses to concede to the other, I will stay in the back cottage. It seems that you are more comfortable in my house than I am. Therefore, you stay in there. I will go up to my room to pack some toiletries and clothes, if any are left, and then I will leave you to enjoy the cottage you created, not the home that I made when I arrived here. Now, if you will excuse me," Elpee boldly stated as she walked past Anna and into the house.

Once inside, Elpee began to feel the draining effects of the energy she had expended to exhibit that display of forceful self-assurance. No bother, she had to go on, and so up the stairs, she went straight into her bedroom, where she approached her dresser, took a deep breath, and opened the top drawer. After moving aside some handkerchiefs, Elpee found what she was looking for. She quickly glanced over at the door, guardedly picked up the snail shell, and stuffed it into her grown-in and pinned-up mane of lion's hair. Not caring what else she would take with her, Elpee began throwing articles of clothing and various other sundries into an old carpetbag, and left her bedroom vowing that she would return. She descended the staircase into the living room and walked past Anna into the back cottage, which would be her new home for an indeterminate amount of time depending on the outcome. Elpee shut the door and waited. She did not know what she was waiting for, but she also did not know what else to do, at least at that very moment.

As the hours passed, Elpee quietly sat on her pottery stool waiting for something – anything – to happen. She had no idea what to expect, and although she felt alone and lonely, she mostly felt fear. Pure, unadulterated fear. There was some crazy, netherworld woman living in her house, and Elpee had wittingly banished herself to an old shed behind that house. She wanted to make her move, but thought it best to wait Anna out and see how the woman would react, if at all, to what she would undoubtedly consider Elpee's outright defiance.

Darkness overcame the house, the shed, and the yard. Fortunately, Elpee kept candles in the old studio, and so she began to light several, mindful of the fact that she must conserve some in case she would be relegated to this dwelling for an extended period. Anna seemed to be enjoying the comforts of Elpee's house, as there were lights on in every room, and the putrid smell of the nightly concoctions Anna called supper wafted out of the open windows. Elpee did not know when she would eat again, but she hoped it would be soon and that it would be in her own home.

Feeling pangs of hunger, Elpee curled up on the floor with only an old shawl to keep her warm, and prayed herself to sleep as she thought of PoliM'aladroit and her courage and belief in the Universe. Every time she woke up, she would remind herself of the fortitude the Princess of ShinyShores had, and she would draw strength from it. It would help her to persevere until the time was right; a time she hoped would come soon.

In the morning, she was awakened by a rustling sound coming from outside the back window of her new quarters. She opened the floor-to-ceiling window to find a cup of freshly steeped English breakfast tea with lots of cream and sugar in it and a bowl of homegrown melon from someone's garden. Despite her dire situation, the unexpected breakfast made Elpee smile. First, there was PoliM'aladroit giving her courage and faith last night, and now danDay-leon providing her with the most delicious tea in the history of all teas. Lest she go hungry, Elpee did not look a gift horse in the mouth and accepted the bowl of diced-up, fresh, homegrown melon, which was evidently from that dyed in the wool scoundrel, Hortense.

After her nourishment, Elpee opened the window and quietly whispered, "Thank you, girls."

She spent most of the day observing Anna's actions and attempting to establish a pattern to them. When she felt confident enough in her assessment of them, Elpee would execute her plan, but because Anna had the advantage over Elpee in most circumstances, it was imperative that Elpee not ever, ever, ever, play it out in her mind. If she did, Anna would then become aware of it, giving her another advantage; the ultimate and conquering advantage. Trying to break her concentration, Elpee envisioned that she wore a rubber band on her wrist and pretended to snap it whenever a thought came into her mind. It was also imperative for Elpee to maintain a positive emotional state so that Anna could not know her real fear and despondency and thereby capitalize on it. Elpee was little aware that it would take many days and many nights before her plan would be carried out.

EVE OF THE APOCALYPSE

As Elpee lay weak and nearly beaten, she felt a pinch. And then another. And then another. And yet one more before she rose from her floor bed. There, standing in front of her, was Alpert, the three princesses, and one *queen*, each with a unique gift for Elpee. First, danDay-leon approached Elpee and gave her a cup of green tea with ginseng, which the frightened and exhausted refugee gladly and graciously accepted. Next, PoliM'al-adroit walked straight to Elpee and directed her to sit on the potter's stool while she drank the potent mixture danDay-leon had concocted. All the while, *Queen* Euterpe, who was silenced by having her mouth bound shut by a piece of midnight blue ribbon, floated around the old cottage, able only to simulate one of her poetry readings. Alpert stood off to the side, leaning against the wall with his arms crossed over his chest. He would stay there saying nothing until all three princesses and one *queen* had accomplished what they had come to do. Hesitantly, Hortense advanced toward Elpee, extending a bowl of nuts and berries with three pieces of red licorice protruding from it. Elpee, although drained, managed a snarl as she snatched the bowl from Hortense's hand.

"That wasn't nice. Take it back, Missy, or I'll take the food back," Hortense said as she reached for the bowl.

"Ladies, please!" Alpert scolded, his eyes pointed directly at Elpee, who was the more guilty party.

Elpee sent another slight snarl in Hortense's direction while also throwing one shoulder up in a show of indifference. She managed to incorporate a hint of a smile into her gestures, but that was as good as it was going to get.

"Whatever!" Hortense proclaimed as she walked away with her arms extended in a gesture of surrender.

Now, it was Alpert's turn.

"There is no more time. You must act now. The sun will be shining brightly all day tomorrow. You need to eat and drink all that you can now because you will need your strength. We will leave you some extra . . . Eat it all. Start your task early because you will need as much time as you can get. The sooner, the better."

"I don't know, Alpert. I am too tired, and maybe Anna is right after all. Maybe I should just accept that this is my lot in life and that everything I wanted is just poop. Maybe I really am who she says," Elpee dejectedly stated.

"Do you remember the last words I spoke to you when I was here last?" Alpert quizzed her.

"Of course I do. You said, 'Figure it out'. Those three words have haunted me ever since," proclaimed the beaten but not yet entirely defeated Elpee.

"There were more than just three words I said as I walked away. Even though I know you believe you are of superior intelligence, let me help you remember."

Alpert waved his hand across her eyes, and as it descended to the level of her chin, she burst into tears.

"You said, 'Figure it out . . . *Elpeè*. You called me by my name for the first time ever."

"I called you by your name, as you say, 'for the first time ever' because that is when you began your ascent to obtaining an identity. That is who you are, Elpee. Are you ready to fight for it? The choice is yours. We came here to support and hopefully encourage you, but you alone must do it. We must go now, but there is plenty of food and beverage to give you strength. The resolve you must provide.

"Good luck, my friend!" Alpert said as all five of them left her alone to fight her battles, both with Anna and her own personal demons.

THE DAWN BREAKS ON A NEW DAY

Elpee spent the rest of the night with her head spinning, wishing she could get some sleep, but knowing that if she failed to do what was necessary, sleeping would be her only option in this life. She ate, drank, and focused on how she felt and what she was about to do. She rationed out the candy from Hortense, saving one piece of licorice that she anticipated she would sit and enjoy when her task was completed.

No longer able to keep from rehearsing the scenario in her mind, Elpee set out to work. She gathered up the materials she had asked to save so that she could make one last mask, and that is precisely what Elpee planned to do. She would have to manage to do that with what Anna had not disposed of and pray that the gods of clay and masks would assist her in her project. Elpee concocted the mixture of powder and water as dry as she thought was functionally possible, hoping to accelerate the drying process, as, without a proper oven, she was dependent on the sun goddess to fire the piece. She paid no attention to what may be occurring in the main house but focused only on what her hands were doing at every given moment.

With the mixture complete, Elpee began to mold it into a mask. At first, she thought she would sculpt a hideous face with grotesque features that would scare all of creation away, but believing in the law of cause and effect, Elpee changed her mind. She made the representation rather nondescript— neither pretty nor ugly, masculine nor feminine, good nor evil, happy nor sad. She knew that when she created the features she could not incorporate any negative traits, for to do so would only come back to her threefold. She would leave the mouth flat – just flat, neither turning the lips up in a smile nor down into a frown.

When certain that the likeness was as neutral as she could make it, Elpee shook herself off and began the final and most important part of the procedure. She reached into her pinned-up hair and felt around until finally, the errant snail shell found its way into her fingers, and then removed it from the tangled mess of tresses. She looked at it for a second, and with all her might and magick, said aloud,

"Return the snail to the earth."

She then placed the shell in the mouth of the mask and molded the clay around it to ensure that it was secured enough to become one with the mud. Very quietly, Elpee opened the window and placed the mask out into the bright sunlight. She knew exactly where to set it, as the gnomes had etched out a landing pad in the grass for her, indicating the precise location for maximum radiational heating.

Elpee took one last drink of tea and ate the remaining red licorice before retiring to one of the wicker rockers and awaiting Anna's inevitable appearance. All Elpee would have to do is keep her away from the mask long enough for the clay to dry sufficiently for its maker to be able to string it up. Elpee held to the belief that once the terracotta hardened and the shell bonded, becoming one with the mask, Anna's days at Cherry Cottage would be over. She did not comprehend the enormity of this undertaking because, although she knew that she was fighting for her life, Elpee failed to recognize that her nemesis was in fact doing the same. Anna would try with all her might to keep herself bound to Elpee for as long as Elpee lived or for all eternity if she did not live; the latter being the choice Anna would prefer.

Elpee rocked and almost forgot the reality of the day and the situation, imagining herself to be in a different time—a time before this and before Anna existed at all. So lost in her pseudo-peace was Elpee, that she failed to hear Anna's approach until she was startlingly made aware of it by her roaring pronouncement.

"Get off my chair, and get out of here. You dirty this place up with your messy hair and your filthy hands," said Anna as she lifted Elpee's hands to look at them. "What is this I see? Is this clay? Did you make another one of those repugnant masks? I knew I should never have allowed you to keep any of that material. Where is it? I want to see it," Anna demanded of Elpee.

"I don't know what you mean, Anna," replied Elpee, feigning innocence despite her inner tremblings.

Anna brought her hand back behind her shoulder, and in one quick forward motion slapped Elpee viciously across the face. The rocking chair moved back and forth so violently that it almost overturned. Elpee, on the verge of tears from pain and anger, stood up and went face-to-face with Anna.

"Don't you ever do that to me or anyone else again, you beast. You want to be a princess, but you are too evil inside to ever be something or someone so noble. You are nothing and never will be because you live off the generosity of other people; good people who believe you and who believe in you. And how do you repay them? With your dishonesty and disloyalty. You are nothing more than a leech . . . A bloodsucker! Your day will come, and I can't wait to see it," Elpee venomously spewed after having been quiet for so long.

"That is something you will never see, my dear, because you will not see the end of this day," Anna retorted as she pushed Elpee back into the chair and headed toward the old cottage.

To distract Anna from going into the pottery shed and perhaps seeing the mask, Elpee yelled to her, "Who do you think you are, you old bat?" as she entered what was once her kitchen. Anna turned immediately and went after Elpee with a savage and irrational vengeance.

"GET OUT OF MY HOUSE! GET OUT RIGHT NOW. YOU HAVE NO RIGHT BEING IN THERE!"

Elpee ignored her and continued further into the interior of the structure. The desperate and determined woman would do almost anything, including infuriating the insanely angry Anna even more, to bide her time while the mask was drying in the sun.

"Come on, Anna, let's sit down and talk. We've both said some ugly things, but we need to put all this behind us so that we can move on. Please, Anna, come sit down," Elpee said while pointing to the couch.

Anna once again pulled her arm around behind her, and in an attempt to strike Elpee for the second time began the forward motion, but Elpee's quick reaction stopped Anna just short of her repeating the violent action.

"Oh, no, you don't!" she said as she clutched Anna's forearm. "No one, especially not you, will ever do that to me again. You may get your wish, Anna. I may die fending you off, but you will never hit me again. Do you understand me?"

HIGH NOON

The fight began in earnest with those words. Anna would not accept Elpee's rebellion, and Elpee would not agree to take Anna's dominance. Elpee used every possible ploy to keep Anna within the confines of the main house. There was no way that Elpee could check the progress of the mask's drying without Anna going outside with her, so she had no alternative but to assume it was not yet cured and continue the battle. Another problem would have to be addressed before this war was over, but Elpee could not think about it now and believed that the proper moment and solution would present itself to her. Currently, Elpee's chief objective was to keep Anna in the house and to keep herself alive.

"Anna, I am going up to my room to see what destruction you have produced up there. Would you care to join me?"

"Don't you dare go into my room. There is nothing in there that belongs to you any longer. It has all been thrown away. All that junk that you had. You were never fit to be a princess or to live in this house. It was I all the time that made you who you were, but you had to go and ruin it all. You thought that you could do a better job of planning your life than I was doing, but you were wrong. You took everything I did – all the plans I had – and began to throw them all away. I could not have that happen. I was not going to live in that stupid and childish world that you wanted to return to. I deserved better than that and your simple, narrow-minded way of living."

"Did it ever occur to you, Anna, that I just might have a say in this matter of how to live my own life? Maybe I like polka dots and peanut butter. SO WHAT! Who are you to tell me? You know who you are? You are my worst nightmare. The thought of living a stifling and regimented life without joy and laughter is a living hell. And let me tell you, Anna, I came from there, and I am not going back!"

"You ungrateful wretch!" Anna yelled back at her. "The only thing I regret is that that other wretch stole your dog. I had plans to dispose of him myself, along with all your other garbage."

Elpee saw red at the statement concerning her beloved Butter and flew at Anna in a rage.

"How dare you say that, you monster! You are a fiend and deserve to rot in hell for all eternity," Elpee shot back as she pushed Anna hard into the fireplace.

Anna, having hit her head on the mantle, toppled forward, which allowed Elpee to get around her and open the doors to the fireplace. As Anna was stumbling to get to her feet, Elpee kept knocking her down and pushing her closer to the opening of the firebox. Eventually, after several of these incidents, Elpee was able to drive Anna all the way into the firebox and close the doors, trapping her inside. Although there were no handles on the inside for Anna to use as a means of escape, Elpee pushed the couch in front of the doors to ensure her imprisonment for the few minutes she needed to check the mask and complete the job.

Sure that Anna was incarcerated in the fireplace, Elpee ran outside and around to the back of the pottery shed. To her relief, the mask was dry, and sitting next to it was a note that read:

Follow the arrow to the yellow yarrow,
And hang me on the tree with the crooked knee.

Elpee scooped up the mask and followed the arrows into her garden. There, she found the yarrow growing at the base of a tree with a peculiar bend to it. Upon closer inspection, she found that a hook had been placed in the crook of the tree, allowing her to hang the mask in such a position that the air would be able to find its way to the face's lips and the snail shell embedded within them. She placed the mask on the hook and said a quick please and thank you to the Universe before returning inside the house.

Elpee was relieved to find that the furious and anxious to retaliate Anna was still confined to the brick prison with glass doors. She knew that she had to let her out of the firebox but was afraid that when she did, Anna would come out with all the fury of a caged animal and actually kill her before the mask could whistle. Having come this far, Elpee had to believe that all would be well, or that she could at least outrun Anna if necessary.

With that reassurance, Elpee pushed the couch out of the way and back into its proper place. Without hesitation and before she could think about it, Elpee flung open the fireplace doors. Anna had been so twisted up in the firebox that it took a moment for her to unfurl herself and exit the cave. After she had returned to an upright position, the crazed woman began what would have been a lunge at Elpee's throat when suddenly and without warning, she was whisked away on a carpet of wind. In the distance, Elpee heard a faint whistle, but a whistle nonetheless. Anna flew out of the house and was propelled to the tree, where she instantaneously and eternally was melded with the mask. There she would remain frozen in time and place for all her days. Elpee, at last, was able to sit down and cry – not only for what was gone but for mostly for what was not.

HOME AGAIN

———

As Elpee sat inside her reclaimed home, she began to feel overwhelmed by everything that had occurred and everything that still needed to transpire. Exhausted and not knowing where to start, she chose to go upstairs and take a relaxing bubble bath. She began by filling the tub with steamy water and then went into the wee closet where, fortunately, hidden was an emergency stash of aromatic salts and bubble juice. After retrieving the ingredients for the bath water, Elpee sprinkled a bit of each into the substantially filled iron vessel.

When Elpee lowered herself into the tub and was fully submerged in the healing water, she unquestionably knew what heaven felt like. The chains that held her purgatory bound were released and she, at last, felt free to wander the earth among women and men of her own ilk. There would be no more definitions or mores to confine her, nor any unrealistic goals and unwanted tasks to perform. The magnitude of it all was incalculable, and there was no need to ponder it now, as all Elpee needed and wanted to do was to bathe in the bubbly water until all the iridescent orbs had vanished.

And so she did!

Basking in the moment, but also afraid of falling asleep, slipping under the water, drowning, and being washed down the drain, Elpee decided to get out of the tub and tackle the wreckage that awaited her. As she went into her reclaimed bedroom to sit on the bed for what was intended to be a minute or two, she instead promptly fell asleep for a very long time.

When Elpee did awaken, she heard the sound of laughter coming from downstairs. She could hear voices rising through the heating grate in the floor of her bedroom. Always curious – well, nosy, actually – Elpee ran down the stairs to find two princesses and one *queen* fussing about the house, removing the darkness and infusing the sunshine everywhere they went. It still did not resemble her cottage, but it thankfully no longer had any semblance of Anna in it. Elpee resigned herself to having to start over – yet again.

The four women gathered in the kitchen with danDay cooking bacon and brewing tea and Euterpe furiously painting something, her entire body a living palette of colors as a result of her efforts. She would not show Elpee what she was doing no matter how much the reinstated princess pleaded. Elpee knew one thing for sure, and that was whatever it was, would have an abundance of polka dots on it.

"PoliM'aladroit, please come out to the porch with me. I want to discuss something with you," Elpee asked of her.

"Of course. danDay-leon, please call us when the preparations are completed," PoliM'aladroit requested on her way out to the front porch while still holding a bowl of smoldering white sage and a colorful folding fan she was using for smudging.

They sat in rockers facing the other.

"Can you explain to me why this all happened? Why did everything have to change from the way it was when we were all together? Why did I have to travel to the land of the adults and then have it change back again?" Elpee asked her.

"Everything changes. You changed. You thought you might want to lead a more mature and conventional life, but you found it to be a mere existence. You missed much of what we all had together and wanted to have some of it back, but to do that required change – change of a different nature. A deeper change."

"Okay, but what about Anna, and what was my lesson in all that?"

"Are you a dope, Elpee? Oh, I hope not. I give you far more credit than the slight amount being a dope warrants, but I will explain nonetheless. Anna was Anna. What you thought was your Faerie goddess-mother was actually some cosmic leech. You must have made a wrong turn in the kaleidoscope and invited her in, or perhaps she was indeed your lesson."

"Thanks for the vote of confidence on my dopiness. I guess I needed to stand my ground for what I believed in and what I wanted without any outside influence or interference, and Anna was my lesson in how to do that," Elpee said, finally seeming to understand. "I get it. No matter what Anna or anyone says, my reality is my reality, and I cannot conform to anyone else's."

"Bacon and tea are served in the dining room," danDay-leon announced.

Elpee and PoliM'aladroit rose, hugged each other, and entered the house. They sat at the table with everyone distracted by the rainbow of colors that encased Euterpe, who was doing nothing else but floating around and giggling aloud.

"I have never seen you unable to speak, Euterpe. What is wrong with you?" asked Elpee.

Queen Euterpe, still chuckling, pointed to the sign that always hung on the wall above the table and over her head. Replacing the previous placard that accented the wall was now a polka dot bedazzled plaque that read, 'If you need helpee, please say Elpee'. They all had a good laugh in between eating, of course.

"I am so happy and grateful to all of you for how you came to my rescue, but there is one thing that is bothering me. Where is Butter? Hortense said she would return him when I got myself together. Well, it's been a little while now, and I haven't seen my Butter yet," Elpee said while alluding to her displeasure with the Princess of Grouse Hollow.

"You owe her an apology. You repeatedly hurt her feelings, and for what reason? Because she took your dog away from Anna and out of harm's way? You owe her a debt of gratitude in addition to an apology, Elpee," PoliM'aladroit stated in response to Elpee's self-centered comment.

After her initial astonishment, Elpee admitted the error of her ways. "You're right. I do owe Hortense an apology and a thank you. She saved Butterball from an unknown fate at Anna's evil hands." When she thought she felt as contrite as any human being possibly could, Elpee again began to get impatient at Butter's continued absence. She immediately felt a sharp pinch inside her arm.

"Ouch! Okay, okay, I'm sorry. The sun rises and sets on that princess. The world is a better place because of her existence . . . Blah, blah, blah. Now, where is my dog?"

danDay-leon cleared her throat to get Elpee's attention and then pointed out the window to the side garden. Elpee jumped up and ran to the window seat to see what danDay was pointing at. There, rolling around in the dirt, were Pippy, the gray creature, and Butter. Elpee jumped off the chair, ran out the front door, pushed open the side gate, and dove onto the ground with all three creatures. The two black ones were licking her from head to toe while the scruffy gray thing sat observing the odd behavior of the other two. When they were all exhausted, except for the gray boy who could not possibly be exhausted from having done nothing, Elpee left them to rest while she went inside to clean up. As she exited the garden and began to climb the stairs into the house, she noticed a box with a note attached to it. Elpee opened the package first and inside it was Elpee's favorite – a peach pie. She then unfastened the envelope that held a message, which read:

You're welcome . . . really
Hortense

Elpee's happiness over Butter's return was overshadowed by Hortense's absence. Elpee knew she had done a lot of damage by her mistrust of the princess, and she just hoped that it was not irreparable. *Where and how will I begin to make it up to Hortense?* Elpee thought. Then she came up with a solution to the dilemma. Elpee would steal Pippy in return. Yes, that is what she would do, she decided. And at that moment, Elpee turned around and went outside, but Pippy was gone. There, hanging on the fence, was another note. This one read:

Too late, Sunshine, but it was a good thought!
Bake me a yellow cake with chocolate icing,
and I'll call it even.
Hortense

Elpee smiled as she went into the house, knowing everything was going to be all right. Very different, but undeniably all right.

The girls were seated at the table in the living room doing a jigsaw puzzle when Elpee returned.

"Where do you all live? You know, there is a lot of explaining to be done around here," Elpee admonished them jokingly, but with serious intent.

"We live right here, at least for tonight. After all the work we did, we are too exhausted to go anywhere else," PoliM'aladroit, the self-proclaimed spokesperson, informed Elpee.

"Fine, but I want answers . . . real answers, sistas," Elpee advised them in no uncertain terms.

They all looked at each other and one by one they spoke up.

"I live in town," said PoliM'aladroit.

"I live across the street," replied danDay-leon.

"As for me, it's hard you see,

"to tell thee, where I be.

"Could be a tent, that's not what I meant.

"Or in a shell, or maybe a bell," proclaimed Euterpe before Elpee interrupted her rant.

"You are all nutballs! Never mind. At such time that you women feel benevolent enough to not mock me, and to also display a degree of honesty when answering my questions, I will listen. However, until that moment, I shall not put up with your shenanigans," declared Elpee, trying to sound regal and commanding.

"Hortense is living in a mansion on the ocean," PoliM'aladroit added.

Exasperated by their nonsense, Elpee just threw her hands up in the air, snickering at what she believed to be her friends' silly sense of humor.

"Oh, and by the way, where is Alpert?" Elpee asked.

"Oh my . . ." danDay-leon commented in a stammering voice that trailed off without explanation.

"Alpert the wizard? Not caught in a blizzard.

"Away he must go, from all that he . . ." Euterpe said before, once again, being cut off this time by PoliM'aladroit's shushing her.

"Now, *that* we must talk about," PoliM'aladroit proclaimed to Elpee, who sat with her mouth agape and her head filled with a million questions.

And so it went!

Brenda Grace de Jong

My Name is Elpee
~ A Trilogy ~

Book 3

Forsaken Paradise;
The Road to Freedom

To those who had faith in me and my ability to navigate the road I chose to travel . . . And to those who questioned my sanity, resolve, and capacity to do so.

To those who, despite the odds, encouraged me, held me up, and caught me when I stumbled . . . And to those who placed obstacles in my way and then challenged my ability to steadily forge onward.

To those who nurtured my weary body, mind, and spirit . . . And to those who counseled me to abandon my path for a less demanding and more orthodox road.

You have all been a part of my story and have helped to shape me into the person I am today.

I thank you all.

Mostly,

I dedicate this book to my 'family'. . . Be you by blood, or bond, or both.

You showed me the infinite value of kinship, which taught me how to integrate independence and interdependence.

You supported me through death, divorce, education, employment, accidents, injuries, and a myriad of other life challenges.

There are no words to express the depth of gratitude and love I feel for you. You have made this all possible.

"Desperation is the raw material of drastic change.
Only those who can leave behind everything they have ever believed
in can hope to escape."

~ William S. Burroughs

PROLOGUE

———

Once upon a time in a faraway land, after the three previous, faraway lands lived a girl/woman named Elpee, who was not always Elpee. She began as someone else before becoming Elpee the first time, and then was convinced she needed to be Grace, but she soon quit that name and became Elpee once again – with a possible middle name of Grace.

She had no friends and then she had many; most of them were not of the human persuasion, but rather they were elves, gnomes, and princesses. Then, for a while, they were no more – returning only after Elpee spent time living among the 'vapid ghouls'. In those days, there was a quirky non-wizard and a Faerie goddess-mother with a seriously egotistical agenda that included stealing Elpee's existence – the very one from which Elpee was attempting to escape. The princesses came and went, and unbeknownst to Elpee, they lived in houses across the street, down the block, and in town. Hortense was Agness, then Carol, and eventually back to Hortense. Elpee, while banished to the back cottage as Anna took over her house and her life, made one more mask, which would save her. Finally, Elpee and her friends met again after Elpee had bound Anna to the clay mask by placing the snail shell in its mouth and hanging it on a tree branch in the castle's garden. Butter #1, Elpee's dog, disappeared in one of the faraway lands and returned (maybe) as Butter #2 in another land.

It appeared that all the creatures, princesses, gnomes, elves, dogs, and masks would reunite in this new(est) faraway land – all except Alpert the non-wizard that is – who to Elpee's knowledge, or lack thereof, was missing in action. Perhaps he would return, and they would all, at last, live happily ever after.

And so would it be?

THE NEW(EST) FARAWAY LAND

As was typical of her life, Elpee had far more questions than she had answers. Whilst she sat in her living room with the self-proclaimed *Queen* Euterpe and the princesses, danDay-leon and PoliM'aladroit, her head swam as she tried to make sense of what these monarchs were telling her. They were speaking in gibberish – matriarchal, monarchal, maybe even majestical gibberish, but gibberish nonetheless.

"Excuse me, ladies, but you speak nonsense. In my absence, did you develop and perfect a language known to and understood only by you to the exclusion of all others?" Elpee asked the princesses.

"What say, you say?

"We say, no say?" Euterpe spewed to Elpee in response to what the *Queen* considered a ridiculous question.

"Thank you for your input, your majesty," Elpee replied. "Would you mind checking on the dogs and perhaps the masks also? Make sure everyone is okay, please, 'terpe."

The poet *Queen*, now having a mission, flew out the door and into the garden. With Euterpe tending to Elpee's requests, the confused woman was better able to understand what was going on now and decipher what had been going on in the parallel world where the other princesses lived while she lived here in hers.

"I can't tell you how much I missed all of you. I don't think I knew that myself for a long time. Things just weren't the same even though I tried to . . . Oh, I don't know! I'm just glad we are all together again," Elpee proclaimed as she fought back the tears.

PoliM'aladroit rose from the couch, and as she approached Elpee to give her a hug, she gracefully stumbled over a grain of sand that was on the floor and just as elegantly she landed on her bottom. Elpee and danDay-leon were serenaded by a cacophony of the most colorful words PoliM'aladroit reserved for these such occasions. Those words, however, were fortunately drowned out by the wails of her little gray creature.

"What the heck is that noise?" a startled Elpee asked.

"It's okay, Macaroni," shouted PoliM'aladroit out the window.

"Who the heck is Macaroni?" a now even more confused Elpee asked.

"I'll make us some tension-tamer tea," a flustered danDay-leon said as she made her way to the kitchen, walking around PoliM'aladroit, who had yet to rise from the place on the floor where she had landed.

"It's my boy," replied a very stately PoliM'aladroit, despite her somewhat disconcerting position on the ground.

"I didn't know it had a name. Macaroni?" asked Elpee.

"Yes," was all PoliM'aladroit replied to the question.

"Why?" asked Elpee just as concisely.

"Because I can remember it."

"Okay," responded Elpee in muddled resignation.

Soon it seemed that all creatures, human or otherwise, had returned to a state of relative calm. PoliM'aladroit had righted herself and was back sitting on the couch, forgetting her reason for having left it in the first place. The little gray creature had stopped his howling, and Elpee was happy to be confused only about the past with the present being resolved – at least for the moment.

"When danDay returns with the tea, may I ask some questions of you both so I can put this all together?" Elpee asked of PoliM'aladroit.

"Certainly. We would be more than willing to do anything we can to help you assimilate," responded PoliM'aladroit.

"Thanks. I need all the help I can get, that's for sure."

Both women waited for their tea in silence, with Elpee seemingly formulating her questions while PoliM'aladroit perused a book. Elpee became bored after completing her mental list and rose to help danDay-leon in the kitchen. When she arrived there, she found the kettle was boiling ferociously, but its boiler was nowhere in sight. In the distance, Elpee heard a snoring sound coming from somewhere outside. She extinguished the flame beneath the burner upon which the kettle sat and left the kitchen to investigate from whence and whom the noise was being generated. There, stretched out in the hammock out cold and sleeping like a baby was danDay-leon. Elpee turned to leave and re-enter the kitchen when the sleeping Princess of Teacup Manor woke herself with a fantastically loud snore.

"Oh my! I just came out here to rest while waiting for the water to boil. Let me check to see if it is done yet," danDay-leon stated to both herself and Elpee as she struggled to extricate herself from the oversized hammock.

"It's boiled, danDay. Do you want to come in, or would you prefer to stay here and rest awhile?"

"Oh, no, dear. I want to join you for tea. It's been so long since we shared any together," said danDay-leon as she entered the kitchen and poured out the warm water that was in the waiting teapot and replaced it with the hot water from the kettle. She then inserted a concoction of tension-taming and various other tea leaves into the pot and carried it onto the front porch, where they would enjoy their infused beverages and each other's company. Elpee carried the other necessary items out there on a tray and placed them on the round barrel table situated between the couch and the rockers. danDay-leon poured the tea into all their cups, and when everyone was done preparing their tea, Elpee began her questions.

WHO'S ON FIRST, WHAT'S ON SECOND . . . ?

"What the heck happened?" Elpee asked in a rather broad sense.

"Perhaps you can be a bit more specific with your questions, as it would be easier to answer them if you did so," PoliM'aladroit requested.

"Where does everyone live?" the princess complied.

"As you thought, danDay-leon lives across the street."

"Hah, I knew it! So Agness *was* Hortense in disguise, but why did she leave and you move in?" Elpee asked of danDay-leon. But, before the Princess of Teacup Manor could answer, PoliM'aladroit continued with her explanation.

"Because you were getting too close to her, inviting her to parties and such. By nature she is elusive, and in this situation, it was even more critical for her to maintain her distance until the time was right for you to change things, if you ever did, which was something we all began to doubt. Your resolve to do so seemed to be in question, and as time dragged on, you became more inquisitive about your surroundings than you were about your life."

Rather than doze off again, danDay-leon jumped into the conversation.

"Hortense needed to get away from you and the situation, so she moved out and I moved in, hoping that we would all be reunited and live close to each other. When you escalated across the street into the yard and the house that day and found out I lived there, we all began to hope that you would make a decision before I also had to move."

"All right, I'm beginning to get it . . . Hortense, Agness, Carol, Hortense, in that order, moved here first – undercover you might say – and then when I got too friendly, she felt it best to move rather than have her cover blown. You, betting that I was going to decide that I didn't quite fit in here, chose to move into her old house. Am I correct so far?" Elpee asked of danDay-leon.

"Right on target!" danDay-leon answered with enthusiasm while clapping her hands together.

"Good! Next question. Where did Hortense go?" Elpee, the inquisitor, asked of no one in particular.

"Princess Hortense of Grouse Hollow,

"lives in a house that's a tough act to follow.

"It lies and looks out on the beach,

"The ocean and waves within her reach," announced a lilting voice that emanated from the garden.

"Really? She lives in that huge house at the end of the block on the ocean?" Elpee posed the question, more to herself than she did to the others. "That's why I always saw Pippy and Butter running on the beach and then disappearing into the dune grass. They were going home. Nice, but . . . It figures she would . . . oh, never mind."

"How do you like your house, danDay?" Elpee continued while trying to absorb the last bit of information.

"It is so quaint and sweet; not as large as yours, but it suits me perfectly," Teacup Manor 's own answered.

"Excellent. I am happy for you, and it is a beautiful and charming house. It has so much character, and I'm sure that your presence will only serve to add more of the same to it," Elpee responded to danDay-leon before turning to PoliM'aladroit and quizzing her.

"And where do you live? In town, you said?"

"Yes, I live in a tiny cottage located behind the general store. I like the activity associated with the town, and I find it very agreeable to live there," PoliM'aladroit responded.

"Well, now that you know where everyone lives, let's make a toast and drink our tea," danDay-leon suggested.

They all raised their cups, but their toast was interrupted when Elpee lowered her arm.

"Wait. Stop. Where is Alpert? You said we needed to talk about him, so where is he?" Elpee asked of the two princesses who were on the porch with her. danDay-leon rose to leave the room, allowing PoliM'aladroit to speak to the question. But before addressing the issue, PoliM'aladroit turned around, walked to the window, and politely requested that Euterpe be silent and allow her to handle the situation.

Euterpe stated her intention to comply by saying, "Whatever you say, "have it your way,

"do as you may,

"I am busy with clay."

"I am sorry, and I appreciate your curiosity, but we cannot discuss Alpert or anything to do with him right now. Please respect this, and do not go snooping around trying to get information. It would be extremely detrimental to him if you did. I will tell you what I know as soon as I am able to," PoliM'aladroit informed Elpee.

"When will that be?" the irritated Elpee asked of her.

"Not until the day after next week," PoliM'aladroit replied.

After expressing a huff and making an unflattering face, Elpee raised her hand holding the teacup to resurrect the forestalled toast. danDay-leon returned to the porch, and they all lifted their cups again, and one by one made a toast.

"To friends."

"To self."

"To us."

"To you and me and the bumblebee," came the salute from the voice in the garden.

MASKS

As each day passed, Elpee became more comfortable with who and where she was and felt a great sense of gratitude to have her old friends back. Slowly – very slowly – some of her questions were being answered, but for others she would have to wait for the answers to reveal themselves to her. During this time, Elpee spent her days trying to recreate, or often merely create, the sense of personality she had given to her cottage before Anna had destroyed it by removing all that was Elpee from it. She cleaned up the masks and did her best to fix any chips they may have acquired in their fall from grace while under Anna's rule. Although Elpee was successful in restoring them to relatively good condition, they seemed lackluster and emotionally flat. She would need to restore them to proper emotional as well as physical health. For days, Elpee pondered how to accomplish these two tasks, and one day, as she contemplated this undertaking, she over-heard them talking among themselves.

"I am feeling blue."

"That's odd. You're usually in the pink."

"Look at him over there. The poor guy is green with envy."

"And Cleo looks as white as a ghost."

"I hope we don't get too much sun or our faces will be as red as beets."

"Someone's in a black mood."

"You're too yellow to tell him."

Ding! Ding! Ding! The bells and whistles went off in Elpee's head when she realized how to cheer them up and bring them back to life.

"Okay, boys and girls, soon you will be all fixed up. Just give me a few days," Elpee advised the gloomy clay faces. She then turned and left them to go into the cottage to make the arrangements.

Once inside, Elpee climbed the stairs leading to her bedroom and went to the small desk in the corner, where she removed her stationery and fountain pen and began to write.

The pleasure of your company, and the request for your assistance,
is hereby extended by the current Princess of Cherry Cottage by the Sea,
Her Majesty, Princess Elpee.
Please bring your friends, your pets, your appetite, and your imagination.
Refreshments will be served, as well as mud pies.
Towels and aprons will be provided on a first come, first served basis,
as supplies are limited.

DATE: Tomorrow
TIME: As much as you can offer
PLACE: Here

In lieu of RSVP, simply attend

Elpee wrote six identical invitations, and when they were completed, she inserted them into six identical envelopes and placed six identically different hand-drawn stamps on them. She then embarked on the task of delivering each one. She decided to leave the easiest ones for last, therefore, she would begin with ShinyShores, PoliM'aladroit's cottage in town.

Elpee and Butter began their delivery mission, and despite his much and often grumbling, Butter cheerfully carried the invitations in his saddlebags – three notes on each side. When they reached their approximate destination, Elpee needed to figure out where exactly PoliM'aladroit's house was. She went behind the general store and looked around, but there were a number of cottages located back there. Suddenly, Elpee heard the familiar and wretched wailing of PoliM'aladroit's small gray creature; the one he made when she was in distress of some sort.

Elpee followed both the noise and Butter, who was now leading the way, to a small yellow house with a green roof and a tangerine-orange door. There they found PoliM'aladroit on top of the building repairing a loose shingle on its roof. However, she, in the process, had nailed her pants to the rooftop, which precipitated a string of 'expletive deletes' to exit from the trapped princess's mouth. Elpee removed an invitation from Butter's backpack before he scooted off to be with his friend, the gray creature, hoping to distract him from his master's audible outburst. Seeing Elpee caused PoliM'aladroit to quiet her ranting and to take a deep breath before speaking. Finally, she said, "I cannot believe I did that. How could I have been so careless as to have nailed my clothes to the roof? Now I will have to shred them to pieces or remove the shingles just to be able to get down. What a shame!" PoliM'aladroit exclaimed as she shook her head in self-exasperation.

"Or you could just take the nails out with the hammer," Elpee suggested.

"Oh . . ." PoliM'aladroit quietly commented on Elpee's simple solution to what she had considered the most complicated of problems.

As the nailed-to-the-roof princess began working to extricate herself, Elpee quickly wished her well, said her goodbyes, and left the invitation in the screen door. She then continued on her way to deliver the other invites.

"Let's go, Butthead," she called to the canine, who quickly, but leisurely, came strolling over to her.

Off Elpee and her sidekick went back in the direction from which they had come. When they arrived at danDay-leon's home, an eerie feeling overcame Elpee as she entered the yard. She remembered the last time she was there, which was after Agness left but before Anna did. A chill ran through Elpee's body as she recalled in fast motion the chain of events that led up to and occurred since that time. Things were still jumbled up, but Elpee knew that in time she would get her facts straight.

In an attempt to de-creep herself, Elpee shook her whole body, and when she felt sufficiently normal, she stopped and stood still. There, standing at the cottage's door looking at her somewhat peculiarly, was its owner.

"Hi," was all Elpee managed to say as she stood there, still dizzy from shaking herself around.

"Are you all right?" danDay-leon asked her. "I thought you were having a reaction to having been bitten by a venomous snake. You weren't, though, were you?"

"No, but thanks for asking."

"That's good. I'm glad to hear it. Come in, please," danDay said, while holding the door open for Elpee and Butter.

Elpee moved forward with a mixture of trepidation and determination. Butter, on the other hand, screeched to a halt and would not enter. Not wanting to deal with one of his moods, but with no choice other than to do just that, Elpee took a deep breath before speaking.

"I want to tell you to get your butt in there right now, mister, but you won't, will you?"

The dog, now lying prone with all four furry legs and feet reaching for the sky, shook his head 'no' in confirmation to her question.

"You won't get arrested, I promise. Auntie danDay is inviting you in."

Unaffected by Elpee's assurances, he lay there stiffly with his eyes appearing to have rolled back in his head. He feebly managed a shake of his head, once again indicating he would not enter the house under his own volition. Elpee gritted her teeth, stomped her feet, and made a distinctive grunting noise before walking over to the rigid and uncooperative dog. She bent down and picked him up, upon which he immediately went limp in her arms. Before attempting to move forward with him, she stood still and took another vitally needed deep breath.

"Why do you always have to play this dead dog routine with me when you don't want to do something? And by the way, Buddy-boy, this will cost you. You haven't lost all the weight from eating that hamburger ice cream, so it's diet time for you, my friend. Hah! You see? You made me pick you up, and now I know you still weigh half a ton. So there, smarty pants!" Elpee declared gleefully.

Her faithful companion went even limper in her arms and stuck his tongue out at her as she carried him into the house. While ignoring him, Elpee placed him on the floor and reached into his saddlebag to remove an envelope. She handed it to danDay and hastily stated, "I don't have time to explain, so just read it yourself, would you? Sorry for the freshness and the rush, but I have more deliveries and a hundred things to do, one of which I hope does not include carrying this slug of a pug around anymore."

"Butter," she continued, "you can walk out on your own four feet, or you can stay with Auntie danDay, and I will have her make you horseradish and jalapeno tea soup for dinner."

Not waiting for the dog to exercise his freedom of choice, Elpee gave danDay a quick peck on the cheek on her way to the door. Butter rose from his position, his ears flattened to his head, and landed a big lick-kiss on his Auntie danDay – a guarantee that he would stay in her good graces.

He continued on, giving his master a smug shrug and a toss of his head as he passed her and went out the door.

As they left danDay-leon's house, the canine took on a slightly pathetic limp, indicating that he was not entirely cured of his most recent near-death experience. To test his degree of fitness, Elpee conducted an experiment though she already knew the results. She said aloud, "Hmm, I wonder if I should deliver the invitations back home or to Hortense's first?"

Butter stopped mid limp with his ears erect and waited for his master's decision.

"I think I will," Elpee said, being deliberately indecisive to extend the dog's anticipation.

His ears were now the size of a donkey's and were ready to capture her words the instant they were spoken if she ever stated them, he thought.

Finally, "Hortense's it is."

Butter, who had been standing like a thoroughbred at the gate, appeared miraculously cured as he broke into a run and headed down the walk in the direction of the ocean. Elpee lagged far behind, choosing a leisurely pace instead. She was in no hurry to see the Princess of Grouse Hollow after all the mean things Elpee had thought and said about her when she stole Butter.

Elpee arrived at the gate of Hortense's mansion about five minutes after she last saw Butter's butt streaking down the walk.

"Hortense?" Elpee called out as she entered the side deck area, but she got no response, and so she tried again.

"Hortense?" Still no answer from the errant princess. Elpee could see Butter and Pippy playing on the beach with what appeared to be no human supervision. Again, Elpee's mind thought the worst. She surprised herself by the awareness of the absence of a pinch she usually felt as a means of correction. *Interesting*, she thought.

Elpee placed the invitation in a planter on Hortense's back step and then went to sit on the bench at the top of the overpass. There she delighted in watching the canine cousins play and roll around in the sand, causing her to stay longer than she should have, considering all she needed to do, but she could not help herself.

When she could procrastinate no longer, Elpee called for Butter to tell him that the play date was over and that it was time to go home. Reluctantly, he left Pippy's side and climbed the stairs to where Elpee sat waiting for him.

"Hi, mister. Did you have fun? I think you did, you special boy. Tomorrow Auntie Hortense is coming over, and you and PippyLou will play in our garden. How about that? Now, though, we need to head home and deliver the rest of the invitations," Elpee told the sand-covered dog as she petted him vigorously, hoping to dislodge some of the granules before they arrived home.

For once, Butter complied without an argument. What a pleasure, Elpee thought as she recalled what an obedient dog he was when they first met and how he had since developed a mind of his own. No bother, he was still the best!

When they arrived at their cottage, Elpee removed the three remaining invitations from Butter's pack and took them behind the pottery shed. She left one at the gnome hole, another in a clearing where the elves dined, and she tied the third to a parchment kite, which she secured to a tree, hoping Euterpe would come by and retrieve it. With all the invitations delivered, Elpee went home and fell asleep on the couch with no thought of food for herself or her dog.

Preparations and Then Some

The next day, Elpee awoke feeling beyond famished. Butter, on the other hand, was quite happy playing with an enormous spider that was sitting quietly in the middle of the living room floor.

"You're going to get in trouble just like the last time. Don't you remember? I am much too busy to rescue you this time," Elpee warned him as she made her way to the kitchen to brew herself some coffee and to toast several slices of bread, which she would slather with black-raspberry preserves.

She prepared the coffee pot, and when it began to brew, she toasted her bread. Soon, but not soon enough for the ravenous Elpee, her breakfast was ready. She placed it on a tray and took it outside onto the deck to indulge all her senses at one time. She wanted to enjoy the way her breakfast felt and tasted while observing the sights, sounds, and smells of early morning. She savored her meal for only as long as it took to partake of it, as there would be no dallying today.

While Elpee was cleaning up the dishes, she began to wonder where Butter was because he was far too quiet for *her* own good. The thought lasted only a split of a split second because she knew where he was; he was in trouble with the spider despite her having cautioned him. After drying her hands, she went into the living room and saw exactly what she had anticipated she would. There, sitting quietly in the middle of the living room floor was Butter with the spider playing with him. Unfortunately, the poor dog was entrapped in the gigantic spider's massive web, and he could do nothing but sit there at the mercy of the tormenting arachnid, whose turn it was to now irritate and harass the instigating canine.

"Butter, didn't I . . . Oh, what's the use? Never mind," Elpee declared in defeat, knowing that getting aggravated would serve absolutely no purpose at all.

She stopped the wooly creature from poking at its captive prey and chased it away before tackling the task of freeing the dog. The spider gave one last nudge to Butter before leaving the house, or at least the living room. Elpee went outside, retrieved a large but manageable branch, and brought it over to Butter, who began yelping at the thought of being beaten to death with a tree while trapped in a cage of spider spit.

"Calm down, buddy. I'm not going to hit you; I'm just going to spin this stuff off you and onto the branch."

He quieted down, and little by little, he gained his freedom until he was up on all fours ready to hug Elpee, who was still holding the giant stick, which held the transferred spider web and now resembled a torch.

"Oh no you don't," she said as she jumped backward, almost falling over. "I love you a lot, but the spider spit has got to go. Sorry. Outside and over to the hose right now, mister."

Unhappily, he complied and sat there waiting for the next torture to be inflicted upon his poor self. After disposing of the spitty stick, Elpee grabbed the bottle of soap that she kept under the sink and the scrub brush from inside the closet before joining him out on the deck. She had no time to spare, and so she spared him not. On with the hose and then with the soap. Scrub-a-dub-dub and once again on with the water tube to rinse away the suds and sand. Elpee had placed his magick carpet on the deck, which he immediately ran to as soon as she stopped squirting and stinging him with the highest-pressure hose he had ever felt. He began rolling around and thrashing about, somehow managing not to hurt himself, but certainly on the verge of doing so at any given second. Elpee gave him a warning before she returned to what she had begun before being interrupted by this Butter-induced delay.

"Butter, DO NOT get off this deck and roll around in the dirt. I mean it!"

While he was floundering all over the deck, Elpee managed to work around him by moving the wicker rockers and slatted table off the wooden platform so that she could set up the long table underneath the overhang. Still dodging the speeding bullet of a dog, its owner put out sixteen loaves of white bread, two gallons of peanut butter, and one gallon of pure grape jelly. Next to the food, Elpee placed seven knives, no plates, and a bunch of acorn cups. The guests would have to share the dining tools, as Anna had disposed of much of Elpee's tableware. She then moved the vat of tea she had sun-brewed the day before into the shade and added ice to it.

Having completed the food preparations, Elpee moved on to other things. She went into the pottery shed, strategically pried open the lid of the window seat, and looked at the stash of paint stored inside it. Elpee's pallet of colors stared back at her, asking to be set free. They were one of the very few things that had escaped Anna's disposal, and it was only due to Elpee's failure to secure a handle on the window seat that caused Anna to overlook its existence. *Happy, happy,* thought Elpee!

The joyous princess propped open the door of the shed, pulled her wagon in, and began loading it with the hidden paint. When the window seat was empty, it was just that – empty. There were no brushes – big or little, new or used – in there, and Elpee did not know where they were. No bother, they would improvise because they were, after all, a resourceful bunch. With everything set up and all the preparations completed, there was nothing left for the woman and her dog to do but rest and wait.

JUST LIKE OLD TIMES

———

Elpee and Butter waited on the front porch for the invitees to arrive. Elpee was a bit less anxious than her canine companion was, as he stood at the screen door looking both ways and shifting his weight from side to side – left – right – left – right. He just could not contain himself or his excitement. Elpee sat on the sofa playing one-person old maid, but Butter would not leave his post at the door until someone – anyone – arrived. Fortunately, just as he was about to explode, he spied PoliM'aladroit walking toward the cottage. He began wagging his stub, which alerted Elpee that a guest would soon be arriving.

Elpee rose and walked to the door in time to greet PoliM'aladroit as she climbed the steps. As was their ritual, Elpee pushed the top of the screen door while Butter pressed against the lower half, allowing their guest to enter. The two princesses exchanged hellos, and the canine tugged on PoliM'aladroit's trousers to get her attention because he had a question for her. She looked down at him, and he asked her by turning his head sideways and expressing an, "Er?"

"He could not come. He is at the salon getting a makeover, poor thing; there is nothing worse. He does, however, send his regrets," PoliM'aladroit said in response to Butter's question regarding the small gray creature's absence.

The disappointed dog resumed his place at the door, waiting for the next guest to appear, and appear she did. *Queen* Euterpe seemed to magickally materialize, making her presence known without any prior sighting of her.

"Butter, Butter, Butter, Ball,

"my, oh, my, you've grown so tall.

"I remember when you could barely crawl.

"When that was, I don't recall," the pink-haired *queen* recited upon her entrance.

The dog smiled up at her despite being unsure whether he should be flattered or embarrassed. As Euterpe was giving him a perfunctory pat on the head, Elpee approached the *Queen* with outstretched arms.

"Euterpe, I am so glad you could come. It's your favorite kind of day because it's all about polka dots. Well, maybe not *all* about polka dots, but something like that. You'll see. Come inside, PoliM'aladroit is here."

Butter remained on his self-appointed stakeout at the screen door and would not be moved from his post. While he waited impatiently, he could hear talking and laughing coming from the opposite side of the house. Curiosity got the better of him, and he left his station to investigate the source of the merriment that did not include him. Some of the gnomes had arrived as well as the elves. In the distance, he spotted a small army of additional gnomes pushing a colossal watermelon in his direction. It was indeed a sight to see, and while he was busy watching it, another familiar voice called out from the opposite side of the house.

"Hello, is anyone home?"

Elpee hurried through the house and to the front door to greet danDay-leon, who stood there laden down with teacups and some delicious raspberry-bergamot tea to fill them with.

"Welcome, and what do you have there, danDay?"

"Just some tea for later and some extra cups that I had in my cupboard. I know that you are a bit short of teacups, so please accept these as an informal housewarming gift," danDay-leon responded as she offered them to the host.

Elpee received the cups and just held them and looked at them for some time in awe of their beauty before responding to danDay-leon.

"danDay, these are so beautiful, I couldn't possibly accept them," she finally expressed to the other princess.

"Please, Elpee, you must, or my feelings will be hurt. You have lost so much at the wicked hands of that evil imposter, Anna, that these will be a nice start for you to begin your new life. Besides, I can't imagine anyone who I would more prefer to have them."

With tears in her eyes and a lump in her throat, Elpee hugged danDay and expressed her gratitude, although her words were barely audible.

All the guests had arrived except Princess Hortense. Butter took his place back at the front door and waited while Elpee gathered the other outside guests onto the deck. Everyone seemed to be reacquainting themselves with each other and exchanging stories of what had happened in their lives since last they met. Elpee stood aside, watched, and listened, so grateful for all of them and for having gotten a good portion of her old life back. What was she thinking when she let it all slip away, believing that aging and the conventional characterizations of growing up were linked by an unwavering definition and that there was no margin for individuality? Elpee shook her head and herself back to reality and to the present, which at this moment did not include her faithful sidekick, Butter. She walked back into the house and found him sitting woefully at the door waiting for their last guests to arrive. Elpee felt so sad for the little guy, and she did after all tell him his cousin PippyLou was coming to play with him in his garden. He just sat there staring dejectedly out the screen door. She went over to him, stroked his head, and gave him a big hug.

"Don't worry, mister, it will be all right," she told him, although she did not know how that would be.

"I'll be right back. Okay?"

The canine was too intent on staring down the road trying to will the missing guests to come that he did not answer.

Elpee hurriedly went outside and found Euterpe.

"'terpe, do me a favor, please. I can't leave the party, so would you please run down to Hortense's house and get her to come here? Butter won't leave the door until she and Pippy get here. Whatever you have to do, get them here, please. Thanks," Elpee asked of her, and abruptly turned to join the other guests before the *Queen* could begin one of her soliloquies.

PARTY TIME

———

Just a few minutes later, as Elpee was gathering everyone around to explain their mission to them, she heard a screaming sound coming from the front porch that she recognized as Butter's excited screech. She quickly made her apologies and ran inside to find him sitting there delighted and gleeful watching Euterpe riding PippyLou as a cowboy would ride a horse. Elpee was not sure if Butter was excited to see Pippy or if he also wanted a ride.

"Thank you, Euterpe, you can get off now and let him . . . Or is it her . . . Oh, I never remember, come in the house before Butter explodes. Where is Hortense?" Elpee asked.

"No way she say,

"she come this way.

"Not today,

"for sure she say," answered *Queen* Euterpe.

"Whatever! I am not in the mood. Come on, let's go and get this show on the road. You boys and girls outside. Hurry, I have some cookies for you," Elpee said as she swung around to return outside and to her guests.

Two dogs, one princess, and one *Queen* exited the house and joined the other frolickers on the deck. It appeared that quite a number of them had already eaten, as the amount of food on the table had drastically diminished, and they were now diving into the watermelon. Because the gnomes had rolled it all the way to the event, the elves offered to cut it up – a chore Elpee chose to close her eyes to, as it involved axes, machetes, wedges, and sledgehammers. While the elves undertook that task, Elpee gathered the paint cans, opened the lids, and put a stirrer of some kind in each.

"Yoo-hoo," Elpee said, trying to get everyone's attention. Although she could be known to be a screamer and to have a big mouth, she was never able to project her voice loud enough to be heard over the din of a crowd of people. She tried again.

"Yoo-hoo, everyone, please listen," she said, and to her surprise they did. All became quiet.

"Thank you so very, very much for coming today. I missed you all tons, and I am glad to have the bunch of you back in my life. Someday, I hope the rocks will also be joining us, but our mission at hand concerns the masks. You see, Anna . . . Er, well, she was a mean, mean woman. She took the masks that I had made and hung in my garden, and she tossed them on the ground into a heap. They have been terribly traumatized and depressed by the treatment they received, and I was hoping we could cheer them up by giving them a makeover," Elpee explained.

Before Elpee could continue any further, in the crowd could be heard the muttered words, "Oh, no. A makeover . . . Nothing worse." It was apparently coming from PoliM'aladroit, who was referencing her little gray creature. Elpee chose to ignore the comment and instead continue with her own discourse.

"There is plenty of paint here, and each can has a stirrer thing in it, but I don't have any brushes, so we will need to figure out how to apply the paint. There are phragmites in the back woods and plenty of other objects we can use, including our hands. Each mask has their own special personality and identity, so please respect that and help them to enhance who they are by brightening them up. Thank you, and now please begin."

Everyone jumped in with both hands and feet, literally, using any or all twenty digits as a means of painting the masks as well as expressing themselves. Elpee was sure that this project would leave everyone indelibly dirty. After Anna had taken the masks down from their appointed stations and tossed them in one big pile, Elpee took the time to carefully separate them, inspect them for any damage, and clean them off before hanging them back up again. She thought that would be sufficient for their needs, and perhaps it was, but positively not for their wants, and that is what the invitees were tending to this day. Each guest had their own technique and color scheme, and Elpee would not interfere with any agreement they had reached with the mask concerning that – excluding Euterpe, that is.

"'terpe, I am sorry to meddle, but I must object to your use of polka dots on everyone. It's beginning to look like an open-air measles ward, and I do have *some* concern for what the neighbors might think."

"Fine, fine, I shall go away.

"You shan't see me again for the rest of the day."

"That's not what I want, and you know it. I would just prefer for the polka dots to be confined to inanimate objects like planters and fences, and maybe even rocks. Remember, they didn't mind that they had spots all over them. Maybe you can begin a new rock family for me, wouldn't that be really nice?" Elpee diplomatically and lovingly asked her friend the *Queen*.

"That would be nice,

"but I have a price.

"Of the watermelon,

"I would like a slice," Euterpe responded, and sat down, waiting in a most regal way to be served her requisite payoff before doing anything further.

Elpee personally got a piece of the fruit and brought it to the reigning *Queen* who was sitting on the bench in the garden that was presently serving as her throne. In a somewhat unstately manner, Euterpe chomped on the piece of watermelon and delighted in spitting the pits in all directions. Elpee just shook her head and went about her business.

Soon, all the food, paint, and gloominess were gone. Everyone was full, the masks were giddy, and Elpee had little cleanup to do because there was nothing left. The dogs had worn each other out and were sleeping in the grass behind the pottery shed. The guests began to depart, each thanking Elpee as she also thanked them. They all – princesses, gnomes, elves, and whomever else was there, just unseeable – vowed their forever friendship and pledged their allegiance to each other and to the common good.

What to do Next

—————

As the days went on, Elpee developed a sensation of melancholia; it was not a depression, but rather a malaise that was neither comfortable nor uncomfortable. It was just a tender, introspective feeling that caused her to retreat and to reflect on her life and her surroundings, both now and in the past. She knew she would have many more trips and side journeys along the way, but this once-waif also believed that she, at last, had arrived at her destination of self. The only thing she had to do was stay. Well, perhaps she would even have to accept, adapt, adjust, align, and most of all, enjoy.

Sometimes Elpee's idea of enjoyment was to have fun, at other times it would be to work, and still at others, it would be about doing just what she was doing now – being silent and listening to the voices both from within and without. This sense of security in herself and the Universe was a new feeling for Elpee. She was confident in the knowledge that she and It were precisely in sync even if it felt less than that.

"So, there is something between laughing 'til you cry and crying 'til you throw up. Excellent!" Elpee said to herself. "I like it. This feeling is . . . Well, it just *is*."

The newly self-redefining princess spent her time quite ordinarily, just as others did. She tidied her house, worked in the garden, visited her friends, and contemplated her existence and her future. Life – it was happening to her.

Butter came and went with PippyLou, but there were no sightings of Hortense. Even when Elpee took Butter to the beach, Pippy would come bounding out of the house to greet him without any sign of its master. Crazy thoughts went through Elpee's head like maybe, Hortense abandoned Pippy, and now the canine was having to fend and forage for itself. It, without doubt, was a crazy thought, because PippyLou was so overindulged by its master that the animal could never, ever survive without human attention being paid to its needs.

Hortense's absence deeply disturbed Elpee because, as much as Hortense was elusive, there was always a sense of her presence, unlike now. Her nonappearance at Elpee's painting party was very distressful, since everyone was together for the first time in an exceedingly long while. There was a visible gap in the landscape that was the friends' reunion. Despite knowing there was nothing she could do, Elpee was saddened by Hortense's invisibility. She missed her and the bantering that occurred between them. Elpee could always count on Hortense for a pithy game of verbal ping-pong, with the winner of the said game ever being in question. Eventually, she would gather up the courage to extend the olive branch by baking Hortense the cake that hopefully would flush her out of hiding, but Elpee was not yet ready for the disappointment if it failed to do that. For now, however, she would continue to do what she was doing by just sitting still, alone and celebrating its quiet merit.

Alpert was another missing piece in the fabric of her life. Elpee wanted to know where he was and why she could not investigate those whereabouts. PoliM'aladroit advised her not to snoop, which to Elpee meant that there was something secret and sinister about his location – a supposition that of course made her even more curious. Oh, poop! She would have to learn to be a bit more patient or perhaps more assertive and just shake it out of PoliM'aladroit. *Excellent idea*, she thought to herself of the latter option, but for now, she would have to choose patience, because that was what was needed for where Elpee was currently located on the planet. Elpee did not feel that she was moving forward or backward, was neither happy nor sad, energetic nor tired, and a myriad of many other opposite feelings. Here is where she was, and so she thought she might as well make friends with the holding zone she found herself in.

After several days of making friends with her present situation, Elpee became bored and decided to get some fresh air for herself. It seemed that Butter was utterly self-sufficient, or at least Pippy-sufficient, since they were more inseparable than ever. How much longer did she need to embrace this limbo-land she was in, she wondered? Elpee did not want to accept, no less be comfortable with the fact that her friends were missing or almost missing. It was unquestionably not a picture that she would paint and hang over the fireplace. Things had to change. Elpee had to change.

Tea Time at Cherry Cottage

———

danDay-leon stopped by Cherry Cottage one day around four o'clock in the afternoon just as Elpee was ready to take a break from her doing nothing.

"Hello, hellllllooooo?" danDay-leon called out, seemingly overlooking the fact that Elpee was standing directly in front of her with nothing separating them but a roll of metal screening that was lightly supported by a wooden frame.

"Hi, danDay," Elpee said to the other princess, causing her to stumble backward. Fortunately, danDay-leon caught herself before she landed where PoliM'aladroit usually did – in the area of her derriere.

"Come in before you kill yourself," Elpee said as she opened the screen door solo because Butter was off somewhere with Pippy.

"It is time for afternoon tea, and I haven't seen you in some time, so I thought I would join you for refreshments," danDay-leon stated while inviting herself to the afternoon ritual.

"I don't always observe the tradition. I apologize because I know you so look forward to it. Perhaps PoliM'aladroit or one of the other neighbors would care to partake in it with you."

"Nonsense! I came here because this is where I want to be, and you are whom I want to have tea with. Now, go and get some of the raspberry-bergamot tea that I brought over last time. I know you must have some left over, and if not, I of course have some kind of leaves stashed upon my person somewhere. Go, and I will fill the kettle," Teacup Manor's princess commanded.

Elpee surrendered to danDay-leon and her instructions by getting the flavored tea from the pantry. She was actually glad that danDay dropped by for a visit, because Elpee recently recognized that although she was friendly and outgoing, she was not naturally a social person as others were.

What was second nature to her friends was a deliberate and concerted effort for Elpee. She thought to herself that she needed to try harder, but
also knew it would not happen; a fact that she both sadly and happily accepted.

Elpee handed the tea leaves to her friend and then began to set up a
tray with cream, sugar, spoons, napkins, and two of the porcelain cups
danDay had given her. danDay-leon poured the boiling water into the
teapot which already contained the tea leaves and placed it on the tray,
after which both women retired to the porch to celebrate afternoon tea.

"I'm sorry, but I haven't any cakes for us," Elpee said apologetically as
she placed the tray on the round barrel table she used for a coffee – or in
this case a tea table.

"As you would say, my dear, 'no bother'," danDay-leon said as she
reached into her oversized duster and extracted warm, just-baked, oatmeal,
raisin, and nut cookies.

Elpee and danDay-leon lifted their cups and drank to each other.

"Thank you so much, danDay. You truly are special."

"As are you, my dear. We all missed you so much and weren't sure if
you were coming back to us. There were moments of doubt, especially
near the end when Anna began taking over your entire life, and you
seemed too tired to fight her to regain it. We were happily incorrect, and
here you and I are now, sharing afternoon tea. What a delight!" danDay-
leon happily proclaimed.

"Where is Alpert?" Elpee abruptly asked, surprising even her own self.

The Princess of Teacup Manor was visibly shaken by Elpee's question,
and in reaction to it began coughing and clearing her throat, wringing her
hands together, and shifting her position on the sofa.

"I must defer to PoliM'aladroit and not discuss it, and I suggest you do
the same. It will all work out in time," danDay-leon finally uttered.

Unlike the others, danDay-leon was a demure character, and Elpee did
not feel comfortable badgering her about Alpert's whereabouts as she may
possibly have done to the others. Although still curious, Elpee changed the
subject and engaged danDay-leon in an entirely different topic of conversation to make her feel more comfortable.

It was well past dark when the two princesses ran out of things to say to
each other and danDay walked across the street to her own home. Elpee

placed the tray on the kitchen counter, where it would remain until the next morning, when she would clean it up before breakfast. She called to Butter, who was lying on his magick carpet on the back deck. He moseyed into the house, and they both climbed the stairs and retired to their respective beds.

INSIDE

In the days that followed the uplifting visit from danDay-leon, Elpee decided to reclaim her home and garden as well as her life. She had mixed emotions about putting in the effort to accomplish this because although it was exciting, it was also overwhelming – physically and emotionally. At times, Elpee felt engulfed and ruled by the anger she felt for Anna at having taken so much of who she was and what she had. At other times, feelings of sadness overtook her when she thought of tending the garden without the help of Hortense. Sometimes, however, she felt showered with a sense of enthusiasm at the prospect of starting over and finding herself, rather than merely playing a role in her own life.

Elpee dedicated one entire day to touring and inventorying the house in which she lived, and with pen and paper in hand, she made lists of what was gone and what she would like each room to have. Missing from the entire house were the old lace curtains that elicited a feeling of warmth and security within Elpee, as well as having added to the charm of the structure. Overall, it appeared that Anna had removed any decoration that had once adorned Elpee's house, especially those things that were in the cherry or polka dot family.

As she toured the four bedrooms, Elpee noted that all the chenille bedspreads were gone, as were the pictures on the walls. The Rose Room no longer housed roses, the Green Room was no longer green, and the front bedroom was no longer even a bedroom. The old four-poster bed that Elpee once had in her own bedroom was gone, but the corner writing desk, for whatever reason, was still present. The upstairs bathroom, which was previously graced with polka dots and mermaids, was now completely barren. Only the large clawfoot bathtub in all its overpowering starkness occupied the room.

Downstairs, the kitchen cupboards were bare, and Elpee's bowl of glass cherries and cherry teapots were nowhere to be found. The dining room built-ins housed little more than the teacups danDay-leon had recently given Elpee as a housewarming gift. The oval braided rug was conspicuously missing from under the dining room table, as were the draw drapes that separated the dining room from the living room. The checkerboard and its pieces no longer sat atop the game table, stripping it of its personality and relegating it to the role of an otherwise ordinary side table. The collection of games and puzzles were severely reduced in number to a mere handful. The saddest of all absences were her books. Missing were all of the beloved volumes of stories that had surrounded Elpee, no matter which faraway land she lived in.

When Elpee was relatively satisfied that the list was complete, she returned to each room, sat on a piece of furniture, and opened her mind to the possibility that she may have overlooked something. She then asked the room to let her know if she forgot anything, and if so to advise her of what it was. As she did this, her brain went into overdrive with reminders, suggestions, and requests coming from all directions. Elpee was not sure if they could all possibly be coming solely from the rooms or if she, too, wanted some additions or changes. No bother. She jotted down notes as quickly as she could, and would take them all under advisement when the time came.

Elpee reassured herself that the restoration would be a labor of love for the house and for herself, because they reflected their individual and mutual souls back to each other and nothing could change that, not even Anna's malevolent attempt to do so.

With a smidgen of excitement, Elpee decided to begin the task immediately. She went to the hall linen closet to investigate what remained in there that she could utilize. In the cubby hole, she found a variety of bed linens, tablecloths, napkins, aprons, towels, and the like that she could possibly put to use. Elpee began by tossing onto the floor all the *stuff* that would soon be appropriately named and gracefully displayed. She found one orange and one black – faded to dark brown actually – bath towel. She took them into the bathroom and strategically placed one on each window. After poofing and draping, Elpee stood back to view her creation.

"Excellent! It looks like an autumn festival should be celebrated in here. Oh, I just can't wait for the weather to get cooler and for the trees to begin shedding their leaves so that I can draw a bath and add a sachet filled with cloves and orange peels along with just a hint of eucalyptus to it," Elpee said aloud. She then clapped her hands and returned to the pile of *stuff*.

Elpee found and extracted enough linens from their hidden existence in the closet to satisfy her immediate objective while giving them a purpose and a life. There was a faded green, seersucker bedspread and a yellowish table runner that would serve in the Green Room. Elpee felt beyond lucky when she discovered a sizeable flowered tablecloth and matching napkins that she could use for a bedspread and window treatment in the Rose Room. Nothing could replace Elpee's peach chenille bedspread, and she would have to accept that and settle for something else right now. She found a pair of old lace curtains in the back of the closet, and although they had some holes in them, they would do for the present time. As for the front bedroom, that would have to wait, since it was not currently a bedroom and would need to be restored to one before Elpee could do any decorating.

Elpee went down the stairs with an armful of linens, tripping on the errantly hanging material, all the while hoping not to make a rapid descent to the bottom in the process. She walked over to the couch, dropped her stock of goods on it, and then proceeded into the kitchen to get a much-needed snack. Anxious to begin the makeovers, Elpee grabbed a plum and a glass of water and quickly returned to the living room. She threw her body onto the couch only to hear a very loud yelping, which caused her to immediately jump up. There, hidden within the pile of *stuff*, was a semi-squished Butter.

"Butterball, are you okay? What are you doing in there, mister?"

"Argh, Argh, Argh," replied the flattened puppy.

No matter what Elpee did to try to comfort him, or how hard she struggled to evaluate his injuries, she was met with failure. He continued wailing as if he had been run over by a steamroller. Suddenly, Elpee heard what sounded like a thunderous herd of pachyderms running toward them. When she turned around, she spotted a hairy black bullet aimed directly at her, and at the exact same moment, she felt its impact. PippyLou ran into her, knocked her over, and was on the couch with his friend doing what she was unable to do – shut him up.

With Pippy's arrival came Butter's recovery. Both canines jumped off the couch, with Butter shedding *stuff* in the process as they ran out the door to play. Elpee shook her head, shook herself, and began to do in the living room what she had done upstairs.

Tea towels were hung on the kitchen window, round and square linen doilies adorned the dining room windows, and various tablecloths decorated the living room. The front porch was bedecked in a variety of aprons – ten in all – with no two patterns being the same.

"Interesting!" Elpee proclaimed as she appraised the appearance of each room.

Done for the day, Elpee threw in the towel, both figuratively and literally, and walked across the street to danDay-leon's in search of some nourishment or at least some tea. danDay answered at Elpee's first knock on the door, opened it, and invited her in.

"Hi," said Elpee. "Can you make me a cup of tea, and do you have anything to eat?'

"Of course," the Princess of Teacup Manor replied.

But, before Elpee could take one step over the threshold, danDay-leon rescinded her invitation by shaking her head, turning around, and walking away. Her repeal was based on Elpee's query as she began to enter. The words she spoke were, "Where's Alpert?"

danDay-leon's answer could be heard coming from inside the house, behind the closed door.

"Ask PoliM'aladroit."

AND OUT

Elpee was utterly pleased with the interior appearance of her cottage even though it was decorated somewhat quirkily. It did not have the charm it once had, but eventually, it would, and at least now it positively did not resemble the bastardized version Anna had left her with. It was Elpee's home, and even if it did not have the old charm, it did have the warmth only a loving inhabitant could create.

With the inside sufficiently completed, it was time for Elpee to tackle the gardens. It was not until Hortense was gone that Elpee realized how much she had depended on her and how she took her contribution for granted. Now it was Elpee alone who would be responsible for weeding and tilling the ground. Unsure if she could, or even wanted to, maintain the grand palette of botanical colors Hortense had created, Elpee thought about her alternatives. She walked around the plot of land to obtain the sense of the vibrational resonance it was emitting. Elpee began embellishing the garden by creatively scattering about the rocks Euterpe had polka-dotted while the others were painting the masks. Unlike when they lined the paths and walkways, the stones now had no mission and were not expected to function as guardians of the garden. They were at present *of* the garden and could just be, much like Elpee. As she picked each one up, they instructed her where they would like to live; some in the shade, some in the sun, while others were just indifferent or undecided and wanted both or neither. Elpee would speak to Euterpe about them because perhaps she had painted some of them with unfitting colors and needed to make a few adjustments. Overall, everyone seemed content, and Elpee felt joyful over their contribution to the landscape.

Next, Elpee thought it might be a good idea to bring the indoor plants outdoors and distribute them amongst the other foliage. There was still a small quantity of plant life that Anna had not disposed of or killed, and

Elpee thought that it would be wise to cleanse them of Anna's aura by placing them in nature.

The task of transporting the plants would have been made easier if the two black canines did not insist on being in on the action by walking in front of Elpee and impeding her progress. One by one, Elpee brought the plants outside and commanded the dogs to leave them alone by explaining that they were not toys and they were already slightly traumatized because of the move. Butter and Pippy reluctantly complied and showed their support of the relocated plants by licking their wounded spirit leaves.

The garden, though different from the one Hortense had created, was happy and alive. The bench in the corner was the focal point of the plot with plants, rocks, and masks in an array of colors and personalities surrounding it. It not only looked good, it felt good. Now, Elpee also had a sense of accomplishment and confidence regarding the cottage's outdoor extension.

The wooden window boxes that were on the front of the house facing the road were bare and looked sadly shabby.

"I don't know what to do with the window boxes," Elpee said to no one in particular.

"Maybe if I paint the wood . . ."

Ding! Ding! Ding! Another enlightening moment for the princess. She summoned Euterpe in her mind, and when that did not work, she text-messaged her. Soon, Elpee saw the *Queen* sauntering down the road toward her.

"'terpe, I need your help. I want to paint flowers for the window boxes," Elpee explained to the *Queen*.

"Paint, paint, what say you, paint?

"The fumes may make us both feel faint.

"Just line the bottom with some rocks,

"and then put some flowers in the box," Euterpe expressed in a lilt.

"No, not the boxes. I want to paint some wooden flowers to put in the window boxes," Elpee said, trying to clarify the request.

"What a sight,

"but all right,

"I will assist you in your plight."

One princess and one *Queen* spent the afternoon painting wooden flowers, mounting them on stick stems, and arranging them in the boxes.

Half of their creations had petals and centers painted as flowers should have, however, the other half was embellished with various sizes and colors of polka dots, most of which were covered with glitter. No bother. Their fabrication was fabulous.

"Thank you for all your help, and by the way, where is Alpert?" Elpee blurted out, but Euterpe quickly cut her off.

"Go I must.

"With all this dust.

"Don't want to rust.

"You see, I trust," she expressed as she departed faster than she had arrived.

"Poop!" declared the disappointed princess.

Done for the day, Elpee went inside to bathe and dine. She turned on the radio and tuned to a channel that offered a coffeehouse blend of music. Happy, happy she felt on her way upstairs until she passed the potted fern that was sitting on the landing floor. It was looking weepy and lonesome and wanted to go outside with the others.

"You can't go outside, you are far too fair and will get sunburned," she tried to explain to the forlorn fern, but she knew her effort was probably in vain.

She continued up the stairs enjoying the music and her new-old cottage. The Princess then bathed, powdered herself unerringly three times with the giant powder puff, and put on her cherry pajamas, the ones that she took with her when she abandoned the house, leaving it with Anna.

"Ah, heavenly," she proclaimed as she descended the stairs, trying to avoid eye contact with the fern.

Dinner was tomato soup and grilled cheese for both Butter and her, after which they both cuddled up on the couch, she with a book and he with a bone. It was not long before they were both asleep. This had become an evening ritual for both Elpee and her pet. After a long day of work, or in his case play, they would come in, have dinner, and relax. Both were enjoying their lives and wanted more of it.

There was only one thing that was casting a pall on the atmosphere of late, and that was the senseless fern that Elpee was trying to save from killing itself. It would not accept the fact that it could not tolerate the direct sunlight and had to remain in the house. It got weepier and weepier until it was weeping real tears and expressed to Elpee that it was not the sunlight it could not tolerate, but rather the desperate loneliness it was experiencing with all its housemates gone.

Finally, Elpee *heard* the fern and took it outside. She placed it in the shadiest area she could find, gave it a big drink of water, a hug, and allowed it to be where it wanted to be. She would always feel sorry for having made this decision, but she would never regret it.

Memory Lane

———

One day several weeks prior, the girls had strategized, philosophized, and organized the details for an upcoming slumber party they wanted to have. It was agreed upon that because Hortense was still not communicating – at least not with Elpee – no one knew where Euterpe lived, and the fact that Elpee had the largest house, the sleepover would take place at Cherry Cottage. They planned to serve a luscious, buffet style, open-house meal at which the gnomes and elves would join them.

On the evening of the event, sizeable people and little people came and went, in and out, and ate and drank. Simon, the head muckety-muck gnome, introduced a new dweller in their tree. Her name was Camby. She had blonde hair and was tall – not gnomish or elfin at all. She was probably almost three feet high, and Elpee did not know how she could manage entering the tree or how anyone else was able to fit inside once she had negotiated the fete. Elpee was curious, but was well mannered enough not to ask any questions and instead modestly welcomed her. She was well spoken and appeared to be well educated as well. Elpee concluded that because Camby was much different from the other woods creatures, she was either adopted or from France.

The expressions and feelings of merriment were overwhelming to Elpee, and it was nothing she had ever experienced in her other faraway land lives. She did not have to think about, ask, or convince herself about the happiness she felt because it came from her heart, not her head. They played games, sang, and danced – alone and with each other. The people who were somewhat short and just not quite able to dance with those who were taller merely stood on the taller person's shoes and were whisked around the outside dance floor by them.

Since Camby was the newest member of the tribe, the veterans had saved the cake for later in the evening rather than serving it directly after dinner, because showing her how it was eaten in their world would be the crowning glory on an already glorious night. Elpee set the cake on the dining room table and went outside to announce that it was time for dessert and to request that everyone come inside. As they entered the house, Elpee provided each of them a utensil to *use*. Some guests were given spoons, while others were supplied with knives due to Elpee's silverware supply shortage, but Camby was fortunate and was presented with a fork. The traditional pineapple upside-down cake was sitting on the table. Everyone gathered around it, raised their utensils, threw them over their left shoulder, and dove face first into the cake. Everyone except Camby, that is. She did not quite get it, and even after it was explained to her, she chose instead to use her fork rather than diving in. Everyone else thought it odd, but they were an affable crew and believed to each her own.

The evening grew late, and everyone was tired, so collectively they all chipped in to tidy up, but in typical fashion, there was little to do because everything there was had been eaten and drunk. When that task was completed, the guests began to leave Elpee's home to return to their own residences. The gnomes retired to the trees and the elves to their own neighborhood, and on their departure Camby was serenaded with an impromptu welcome song by all the partiers as she left with the other gnomes.

The three princesses and one *Queen* retired to the living room to reminisce about the good and the bad old times. They recalled some of the antics and pranks they had engaged in. Elpee recounted the time she left the faraway land where she had met them in search of a more mature world and how that world almost destroyed her. They each took turns telling stories about both those lands and how much they missed Elpee when she lived in the last one when they could only see her from a distance.

"I am so grateful for all of you – including the very obviously missing Alpert and Hortense – for saving me from Anna and that place," Elpee said.

Euterpe, in a show of emotion, walked directly over to Elpee, sat on her lap, and began to explain how she felt.

"I was so sad that Anna was so bad.

"But, what could I do? It could only be you,

"who could beat her up and send her away

"and cast her in clay for a year and a day."

"I know, 'terpe. You couldn't do anything until I was ready, but I know you wanted to do something and would have if you could. Thank you for caring about me," Elpee said to *Queen* Euterpe.

Although the other two princesses had already expressed their concern to Elpee when she first returned here, it did not stop any of them from reviewing and reliving the events that changed all their lives. They all soon fell asleep, danDay-leon in mid-sentence, without any of them ever climbing the stairs to the bedrooms.

TROUBLE CAME FOR A VISIT

It was now time for Elpee to begin planning her future, or at least to consider planning it. The interior of her house was as complete as it could be for the current time, and the gardens were spectacular – precisely as she had wanted them to be. Therefore, with nothing much left to do, Elpee needed to devise a strategy that included who, what, when, where, and why. She decided to walk to the bay and contemplate these questions on the way.

"Butter, do you want to go for a walk?" Elpee called to the dog, who immediately came flying into the house and did a perfect slide, stopping right next to her.

"Good boy!" she said, bending down to pet him.

"Get your leash," Elpee instructed him when she was done petting him and stood up.

Butter left her side and ran to the front door, where in a basket on the floor Elpee stored sunglasses, gloves, bug spray, and his leash. He delicately pulled the lead, which was fashioned from hemp, out of the basket with his teeth. He would yank a length then stop and drop it, and return to the basket to retrieve another stretch and so on. When the entire leash was on the floor, Butter would sink his teeth into what appeared to be a predetermined section and waited for his master to help him open the door. As she arrived there, he pushed his butt against the lower half, she grabbed the handle, and out they went for their stroll. When they reached the walkway, Butter automatically turned left toward the ocean.

"This way, mister. We're not going to the ocean today. We're going to the bay and then to the post office to check our mail," Elpee said, correcting her furry friend.

Butter complied without arguing, turned around, and began walking north while holding the leash in his mouth. With the majority of the rope dragging behind him, they continued their trek until they reached their destination, where Elpee then took it from his mouth so that he could play unencumbered. His unfailingly devoted and well-trained master found him several rocks that she gave to him, one at a time, to toss around in the shallow water. He batted each stone back and forth until it was lost and would then come to Elpee begging either for help in finding it or providing him with a replacement. She always opted for the standby, and once she gave it to him, he would begin the exercise all over again.

Elpee had intended to use this time to arrange her thoughts, but she was so delightfully distracted by her dog's antics that all thinking of the future went out of her head. She could not help herself because he put on such a show that she sat and watched him until she ran out of her supply of rocks. Elpee did not answer any of the 'W' questions she had intended to, nor did she even think about them. Instead, she relaxed and had a good time watching and laughing at Butter.

"Let's go, Butterball. I have to go to the Post Office, and besides, your paws must be as wrinkled as prunes by now from spending all that time in the water."

Reluctantly, he complied, got out of the water, and shook himself off. Elpee placed the leash around his neck, and the two of them began their walk into town. As they passed stores, Elpee said hello to the owners or customers, and as they approached the bakery, Butter accelerated his pace, knowing that a delicacy awaited him there. Henry, the owner, always came out and gave the dog a special treat just for being Butter, and this time was no exception. On today's menu were mini peanut butter pop-ems, which only added to Elpee's delight as she watched the dog eat them and then try to get the peanut butter off the roof of his mouth. She courteously thanked Henry for both Butter and herself before continuing on to their next stop.

The Post Office was directly across the square from the bakery. Elpee and Butter walked the short distance, and when they arrived there, she tied him to a tree while she went inside. Elpee strode over to her ancient, keyless, brass post office box and began turning the tumbler. To remember the combination, Elpee created and memorized the code-phrase, '*i*t's *n*ot *f*antasy, *r*eal *l*eprechauns *r*ule', meaning to turn the tumbler to I, N, F – Right, Left, Right. It was always a surprise to her if the door opened on the first try, and when it did this time, Elpee was certain that it was her lucky day. For a few seconds before extracting the mail, she fantasized about leprechauns and imagined that there was a pot of gold, or at least something favorable, waiting for her inside that small metal vault. She reached in and pulled out an envelope whose flap was sealed shut with wax and the initial 'C'. Elpee's body stiffened as she looked at the letter and instantly recognized the handwriting. Perhaps the leprechauns had not favored her this day. As she left the building with a scowl on her face, Elpee muttered under her breath, "Great! My long-lost cousin, Chucklpe."

WHO GOES THERE ... UNDER THE SINK?

Elpee put the unopened letter in her pocket and then untied Butter while wondering when or where she should read it, or for that matter, whether she should read it at all. Since she was in town, Elpee decided to visit PoliM'aladroit, knowing that if she chose to, she could open Chucklpe's letter there. Besides, she thought Butter and the small gray creature could play together.

"Let's go, Buddy-boy, we're going to Auntie Pol's."

The dog put some pep in his step upon hearing the news, and quickly they were both behind the general store and at PoliM'aladroit's house. Elpee knocked on the front door by using the trunk of a massive brass knocker, which was fashioned in the shape of an elephant. There was no answer to her rapping, so Elpee lifted the elephant's proboscis and once again banged on the door with it. With still no response to her continual banging on the door, Elpee became alarmed because PoliM'aladroit's bicycle was in its rack near the walk and she could hear the gray boy making noises inside the house. PoliM'aladroit never left home without one or the other, which prompted Elpee to investigate the surroundings, hoping all the while that her friend was safe.

She walked around to the left side of the house and looked in the living room window, but saw nothing. As she continued on her way to the back of the house, Butter got excited at seeing his little friend and began tugging on the leash.

"Hold on, mister, I have to check things out first. You need to stay here for a minute," Elpee told the boy as she secured the end of the leash over the picket fence that separated the neighboring backyards.

Elpee looked in one of the kitchen windows and saw nothing unusual other than that the cabinet doors beneath the sink were open. She called PoliM'aladroit's name and heard a muffled noise in response. "Uh-oh," she murmured. Frightened to go in and afraid not to, Elpee took a deep breath and went into the house, ready to take on the direst of demons if need be. As she entered, Elpee saw two feet with a shoe on each of them protruding from underneath the sink. She walked over to the feet, and wearing her best impersonation of courage, looked to see to whom they belonged while hoping that their owner was still breathing.

"PoliM'aladroit, what in the dickens are you doing under the sink, and why didn't you answer me?" Elpee asked her in a most chastising of ways.

The Princess of ShinyShores moved her mouth, but no words came out. She did, however, manage to express to Elpee that she was stuck where she was and needed assistance to be extricated. Elpee pulled on one leg and then the other with no luck – PoliM'aladroit remained wedged where she was under the sink. Elpee repositioned herself, grabbed both of the stuck princess's legs, tucked the ankles under her own arms, and pulled with all her might, only to wind up on the floor when PoliM'aladroit's shoes gave way before she did.

With one last possible solution in mind, Elpee brought Butter – leash and all – inside, put another leash on the small gray creature, then secured one animal to each of PoliM'aladroit's legs, and told them to pull. Again, no luck, as they merely looked at Elpee with quizzical expressions on their faces. Elpee then stood in front of the animals and urged them to come to her, but that too bore no results. She was out of ideas and was ready to call the fire department, that is if the town had a fire department, which she told herself was something she would have to research if and when this fiasco was over. The gray creature lay sadly on the floor by his mistress when all of a sudden the sound of the ice cream truck alerted Butter. He bolted to the front door, immediately dislodging the stuck princess much like a cork from a bottle, and dragged both her and the gray boy across the floor behind him.

"Not now, Butter, but thank you so much for getting Auntie Pol out from under the sink. And what in all heaven, may I ask, were you doing under there?" Elpee, in one uninterrupted breath, questioned PoliM'aladroit.

"Yes, thank you, dear boy, for rescuing me. I shudder to think what would have happened to me and my boy had you not come just to free me. Thank you so much, Butter," PoliM'aladroit declared as she hugged him while she remained on the floor.

Feeling as if she had absolutely no part in PoliM'aladroit's search and rescue, Elpee thought she might as well adopt the role of the top prosecutor.

"Enough with these shenanigans, I say. The last time I was here, you had nailed yourself to the roof, and now you lodged yourself in a kitchen cabinet. You need to grow up, Missy, and act your age. And by the way, you are very welcome for the extrication from that cabinet. Where is Alpert? What in the heaven's name were you doing under there anyway? I want answers."

"I dropped something in the sink, and it went down the drain. I was merely trying to retrieve it by disconnecting the drainpipe under the sink, and something went wrong," PoliM'aladroit explained.

"What happened is that you got stuck. What in the world was so important that you would attempt doing what you did?" Elpee asked.

"I would rather not say," the other princess answered in what was a weak attempt to at least sound regal while still seated clumsily on the floor.

Elpee said no more, but because of the intolerant expression on the Princess of Cherry Cottage's face, PoliM'aladroit sheepishly responded, "A safety pin."

Before Elpee could comment on the absurdity of the answer, PoliM'aladroit rose to a standing position and advised Elpee that there would be no more discussion of her mishap or of Alpert and his whereabouts.

READING THE LETTER

———

After PoliM'aladroit regained her composure and use of her body, she offered Elpee some refreshments. Elpee accepted a glass of lemonade, proceeded to add nine spoonsful of sugar to the glass, tasted it, and then added several more before sampling it again. Ah, perfect! Both princesses went out the back door and sat on the glider PoliM'aladroit had in her yard. The canine cousins were resting in the grass, the small gray creature more so, as Butter was rolling around on it, enjoying its texture.

Elpee started the conversation with the specific reason she came to ShinyShores in the first place.

"PoliM'aladroit, I just came from the Post Office, where I discovered a letter from my cousin, Chucklpe, inside the box. I'm afraid to open it, so I thought I would come here for moral support," Elpee explained as her friend listened intently, encouraging Elpee to continue her explanation.

"I was not aware you had a cousin, my dear."

"That's because he is a vagabond. Well, I shouldn't say that about him, because I really am not sure he is a drifter, only that he appears and disappears and most of the time no one knows where he is. For all I know, he could be living down the street from me," Elpee briefly explained to PoliM'aladroit.

"Why is it that you are afraid to open it?" the other woman asked her.

"Because Chucklpe only makes his existence known when there is either a funeral or a wedding, and I fear bad news, even if it is from afar. And he's weird because flowers always accompany him when he visits, I don't know why. I guess maybe because he only shows up for occasions that warrant them."

"We have all been here for you and each other for quite some time now, so please be assured that no matter how dire the information contained in that letter may be, you have our support. I am sure I can say that for all the other princesses as well," PoliM'aladroit guaranteed Elpee.

"All except Hortense, that is. I'm sure you can't speak for her, and I am equally as sure that her support would be absent. But that is another story for another day. I can't imagine who could have died, there are so few of us left," Elpee commented emotionally.

"Well, shall we continue your agony, or should we open it and read the contents?" PoliM'aladroit inquired of Elpee.

"I think I would prefer to prolong the anguish a bit longer. I am not quite ready to face the cruel reality yet. Let's take the boys for a walk, and then when we return, I will open it. Besides, they deserve a treat for their use of life-saving skills on you," Elpee suggested.

"Excellent idea! Let me retrieve my shoes, and then we will go," PoliM'aladroit answered.

In short order, both women and both animals were on their way to the market to purchase a reward for the canine cousins. The gratefully extricated princess insisted it was her treat and went inside. When she returned, she held in her hand several scraps of meat for them, which they played with for several minutes before actually chewing on and swallowing them.

All four people and dogs strolled through the busy streets of the town, saying hello to neighbors and looking in the store windows as they passed them. They discussed the weather and all matters of superfluous fluff to avoid the mention of the letter, but PoliM'aladroit would not be accommodating for much longer. Her patience for Elpee's stall tactics was wearing thin, and she also wanted to retrieve the errant safety pin that was trapped in her drainpipe, which she could only do after Elpee left. They had almost completed the loop around town and its square in the middle, and would soon be returning to PoliM'aladroit's front gate.

"In we go," PoliM'aladroit directed the other three entities as she held the gate open for them. Everyone complied, although Elpee entered most hesitantly as she shuffled and dragged her feet while humming and making unpleasant faces. Once all four of them were inside the house, its owner shooed the four-legged beings into the backyard and then sat on her sofa, awaiting Elpee's recital. Elpee needed no further prompting to at last read the letter, as PoliM'aladroit's body language said it all. Elpee also sat, choosing the floral wing chair located in the corner by the bay window. She unsealed the envelope, removed the contents, and took a deep breath before beginning to read it aloud.

"Dear Cousin Elpee,

"I hope, actually, I know, that this letter will find you well and in good health, as I reside down the street from you. You see, I am living in a splendid cottage on the ocean and soon plan to move into its grander parent next door. I was on my way to visit you when I spotted a dazzling garden, which I needed to explore. It turns out that the garden's owner, like myself, is enamored with every variety of flora. The rest is, as they say, what Faerie tales are made of, cousin. Fate has brought me to my soul mate, and we will soon be married. Perhaps you know her. Her name is Hortense. Our invitations will be mailed shortly, but please reserve the date. We will be joined in wedded bliss on October 31 of this year. Details to follow. Bye-bye now!

"Your loving cousin,

"Chucklpe"

Both of the princesses remained seated with their eyes glazed over and their mouths agape. Elpee spoke first with a series of not so pretty words.

"Unbelievable. Well, of course it is believable. Anything is believable when it concerns those two scoundrels. Married? Hah! I told you he was a dirty, no good so-and-so, and the other one . . . Well, words could not begin to describe the degree of loathsomeness she possesses. No wonder she stopped tending my garden, she was too busy with that chucklehead, Chucklpe. I guess I didn't make her the cake in a timely enough fashion to suit her. Well, let me tell you something, I am glad I didn't make it, and I never will."

Elpee was not even close to concluding her diatribe, and PoliM'aladroit dared not move from her position on the couch lest the Princess of Cherry Cottage lose her mind even further. She sat there motionless while Elpee continued her discourse.

"And another thing! I felt so bad for thinking ill of Hortense when I found out why she stole Butter. Well, let me tell you a thing or two, I was absolutely right, and I should have burnt her at the stake. Chucklpe is . . . Oh, I don't really know what he is except that he suckers you in, sucks the life out of you, and then disappears. In any event, he is Hortense's problem, and may they live happily ever after, but let me tell you I won't be going to that wedding. No siree, bob! Blah, blah, blah," Elpee said, attempting to finish the sentence before pausing, as she desperately needed to come up for air.

Just as PoliM'aladroit was about to speak, Elpee interjected.

"I'm done. Thank you for listening, and have a good night. Where is Alpert? Be careful trying to retrieve your safety pin," Elpee concluded as she turned and went out the back door, calling for Butter on her way.

SHUT UP!

Elpee was beside herself, knowing that that rascal Chucklpe was living right here in her hometown. She was even more beside herself thinking about him living down the walk from her. Elpee was so beside herself thinking of him duping her friend Hortense into marrying him that she was beside someone else. She was so out of her own time and space that she could not think straight. She wanted to do something but did not know what. Hortense clearly wanted no contact with her, so that eliminated Elpee's option of enlightening the soon-to-be bride on the subject of her wayward cousin, Chucklpe.

The seething princess was not thinking rationally, because she spent every waking hour contemplating ways to get rid of Chucklpe or to warn Hortense of what a dirty no-good scoundrel he was. Sure, he always came with flowers because that was his calling card; his signature, you might say, but those flowers were ever held by an empty vase. Then, Elpee began to wonder why she was trying to protect Hortense. After all, wasn't she being the rudest of all rudes to turn her back on Elpee in the way she did? Elpee made a grave mistake by misjudging Hortense's character, both now and when she stole Butter. She knew that people made mistakes, and that that is how living creatures usually learned, and so Elpee tried to convince herself that people should be encouraged to make errors in order to learn the lessons that resulted from having made them. She knew that her hypothesis was beyond far-reaching and was merely a selfish and self-serving attitude on her part. Still and all, Elpee believed Hortense carried this resentment excessively far. Fine, she thought, let them have each other – who cared, anyway?

When she stopped thinking about Chucklpe, Elpee's thinking would turn to Hortense, then back to Chucklpe and so on. She went about her chores being less than gentle with the items she encountered in the process. From the walk, passersby could hear a cacophony of banging, slamming, and thudding coming from inside Cherry Cottage. Elpee chose to discuss this with no one, but rather to find within herself the solution that would give her some peace of mind and a resolution to this problem.

At night, Elpee would sit rocking in the chair in her bedroom, attempting to concentrate on one of her much-loved books without success. The only thing that she managed to accomplish was to rock the chair so fast, and so hard, that it left a permanent impression in the wainscoted wall behind her from having hit it so often and so vigorously. Night after night, Elpee returned to the same ritual only to have her mind wander to either Hortense or Chucklpe rather than focusing on the literature. In an attempt to quiet her mind, Elpee tried to recite famous speeches. She began with her favorite, the 'Who's on First, What's on Second, and I Don't Know's on Third?' routine, but began to giggle, which was a welcome change from her current black mood. However, finding sleep was the issue at hand. She then began to recite the more somber 'Gettysburg Address', followed by Sojourner Truth's 1851 'Ain't I a Woman?' By the time Elpee began Lou Gehrig's farewell to baseball speech, she had fallen soundly asleep – that is until the noise started.

Elpee was awakened that night, and every night thereafter, to the relentless sound of something loud and bothersome. It was a noise she could not identify nor define, but despised nonetheless. It went on, and on, and on. It made her teeth hurt, her skin crawl, and her already threadbare nerves unravel even further. One night, in desperation, she yelled out the window for the powers that be to please quiet the incessant disruption of the evening stillness. As she sat back on her bed, Elpee thought she heard laughing in addition to the usual insufferable noise. At this point, she realized that her only solution might be to accept the clamor before she collapsed from exhaustion. And she eventually did just that and managed to obtain some rest while still feeling disdain for the disruption.

Elpee made no effort at communication with PoliM'aladroit since the day she read the letter at ShinyShores because she was too busy having hissy fits over the author and its contents. PoliM'aladroit left Elpee alone with her anger for her to either conquer or be conquered by it. Truth be told, PoliM'aladroit was still occupied with trying to retrieve her safety pin and had little time for anything else. In the midst of one of those hissy fits, danDay-leon, who could contain her curiosity no longer, ventured across the street under the guise of sharing tea and knocked on Elpee's screen door. Just as she finished rapping on the wooden frame, an object flew past her eyes and landed out the window on the other side.

"Oh, my," danDay-leon commented while wondering if her own demise would be the price she might have to pay for her nosiness.

Elpee came to the door and invited her in, causing danDay to question whether she should accept the invitation or not. However, she did.

"What in blazes is going on here, Elpee? All I hear is ugly coming from out of this house. It is not like you, and quite frankly, I don't like it. I don't like any of it. I miss everything about what were you and this cottage. Your anger and energy are destroying both of you, and it is beginning to leak across the street, and I will not have that. Now, stop it and don't be a hater," danDay-leon told the angry and out of control princess. "And by the way, you look awful. Are you sleeping?"

"No. There is this indescribable noise every night, and it doesn't stop. It's wearing me down," Elpee whined.

"Sit down," danDay-leon commanded. "Tea is the answer, and I will make it. That is an order, Missy."

Elpee, too tired to toss one more object or throw out another barb, fell into the down sofa and waited for the tea, which danDay-leon served in short order.

Both princesses drank the brew in silence while still enjoying each other's company. When Elpee finished the last sip from her cup, the Princess of Teacup Manor took it from her and began examining the re- maining leaves. She swirled the teacup round and round and gazed inside with each turn.

"If you tell me you see a kaleidoscope again, I swear danDay, I will not be responsible for my actions," Elpee warned her.

"Don't be ridiculous . . . A kaleidoscope? Well, I never," danDay-leon scoffed. "I see good things. Lots and lots of good things and spiders."

"What? Have you completely lost your mind? Good things and spi- ders? Here we go again with your amateur seering. Just what I need, more spiders so Butter can play with them and get all gooey from their spit."

"I'm only trying to help you, and you ridicule my talents," danDay said to Elpee while trying to hold back tears.

"I'm sorry, danDay. I didn't mean to hurt you," Elpee, feeling horrible, said as she hugged the other princess.

"Thank you for the tea and the reading. Most of all, thank you for telling me about the ugly. I don't want to be a hater. I love you."

A Whole Lotta Crying Going On

Elpee tried her best, with her heart and soul, and all her might, to elimi-
nate the fear and hatred she felt toward Chucklpe. He was a bad seed, and
there was nothing she could do about it. No matter how hard she had
tried in the past, Elpee was never able to change genetics or history, so why
would she entertain the possibility now? Given the absolute nature of both
those facts, the Princess of Cherry Cottage put her focus on tolerating the
situation while also hoping to build on it and extend that mental and
physical energy to achieve a level of acceptance. Hortense was her own
person who made her own decisions and mistakes and survived them
both. If she chose to marry Cousin Chucklpe, so be it!

Since danDay-leon's visit, Elpee spent much of her time contemplating
things that danDay had said to her. Elpee certainly did not want to be a
hater. She had seen what resentments and anger had done to people; how
it ate them up and drew every molecule of joy and peace from their souls,
leaving them empty except for the never-ending torment that lived within
them. The existence that those tortured souls must have felt was not something Elpee ever wanted to experience if she had the choice. Ruminating
about Chucklpe and his presence in town was counterproductive to how
Elpee wished to live her life. She had to let go of the anger she felt for him
as well as the concern she felt for Hortense.

If only she could get some sleep, Elpee thought, she would be able to
handle all this nonsense better, but the noise from outside was an unnerving and unremitting symphony of squeaking, slurping, giggling, and
squealing. The sleep-deprived princess was befuddled and did not know
how to either quiet the clamor or sleep through it. Maybe, she thought,
she could tiptoe down the stairs when the noise began and quietly sneak
outside to find the source. That was only a fleeting thought, as Elpee
quickly realized that she was way too chicken to attempt doing any such

thing. She entertained sleeping somewhere else, but danDay-leon snored too loudly for Elpee to sleep over at her cottage, PoliM'aladroit's creature and Butter would be up all night playing with each other, and who knew where Euterpe called home. Needless to say, Hortense was not even a remote possibility of an option in Elpee's mind. She would just have to . . . Well, she really did not know what she would have to. She was out of options, exhausted, and trying not to be disordered and disagreeable. What to do...what to do?

While contemplating the lack of solutions, Elpee heard yet another noise coming from outside, this time from in front of the house and in the daylight. Vroom, vroom, vroom came a rattling noise from far down the walk. It got noticeably louder as it approached Elpee's cottage, so loud in fact, that Elpee needed to cover her ears and Butter found it necessary to sing its praises in the form of a screech. Just when Elpee believed her eardrums would rupture and her brain implode, the noise ceased. She took her hands away from her ears and opened her eyes, which she had unknowingly closed, and looked out the upstairs front window. There, stopped directly in front of her house and taking up the entire walk from side to side, was a pay-loader.

"What on Earth?" Elpee said as she looked toward the heavens. "Please tell me that whoever it belongs to is not here to demolish my home."

Elpee cast her eyes away from the above and returned them to the five-and-a-half-foot range the window allowed her to see before she peered down and espied a swatch of wild pink hair flying around the far side of the machine.

"Oh, happy days and hallelujah, it's only Euterpe . . . Well, I *think* it's happy days and hallelujah . . . Ya never knows with that one," Elpee proclaimed with questionable relief.

"Hello my cousin, do you like my ride?

"I've been a-buzzin' around the countryside," Euterpe asked with a childish smirk on her face.

"'terpe, where did you get this piece of earth-moving equipment, and why? Did you steal it?" Elpee asked, not thinking that she had not even greeted *Queen* Euterpe first.

"My feelings get hurt when you act so curt.

"Not even a greeting, before such a beating.

"I feel such sorrow, for I only did borrow,

"this machine from the canteen,

"to fix a hole from a troll."

"I'm sorry, Euterpe," Elpee began to say as she moved toward the Queen to hug her in conjunction with her apology.

"I don't know what's wrong with me. I am so rude. I am so tired . . ." Elpee managed to sputter out before breaking out into a full-blown bout of weeping.

Now it was Euterpe's turn to embrace Elpee.

"Please don't cry,

"or I shall die,

"to think that I,

"did make you cry."

"WAH, WAH, WAH."

Sniffle, snort, sniffle.

"WAH, WAH."

Cough, cough, snort, choke.

Sounds of all sorts were being emitted from Elpee's nose, throat, and mouth, as well as a veritable waterfall of tears pouring forth from her eyes. She could not stop herself, and Euterpe felt incapable of helping her friend.

"Wwwwhere'ss Aaalllpppert?" Elpee struggled to ask in response to her not receiving his usual 'get a grip' statement in the form of a sharp pinch.

"Ohhh, I cannot say,

"not on this day.

"Do you want to play,

"or shall I go away?" the poor, upset, and now fearful Euterpe stammered back at her.

Both women hugged each other, not knowing whom they felt worse for, themselves or the other of them. As they embraced in unison, they both let out wails unique to them.

"WAH, WAH, WAH."

"Boo-hoo. Cry-cry.

"Sob-sob. My-my."

"WAH. WAH."

"Shut up, I say,

"I want to play.

"Cry no more,

"your throat'll be sore.

"Dry your eyes, and blow your nose.

"No more sighs, forget your woes.

"Off we go, on the truck.

"We'll have some fun, with any luck.

"Bring the dog, he wants to come.

"Make him sit in the back and give him a plum," instructed Euterpe.

Not knowing what else to do, Elpee complied. She went inside, got some tissues, and blew her nose. She then called for Butter, who came running, and in no time Elpee and her canine companion were riding along with Euterpe in the pay-loader. Elpee did not know where the *Queen* was going, she just hoped it would not land them both in jail.

LULLABY AND GOODNIGHT

———

Euterpe drove the monster machine down the road faster than she probably should have and the motion, or perhaps the fear of incarceration, caused Elpee to immediately fall asleep. She rested in the front seat next to Euterpe with her head bobbing back and forth and her mouth agape. If Elpee was snoring, it could not be heard over the deafening clamor of the pay-loader. The *Queen* laughed each time she hit a bump or rut in the road, and Elpee's body was catapulted off the seat and into midair. On one of these exceedingly violent hurls, the princess's body did a somersault, and upon its return from the atmosphere above the truck, landed in the back seat. Poor Butter was nearly squished by the descending body, but he managed to jump, just in the nick of time, into the front seat to take his master's place.

"Let's get your friend and ride on the sand,
"we'll drive on the beach 'til we hit dry land.
"Your mother will sleep, and the secret will keep,
"until it is time to be done with this crime," Euterpe said to Butter.

The word *crime* made his ears stand up and his lips flap, out of the terror of being jailed for what they were doing. For reasons known only to him, the canine was frightened by only one thing on the planet, and that was jail. Euterpe, seeing the distress on the animal's face, attempted to calm him down.

"Don't be scared you, little boy,
"we'll get your friend and a toy.
"You two can play while I drive,
"until the place, we do arrive.
"I only kid about the crime,
"sometimes I just can't help but rhyme."

The *Queen* paid no more attention to the canine sitting beside her. She merely stopped in front of Hortense's mansion and yelled for Pippy.

"Pippy, oh, PippyLou.

"Your friend Butter is here for you."

Out of the house like a rocket came a grotesque, beast-like creature. It was some other kind of being who walked to the truck on two legs with Pippy next to him on a leash.

"Hello, my name is Chucklpe, and this is my fiancée's dog, Pippin. Who are you?"

"Fiancé, my hiney, Hortense must be blindey.

"The dog's name is Pippy. Got that, Zippy?

"Now give him to me, or I'll bite your knee.

"Ta-ta, for now, is all I say.

"You really need to get out of my way," *Queen* Euterpe commanded rather regally of the ominous-looking man as Pippy jumped up and into the front seat on top of Butter, who did not avoid being squished this time.

Astonishingly, Elpee slept through all the stops and starts, bumps, and conversations. Soon it would be time to return to her cottage to view the result of all the work that was being done there while the two women and two dogs rode the beach. Every few miles Euterpe would stop their forward motion, lower the bucket, and scoop a mound of sand for the dogs to climb up, down, roll around, and play on. With the sun getting lower in the sky, it was time to head back to Cherry Cottage, which by now was almost a proper castle, and awaken Elpee to the surprise that awaited her.

As they pulled up in front of the cottage, both dogs jumped out and ran up to the door. Pippy grabbed the handle with her, or his teeth, and Butter pushed the bottom open with his butt, letting themselves into the house. They waited impatiently for the *Queen* to wake up the princess and for both women to enter the house.

"You must wake up and go inside,

"you slept for the entire ride.

"You were so sleepy I must say,

"now go inside, be on your way."

Once again, Elpee obediently climbed out of the earthmover and went inside her darkened home. There she was met with at least five hundred pairs of beady, black eyes set against a background of white staring at her.

Afraid to move, the princess froze in place, as she thought that it was another kaleidoscope moment. She was overcome with fear because she did not want to go back into that black hole and she certainly did not want to move again. She wanted to stay at the cottage and live in the house that she fought so hard to reclaim from Anna.

"Not the kaleidoscope, please, oh, please," Elpee pleaded aloud to the Universe.

From somewhere beyond her field of vision came a voice that said, "You are right. It was in the tea leaves, just as the kaleidoscope was, but it is not the same."

"Spiders?" Elpee asked.

The answer to her question was a nonverbal, deafening noise, followed by Euterpe's giggling. It was the same earsplitting noise that kept Elpee awake night after night. What had Euterpe and the spiders been doing out there, she wondered?

To combat the darkness, danDay-leon and PoliM'aladroit each lit lamps that were located around the living room. The spiders parted, and Elpee was able to see the reason for the nightly noise. While Euterpe took her on their joyride, her arachnid friends hung their most beautiful spider-spun lace curtains in all the windows of the cottage. Even the junior spiders shared in making the curtains, and although the ones that adorned the downstairs bathroom window were somewhat askew, they were uniquely beautiful.

CALLED ON THE CARPET

To celebrate her new, old house and to express her appreciation, Elpee invited the two princesses and one *Queen* to stay for cheese and crackers and a freshly brewed pot of tea. She also encouraged the spiders, the two dogs, and the small gray creature to play with each other.

"Go ahead, Butterball. You can go play with your eight-legged friends. I don't mind. Show your cousin Pippy how to do it. I don't think he or she has ever had a spider pal before," Elpee said, giving Butter permission to get slobbered up.

PippyLou jumped right into the action, perhaps too eagerly, because the target of his/her attention immediately spun a rope-like web onto the animal's face, causing it to jump backward in defense. With his/her beautiful black face and brown eyes stained by the netting that covered them, Pippy decided to sit out that game and only watch.

"I met a man at Hortense's house,
"who had a face just like a grouse.
"He had feathered legs and feathered feet,
"I do not deem him very sweet.
"He called the big dog by the name of Pippin.
"I really wanted to give him a whippin'.
"And, Hortense wants to marry him?
"Her chance for happiness is mighty slim," Euterpe pronounced.

"I DON'T CARE. I DON'T CARE, I DON'T CARE!" Elpee kept repeating over and over as she stuffed her fingers into her ears to avoid hearing anything further about her rogue cousin.

Elpee could see the other women's mouths moving but happily could not hear what they were saying. Her eyes went from woman to woman, focusing on the one whose lips were currently moving, and continued this until they appeared to have exhausted the conversation.

"I will not entertain any conversation that involves Chucklpe, Hortense, marriage, or any combination thereof. If you ladies would like to continue your discussion, please take it elsewhere, as . . . I DON'T CARE!"

"My dear, we were discussing how beautiful your house looks, and in so short a time," responded danDay-leon.

"Oh . . ." was all Elpee could say to that pronouncement. They each shook their heads at her, as if implying that an apology might be in order

In unison, they smiled and nodded at her in a show of agreement for accepting her unspoken admission of guilt. With that out of the way, Elpee felt free to blurt out, "Where's Alpert?"

Again in harmony, all of the women's smiles faded into scowls, and their nods were replaced with heads that were shaking back and forth in displeasure.

Frustrated, she stood with her hands on her hips and decried, "Come on. I want to know where he is. I have a right to know. What is it with all the secrets, and why only when it concerns me? You all seem to know what is going on. It's not right . . . Not fair, I tell you. Spit it out, ladies, give me the info," Elpee said, half out of exasperation and half with an air of confidence that she hoped would bully them into telling her.

Euterpe danced around singing to herself, while danDay-leon kept sipping her tea if indeed there was any left in her cup. PoliM'aladroit was the only one who even acknowledged Elpee's discourse.

"My dear, I told you we could not speak on this issue until the day after next week. Now, let us drop it until that time."

"And when in blue blazes is that, PoliM'aladroit?" Elpee asked as she stood defiantly in front of the senior princess with her hands on her hips, expecting an answer.

The princess of ShinyShores disregarded Elpee's question, which infuriated the red-faced princess of Cherry Cottage even more.

"That's it. I'm calling you on the carpet, PoliM'aladroit," Elpee warned her.

"What exactly does that phrase mean, dear? I never quite understood its connotation," asked danDay-leon.

"I have no idea, but for now it means that tomorrow morning is the 'day after next week' and we will all meet again then to air the dirty laundry. I mean it, ladies. I have rights, you know?" Elpee concluded as she sat down with her hands still on her hips.

REALITY

———

Elpee woke early the next morning in excited anticipation of hearing news regarding Alpert and his whereabouts. She sat on the porch sofa waiting for her friends to arrive but would get restless and wander about the rest of her home, taking in its newfound warmth and charm before ultimately returning to the porch to again wait. Elpee knew danDay-leon would not arrive a minute before the other two women, lest the truth be squeezed out of her by the overly nosy Princess of Cherry Cottage. danDay would remain by her window, peering out of it to see when the time was right for her to walk across the street to join the others.

The first to arrive was Euterpe on another borrowed mode of transportation. This time, the *Queen* had absconded with someone's scooter and was spotted by Elpee riding it back and forth in front of her house.

"Come on in, 'terpe. Put the scooter in the yard before someone steals your stolen goods."

"I borrow,

"'til tomorrow,

"with no trace of sorrow,

"for that which I borrow.

"So there, mon frère!" Euterpe stated as she entered the house and sat down emphatically.

Elpee sat lovingly next to her, noticeably trying to charm her, which prompted the *Queen* to declare, "I shall not say,

"until the day,

"that PoliM'aladroit comes to stay.

"My lips are sealed,

"and can't be peeled,

"No way José,

they're shut to stay."

"Oh, poop!" was Elpee's response.

Soon enough, what appeared to be the guest of honor along with her small gray creature arrived on her bicycle, disembarking in the usual manner – a sideways stumble ending with her derriere on the ground. It was becoming the norm for PoliM'aladroit to exit from her transporter in that way, and were it not for danDay-leon crossing the walk at the same time, PoliM'aladroit would have been left to negotiate the up-righting of herself alone; a choice she would have preferred to accepting another's help to do so.

When all the women were inside the house, all the dogs within the garden, and all the vehicles in the yard, the conference could then begin. Elpee suggested that they sit at the dining room table to be able to face one another. They all agreed and sat on the newly cushioned, but ancient, Chippendale dining chairs. Not that she wanted any of them to be deprived, but Elpee chose not to serve refreshments while they discussed the matter, as it might serve as a distraction or a diversion, and she wanted everyone's full attention and disclosure.

"I know you two," Elpee began her well-rehearsed speech while looking at danDay-leon and Euterpe, "will defer to PoliM'aladroit to explain the secrecy of Alpert's location . . . Like he committed the crime of the century or something."

With the pronouncement of those words, danDay-leon began furiously fanning herself with her hand, and Euterpe started whispering to herself in verse.

"WHAT? What did I say? Somebody say something," Elpee anxiously asked all of them.

danDay-leon kept fanning, and Euterpe kept burbling, leaving Elpee to pose her questions and comments directly to the Princess of ShinyShores.

"Okay, PoliM'aladroit, it looks like you and I will be the only participants in this exchange of words, so I have asked my question more times than I can remember and I have deemed this day to be the day after next week. Therefore, it is now your turn to speak. Hopefully, you will forthrightly answer me," Elpee said candidly.

Sitting rigidly straight in her chair, PoliM'aladroit looked directly at Elpee and said, "Jail. Alpert is in jail."

"Excuse me? Could you repeat that?" Elpee quakingly asked of her.

"I said Alpert is in jail. Incarcerated, prison, penitentiary, the slammer, the big house," PoliM'aladroit said, in compliance with Elpee's request.

"I think I get that part of it. Now, may I ask why? I mean, what could he have done that was so terrible that he is behind bars for?" Elpee asked.

"Well," PoliM'aladroit said, "here is where it gets sticky."

"Shtickey shmickey!

"Because of you and the clay,

"Alpert was sent far away," Euterpe announced when it became too torturous and she could hold her tongue no longer.

"Euterpe, why would you say that so brashly?" scolded PoliM'aladroit. "I was taking my time and trying to be gentle with my explanation."

"There is no time better than now,

"to discuss the crime and to help him how.

"Poor Elpee waits for us to tell,

"how Alpert wound up in the bowels of hell.

"She has a right to help us fight,

"so let's go with the flow and get on with the show," Euterpe stated, defending herself.

"'terpe is right. Enough dancing around the issue. If Alpert's in trouble, I want to help him, and as soon as possible, especially if it is my fault or because of me. Oh, stop babying me, PoliM'aladroit," Elpee said, with tears of frustration showing in her eyes.

"All right, my dear, I will explain it to you as best as I can," said PoliM'aladroit to the forlorn Princess of Cherry Cottage.

THE GORY DETAILS

"You see, although Alpert is not a *wizard* in the true sense of the word, he is bound by their rules and code of ethics, which addresses, as Anna put it, their 'chain of command'. Anna knew very well the rules and pecking order of the white wizards, and she chose to use that knowledge in the blackest of manners to satisfy her own needs while destroying others in the process. How she came to you in the first place when you were spit out of the kaleidoscope, I don't know, but when she came to you after that, she told you that there was a chain of command, which was true, and that Alpert sent her—*that* was *not* true. She could never reveal herself to Alpert because Anna knew that he would be onto her. So that is why, when that she-devil appeared to you in the woods, she told you that she could only come to you if Alpert were to leave. And later when she found out that Alpert was on another case and was therefore unavailable, she began her invasion and showed her true self by commencing to take over your life, knowing there was nothing Alpert could do to rescue you."

Taking a deep breath, PoliM'aladroit paused and shifted in her seat. "May I have a glass of water before I continue, please?"

Not at all happy with the interruption in the explanation, Elpee grudgingly went into the kitchen and returned with a pitcher of ice water and a stack of glasses that she placed on the table. She thought that by doing so, there would be water enough for all of them, thereby avoiding any further interruptions. PoliM'aladroit poured herself a glass, took a long swig, placed the glass back on the table, and continued.

"Where was I?" PoliM'aladroit asked.

"Anna knew Alpert was busy and couldn't help me – " Elpee began, but having jarred PoliM'aladroit's memory sufficiently, was cut off by her.

"Oh, yes, I remember now. So, Anna, believing she was in a win-win position, jumped in headlong and took over."

"Wait," Elpee interrupted. "What do you mean she was in a 'win-win' position?"

"Because Alpert was engaged in a case elsewhere, she had free rein over your home and your life, putting her in a winning position."

"And the other win?" Elpee once again interrupted.

"She did not believe that Alpert would abandon his duty by leaving his other case, which technically he did not because he got a resident non-wizard to replace him. She firmly believed he would not do this because she knew the consequences he would face if he did."

"Jail?"

"Worse, my dear. You see, jail was just the beginning, but we will get to that in a moment. So, Anna believed that if Alpert did not come, she was the victor, and if he did come she would also prevail because he would be ruined. The one thing she did not take into account was your spirit and resolve. She viewed you as the poor and weak misguided soul she met long ago, certainly not a force to be reckoned with, no less defeated by. The way in which you accomplished that was brilliant, I must say, using her own calling card, the whistle, to cast her in clay for all eternity."

"Thanks, PoliM'aladroit, but can we get back to Alpert, please?"

"Humph. Fine. After we left you that night when we all visited, Alpert was arrested, and we did not know his fate until recently. DO NOT ASK ME HOW," the Princess of ShinyShores, admonished Elpee by holding her hand up in a gesture of warning. "I will not say because it is irrelevant. He was given three options in jail. The first was to give up his position for all eternity. The second choice was to retain his position and not return here for all eternity. And, in the absence of the first two, the third was to remain in jail . . . As you may guess . . . For all eternity."

"Oh, my! I don't know what to think or say. What should we do?" Elpee asked, more of herself than of any of the other princesses.

"There is nothing we can do. Alpert made his choice," PoliM'aladroit stated dispassionately. "The die has been cast."

"Poop! I'm not so sure that's true. Perhaps it is quite the opposite, that he has made no choice and therefore remains in prison by default."

"What do you mean by that?" asked danDay-leon.

"I mean, if he made a decision to remain in jail, then what PoliM'al-adroit said may be true. Or, if he consciously made a decision *not to* make a decision, then it would be true again. But, I don't believe either instance is accurate. As a matter of fact, I know they are not the truth. I know Alpert, and I know he is feeling defeated and demoralized by allowing someone like Anna to snare him the way she did. I also know that he cares enough about all of us to not opt for door number two, or he would never have come here with all of you to rescue me," explained Elpee.

"I am beginning to understand your concept, but you will need to expand on it a bit further for me to agree with you on it," PoliM'aladroit said.

"I agree," seconded danDay-leon.

"Tell us, Elpee,

"we need helpee.

"Remember the sign?

"Help us make our thoughts align," chimed in *Queen* Euterpe.

"What I'm saying is that Alpert is paralyzed right now. He can't make a decision because he is incapable. The dear man is too emotionally frayed to do anything. He is in more of a jail in his mind than the one that imprisons his body. We need to help him, or his spirit will surely die long before his body does." Elpee could say no more. She had pleaded her case, and it was now the other princesses' turn to speak to her proposal.

"What can we do? What if what we decide to do is the wrong decision?" asked danDay-leon.

"Do you think he wants to remain in jail? Do you think that is his decision?" Elpee asked in return.

"No."

"Well, do you think he never wants to come here and see us again?" Elpee asked danDay-leon.

"I don't think so, but what if he wants to stay a wizard?" danDay-leon waveringly replied.

"If he had wanted to stay a wizard he would have told them that and been out of jail already," Elpee explained to the confused princess.

"Oh, I don't know. What if . . ." danDay-leon seemed at a loss for words and could not continue.

"danDay, you have got to do better than, 'Oh, I don't know' and 'What if.' Our friend's life and sanity are on the line. We have to do something, and if you all won't help me, I will just have to do it myself," Elpee asserted to all of the potential accomplices as she stood up boldly with visible conviction and determination.

danDay fiddled and was unsure of what to do or say as Euterpe flitted her usual flit-self, and PoliM'aladroit quietly asked Elpee, "What do you propose we do, my dear?"

"Bust him out, of course!"

THE WORLD ACCORDING TO THE *QUEEN*

———————

All the princesses waited for some profound words of wisdom to come spewing from the other's lips, but none came. danDay-leon's eyes grew more prominent with the look of trepidation fixed in them. Elpee sat back down in her chair, just staring at PoliM'aladroit, ready to catch the first syllable that she uttered, and Euterpe fluttered about humming, dancing, and giggling to herself. Just as Elpee felt that she might explode, a voice rang out and began speaking in verse as only Euterpe could.

"Let's go, let's go, we have seeds to sow.

"I can wait no more, my brain is sore.

"So, please let's hurry, no need to worry.

"Let's be on our way. We'll be there in a day.

"Thursday is good, and we'll all wear a hood.

"'Tis All Hallow's Eve and a good time to leave.

"We will go get the wizard and leave them a gizzard.

"It's to show our thanks and avoid any pranks.

"Besides, it's the date for Hortense and mate,

"to tie the knot, right here on the spot.

"So what do you say? Shall we be on our way?

"No need for delay. Let's seize the day."

Everyone in the room, especially Elpee, looked at Euterpe in astonishment. Individually, danDay-leon now had eyes the shape and size of dinner plates, Elpee was frozen in place with her mouth agape, and PoliM'aladroit took it upon herself to break the silence.

"What is that you say, my dear? Oh, that is right . . . It should come as no surprise, as Elpee's cousin, Chucklpe, did give that date in his letter to her. All the same, is it so that the Princess of Grouse Hollow is to be wed on Thursday of the next week?" she asked.

"That's what I said.

"Why is Elpee so red?

"Is she right in the head,

"or should she go to bed?"

Without waiting or giving anyone a chance to respond, *Queen* Euterpe continued with a shrug of her shoulders.

"No bother, say me, it is about to be,

"wedded bliss for she and Chucklpe.

"As the moon rises upon the ocean,

"it will be time to put our thing in motion.

"I will gather the goods and make a potion,

"that will help us cause a great commotion.

"We'll be away from here when the lovebirds wed,

"I know it's an occasion that Elpee dread . . . s,

"so, off we will be, to the land of the dead,

"in order to find the wizard instead."

Appearing out of breath and dizzy from all her thinking, Euterpe swooned onto the couch. Once again, all the women remained silent, which was a most unusual occurrence for them. Finally, Elpee awoke from her traumatically induced coma-like state and began ranting and raving, as Alpert would say, 'like a banshee'.

"Are you sure they are going to get married? I don't believe it, not for a moment! I don't care what that chucklehead said in his letter. Neither of them can commit for the long-term. He has done this so many times before, and for heaven's sake Hortense can't even commit to a friendship, do you really think she can commit to a marital union? POOP! I just don't believe it. And another thing, Cousin Chucklpe just blows into town when the mood suits him and leaves just as quickly and unexpectedly. The only thing stable about him is the destruction he leaves in his wake when he has taken all he can from his latest victim."

After taking a breath, Elpee continued. "Well, you know what? That self-centered, inconsiderate, shadow of a person that Hortense is may just deserve the likes of someone of equal standards just like Chucklpe. Good! Let her see what it feels like to be on the receiving end of being used up and abandoned. Let them be tied to each other for as long as they both live, it will save me the trouble of wanting to torture her because I know he will be doing a good enough job of it!

"And another thing," Elpee continued, "how appropriate they should marry on Halloween. That's a statement in and of itself. I just want to . . . To . . ."

Stopping Elpee from expelling any more volumes of venom, PoliM'aladroit changed the subject to the current situation and advised them that a problem existed.

"How are we to stage this rescue of Alpert when we do not even know where he is?"

Not having directed the question to anyone in particular, PoliM'aladroit began to look around the room, hoping for some input on where to initiate the search, when *Queen* Euterpe, apparently having recovered from her swoon, shot up and began anew.

"You're wrong, dear Princess of ShinyShores,
"*Queen* Euterpe knows exactly the doors,
"that need to be opened and where they are.
"Since none of you fly, we will need a car."

"How do you know such a thing?" asked danDay-leon.

"Don't bother yourself over silly things,
"I know enough people and can pull some strings.
"I was just there last week to say hello,
"and on my way out I stubbed my toe . . . Wanna see?" Euterpe asked as she began raising her foot off the floor in preparation for exposing the injured digit.

"NO. I DON'T WANT TO SEE! You have seen him? Visited him? Where? And why didn't you tell us?" asked a frustrated and confused Elpee.

"He is my friend and my support I lend,
"by visiting him so his mood won't descend.
"Any of you could have done the same,
"just because I did, I get the blame?
"It is not a fair thing that you do that to me,
"I forgive you all and will take you to he.
"But not a day, a moment, or a second before,
"the moon is full, the tide high on the shore.
"That in case you don't know is October three one.
"It will be a day that is absent of any sun.
"At half-past something, we will have to go,
"you girls must hurry and not be slow.

"We can't be late,
"or we'll miss the gate.
"And it will close,
"that's all I'll disclose.
"So, goodbye, my friends,
"I accept your amends.
"Say no more of the slight,
"everything is all right.
"But prepare you must,
"you have my trust.
"You girls make a plan,
"and I'll secure the van.
"Ta-ta for now, no need to bow!"

As the last syllable was expelled from her mouth, Euterpe turned and flew out the door, and was not to be seen again until Thursday, October 31, at precisely half-past something.

IN THE WAKE OF THE TORNADO

The three princesses were left spinning in a cloud of dust as *Queen* Euterpe exited on the wings of the wind. The first princess to stop spinning was PoliM'aladroit, who, when she did, abruptly fell over and onto the floor. danDay-leon wobbled sideways for some time before gently coming to rest on the sofa. Poor Elpee, however, kept spinning in circles, picking up speed with each revolution until she was an unstoppable flash of a human top that was ricocheting off walls, which helped propel her into another room – and another – and another. PoliM'aladroit and danDay-leon could do nothing to stop Elpee and the momentum she was gaining. As PoliM'aladroit struggled to get out of the way to avoid being stomped on, danDay ran upstairs, pulled the blanket off a bed, and ran back down the stairs as quickly as she could. She found PoliM'aladroit and gray boy atop the dining room table in an attempt to stay out of harm's way while the two black dogs chased the human top through the house.

"Come here, PoliM'aladroit," commanded danDay-leon. "Hold the other side of this blanket and we'll snare her the next time she comes around."

PoliM'aladroit reluctantly got off the table and grabbed an end of the blanket. Both princesses held a side of the fabric and braced themselves for the return of the human rocket.

"Here she comes," screamed danDay-leon, and with that, they caught the runaway princess and Butter, and Pippy, and eventually themselves, as the speed and forward motion spun everyone into the blanket, creating a giant shroud for them all.

"MMMMMMMmmM"

"shp, shh, sheh"

"Arghf, Arghf"

"AOOOOH"

"WAH"

A cacophony of muffled bellows overflowed from inside the cloth cave.
wiggle, wiggle, wiggle
thump, thump, thump
wiggle, thump, wiggle
thump, thump, wiggle

A wiggle and a thump and another thump and one more wiggle and PoliM'aladroit was either born from the cloth or resurrected from the shroud. Her birth/rebirth in turn afforded the same opportunity for her siblings in the winding sheet. One by one, they extricated themselves, until at last, all five of them were sitting on Elpee's living room floor. They were quite the sight to behold after having been windblown, tumbled, tussled, and wrapped. When they came to their senses, they looked at each other and laughed, all except Elpee, who was green and appeared to be suffering from vertigo as a result of her cyclonic adventure. Both PoliM'aladroit and danDay-leon, having regained their composure, lifted each other off the floor and then guided Elpee to the sofa. They propped her up and positioned pillows all around her, hoping that soon she would recover. Elpee remained in that position, and eventually, an ashen gray color replaced her earlier green complexion. She did not move or speak to the others because she was afraid to shift anything on her body. She planned to remain exactly where she was for the rest of her natural life.

After hours of failed attempts to communicate with Elpee, danDay-leon again untypically took command of the situation. She wrote something on a piece of paper and walked toward Elpee's dog and said, "Butter, go to the gnome hole and give this note to Simon, and if he is unavailable, give it to Camby and only Camby."

The little black dog turned his head and emitted a squeak, "eerrrr?"

"Because she is from France, or so Elpee says, and she may be savvy in these matters," she answered him as she tied the note to his collar.

"And you, Miss Pippy, stay here with us. We don't need the two of you gallivanting all over creation when there is a mission right here that needs to be accomplished," danDay advised the large black dog, who immediately and deliberately threw itself on the floor in protest while expelling a giant sigh.

"Go! Stay!" danDay-leon said while pointing at the appropriate dogs for each command.

And so they did!

POLIM'ALADROIT GETS NOSY

Not wanting to look as if she lacked in her intuition or knowledge, PoliM'aladroit said nothing, but wondered nonetheless, what danDay-leon was up to. To appear knowledgeable, yet at the same time disinterested, PoliM'aladroit fawned over the stiff and gray Princess of Cherry Cottage, who remained immobile and rigid on the sofa. In the quietness, time seemed to pass very slowly as they waited for Butter to return home. danDay-leon was busy doing something out in the kitchen, and PoliM'aladroit tried to figure out what it was. Dare she swallow her pride and ask danDay-leon, she quizzed herself? No sooner had the thought been born than a very audible "No" was expelled from PoliM'aladroit's lips. There was her answer! She would just have to wait to see what it was all about. That, although a simple concept, was definitely easier said than done for the princess, who was normally the one in charge of the goings-on.

All the clattering that danDay-leon was doing out in the kitchen made it harder for PoliM'aladroit to exercise patience. It was entirely the same as Chinese water torture, but altogether different of course. Nonetheless, be it the same or different, the effects were just as maddening to its victim, which in this case was PoliM'aladroit.

She sat on her hands, hummed in her head, rolled her eyes, and when she began shaking her whole body, PoliM'aladroit realized she had adopted poor Elpee's persona in the ill princess's absence. How on Earth could that have happened to her, PoliM'aladroit wondered? She dearly loved the Princess of Cherry Cottage, but she, in no way, shape, or form wanted to emulate her, so ShinyShores' own princess took it as a sign to leave the room in which Elpee remained catatonic. She rose and walked to the kitchen, which also gave PoliM'aladroit an opportunity to spy on danDay-leon and to investigate just what was going on.

When she entered the kitchen, she found danDay-leon profoundly engrossed in what she was doing. There were pots and pans, rubber tubing, strainers, and infusers everywhere. A crock of wildflower honey was slowly being warmed in a double boiler on the stove, while lying open on the counter was a linen handkerchief and a length of satin ribbon sitting beside it. Unwilling to ask any questions, PoliM'aladroit closely observed danDay-leon's every movement in an attempt to decipher the purpose of the ritual she was witnessing. The Princess of Teacup Manor went outside and disappeared off to the south side of the yard, and while she was gone, PoliM'aladroit snooped around the kitchen, trying to uncover the mystery, but because their inclinations were so very different from each other, PoliM'aladroit knew it would be hopeless. She, once again, would have to either ask or wait, and once again, she chose the latter.

Shortly after PoliM'aladroit's latest decision to wait was made, danDay-leon re-entered the kitchen with an armful of flowers and what appeared to be weeds. She placed them all on the kitchen table that she had cleared earlier and began snipping away at them.

"A bit of lavender, a pinch of cinnamon, a dash of geranium, and a worm's eyelash of sage," danDay-leon uttered aloud. "Any suggestions?" danDay-leon naively asked the other princess, whom she believed to be equally and as intently present as she was.

"Before I am able to supply you with any suggestions, what, may I ask, is it for?" PoliM'aladroit replied.

"The sachets, of course!" responded danDay-leon most indignantly, having felt mocked by PoliM'aladroit's question to her question. Before danDay had a chance to lose her mind completely, Butter came prancing in the kitchen door and sat down, waiting to be relieved of his overly filled saddlebags.

"Thank you, my boy!" danDay exclaimed as she bent down to release him from his burden. "You are such a good boy. Did you get everything, and if so, are there instructions with them for me?"

Butter nodded his head in the affirmative and was ready for some playtime with Pippy when his thought process was interrupted by danDay-leon's continued conversation with him.

"You must go inside and sit with your master; she should not be left alone. *Someone* else was sitting with her, BUT . . . She got too nosy and left the princess by herself so that she could satisfy her own curiosity. I won't be long in doing this because *someone* is going to help me prepare these flowers and herbs. Now scoot! Inside on the couch."

Reluctantly, Butter complied, and PippyLou joined him in the living room where they both sat looking at the bug-eyed princess.

"Make yourself useful and construct some sachets. There are more handkerchiefs and ribbons in my bag. Remember, a bit, a pinch, a dash, and a worm's eyelash – lavender, cinnamon, geranium, and sage. Leave approximately half the amount of each herb, and I will place them in a bowl of spring water," danDay-leon ordered PoliM'aladroit, as she herself separated what was given to her by Butter. There was ginger root, lemon verbena, lemongrass, and several other ingredients of which she was not familiar. danDay studied the directions Camby and Simon enclosed, and made sure she followed them to a tee. Surprisingly, PoliM'aladroit got the knack of what she needed to do rather quickly and was done before the other princess was. She awaited further instructions before doing anything else, and when danDay-leon could see out of the corner of her eye that PoliM'aladroit had completed her task, she said, "Please bring half of the sachets into where Elpee is and surround her with them. Then, take the rest upstairs along with the remainder of the herbs, which you will need to place in a bowl of spring water."

PoliM'aladroit, acting thoroughly out of character, wholly complied without clamoring.

THE POTION IS BREWED

By the time PoliM'aladroit returned from upstairs, where she had garnished Elpee's bedroom with sachets galore and placed the bowl of herbs and spring water on the dresser, danDay-leon was done in the kitchen. The two princesses met again in Elpee's living room and would shortly join forces to help the bedraggled princess regain a degree of normalcy. They each took a side, danDay-leon on Elpee's right and PoliM'aladroit on her left.

"Open your mouth, dear. I've made some delicious tea for you. It will make you feel better," danDay encouraged Elpee, to no avail. Elpee remained motionless, not daring to move even her eyes.

PoliM'aladroit then attempted to coax her, "Please open your mouth and drink this wonderful blend of tea danDay-leon prepared just for you."

Once again, there was no response from the bug-eyed princess. This tag-team approach at persuasion being used by danDay-leon and PoliM'aladroit was futile, and Butter was getting restless. He felt he deserved a reward for abandoning his friend to do their bidding and could contain himself no longer. Unlike his usual gut-wrenching, ear-piercing clamor, Butter began barking a most unusual bark, to which Pippy responded in kind. Soon, the canines were communicating via a bark-a-rama that could not be silenced by either of the princesses who were able to speak.

Suddenly, all the barking and such stopped. Both black dogs jumped on the sofa until they pulled and pushed the catatonic princess to the floor, causing danDay-leon and PoliM'aladroit to resemble Elpee in her frozen gaze. With Elpee flat out like a pinwheel that was pasted to the floorboards, Butter stood between her arms that were extended over her head in the shape of a V, while PippyLou did the same with her lower extremities. She resembled Da Vinci's Vitruvian Man as the dogs slowly began to walk in a counterclockwise direction, forming a circle around her. They dug their paws in as best as they could, pushing the rigid princess along in the process until they gained the momentum they needed. One revolution, two revolutions, three, four, five, and they were off, each dog chasing the other until they reached speeds never attempted by dog or princess before. As they ran in circles, Elpee spun with them, faster and faster, until they heard a voice coming from the vortex.

"HEY! KNOCK IT OFF!"

The animals slowed down as quickly as they could and soon came to a stop, and with that stop, Elpee immediately stood up and looked around the room at all its inhabitants.

"Thanks, boy, and you. You spun me backward and undid what Euterpe did. COOOOOL!" Elpee said. "You'd better do the same for yourselves, though, 'cause you both look a little washed out . . . Kinda pale, actually."

With a little encouragement and direction from Elpee, Pippy and Butter began chasing each other's tails and spinning themselves right. The other two princesses could do little more than shake their heads in amazement as they returned to the kitchen with the undrunk potion. Elpee remained in the living room to monitor the canines' progress and to ensure that they did not over spin backward in their effort to right themselves. She could not watch them directly because she was not yet far enough removed from her own spinning session, so she surveyed their progress from their reflection in the mirror that hung over the fireplace. As she glanced into it, her mind wandered to one of the faraway lands in which she lived and how her house there was equipped with mirrors that never reflected anything ugly back to her. Elpee snapped herself out of what could have been a long journey that would take her to times and places better not revisited at this moment. Pippy and Butter were slowing down and were almost stopped when she returned to real time in her living room.

"Okay, animals, five minutes of rest out in the fresh air and then you two can go play. But I want you both to rest for the whole five minutes to give your brains a chance to do what brains need to do after you've put them in a body spinner," Elpee advised the anxious dogs as they headed out the back door to reluctantly comply with her conditions.

"And don't be rolling your eyes at me either. That will slow your brains' progress down," Elpee told them before lowering her voice to a frightful tone. "Or worse, I fear."

Both dogs abruptly stopped and turned to look at her, concerned about their already fragile wits.

"Only kidding!" the master and aunt-master snickered as she playfully assured them. Thinking it not one bit funny, both dogs wrinkled their noses, curled their lips up at her, and ran out the door, casting off her admonishments as silly talk.

Elpee joined danDay-leon and PoliM'aladroit in the kitchen, where they were cleaning up the mess made from brewing the tea concoction.

"Are you ready?" Elpee asked them.

"Ready? For what, my dear?" PoliM'aladroit asked.

"Duh. To get Alpert," she responded irreverently, but not maliciously, while rolling her eyes at them.

"We must wait until Thursday when Euterpe returns for us," PoliM'aladroit advised her.

"Oh, come on . . . Let's go. I can't wait 'til then. And besides, you know how Euterpe can try your patience, and unnerve danDay. I think . . ."

"She most certainly does not try my patience," replied the Princess of ShinyShores. "However, if you would like to discuss people who *do* try my patience, I am more than willing to do so."

Understanding what and whom PoliM'aladroit was referring to, Elpee exited the kitchen, as she thought it was best to let sleeping dogs lie, at least for now.

THE MAJESTIC FERN

———

Elpee went out the screen door on the front porch and turned left into the gated area to inspect the state of her garden. As she entered the planting area, Elpee realized that it might be a prudent decision not to leave straight away on their trip to break Alpert out, since the garden surely needed some tending. The season had been somewhat mild, and she was deceived into thinking there was more time than there actually was to accomplish that task. Since Hortense abandoned her friends and Elpee's garden, the mistress of Cherry Cottage just could not get a handle on things.

"And how are you, madam?" Elpee asked Edith, the mask with the purple beret that hung low on the neighbor's fence.

"I see. Well, no bother, I will retire you to the south of France for the winter by tomorrow at the latest. Thank you for your understanding, and my apologies for not making those arrangements sooner. Have a lovely evening," Elpee said before going to the next mask, and the next, and so on.

The Princess checked all the masks and advised them that they would be vacationing for the winter in their paradise of choice. Cleo, of course, chose Egypt; *the boys* wanted to go back to Brooklyn so they could call each other Measles Mug, Captain Cauliflower Head, and Chief My Face is Dripping, freely and unnoticed; while the rest of the crew wanted to visit their families at home. She would send them all on their way, via the pottery shed in the backyard tomorrow morning. Although Anna disposed of all the supplies Elpee had in the back cottage, the shelves and storage cabinets remained intact.

As she walked along the boardwalk, Elpee viewed the rocks and heard the muffled grumbling of the usual malcontents.

"Vacation time! Starting tomorrow, all of you who want a respite can take one. There will be no more traffic or visitors for you to be bothered with, so you can all relax come sundown tomorrow," Elpee announced over their complaining.

She continued on to inspect the remainder of Cherry Cottage's gardens and spotted the houseplants, which she had neglected to return to their proper places inside the cottage.

"OH MY, OH, MY, OH MY. OH MY! I am sorry. Hurry, hurry, let's get inside before you catch your deaths of cold," she cried.

Quickly, Elpee filled her arms with as many of the potted greeneries as she could carry at one time and began transporting them indoors. It seemed that her concern was for naught, because they were all hale and hearty and none were worse for the extended season they were given. After securing all the plants inside, Elpee made one last trip to the garden for a final inspection. There, off in shady corner, she spotted the fern who had insisted that she treat it like its brother and sister plants and that it be allowed to live in its natural habitat. It did not, however, fare as well as its siblings had, and appeared pale, weak, and sickly. Elpee bent to pick it up and hug it back to strength, but the fern recoiled at her touch.

"What?" she asked. "I'm not going to hurt you. I am only going to bring you inside with the others and make you a nice warm mixture of fish oil emollient to make you stronger."

The fern would not hear of it and would not budge no matter how much Elpee tried to coax it to move indoors. Finally, exasperated and in desperation, Elpee sat on the damp ground next to the fern and put her arm around it lovingly.

"I am so sorry. I did this to you. I should never have put you out here. The summer took its toll on you and then I was derelict in returning you to the house, and you must have caught a chill, and now . . . Oh, it's all my fault," the forlorn princess said as she wept with both her arms now around the fern.

As she sat there, she could see through her tears that something was happening around her. All the creatures of the garden gathered around to where the fern and Elpee were seated. They were busily going about some sort of business that Elpee could not figure out, nor did she care to. The worms wriggled, the ants pulled, and the beetles chewed as they carved a discernable message into the grass. As Elpee waited, she continued talking to the fern, expressing her guilt while at the same time trying to persuade it to come into the cottage. She promised all sorts of things, but the plant would not be swayed. The insects parted ways and returned to whence they had come. Elpee released her grip on the fern, dried her eyes, and began to read what they wrote.

"YOU DID NOTHING WRONG AND EVERYTHING RIGHT. YOU LOVED ME ENOUGH TO GIVE ME THE GIFT OF LIFE WHEN OTHERS DOOMED ME TO A MERE EXISTENCE. YOU RESPECTED MY WISHES AND AFFORDED ME THE OPPORTUNITY TO EXPERIENCE FREEDOM. IF IT ALL ENDED TOMORROW, I WOULD REGRET NOTHING AND NEITHER SHOULD YOU. THANK YOU, MY FRIEND."

Knowing that there was nothing else she could say or do to change the fern's mind, Elpee resigned herself to the inevitable. Despite the pain she felt at the fern's decision, Elpee knew that all she could do was respect its wishes and allow it to live its life the way it chose. She went inside and upstairs to the hall closet, where she found a dark green blanket she knew was hidden in the back. She took it out, went back outside to the fern, and gently placed it around it to shelter it from the evening's dipping temperatures.

"I hope you don't mind that I put the blanket around you. I chose this one especially for you because it's deep forest green, the color of the most majestic of ferns, just like you are. Thank you for being so faithful and for the kind words you expressed to me. I will never forget them. Sleep well, my friend," Elpee said before giving the fern one last hug and going into the house alone.

PRAY-EMBRACE?

———

The next few days dragged by for Elpee even though she was busy preparing to bust her friend, Alpert, out of jail. She was anxious to get there – wherever 'there' was. Euterpe did not give her or the other princesses any details of where they were going or how long it would take them to get there. She would have to wait, impatiently or not, and accept that she had no control over the situation, and even if she did, she should not have, because she did not know what to do.

Elpee went out to the south garden multiple times every day to check on the condition of the fern, and each of those times it appeared weaker and frailer than the previous one. On those visits, Elpee, in her determination to honor the fern's wishes, never again broached the subject of returning it to its place on the staircase landing. One warm afternoon, the Princess of Cherry Cottage spread a blanket on the ground near the fern and lay there in the sun for some time, reaching over occasionally to touch its brittle leaves. While lying there, Elpee focused positive energy on and toward the fern, hoping to heal it despite what she knew was a dismal prospect, but she needed to try.

Soon, she and the other princesses would be leaving to rescue Alpert, and where she was once excited at the prospect, she now felt torn and frightened. As much as Elpee wanted to go to the wizard, she hesitated to leave the plant for fear it would die of neglect while she was away. Elpee should be doing more to prepare for the trip, but she could not tear herself away from the garden until two days before their departure date when danDay-leon walked across the street and entered Elpee's garden.

"Are you all ready for our trip? Have you packed? Are you excited? Or scared? Why are you sitting on the ground in your garden on October twenty-ninth?" danDay-leon asked her.

"No, I haven't packed. I don't know what to bring or how much," Elpee answered.

"Well, I am bringing one of everything so that I will have enough."

"That's a good idea, but what if Euterpe returns with a go-kart for us to get there in? There won't be any room for all that stuff, danDay."

"Hmm. I will have to think about that. You really should not be sitting on the damp ground. What if you catch a cold and are unable to go? Get up, dear, go inside and pack a bag. Our time to leave will be here before you know it," danDay-leon said before turning around to leave and return to her own house.

Elpee was just as glad that danDay-leon left without pressing her further for an answer about her reason for sitting on the ground. She felt that it was personal and private between the fern and her, and she did not want to discuss it with anyone else. danDay-leon was correct in that the ground was damp despite the warmer temperatures that afternoon, and Elpee knew it was time for her to go inside for the evening. She tucked the blanket snugly around the fern before giving it a good-night hug and retreating to the indoors.

Once inside, Elpee made herself a liverwurst sandwich on rye bread and placed it on a tray next to cheese snacks and a root beer soda. She had intended to eat in the living room but changed her mind and instead carried the tray to the dining room, where she placed it on the table. Elpee sat down, arranged her dinner in front of her, and began to eat. She had little appetite but knew the importance of keeping up her strength for the perilous expedition she and the others were about to undertake. As she sat there staring at her sandwich, Elpee was overcome with anger at the fern for refusing to come into the house, in essence, signing its own death warrant. Maybe, she thought, she should be kidnaping the fern instead of Alpert.

As she sat at the table, pushing her sandwich around on its plate, Elpee looked about the room, and her eyes glanced up at the sign hanging on the wall over the table. The words read, 'Pray-Embrace', or at least in Elpee's mind's eye that was the message it was delivering to her. Elpee blinked her eyes and shook her head before looking again at the sign, which now clearly read as it always had, 'Say Grace'.

"What the heck? Maybe I need glasses or something. Oh wait, I already have them," Elpee asked and answered herself aloud. "'Pray-Embrace', what the devil does that mean? Oh, poop! Who cares anyway? My eyes were just playing tricks on me. I can't eat any more of this sandwich now. I'll wrap it up and save it for later."

After tending to the chores in the kitchen, Elpee, on her way into the living room, passed Butter, who was lying on his bed in front of the heater. He loved to be warm and basked in the heat whenever and wherever he found it. She went upstairs to begin packing, for tomorrow was Wednesday, and Euterpe was returning for them on Thursday. Before entering her bedroom, Elpee stopped briefly in the doorway and smiled. As typical and to her liking, her bed was laden with a swarm of pillows and books, which were strewn about its almost entire surface. She pushed some of her reading material aside to make room for the suitcase she needed to pack. In no mood to attend to this task, Elpee haphazardly placed a change of clothes, as well as her toiletries, inside the traveling drawer. She then began to move the unlocked valise to the rocking chair by the window, but as she passed her writing desk, Elpee tripped on a bone of Butter's and grabbed the desk to keep from falling. As she took hold of a handle on one of the drawers, she inadvertently opened it to find letters upon letters addressed to the Princess of Cherry Cottage by the Sea. Elpee had never seen these correspondences before, and they had all been torn open, unlike Elpee's custom of neatly unsealing her mail with an antique silver and crystal letter opener. Before the addressee of these letters could do anything with the communications, she relocated the suitcase to the rocking chair, then picked up a pile of letters and went downstairs to begin sifting through them.

THE LETTERS . . . NUMBER TWO

Elpee dropped the envelopes on the couch, put a kettle of water on the stove for tea, and lit the fire that she had previously built in the fireplace. When the tea was made, Elpee retired with it to the couch and began reviewing the letters one by one. She did not recognize the handwriting as anyone's she knew and was surprised when she opened the first one, and the signature on it was Alpert's. Elpee read it only in bits and pieces, as she was anxious to move on to the next one. Its contents revealed some sort of concern Alpert had surrounding Elpee. She picked up the next letter, and its author and subject were identical to the previous one; it was Alpert, and he again expressed an unease regarding her.

Elpee knew the handwriting on the next letter as soon as she removed it from its envelope.

Hello My Dear,

No noise I hear, I searched the rear,
you did not appear, how very queer.
It is quite clear you are nowhere near.
Perhaps I fear, you are in Zaire.
What say you, doll face,
did you pack a suitcase,
before you left without a trace?
If that's the case, I must erase,
your pretty face, from my database.
Never you mind, I'm much too kind,
quite refined, and with these combined,
I am not inclined to have your name redlined.

Forget it all, tomorrow I'll call,
so don't be AWOL, or there'll be a brawl.

Ta-ta for now!

Euterpe, the *Queen*

Letter after letter read the same except for the author's names. Most of them expressed curiosity and worry, not so much for where Elpee was, but rather for her lack of response to them. Although it was not out of the ordinary for Elpee not to be at home, her failure to reply to their notes in a timely fashion was unusual and alarming. Having read several letters from each of the princesses, except Hortense of course, and an equal amount from Alpert, Elpee decided to put them aside and go for a much-needed walk before the sun went down. The princess was anything but princessly, as the ire that was generated by the she-demon, Anna, and her interception of Elpee's communication with the outside world built within her.

As she exited the cottage, Elpee had to refuse Butter's generous offer to go with her, for she needed time that was undistracted to think and clear the anger from her head and heart. As she walked to the beach, fleeting thoughts entered Elpee's consciousness before they were able to amalgamate and exit her mouth.

"So long ago, back in that place I came from, I used to look out those cloudy windows and wonder on which side the danger existed. I was taught that the monsters lived outside those windows, and that's why I came here – to be safe and happy, but then it happened again. They were wrong – the monsters live within and among us, if we allow them to. How could it happen again? How could I *let* it happen? I am so angry! I am angry with myself that I was duped by that devil and that I allowed someone to come into my home and make it and me unsafe. I feel like such a dope . . . A failure. I don't think I will ever get this life thing down. I just don't."

Elpee spent as much time as she could indulging her anger with and disappointment in herself before forcing herself to return home to the duties that awaited her there. As she walked up the stairs from the ocean, Elpee tried with all her might not to look at Hortense's house at the top of the dunes, but she was unsuccessful. Her glance in that direction revealed that the building appeared to be winterized, with everything secured and the storm shutters down as if she had gone somewhere for the winter.

"She's probably going off to sail the seven seas with that nitwit cousin of mine. An extended honeymoon, I suppose."

Elpee stopped in her tracks, looked away from Hortense's house, took a breath, and reminded herself, "Don't go there, Elpee! You don't want to add fuel to a fire you are trying to extinguish. Yes . . . Yes, you're right. Of course I don't. Thank you," she said aloud to herself, the Universe, and the goddess of common sense.

After meandering back to the cottage, Elpee arrived at her home in a somewhat better mood than she had been in when she left it. Butter greeted her at the screen door by dropping another torn open envelope addressed to her at her feet before turning his butt to her and promptly exiting.

"Butter, I can't take you everywhere, every time. I'm sorry you're angry, but I had to go alone," Elpee replied to his visible butt snub, but he was gone.

"What is this? I'm done reading these stupid letters that only serve to make me feel bad about myself and my inability to judge characters wisely."

With that said, Butter stuck his head out the living room door and onto the porch where his master had migrated to and was now sitting on a rocker with the envelope in her hand.

"Grrrrr . . ."

"Okay! I'll read it, but don't get fresh or demanding with me, mister."

After hearing his master's conditional concession, he once again turned his butt to her, went back into the living room, and returned to his previous location close to the heater.

Elpee removed the letter from the envelope and began reading what she now recognized as Alpert's bold script.

Anna,

I am addressing you directly in this letter, as I know you have read all the ones that I previously have sent to the rightful inhabitant of Cherry Cottage. I am equally sure, at this point, that those letters never reached their intended recipient. As you know, through intercepting my previous correspondence, I am unable, at this time, to venture beyond my current post without sustaining the direst of consequences; therefore, it appears that you have one-upped me. You made sure that I would be otherwise engaged be-fore you executed your plan to relieve the title-holder of Cherry Cottage of her residence and identity. You, being evil incarnate, knew exactly the ways in which to execute this deed by preying on her in the very way that she was accustomed to being preyed upon before she made this her home. I warn you that despite the fact that I am duty-bound elsewhere, should any harm come to Elpee, I will spend all eternity hunting you down, and I will return you to the bowels of hell from whence you came.

J. Alpert VII

As Elpee finished the letter, she began to weep. Anna had perpetrated the perfect hoax on both of them. She realized that it was not her fault, and that Anna had been playing both sides because she was the only one with all the information. She duped even Alpert despite his knowledge and warnings to Elpee about Anna's evilness. He assumed that Elpee was reading the letters in which he disclosed his concern for her and his in-ability to assist her. Alpert unknowingly gave Anna the information that allowed her to do what she did, and in his remorse for having done so, he chose to become derelict in his duties and return to Cherry Cottage with the princesses for a short time the night before Anna's demise.

Overwhelmed with facts and emotion, Elpee locked up the house, gave Butter a carrot, and retired upstairs to her bedroom, where she got under the covers and promptly fell asleep.

WEDNESDAY – THE DAY BEFORE

Elpee awoke refreshed and renewed. All the pieces had fallen into place, and she now understood how everyone had gotten to where they were so she could focus on tomorrow and Alpert's rescue. She went downstairs and made herself a good, strong pot of coffee using her French press machine, which was a gift from Camby, the tall gnome who was either adopted or from France. While the water for the press was boiling on the stove, Elpee let Butter out the back door and off he went, disappearing into the back forest area where the gnomes lived. She would let him play while she drank her coffee, and when done, she would call him into the house for his delicious breakfast of rice, chicken, lettuce, and some dry kibble stuff with warm water poured over it. He then would be treated with a breakfast-dessert of mashed banana.

Elpee poured herself a cup of the dark brown liquid and sat at the dining room table rather than going outside on the back deck or onto the front porch, both of which were too nippy now that is was the end of October. By mid-September, Elpee had abandoned her early morning ritual of having coffee in either place. Soon, she would be having her morning victuals in front of the fireplace. It was a chilly and drafty old house, and she needed to accommodate its nature by moving about and changing her routines within it as the seasons changed. No bother, she thought. She was lucky to have a house large enough to enable her to do that.

As she sat there, her thoughts were on everything, yet nothing at all. Elpee mindlessly looked about and once again believed the sign on the wall conveyed the message, 'Pray-Embrace',

"What the heck? YOU DO NOT SAY THAT! NO, YOU DO NOT! DO YOU HEAR ME?" she loudly commanded the scripture board that hung above her head. "Besides, I don't even know what that means . . . 'Pray-Embrace'. It's stupid, just stupid, I tell you."

Not bothering to look or say anything more, Elpee picked up her coffee cup, went into the living room, and sat on a chair that was out of sight of the dining room altogether. Before rounding up Butter for his morning meal, she tried to clear her mind and concentrate on what needed to be done in preparation for tomorrow's great escape. She went over the checklist in her head and decided that she was as prepared as she was able to be with the information she had, which was basically nothing. When, where, how, how long? None of these questions had answers to which Elpee was privy. She did not even know at what time Euterpe was arriving, or just as importantly, in what manner of transportation they would be traveling. The only thing that mattered was that she did come and that they would be able to rescue Alpert. Being away for Hortense and Chucklpe's wedding was also an added bonus for Elpee. When the princess felt assured that everything was under control, she went to the kitchen, prepared the conglomeration of chow for the canine, and called for him to come into the house to eat it. It took quite some time before the boy responded by returning home from wherever he was playing, but that had become standard for the pooch.

After his first course was finished, Butter waited impatiently for his dessert, as that was the only part of the meal he truly enjoyed. Elpee re-trieved his breakfast bowl from its dining room in the corner of the kitchen floor and began mashing a length of banana in it. Before she could return the banana-laden container to Butter, Elpee had to roll two capsules of natural herbs around in the mush and let him lick it off her fingers. She did not know what these pills were, but danDay-leon gave them to her with instructions to dole out two with breakfast and one with his dinner. On blind faith, Elpee followed those instructions be-cause she knew danDay loved Butterball and would only do good things for him. Elpee could never forget the one last detail that would complete the breakfast tradition, only because her little dog mate would not allow her to. Butter sat by the kitchen sink until his master gave him his ham-burger-flavored, chewable vitamin. His final swallow signaled his exit straight out the back door, where he would go looking for entertainment and his next adventure.

With her coffee drank and Butter fed, Elpee was free to set about exe-cuting all the last-minute details before bringing her suitcase downstairs, where it would sit until tomorrow, when she and it would join Euterpe and the other princesses. She dusted and vacuumed, swept and mopped, and cleaned and straightened. She watered the plants, packed some snacks, and was ready to go, with the exception of one last task she needed to complete. Elpee had to tend to ensuring that the fern was warm and had enough nourishment. The self-taught gardener, determined that she would nurture it back to health and perhaps coax it back into the house, went out to the rear potting shed to fetch the liquid potion she had concocted to nourish the fern.

Elpee, with a fresh cup of coffee and the jar of herbal nutrition in her hands, went outside and around the house toward the front garden where the fern resided. It was not her standard route, and it felt somewhat disorienting to Elpee. From that approach, she could not see the fern; however, she continued on the wooden boardwalk leading to the patch of plants where she knew the plant was. Elpee stopped suddenly as she neared the fern, afraid to advance any further, but she made her feet move in the compulsory forward motion until she reached her destination. There at her feet was what once was her majestic fern. Involuntarily, Elpee dropped her coffee cup and then placed the glass container she was carrying on the ground next to it. She joined both pieces of pottery on the damp earth and knelt down to get closer to the fern until she could see it was no more. Immediately, Elpee's heart began racing, tears filled her eyes, and she became overcome with sadness and guilt for having let this happen.

"Oh, why didn't I take you inside and protect you? This is all my fault. How could I have been so irresponsible?" Elpee whispered as she patted the blanket that enveloped the now gone fern. Softly, the wind delivered to her the words, '*You did nothing wrong and everything right. I regret nothing and neither should you. Thank you, my friend*'.

As Elpee sat on the ground weeping, danDay-leon came out of her house and walked to the enclosure that contained Elpee and asked, "My dear, what is it? I saw you from my kitchen window and came to see why indeed you are once again sitting on the cold ground, this time weeping."

"My fern died. I wanted it to come into the house like the others, but it would not hear of it. It told me that it wanted to stay out here and experience freedom and that if it all ended tomorrow, it would have no regrets because of that experience. Oh, danDay . . . I feel like a bad mother. What am I going to do?"

"You are going to sit on the ground and say your goodbyes. I will go make us a pot of tea, and when I return with it, you must then come into the house with me. That is what you will do," danDay-leon instructed her as she sharply turned around and returned to where she had come from.

TEA AND TISSUES

Elpee stayed seated on the ground next to the fern, shivering from both the cold and her emotions, but she wanted to remain with her friend until the very last minute when danDay would return and command her indoors. Unconsciously, Elpee began speaking to the fern, or perhaps her monologue was directed more at herself.

"I don't know what to say . . . I feel so sad and guilty. Why did I listen to you and leave you out here? Why did I bring you out here at all? Yeah, sure, you wanted to live outside and wouldn't listen to me when I hesitated to honor your request, but I should have known better. I hate this! Why does everyone – even plants – have to swim against the tide and do things their way despite the pain it causes the people they leave behind? Why can't you all see that you have no right to walk into someone's life, steal their heart, and then just walk away? It's not fair. What did I ever do to deserve to be abandoned over and over again? The only thing I ever did was love you, and you all left me and never looked back...All of you."

Elpee sat there sobbing and mumbling question upon question to people and things that were unseen and unable to answer because they were no longer with her. Perhaps she was asking the wrong people or the wrong questions, but most of all maybe there were really no questions, only answers.

Unseen, danDay-leon approached Elpee and touched her shoulder, indicating it was time to go into the house. Mechanically, Elpee responded and rose up to meet danDay's outstretched hand. Together, the two princesses walked into the cottage, where danDay-leon had lit a fire in the fireplace when she returned from her own small house with the pot of tea. She steered the shaking Elpee to the rocking chair nearest the hearth, and when she was seated, danDay-leon placed a shawl around the broken princess's shoulders and an afghan on her lap.

"You just sit here and warm up, and I'll bring the tea to you," danDay instructed Elpee.

As the upright princess was preparing the tea tray in the kitchen, the seated princess began yelling, without pause, from the living room.

"I NEED A TISSUE. I NEED A TISSUE. I NEED A TISSUE. I NEED . . . "

Hurriedly, danDay-leon returned to the living room with a look on her face that immediately stopped Elpee's hollering.

"I'm sorry, danDay, but I am so bundled up here I can't move, and my nose is running . . . a lot," Elpee replied in a soft and repentant voice.

Still, with a look of stern impatience on her face, danDay-leon placed the box of tissues on Elpee's lap and sharply spun around to return to the kitchen while uttering quite audibly, "Alpert was certainly right – she screams like a banshee! I do not know why she cannot simply make a statement, or ask a question without such urgency and earsplitting volume to boot. Will she ever learn to temper that disposition of hers? I wonder."

Elpee sat sniffling and feeling quite ashamed of herself . . . Well, not really. She thought that she *should* feel quite ashamed of herself, but she didn't because she did not understand what all the fuss was about. *No bother*, she thought; she felt too sad to try to figure out why danDay-leon was upset. Elpee sat there rocking away while revisiting the life and death of the fern, along with all the other lives and deaths that had occurred in her time on this earth. Depleted of tears, all the spent princess could do was sit there and rock while feeling emotionally exhausted and abandoned by the Universe. She could not understand why they all had to leave her. Before Elpee could slip any further into the abyss of self-pity, danDay-leon entered the living room with the tray of tea.

"Here we go. Try to un-cocoon yourself a bit so that you can get an arm out to hold the teacup," danDay instructed Elpee while she poured the tea into the cups.

By the time her teacup was filled with the cinnamon, apple, and honey tea, Elpee had sufficiently freed herself to accept it from its maker.

"Thank you, danDay, and I'm sorry for hollering before, it's just . . ."

Once again, Elpee was cut off by danDay-leon, this time by her shaking her head at Elpee in a gesture indicating that all conversation must cease. Elpee acquiesced and sat back in the chair with her tea. The two princesses sat in front of the hearth, silently sipping the always perfectly spiced warm liquid from the delicate, china cups.

Feelings Aren't Fact . . . But Tea Leaves Are

danDay-leon was the first to break the silence by saying, "So, tomorrow we are off to rescue our friend, and hopefully we will be well rested and prepared. Most importantly, I hope that Euterpe will be on time and in a mode of transportation that has not been illegally appropriated by her. Although, now that I am thinking about it, how else would she be able to obtain our ride but in that fashion? I suppose that matters little compared to the weight the success of our mission itself holds."

"Oh, danDay, I wish I was in a better frame of mind on the eve of our mission, but the death of the fern just leaves me vacant," Elpee said.

"Hush, Elpee. It's the circle of life . . . The natural order of things. Everyone and everything has a beginning and an end, and usually a middle in between. It is not personal. It is simply what we all are ordained to do. Nothing more, nothing less," danDay-leon responded.

"So I should just accept it? That's it?"

"Yes or no, whatever you choose. It is the way it is, and you can continue to resist and take it as a personal affront that the Universe has conveyed specifically and only upon you, or you can accept it for what it is. The choice is entirely yours on how you would like to deal with it."

Elpee barely listened to the words that were expelled from danDay-leon's mouth as she drowned them out in her head with her usual 'blah, blah, blah'.

"You can also choose to hear what I am saying, or tune me out. That choice is also yours," danDay-leon counseled Elpee.

"Okay, I know you are right, but it still feels personal."

"Feelings are not facts, my dear. What a silly girl to think they are," danDay-leon advised Elpee as she giggled and shook her head.

"Huh?" Elpee asked.

"Just because you feel a certain thing or a certain way does not necessarily mean that it is true. Do you remember when my feelings were hurt because I thought you were mocking me for reading your tea leaves? Well, even though I felt that way, you assured me that it was not so. Therefore, as you pointed out to me, my feelings were indeed not fact. Do you understand?" danDay-leon asked Elpee.

"I think I do. Give me a little time to absorb it," Elpee asked in return.

"Certainly," danDay-leon responded. "But let us take ourselves upstairs to finish your packing while you take in the concept, and when we come back downstairs, I will read your tea leaves."

"Okay," Elpee answered as she rose from her chair and headed up the staircase with danDay-leon in tow.

When the two princesses reached the top of the stairs and turned right on the landing, they climbed the last twenty-seven steps to the second floor that revealed Elpee's bedroom on the left.

"What a peaceful room this is," danDay-leon said as she exhaled an approving sigh. "You have done such a fine job of restoring it since its reclamation from Anna."

"Thank you. My suitcase is on the chair. I think I have everything I will need, but since I don't know where we are going or for how long, it will have to do."

"Very well, but I have packed significantly more than you have, so if you need something, you can borrow it from me. What are all these envelopes doing on the desk?" danDay-leon asked.

Elpee had not bothered to return the letters to the drawers in which they had been stored, but instead, after having read them, she simply tossed them on the top of the desk until she decided their fate. Elpee briefly explained to danDay how she came to finding the intercepted correspondence and her feelings about it. Both princesses sat on the bed and discussed the events leading up to Alpert's visit that prompted his current incarceration. Before Elpee became overcome with anger and lost her mind again, danDay-leon suggested that they go back into the living room to uncover the message for Elpee that was hidden in her tea leaves.

"You go down the stairs first," Elpee instructed the other princess as she lugged the suitcase alongside her, "this way, in case I fall, you will soften my landing. Only kidding!!"

danDay-leon snickered at the other princess's often inappropriate, but undoubtedly innocent, sense of humor.

Once back down in the living room, the resident soothsayer picked up Elpee's teacup and began swirling around the remnants that remained within it.

"What do you see?" Elpee asked.

"Be patient, it is a bit jumbled," was danDay's response.

"Hmmm, that is exactly it! It's a jumble . . . A word jumble. Get a pencil and paper and write this down," danDay-leon instructed Elpee, who, without delay, went to the drawer in the right built-in, retrieved those instruments, and returned, awaiting further instructions.

"It is two words. Write these letters down . . . R p y a b m r e c a e. All right, that is all."

"Okay, so what the heck does this mean? This is stupid! I guess I should be grateful that it is not a kaleidoscope or spiders," Elpee frustratedly proclaimed.

Before turning to leave and return to her own home to complete her packing, danDay-leon looked directly at Elpee and stated, "P R A Y E M B R A C E. That is what it says," and she was gone.

Pray and Embrace

After Elpee recovered from hearing the message the tea leaves held and feeling the ire it inspired by its veiled meaning, she and Butter went for a walk down by the ocean. The house that sat on the dunes still looked vacant and plainly appeared absent of any wedding preparations. Elpee, determined not to investigate, continued down the stairs of the overpass and onto the sand where Butter, as he always did, ran to the water and began barking frantically at the waves. She wondered if her canine companion was trying to tell the waves to stop, something she often attempted to do in her head, but without success.

As the dog ran in and out of the ocean, communicating his message to the waves, Elpee sat on the sand and removed a pocket-sized dictionary she had snatched from a shelf in the living room on her way out of the house. She opened the page to the letter P and then continued to the next letter until she had spelled out the word 'pray'. It was defined as: *to implore, to call upon, to contemplate.*

Next, Elpee researched the meaning of the word 'embrace', and the entry next to it stated: *to hug, encircle.* This left Elpee just as clueless as she was before trying to research the meanings of the words individually and combine them collectively to then decode the cryptic saying.

"I have tried to implore a hug and call upon encirclement, but they left anyway. Oh, this is just aggravating me even more," Elpee yelled out in frustration as she threw the book down on the sand just as Butter came running at her. He stopped just short of crashing into his master but did not avoid a collision with the dictionary, which he sent propelling into the air. When the book of words came to rest back on terra sanda, it appeared that all the words on the pages had been sandblasted away, leaving only these three: *accept, adopt, and support.*

DING . . . DING . . . DING! It was one of those overwhelmingly bright moments of recognition for Elpee. A time when she finally understood that which had eluded her for what felt like centuries and had caused her to act out on her least attractive character traits, such as impatience, intolerance, resentment, frustration, and anger, to name a few.

"To implore acceptance. To call upon adoption. To contemplate support. I get it, danDay was right . . . It was not personal or about me! It was about them, doing what they needed to do for themselves, not what I thought they were doing against me. Pray-Embrace means to accept their choices and to support them in those decisions even if I don't agree, or maybe, especially if I don't agree," Elpee said to the sand-encased dog, who, at that moment, looked very much like a breaded pork chop.

"I still hate it, but I understand it. Come on, Butthead, let's go yell at the waves before we go home."

And so they did!

OCTOBER THREE ONE

Butter and Elpee spent a pleasant evening with each other when they returned home from their adventure at the beach. They both, at the insistence of the other, dined on peanut butter and banana sandwiches while watching television in the living room. Shortly after completing their dining experience, human and canine nestled themselves on the couch and promptly fell asleep until a knocking noise woke them both. Startled, Elpee jumped up and went to the front door to find PoliM'aladroit and her little gray creature standing there.

"Hello, my dear. I hope you don't mind that we are here to await our ride. Did I wake you? Oh, my. I am so sorry, but it really is time that you rose and got ready for our trip. It is a cloudy day out, just as Euterpe predicted it would be. I wonder where danDay-leon is. Do you think she will come over here and wait with us? Perhaps I should go over there and invite her to do that," PoliM'aladroit spoke without hesitation or pausing, leaving Elpee no alternative but to listen to her rambling on – and on – and on – and on.

"That's a good idea, PoliM'aladroit. Why don't you go over to danDay's and invite her to wait with us while I make some coffee and feed the boy?" Elpee asked.

Without answering Elpee's question, PoliM'aladroit and the gray boy walked across the street and knocked on danDay-leon's door. This allowed Elpee time to put up a pot of coffee, let Butter out, and prepare his rice and chicken concoction.

When Elpee finished making Butter's breakfast, she rounded him up and back into the house so that she could utilize the time that was still needed to complete the coffee's brewing process. She went to the upstairs bathroom and began drawing a bath, into which she added lavender and frankincense oil. With the bathtub filling, Elpee ran back downstairs to give Butter his breakfast dessert of banana and herbs, then poured herself a cup of strong, hot coffee. It was a bleak day, but it was unseasonably warm, which allowed Elpee to enjoy, although hastily, her coffee on the front porch. As she sipped from the hand-painted coffee mug, Elpee contemplated the day and what it would hold in store. She prayed that it would be without event and produce a positive outcome that would allow Alpert and his entire rescue team to be home by evening.

Not knowing exactly when Euterpe was arriving, Elpee decided not to finish her coffee, but rather to go upstairs to bathe and dress. She laid out a pair of sage green overalls that had a blue hand-painted design on the bib and a green and blue thermal shirt to wear underneath them. Elpee was unsure of which shoes to wear, but she favored the yellow high-tops she usually sported with multicolored argyle socks. Quickly, she went into the bath, and just as speedily she got out, dressed, and returned downstairs to wait for the other princesses.

When Elpee arrived in the kitchen to prepare another cup of coffee for herself, she found Butter outside playing with a squirrel. No matter how much Elpee warned Butterball not to befriend all creatures great and small, he could not help himself. Where once he would not leave her side, he had now come into his own right and was a balanced and well-adjusted little dog. There was no sense reprimanding him, but she felt the need to warn him and inform him that they would be leaving when his *Queen* aunt arrived to take them to Alpert.

"Be careful, Butter! And you, Mr. Squirrel, don't be mean to my boy. Play nice with each other . . . PLEASE," Elpee implored them, knowing there was no time for her to undo the results of a catastrophe, should one occur.

"Butter, please be ready to leave when Aunt Euterpe comes to pick us up. Your other aunts will be here and ready to go, so don't delay us. Thank you. You may resume playing . . . Carefully!"

That being said and with everything in order, Elpee felt free to return inside to the living room, where she would finish her now cold cup of coffee while waiting to take the show on the road.

AND ANOTHER THING

No sooner had Elpee sat down on the couch and been enveloped into its downiness than PoliM'aladroit and danDay-leon arrived at her door and let themselves in. The princess of Cherry Cottage remained where she was and did not get up to greet them, mostly because it was too difficult to rise from the quicksand-like grip the down had on her. The other women did not seem to mind; as a matter of fact, it appeared that they did not even see her buried as she was.

"Elpeeeeee. Elpeeeeeee," sang out one princess.

"Oh, Elllllpee, Elllllpee," rang out the other.

"I am right here under both of your noses. Humph," the dejected princess, feeling invisible, retorted.

"Oh, my dear, we didn't see you down there. You look like you were swallowed up in the couch cushions," chuckled danDay-leon in response.

PoliM'aladroit shook her head and took a seat in one of the rocking chairs, once again puzzled by what she perceived as Elpee's zany antics.

"Don't you shake your head at *my* zany antics. You are the one who nailed yourself to the roof and got wedged under your sink in search of a safety pin. A fine example of sanity you set!" Elpee verbally responded to PoliM'aladroit's unspoken assessment of her.

Neither PoliM'aladroit nor danDay-leon said another word, sensing that there was more to what Elpee was not saying that there was to what she was saying. All three princesses sat in silence before Elpee struggled to rise from the couch and began to speak.

"I killed my fern."

There was no reaction from either of the other princesses. It appeared that they were waiting for some additional information before questioning or commenting on Elpee's statement.

"Okay, maybe I should say that my fern died, or my fern is dead, or there is no need to take the fern in the house now, or . . ."

"What are you talking about, Elpee?" PoliM'aladroit questioned the rambling Elpee.

"I'm talking about the fact that I feel horrible and responsible that my fern is dead because I didn't, or it wouldn't allow me to, take it in the house," Elpee answered through quivering lips before continuing.

"Pray . . . Embrace, you know . . . To accept and support the fern's decision to live how it chose to, even knowing that it would probably be a fatal choice. I figured it out, but it still feels rotten, and I wish I could be given another chance to do it over again. I hate to say it, but even knowing the 'Pray-Embrace' thing, I probably would have done it differently and taken it inside. I hate those two stupid words, and I am tired of seeing them everywhere . . . Books . . . Worm words... In my kitchen."

Having little understanding of what Elpee was pontificating about, but knowing that she was not even close to being done with her ranting fit, PoliM'aladroit and danDay-leon continued rocking and waiting for the encore performance to begin, which it did right on schedule.

"And another thing! If all creatures, whether plant, human, animal, mineral, vegetable, or table, have the right to exercise *their* freedom and I am expected to accept it under the 'Pray-Embrace' law, then *I* have the same right to exercise *my* freedom. I could have – maybe even should have – chosen to bring the plant inside and let *it* be governed by that 'Pray-Embrace' edict. Let *them* see how it feels. So there!"

Deciding that this diatribe must end, PoliM'aladroit stood up and stated, "It doesn't work that way, and you know it. Once you know something, you can never not know it. So, to implore acceptance, I say to you your own words, 'Pray-Embrace'. Learn the lesson, or repeat it, that is up to you. Now, let us be done with this. I am, however, sorry for your loss, but you did a noble and generous thing by giving something you cared for so intensely the freedom it requested so that it could live out its life on its own terms, despite your wanting to do quite the opposite."

She took a breath and allowed the correct amount of seconds to pass before saying, "Now, let's play cards while we wait for Euterpe, shall we?"

"Okay," Elpee immediately responded with resignation, as danDay-leon replied in kind, using the same word, but with a lilt of surprise at the manner in which the conversation between her two friends ended so abruptly and amicably.

Half Past Something

The women sat at the kitchen table playing one-million rummy as the canines ran around in the backyard with Butter's new friend, Mr. Squirrel. It was somewhat difficult to distinguish the newcomer friend from PoliM'aladroit's little creature, as they both were the same steely color and they both jumped around in an equally deliberate and fragmented way. Unlike Butter or Pippy, there was nothing fluid in their movements, but they accomplished their tasks all the same.

Pippy's visits were far less frequent recently, causing what seemed to be more distress for Elpee than it did for Butter. She missed the big black lug, and it surprised her that Butter was not sulking more at his/her absence, but lately, he seemed to be finding his pleasures in the forest behind the back cottage. He was never very discerning about his playmates, and heaven only knows what creatures he would spot to play with back there, but he seemed content, and that relieved Elpee's worries about any separation anxiety he may be having.

danDay-leon was in the lead with eight hundred thousand, seven hundred, and thirty-five points when the three princesses heard the commotion being generated from outside on the walk. All three women jumped up and ran to the front door, with PoliM'aladroit overturning her chair while stumbling to get there. An awkward and most peculiar contraption that Euterpe secured to transport the four women from Cherry Cottage to the place in which Alpert was being detained greeted them. The princesses stared in disbelief at Euterpe, who was sitting in a rowboat that was outfitted with wheels beneath its hull. Seeing the looks of shock on their faces, the *Queen* responded quite indignantly.

"Don't stare like that at me, I say,
"all three of you I see today.
"Have no idea of how to go,

"or even made a vow, you know.
"To find a way for us to flee,
"I should have stolen a bus, I see,
"too bad for you, and shame on me,
"it's one long pew, get in, you'll see.
"I will say no more, I am hurt to the core."

Sensing and seeing the disappointment Euterpe was both feeling and displaying at their reactions to the wheeled boat, the three princesses rapidly approached the *Queen* and began hugging her as they spouted apologies and explanations galore. Euterpe tried to be resistant to their acts of contrition, but she caved in quickly and started dancing around and giggling like the child that she was. Elpee and PoliM'aladroit rounded up the dogs, and soon all of the travelers were on the boat with their appointed accessories and were ready to go.

Euterpe steered the boat south with the intention of making a right turn at the last walk so they would be able to reverse their direction, as their final destination was one hundred and eighty degrees north of their current heading. Before the boat, its passengers, and cargo were one house south of Elpee's cottage, the princess herself asked the *Queen*, "Where are we going? Do we have to cross the ocean?"

"No my friend,
"to turn around, I intend,
"at the end of the walk,
"we will stop and talk.
"We'll turn to the right,
"no ocean in sight."

"Why are we going this way if we are not going on the water? Why are we turning right before then? Are we turning around? What are we doing? I don't understand. If we are going down there to turn around, why don't we just do it here? Could you please explain it to me? I just don't get it," Elpee hysterically questioned Euterpe.

"Oh please be quiet,
"and put your mouth on a diet.
"We are on our way,
"to go to the bay.
"So, no more objections,
"or additional questions," the pilot *Queen* declared.

"NO!" Elpee loudly objected.

A total of ten eyeballs, of various shades, shapes, and sizes instantaneously and simultaneously focused on the loud and overly emotional Princess Elpee, who cracked under the ocular pressure of her boat mates. For what appeared to be no apparent rhyme or reason she sat there on the verge of tears, with her body shaking, and her lower lip quivering sonically. She did not move, at least voluntarily, nor did she offer any explanation for her sudden outburst. Three sets of human and two sets of canine eyes continued their gaze upon the quaking princess, waiting in vain for more words to be expelled from her mouth. Having little time and patience for what seemed to be drivel, *Queen* Euterpe proceeded to give Elpee a piece of her mind (as if she had any to spare).

"Why do you yell so loud, I ask?

"We need to go complete our task.

"So, just sit there, because it's only fair,

"to the rest of us with no time to spare."

"Bu . . . Bu . . . Bubu . . . Bubut, I don't want to go past Hortense's house if we don't have to, please. If we are going to the bay, can't we just turn around here, so we don't have to go down there and see the wedding going on? I do not want to see my friend or my cousin, Chucklpe," Elpee managed to say through sniffles and hiccoughed breaths.

Without saying a word, the living vessels that held the ten eyeballs rose in unison and exited the boat in which they were seated. They stood on either side of the vehicle, which prompted Elpee to do the same. Everyone and everything were now standing on the walk several houses south of their starting point at Cherry Cottage. The humans grabbed a portion of the wheeled boat that was parallel to them and proceeded to turn it one hundred eighty degrees from its current attitudinal position. That was no easy fete, as the walks were narrow and not built for such maneuvers, hence the reason Euterpe had planned to continue south before a turnaround was attempted. As she aided in the joint effort, evidently not happy about reversing the boat, and out of poetic sorts, Euterpe mumbled gibberish under her breath.

"Whatever, whatever! Who cares, says me,

"we'll need a lever, to shoot us to he.

"It's quite an endeavor to get to the sea.

"It's time to go, hurry we must,

"oh woe, oh woe, or Alpert will rust.

"The boat we'll row, and in goddess we'll trust.

"WE HAVE TO GO, no time to play,

"so get in and row, down to the bay,

"if the tide is high, we'll be on our way," Euterpe assertively declared, while looking at everyone with a scowl on her face.

Arrested for Being Stupid

Having grumbled in her lowest possible tone of voice, Euterpe seemed to have set the others straight on their mission regarding the need to get serious and to step up their pace. Micro-inch by micro-inch and step by step, the humans were able to turn the boat around until it faced the direction in which they needed to head. It took less time to realign than anyone thought, probably out of fear of what *Queen* Euterpe would do if they did anything less than use breakneck speed. Euterpe was not at all an angry or mean-spirited person, and under normal circumstances, not one to be feared; however, these were anything but normal conditions, and Euterpe was one thing if anything at all, and that was cuckoo.

Butter and the gray boy had taken advantage of the downtime and had gone off to frolic in the sandpit Elpee had built, believing that if she gave them a proper home, all the fleas in the area would choose to live there rather than on any of them. With the boat directionally correct, the people stepped back into it and coaxed the two canines to join them. After huffing and puffing at having his recreational activities interrupted, Butter reluctantly jumped into the boat, with his sidekick immediately following him. The *Queen* at the helm directed all the princesses to pick up their oars and begin rowing anew by pushing the boat along on its attached wheels. Everyone complied, including the recovered Princess Elpee, who under her breath mumbled, "I don't know why *Euturpentine* the *Queen* has to be so very mean," causing her to expel an audible giggle, to the surprise of the other inhabitants.

"I must say, my dear, that you have a most unique quality and uncanny ability to amuse yourself more than anyone else I have ever seen. It truly is astonishing how you can break into laughter for reasons known only to you, and in a matter of seconds have an uninformed audience participating in the laugh-fest right along with you," danDay-leon pro-claimed in amazement.

PoliM'aladroit expanded on danDay-leon's assessment of Elpee by saying, "It is true, my friend. I often wonder what possible scenarios exist within your head that create in you such a sense of hilarity. Your laughter spills over into the lives and psyches of other unsuspecting people, who seem to have no choice other than to laugh with you for no apparent reason, and suddenly everyone is laughing at nothing. I don't understand how that happens."

Euterpe, who was impatient to move on and still somewhat perturbed by the necessity to reorient the boat, turned around and commented as politely as she could.

"First you cry, and then you laugh,
"you treat us like the wait staff.
"You'd better be wary,
"or you'll sing like a canary,
"and you'll be doing a bid, for being stu-pid."

"I AM NOT STUPID!" Elpee hollered out, and then followed that declaration with a much more quiet statement of, "You big dope. Why are you being like that? All of a sudden, you have to be all serious and *Queen*ly! Well, it is stupid and bossy, and no one is the boss of me, not even you, your majesty," she continued as she feigned a curtsey.

"Don't get on my nerves, any more than you are,
"or I'll put your head in a mason jar.
"Laughing, crying, blar, blar, blar,
"it's all about you and this trolley car.
"Grow up and cope and stop being a dope.
"Others need help, so stifle your yelp,
"give up control and shut your pie hole.
"I AM THE *QUEEN*, and you're a string bean!"

ON THE LAUNCH PAD

Elpee's head, as well as those of the other travelers, was still reeling by the time they reached their destination. None of them, including the canine companions, could comprehend the change in Euterpe's personality and the way in which she presented herself. The wheeled boat had barely come to a stop when the *Queen* ordered them out.

"Get out of the boat and please take note,
"of where we be and what you see.
"For it won't be long 'til we sing our song,
"and be on our way to the next soiree.
"Get the bubbles for the dogguns, and place on their noggins.
"They must leave their toys; we can have no noise.
"As we cross through time, you must take a breath,
"and hold it for nine, to avoid certain death."

Everyone robotically exited the boat on command as if they had all been drugged and had no individual or personal thought processes. Perhaps they were drugged, thought Elpee. Maybe Euterpe put some kind of magickal medicine in the juice she passed around for them to drink on their ride here. That would explain why all the princesses and canines were moving in unison as if sharing a single brain – a brain that was altered by Euterpe's herbs. Elpee's brain was processing this information and its feasibility when a startling fact came to her mind. Euterpe did not pass around any juice on their trip, so Elpee had to admit defeat on the drugged fruit juice theory. Maybe they were all afraid of her, or perhaps still, they were taking direction. Hmmm.

"Oh, I wish my brain would take a holiday," Elpee sputtered as she walked over to what she assumed were the head bubbles for Butter and gray boy that Euterpe had spoken of. She had picked one up for Butter and was reaching for a second one to give to PoliM'aladroit when from behind her she heard her friend's voice calling her own dog.

"Macaroni, come here, my boy. I need to place this diving device on your head." After a few seconds of silence, PoliM'aladroit continued speaking as if answering a question posed to her by the little gray creature, "I am not clear on its purpose or why it must be done. I am simply following directions."

Shaking her head, Elpee surrendered to the fact that she had no idea who was who, or what was what, and instead decided to focus on getting to and rescuing Alpert, a task she had sadly lost sight of. Elpee was able to do that for a microsecond before turning her attention to the confusing fact that there was one oversized bubble remaining after she and PoliM'aladroit took theirs when suddenly she heard a voice coming from behind her.

"I'll get it, sunshine. Don't put yourself out."

Elpee was frozen in place, unsure of how to react or what to say, but then turned around and instinctively ran to her friend and threw her arms around her.

"Oh, Hortense, how are you? I've missed you so much . . . And the gardens, oh, they are in terrible shape. I'm sorry for mistrusting you and for thinking that you stole Butterball. I should have known better . . . That you would never do anything like that to me. Now I know that you were hiding him from Anna, but I should never have doubted you in the first place. Please forgive me, but of course, I understand if you don't. Oh, what can I do to make it up to you . . . Probably nothing, right? I know even making a cake wouldn't do. How did you get here and . . . Uh-oh . . . I forgot, today is your wedding day. Why are you here and where is that scoundr . . . I mean, where is Chucklpe?" Elpee said, and asked, and said, and asked again.

Hortense, despite not wanting to answer Elpee's questions, was relieved that the Princess of Cherry Cottage had at last shut up. Hortense bent down to pick up the bubble she would soon put on Pippy's head before she addressed Elpee in her usual aloof and somewhat impersonal manner, "Don't worry about it. It doesn't matter, and I don't want a cake anyway. I am not getting married today, and I don't want to talk about it," was all that Hortense said to her.

Elpee was initially gleeful to hear that the wedding was off, because that meant Chucklpe must have flown the coop and was gone from his most current residence, but then she felt sorry for her friend, which she expressed to her with an additional hug. Hortense was as receptive to Elpee's mushiness as she could be, but managed to free herself quickly to allow everyone to be ready for his or her impending mission. Hortense moved toward Euterpe and spoke with her briefly before addressing the others.

"Everyone, follow me back to the boat we came here on. We need to move it to the invisible line that is painted on the dock, and when we get it in place, we will have to pick it up and remove the wheels. Then, everyone needs to get back in the boat, make sure the animals have their head bubbles on, and get ready. As we enter the gate, you will need to hold your breath to the count of nine. This is very, very important. Don't ask why. Just do it," Hortense dispassionately instructed them all.

"Excuse me," interrupted Elpee while raising her hand as if she were a student in a classroom, "but why are *you* telling us, and why are *you* here, and one more thing . . . How do *you* know this stuff?"

"I have been asked to because we don't have time for 'terpe to give the instructions. I know this *stuff*, because I have been there, and I am here because I am going back. Okay, can we move on now?" Hortense pointedly asked after answering Elpee's questions.

Elpee was quickly reminded of why she was angry with Hortense in the first place and answered her question just as snidely, "Whatever."

From the Light –
To the Dark – To the Light

The four princesses, one *Queen*, two canines, and one small gray creature reassembled on the now de-wheeled and repositioned boat that faced north while they waited as darkness descended upon them. It was evident that the animals were not happy with the giant diving bubble apparatus their owners had placed on their heads, nor were the human inhabitants who sat rigidly waiting, most of them not knowing why or for what.

They waited for what seemed like an eternity until suddenly a light from behind them illuminated the sky. It was the full moon to the south that was shining on the ocean and reflecting its light and energy upon them. Within seconds, the boat was being transported to a different time and place that was anything but illuminated.

"TAKE A DEEP BREATH AND HOLD IT FOR A COUNT OF NINE," Hortense yelled to her fellow voyagers.

All traces of the moon and its light disappeared, leaving only its incalculable energy – an energy that would carry them to Alpert. Elpee had never known such darkness and stillness in all her existence. Unlike the kaleidoscope, which was colorful and left her battered by its intense motion and emotion, this journey was static, obscure, and tranquil. She felt no movement or life, and no force other than that which initially propelled them through the gateway. The only sensation that Elpee felt was the intense awareness of her own existence. She could feel every organ and cell within her body and was acutely aware of how they worked together and how very fragile they actually were. Elpee, as well as the others on this passage, could sense how delicate a line it was that tethered them to the land of the living and how without difficulty that tie could be severed. It was getting increasingly more difficult for Elpee to hold her breath, but she knew to not do so would be to cross that line into eternity.

Elpee's heart was beating in her ears, and her lungs were screaming for oxygen, but she still felt no sense of anything else around her. She thought she could not stand it for one more second, and that she would succumb to a sure death, when gently the darkness lifted and a new day dawned.

Elpee assumed that she and the other people on the boat were lifted out of the dark just at the count of nine. They had successfully navigated the gateway and survived the passage through the land of the dead. For a moment everyone just sat there, not daring to move, unsure of how or where to do so if they indeed opted to. Somehow and somewhere during their voyage, they all turned around on the boat and were now sitting in the same order but in the opposite direction from the one in which they had begun their expedition. What they faced ahead was far different from the landscape they had left behind. For as far as the eye could see there were snowcapped mountains and valleys that were dappled with winding rivers. Elpee was used to the extreme opposite scenery and was in awe of the magnitude and strength this current one possessed.

Finally, Euterpe, who spoke nothing like the *Queen* of old, rose and began giving instructions to the others.

"Well, ladies and gentlemen, it is time to take off the animals' head bubbles and be on our way. Come along, hurry up, everyone."

"What the heck? Did someone take over Euterpe's body?" Elpee said to no one and to everyone.

"What do you mean? Oh, that! No, I haven't been possessed, you silly thing. Now let's go," Euterpe responded.

"But you are talking normally . . . Not rhyming. How come? How can that be? I don't get it. Was it something . . . ?" Elpee squeaked out before being interrupted by the *Queen*.

"Fine! You want a rhyme? Then give me a dime.

"Nothing is free, as you will soon see.

"We need to hurry, let's catch a surrey.

"It will take less time, now give me the dime!" Euterpe gruffly stated in trying to prove her point to Elpee.

"Okay, I see you still have it, but I don't get how it went away or why . . ." Elpee began, but was again interrupted, this time by danDayleon, who escorted her in the direction of the waiting carriage.

All the humans and the de-bubbled animals squeezed in for their ride to rescue Alpert.

Up, Up, Up and Inside the Mountain

There was so little room for the rescuers inside the carriage that is was necessary for them to coordinate their movements and their speech, as it was only possible for one person or animal to move or speak at a time. Euterpe began by explaining what she knew that the others did not.

"We all know that Alpert got here by breaking the rules as outlined in the Wizard's Handbook. And we all know that he was given a choice of never returning to our land, or giving up his position – whatever that is – to be set free. To date, he has chosen neither of the first two and has remained in prison, either by choice or by default. You all came here with the intention of breaking him out of jail; however, in the interim, another option has been explored as a viable solution."

When Euterpe stopped momentarily to take a breath, Elpee jumped in. "Well, what is it? Tell us."

"Not yet. It can't be discussed until after we arrive because the possibility is still quite uncertain. Some details need to be worked out before we can speak openly about it. Please don't jeopardize Alpert's dismissal from jail by pushing to know something that is not ready to be known," Euterpe adamantly responded.

Elpee, feeling exasperated at Euterpe's admonishment, threw herself back against the seat cushion, if only in her head. None of the women spoke for the rest of the journey, wondering in their minds also, but knowing the time had not yet come to openly ask those questions. The carriage seemed to be going in circles, and for an instant, Elpee had flashbacks of her spinning like a top back at her cottage, and if she could, she would have shaken herself and her thoughts off, but she was not able to move. Just as she thought she could take it no longer, the vehicle stopped, and Euterpe exited it.

"Come on, ladies and gentlemen," she said as she held the door to the carriage open and helped each of her sisters out and onto the road.

"Where are we?" asked Elpee.

"We are at the base of the mountain where Alpert is being held," answered Euterpe.

"Oh, good, he's at the base," said Elpee, happy that they would not have to climb the mammoth mountain.

"No, silly. *We* are at the base of the mountain where he is being held . . . At the top," Euterpe chuckled back at her.

"Huh?"

"Huh?"

"Huh?"

"Errrrr?"

"Errrrr?"

"Well, it appears that all castles are accounted for. Follow me, ladies and gentlemen," Euterpe said as she walked to what appeared to be a cave within the mountain. Once everyone was there, Euterpe removed a rock from the side of the mountain and pushed on the wall behind it. Magickally, the wall of rock slid to one side, and a chasm appeared within the edifice. Euterpe motioned for them to follow her, and of course, they did. Just as the last passenger stepped into the vault, the hefty wall that had moments earlier opened and allowed them access slammed shut behind them. Simultaneously, a door of similar dimensions directly across from its sister opened, and into that opening Euterpe sashayed. The others, not knowing what else to do, followed her lead and also exited their current vault. What they saw took their breath away with its enormity and beauty. They were somehow on the mountaintop, and its splendor was overwhelming – but so was its aloneness.

THEY ARE OFF TO SEE THE WIZARD – NOT

Waiting for them upon their arrival was a slab of wood that appeared to be made of teak and was dressed in a beautiful, hand-painted silk cloth. Teacups made from porcelain so faint that they were translucent were set upon the table. In its center was what appeared to be a single teapot, but upon closer inspection revealed itself to be a number of smaller wedge-shaped cylinders that fit together to fashion the appearance of one large container.

Euterpe motioned for everyone to sit down and enjoy the refreshments that were provided to them.

"I have to leave you now to see Alpert. I won't be long, but please, sit down and have some tea. It is the finest tea in the world, and I think that once you taste it, you will agree. I am sure even you, danDay-leon, will attest to that fact."

Euterpe, signaling that she would entertain no questions, raised her hand to the other princesses as she briskly walked away and into a valley.

The women remained silent as they experimented with the different teas and the exotic flavors they provided. It was certainly a sensory experience to savor such vivid flavors while in a place that was so devoid of life. Although she remained quiet, Elpee had a million questions bouncing around inside her skull, the foremost one being about the absence of people in such an exquisite place and how that possibly could be. She also wondered if the others felt the same way, but for some reason were failing to express it. The silence and solitude were deafening to Elpee; it was louder than any noise she had ever heard. In her isolation, Elpee reviewed the preconceived images she had formulated surrounding Alpert's prison and its appearance. They were not at all like this reality, and nothing could have prepared her for what she was now seeing and feeling. She knew she personally could not endure, for any length of time, an environment such as this one despite all its beauty and riches, reinforcing the need to free Alpert at any cost.

Deep in thought, which seemed to be the only lifestyle choice afforded to anyone here, Elpee was grateful for Euterpe's return. She walked directly to Elpee and addressed her alone.

"You have to come with me to see Alpert," Euterpe said as she extended her hand, indicating Elpee should do so at that moment.

Without questioning Euterpe, Elpee rose and followed her. They traveled through paths and gardens resplendent with wildflowers and greenery whose colors and fragrances were intoxicating to the senses. As they continued on their walk to Alpert, they came across another garden as brilliant and plentiful as the previous one. This one, however, was laden with hundreds of dragonflies droning around and being swept along by the breezes. Thinking she might have been mistaken in her harsh assessment of this world, Elpee reached out to touch a brilliant orange flower on which one of the flying creatures was resting. As she neared the blossom, her hand became painfully cold and numb, and she was unable to feel it. Her hand sensed nothing but icy numbness as it went right through the flower as if it did not even exist. At first, it shocked Elpee, who instinctively pulled her hand back before trying again and faring no better. Her hand felt nothing but a deadening cold as she approached the bud, yet there was a haunting curiosity surrounding them that called to her. Knowing how Elpee felt, Euterpe reached out to her and began to explain.

"I know you are confused. I was too, but I have come to understand. I know now that there are more prisons than just those made with iron bars. Although this is all so beautiful, it's also an illusion. So little of what is here is real, and you live in doubt every minute, wondering what is, and what isn't genuine. Even when you do find something that you can actually smell or touch, there is no one to share it with. It is a solitary experience in an unending solitary existence. This is the worst kind of prison I can imagine. It is a prison of the soul."

Euterpe's explanation that Alpert was doomed to this illusionary, beautiful hell for all eternity, combined with the same unreality Elpee experienced in her first home from which she had fled, overwhelmed Elpee. The broken princess began sobbing an empty and guttural weeping that could be felt by human beings on a primal level. Euterpe gathered Elpee in her arms and let her cry for a brief spell before pulling away and wiping her friend's tear-ridden face.

"Come on, my dear. We have work to do."

The two women walked arm in arm through the last garden—the one that would lead them to Alpert.

J. ALPERT VII (?)

Soon, Elpee and Euterpe were standing in front of what appeared to be an old, Irish cottage with a sod roof and the sweet smell of cherry wood wafting from the chimney. Euterpe knocked on the door and was greeted by an old, gaunt, and frail man. The person standing before the *Queen* and the princess was not someone that Elpee recognized, although she knew it was Alpert. She aggressively approached him but was stopped by Euterpe, who grabbed Elpee's arm, keeping her from moving forward in such a manner. Elpee turned to Euterpe with a questioning look on her face, to which the *Queen* responded by gently addressing Alpert, "Alpert, you wanted to speak with Elpee. Well, here she is."

"Oh, my dear, Elpee, I am so grateful that you survived your ordeal at the hands of that monster, Anna, and I am equally as sorry for having placed you directly in her clutches. I don't know how you could ever possibly forgive me for having put you in such peril," Alpert softly uttered to Elpee.

Despite Euterpe's attempt at advising Elpee to be gentle with the somewhat shattered Alpert, Elpee whacked Alpert on the shoulder and proclaimed, "Are you out of your mind, Alpert? I am the one who has been walking around in a constant state of guilt and contrition for your being here. It was all *my* fault that you came to me that night when you were on another case. I don't know how you can forgive *me*!"

"Okay, kids, let's wind this up," Euterpe said. She turned to Elpee and asked, "Do you, Elpee, take this man, Alpert, at his word, that he is sorry and wants you to forgive him?"

"I do," answered Elpee.

"And do you, Alpert, take this woman at her word, that she is sorry and wants you to forgive her?"

"I do," answered Alpert.

"By the powers vested in me by the laws of the great Universe, I now pronounce you both forgiven. You may do whatever," Euterpe proclaimed with her hands flailing about, having ended her officiating.

Alpert and Elpee cautiously approached each other and gingerly hugged.

"Well, now that the air is clear between you two, and you both seem committed to moving forward, I think it would be safe for me to assume that all systems are go to get you out of here. Is that right?" Euterpe asked, directing the question to Alpert.

"If nothing has changed regarding the details, and the terms remain the same, I am more than willing to move beyond the stagnant orifice that keeps me bound here," Alpert replied in what Elpee thought to be a curiously sad manner.

"Good. Elpee and I will leave you now, and I will arrange everything. Get ready, Alpert, because it won't take long on my end to prepare for your release and our departure. I'll see you very shortly on the other side of this mountain," Euterpe said to Alpert.

"Come along, Elpee," the *Queen* harshly instructed Elpee.

"Why are you so mean? And what were you talking about back there with Alpert? What details and terms?" asked Elpee.

"I am not mean. I am just pressed for time to keep on schedule and to make this happen – a happening I am not all that pleased with, I must say, but the decisions are not mine," Euterpe answered, stopping abruptly when she realized that she was saying more than she wanted to.

"You're not going to tell me, are you?" Elpee pried.

"No."

The Terms of Release

———

Not knowing where they were going or how to get there, Elpee followed closely behind the emotionally distant Euterpe as they made their way back to the others by returning through the gardens that, for some reason, curiously drew Elpee in. As they approached their starting point, it seemed to Elpee that time had stood still. The women and the animals were seated in the same positions where and how they had been when she and Euterpe left them before going to see Alpert. There was a visible and audible pall over everyone and everything, and in contrast to it, Elpee's sense of awareness became radically heightened. She could not wait for the completion of whatever it was that needed to be done to free Alpert so that they all could leave what she perceived to be this goddess-forsaken paradise.

"When can we get out of here?" asked Elpee. "This place gives me the creeps. How could it be so pretty and yet so ugly?" she asked the other princesses, who sat at the table as if in mourning rather than celebration.

The sense of discomfort within Elpee rose proportionately to the amount of time that passed among them in silence. She tried to calm herself and steady her racing heart, but Elpee had a feeling of impending doom that she could not quell, and finally, she expressed it to the others.

"I feel like I can't breathe. Does anyone else feel that way? What's going on here?" she asked them, but they did not answer her.

"You all look like you are in shock, like somebody died, and I feel like I've been shocked with an electric probe. Somebody, say something!" the overly excited princess commanded.

Euterpe broke the silence by saying, "I am sorry that we don't have time to explain, but we don't, and I'm sorry, but you'll have to deal with that fact. I truly wish there was another way, or that there was more time, but there isn't. While you and I were with Alpert, the others were given the details of his release and how it will come about. Now, it's only you that doesn't know, and I really don't know how to begin to tell you." Euterpe, for once at a loss for words, began the explanation.

She again attempted to reveal the terms but remained unsuccessful in disclosing the information that Elpee was painfully waiting for. The tension was ricocheting off the mountains and gaining an ugly momentum when, at last, Hortense stepped in and made a declaration that blindsided the already emotionally beaten Elpee, "Alpert is leaving here and going back with all of you, but I'm not."

"What?" Elpee asked, knowing Hortense well enough to know that there was no suggestion of humor in her statement.

"It was an alternative that no one thought of until I did. So the *Queen* and I cut a deal with the guys in charge here, and that's it. Alpert is free to go," Hortense answered.

"Why?" asked Elpee.

"Why not? He wants to go, and I can help him do that, so why not?"

"Why not? You selfish human being! The degree to which you can disappoint people never ceases to amaze me. Sometimes, in fact, most times, it isn't about you and your self-centered wants and needs. Other people factor into the equation too, Hortense. You sashay in, make friends, stay a while, and then disappear for some unknown reason, at least unknown to the people you desert, and you feel you have no need to explain. There is no communication with you . . . It is impossible, because only one person shows up for the dialogue, and that person isn't you. People live out their lives with unanswered questions, mostly about themselves and what – if anything – they did to contribute to your disappearance, all because you choose the coward's way. You run. You always run. And that, my friend, is 'why not'."

"I'm sorry you feel that way, but it is what it is," Hortense said as she turned and walked away, tossing a wave at the others as she passed the table at which they sat.

THE *QUEEN* 'RULES'

None of the others knew what to say or how to act after witnessing Elpee's tirade, which was filled with a lifetime of anger and love for all Elpee had known, lost, and that which she never had. Nor did they know how to respond to Hortense's non-reaction to it. The moment was so telling that everyone lost sight of their decaying surroundings and the reason why they had initially set sail for this realm. As much as Elpee wanted Alpert to be freed, she also wanted to leave immediately, with or without him. The pain that was springing from her being was palpable to the others, who bore not only their pain but Elpee's as well.

"I feel your pain. I really do, and I wish there were something I could do to help you bear it," danDay-leon said as she rose from the table and approached Elpee, who stood rigidly with her lips pursed – a gesture she made when she was unreachable.

When it was evident that Elpee was intractable in her introspection and entirely unmoved by danDay-leon's empathetic gesture, PoliM'aladroit made an equally unaccepted attempt at consoling her.

"My dear, I am truly sorry for what occurred here and for the unfortunate outcome of our losing Hortense, but . . . " PoliM'aladroit's words only served to interrupt the inventory taking that was happening in Elpee's head, which was detectable by the leer Elpee shot at her. Sensing that the words needed to soothe Elpee were absent or inadequate, PoliM'aladroit returned to the table.

"Okay, okay, I will give it a try,

"of course it makes sense that you want to cry.

"I have no words to help you out,

"but you will be fine, I have no doubt.

"Soon we'll go, and be out of this place.

"and now is the time to 'Pray - Embrace'."

Those two words *pray* and *embrace* altered Elpee's consciousness by reminding her of all the instances in which that eleven-letter verse appeared to her in the real world of plants, tea leaves, dictionaries, and wall plaques.

Fortunately, the presence of those two words created such angst in Elpee whenever they had appeared, that it eventually forced her to research their definitions. She then needed to formulate a connecting thought from those two descriptions – a connection that would help her here and now.

PoliM'aladroit and danDay-leon sat back down at the table while Euterpe continued walking into the foliage and to the place where she would finalize Alpert's release. There was noticeable tension permeating the already emotionally dense atmosphere. The two women at the table sat in silence, neither speaking to, nor looking at, the other, but both wishing that they were at least back on the wheeled boat if not already home. Neither princess ever thought that the rescue of Alpert would seem insignificant compared to the other events that surrounded and would result from it.

Elpee Alone

Elpee stood alone contemplating Euterpe's words while the other women minded their own business and tended to their own sorrows and needs. Though she was still stinging from Hortense's pronouncement, Elpee knew there was a profound message in Euterpe's rhyming words that would help her come to some kind of terms with the situation that currently existed.

"Pray," she said aloud.

"To implore, to call upon, to contemplate," Elpee continued.

"Embrace . . . To accept, to adopt, to support. To call upon acceptance . . . To implore support . . . To contemplate adoption. Just like the fern, I suppose. I needed to find acceptance in its need to live in freedom, on its own terms, and in its own way despite the potential consequences. That decision cost the fern its life. But, to find peace, I needed to support its right to do that, no matter how much I disagreed or feared the outcome. Was that just a test for this? That I needed to learn how to pray and embrace on a plant level because I would need to apply it to human beings in the future?" Elpee continued speaking to herself as she walked in large circles, a ritual she had practiced for years when contemplating the questions of the Universe.

Then Elpee thought about the seeds she had planted with Alpert that day so very long ago. She also remembered going up the mountain in the land where she believed everything was real and looking for, but not finding, them. Questions and answers fluttered around inside Elpee's head, some of which she expressed verbally, but most were silent.

"Were the flowers I saw up the mountain the result of the seeds Alpert and I planted when I lived in Cherry Castle?"

danDay-leon and PoliM'aladroit could hear a droning buzz coming from Elpee's direction, as the din of her words were being expressed in a circular motion to coincide with their speaker's movement. The sound had an ominous tone to it, leaving the two seated princesses unnerved, but there was nothing that they could do about it, even if they knew what that would be.

"But they were nothing like I thought they would be," Elpee muttered softly. "They were not even real . . . Or were they? Maybe I just adopted the perception of the others and accepted their assessment of this place."

Soon, Elpee stopped her solo interrogative and confidently walked directly to the women at the table.

"I will meet you all at the boat. Euterpe and Alpert," Elpee stated.

"But do you know where it is and how to get there?" asked danDay-leon.

"I'll figure it out. Move a rock . . . Push a button . . . Whatever. How hard can it be?"

"My dear, I think it would be better for all of us to stay here and wait for Euterpe and her directions," spoke PoliM'aladroit.

"No, I gotta go. I want to make sure all the preparations are completed so that when the rest of you get there, it will be time for us to realize the purpose of our mission," Elpee definitively stated before slowly turning to leave, signaling Butter to follow her.

PoliM'aladroit and danDay-leon watched Elpee walk away from them, her silhouette getting smaller and smaller until it eventually disappeared. When Elpee was fully out of sight, the fretful and less than regal princesses turned their focus to the direction in which Euterpe had earlier proceeded, hoping for her quick return.

Elpee, meanwhile, headed into the direction she believed to be correct, all the while reviewing conversations and lessons she was exposed to in all her other lands. The determined and focused princess knew that when they left home, they were directed north with the full moon to the south and behind them. She also remembered that when they arrived here, they were all turned around and were facing the opposite direction from their original course. Therefore, she concluded, she would need to make her way north to find the water and the boat on which they had arrived. In this world where everything was unfamiliar, it appeared that distance was also without significance, at least not in the sense that Elpee was familiar with. No sooner had she ascertained the direction in which she needed to travel, than she was at her destination.

Elpee spied the boat that had carried them to this place and in no time – literally no time – she was beside it preparing it for what was next.

THE TRIP HOME

danDay-leon and PoliM'aladroit sat impatiently waiting for direction of any kind, from anyone, while feeling somewhat responsible for Elpee's headstrong disappearance. danDay-leon was visibly uneasy, and PoliM'aladroit was not far behind her on the discomfort scale. Despite its beauty, the place held nothing for either of them, and because of its emptiness, it probably was barren for anyone at all. Regardless of the problems or concerns they faced at home, it was a far better place to live than this perpetually lifeless shell.

Fortunately for the two princesses, Euterpe returned in less time than either of them had anticipated. She whisked in like a broom on dirt, almost scooping them up on the way.

"Come on, ladies, it's time to go. Everything is finalized, and Alpert will meet us at the water," Euterpe announced before continuing with her question.

"Where's Elpee?"

Without explanation or apology, PoliM'aladroit answered, "She went to the boat to ready it for our return voyage."

Although Euterpe would have liked to comment on PoliM'aladroit's pronouncement, they had no time to waste. She took the lead in their trek to the boat while the other two women followed closely behind. They asked nothing of the *Queen* – not where they were going, or why they were walking rather than taking a carriage as they had on their way here.

"Because there are two less humans and two less canines, okay? So, even if that doesn't make sense as to why we're walking, it's still my answer, and that's all there is to it," Euterpe responded aloud to the unspoken question.

Just as the trip to the boat was made quickly by Elpee, it seemed to take no time for the remainder of their party to spot her. Lickety-split they saw her and Butter in the distance sitting on the grass not very far from the launching pad. The three women continued their forward momentum, but unlike before, they now seemed to be making no progress through the power of their own peds. They did, however, get closer to Elpee with each step, but it was because it was Elpee who was advancing and moving them closer to each other.

"What's going on? Why didn't you wait for me to come back and go with the rest of us?" Euterpe asked Elpee the first of many questions.

"I wanted to make sure everything down here was as it should be for when the rest of you arrived," answered Elpee.

"Well, that wasn't really necessary, but thank you anyway. Everything should be as we left it, so all we needed to do was jump in as soon as Alpert arrived," Euterpe replied.

"I cannot wait to be home in my own cottage with my little Macaroni," PoliM'aladroit said as she cradled the little gray creature in her arms.

"I concur, my sister princess. This hideous mask of a paradise, that is in fact possessed and forsaken, jangles my nerves. It is not normal the way everything is unreal here . . . Time, place, distance, happiness. Oh, I can't go on any further. You all know what I mean," danDay-leon said in agreement with PoliM'aladroit's wish to be home.

"Well, soon that will be a reality. All we need is Alpert, who I hope gets here soon and we can all be off," Euterpe said.

"Well, we cannot 'all be off,' Euterpe," Elpee reminded the *Queen*, who immediately reacted in a way Elpee did not allow to develop any further than its initial hint at evasion.

"What do you mean, Elpee? Alpert? He should be here any second," Euterpe asked, knowing full well it was an empty question, as Elpee was not alluding to Alpert.

"No 'terpe, I am not referring to Alpert, who by the way, is waiting down by the water. I mean Hortense and PippyLou. I just want to remind you of that fact, lest you think we, as a group, were made whole by this trip," Elpee emphasized.

"Oh, I know that, Elpee, and I never meant to insinuate that our returning without Hortense was an incidental occurrence to rescuing Alpert. Of course, I feel terrible that she made the decision to stay here and even worse that we will be leaving without her, but as I said to you when this all happened, 'pray and embrace'. That's what I have to do. That's what we all must do," Euterpe explained.

"Pray and embrace. So true, what you say, my sister, and I am glad you feel that way, because I need to discuss something with you, and I hope you will still feel the same way when I am done," Elpee proclaimed to Euterpe before turning away and beckoning Alpert to join them.

IT IS ELPEE'S TURN

The two princesses and one *Queen* stood before Elpee in astonishment, wondering why she chose to take this precious time to have a discussion with them when it would serve them better for her to do so when they returned home. In a distorted contrast to their previous senses of emptiness, everyone was now on edge and wanted to leave this very distressing, goddess-abandoned place.

"I thought long and hard about the 'Pray-Embrace' theory . . . Literally long and hard, both at home and now here since you spoke those words to me earlier. I, for the first time, truly understand those words and what they represent. I can feel what they mean down to the depths of my soul, and again, for the first time I don't question anything about their significance," Elpee began her dissertation.

"Must we do this now?" asked danDay-leon, impatiently.

"Yes, my dear. Can't this discussion wait until we arrive home?" added PoliM'aladroit.

Elpee adamantly shook her head as they spoke, indicating the matter at hand was urgent and could not wait.

"No, it's not possible for this discussion to be postponed; it cannot be had later for reasons that will soon be revealed. Those two small words – pray and embrace – have laid the foundation upon which the present is rooted, and if you are unable to acknowledge the present as it exists, there will be no future as you identify it to be. I have had an ethereal involvement with those words and now fully understand the importance of their meaning and have come to realize that we *all* must pray and embrace if we are to separately, and perhaps collectively, be at home," Elpee said.

Everyone looked at her and each other in confusion while trying to understand the meaning in what she was saying, much as Elpee had felt when those words presented themselves to her back home. Alpert, who was now standing next to Elpee, completed the group of travelers scheduled to leave, all of whom looked uneasy with the thick and mysterious mood that pervaded their environment.

"Very simply, I must tell you all that I have exercised my right to use the 'Pray-Embrace' rule. I support Hortense's decision to remain here to obtain Alpert's freedom, but I also reject it unequivocally," Elpee said before turning to PoliM'aladroit and directing her next words to her.

"Back at my cottage before we left, you said to me that it didn't work that way, but you were wrong, my esteemed friend. It does indeed work that way. You were assuming that I would continue to blindly accept other's decisions even if they were an incorrect determination for me. I am as much entitled to exercise my freedom as anyone, or anything else is, at which point if my choices affect them, they in turn also can choose to adopt the 'Pray-Embrace' rule . . . Or not. You also said that 'once you know something, you can never not know it.' That, however, is entirely true. I recognize that the choices are mine, as are the consequences. I know I am free to execute a plan and that it is better implemented under the umbrella of consciousness than under the guise of ignorance."

With the exception of Alpert and Elpee herself, the others stood there listening to and looking at Elpee as if they were in an even more foreign land than they already were, and that she was speaking a dialect unbeknownst to them. Although they all still felt the critical need to leave, it was overshadowed, to a degree, by the message that Elpee was alluding to, but was not explicitly stating.

"I am sorry if I am confusing all of you with what I am saying, or perhaps by the way I am saying it, but it will all become clear in a minute," she said. Elpee then turned to Alpert and quietly whispered, "Perhaps they will long for these moments of ambiguity when they do know.

"Alpert is not a part of this, and just as Euterpe and Hortense consulted each other about the exchange of prisoners, Alpert and I discussed this matter. He is only recently aware of my plan and certainly had no part in it. Why would he have?"

Afraid that they would be sucked up into some vortex, or overstay their welcome, Euterpe jumped into the conversation and began directing comments and questions to Elpee.

"Elpee, sweetheart, I don't understand your words, no less what they are supposed to mean, but I suggest that we go now before something happens and we all get stranded here. We can discuss this all later, okay?" Euterpe said as she turned and began walking toward the water. The other two women nodded their heads and started following her.

"I suppose your way is as good as any . . . maybe even better than some, but not as good as others," Elpee responded as she put her arm in Alpert's arm and guided them both in the direction of the water.

ON THE DOCK

———

The entire party, consisting of Elpee, Alpert, Euterpe, danDay-leon, PoliM'aladroit, Butter, and the small gray creature, aka Macaroni, made their way to the water where they had parked the boat that was slated to carry them home.

The three women and two animals walked abreast, as if going into battle, while Elpee and Alpert held up the rear by a few steps. As the women neared the dock area, they began looking right and left in search of something. Their paces quickened as they drew closer to the launching area, and Elpee knew it was time for her to accelerate her own speed in order to join them. As she reached her sisters, she was inundated by a cacophony of questions.

"What is going on here?"

"Didn't you say you were securing everything?"

"What did you do when you came down here?"

"You said that you were going to ready everything?"

"What happened?

The din was deafening, and Elpee let the energy of the inquiries ebb until it was almost extinguished. In due course, the noise subsided to a level by which she could speak to the questions and have the explanations capable of being heard. She took a deep breath and made her announcement.

"The boat is gone. I have destroyed it."

Before continuing, Elpee took the opportunity to gather herself and take another breath while the others stood staring at her, some appearing more shocked than others.

"We started this adventure together back in the days of Cherry Castle, and we will continue this adventure together, in whatever land it is that we are now in. I find this place to be charismatic, and although it is quite different than what I have been used to, I have decided to stay here . . . At least for a while. I will not allow it to end any other way. All of you united to aid me in defeating Anna, and that caused us to lose one of our own – Alpert. Now, we have all come together to rescue him from this place, but certainly not at the expense of another of us. No one of us is greater or lesser than the whole. You have, everyone, taught me that," Elpee orated.

Each face that peered back at Elpee told a different tale. Despite their amalgamated astonishment at what had just taken place, none of the women appeared distressed by the outcome of Elpee's actions. A soundless contentment shrouded the atmosphere and its inhabitants. The four princesses and one *queen* gathered together and formed a circle, holding each other close physically and spiritually. An invisible bond that did not exist previously could be felt between these individuals as they meshed with each other on the wooden platform that had greeted them on their arrival. The women who landed on this shore were gone, and a new group had united to form a shared sisterhood through their hard-fought battles with themselves and their personal demons.

When the women let go of their hold on each other and separated, the sun in response reflected a warmth that replaced the icy chill, which had earlier engulfed the land. The melodious sounds of all nature's creatures filled the air, supplanting the earlier deafening silence, and the air was bursting with the sweet fragrances of the plentiful assortment of flora that surrounded them. In response to the drastic change that was taking place around them, Elpee pronounced to the Universe and her fellow travelers . . .

"Pray-Embrace, my friends."

And so, together they each did!

ELPEE AND ALPERT – THE LESSONS

As Elpee walked away from the water with Alpert, she clung tightly to his arm in a gesture of affection and appreciation for this silly wizard-man who patiently guided her and presented her with almost infinite lessons and options in the most peculiar of ways.

"Alpert, remember when you said that I lacked the ability to trust myself and my instincts?"

"Yes."

"Well, somehow I think you were right," Elpee professed.

"And, heavens, what would make you proclaim such an insightful declaration as that?" countered Alpert in contrived astonishment.

"Because, as much as it pains me to admit it, most of the times you were on target, but I didn't see it. Your visual displays were very effective tools in making that happen, I must say."

"Oh, please do elaborate," the immodest wizard entreated, more in search of obtaining compliments than in listening to Elpee's explanations.

"I am not a dummy, Alpert. You and I have been around a while together, so give me some credit, please," she replied to him, more as a demand than a request. "When the others and I first arrived here, I was in agreement with them, that this was truly a barren hell – that everything was unreal, and that you were half dead."

"And now you don't?" quizzed the quirky man who was walking alongside Elpee.

"Ummm, no. And how silly to ask me that when you are standing here looking anything but old, gaunt, and frail. You are seven feet tall and dapper as ever. The flowers were a nice touch too, but there was something about them that disturbed me. I could not reconcile that they could be so beautiful and yet utterly devoid of life. And then I realized that they were the product of the seeds I – or rather we – planted on the hill several lifetimes ago. I didn't fall for the chill either . . . Well, maybe at first, but it was a good test of my believing in my instincts."

"I did not lie. The seeds you planted that day were to sprout when you arrived home and were united with all that you love," responded Alpert to Elpee.

"I am not sure if the others are believing this to be what they say it is or if they are part of this final life lesson of mine, and perhaps the answer to that wonderment is completely of no consequence," Elpee continued.

"And your point?" the ever-pressing Albert inquired of her.

"Euterpe gave it away several times. When we were coming to see you, and I touched the flowers, she told me she knew how I felt and that everything was an illusion – which I now am certain we ourselves create – and she said that a solitary existence, if we choose to live that way, is a prison of the soul. Also, when she told me to Pray-Embrace the decision, which was arranged for your release, it made me realize that I was, once again, falling into other people's realities rather than defining my own. I have the right to decide for myself what is real, and they can come along for the ride or choose not to. And finally, she said that the decision to sacrifice Hortense for you was not solely hers; a happening that seemed to irritate her by having to play the charade. So, if I had to guess, I would say that Euterpe was an active player in this lesson by providing me with messages," Elpee stated her calculations.

"Brilliant, my little student! And the others?"

"Well, aside from you and Euterpe staging this whole giant lesson thing, I would say that Hortense was in on it too. That whole charade of running off to marry Cousin Chucklpe was to prod me to get angry enough to make some changes. ALSO, the big clue was when she asked why she should not trade places with you and disappear from my life. She knew that her flippant attitude of nonchalantly disappearing would push me to the point of saying, 'No more' to tolerating the role of being an extra in anyone's life and believing that everything was my fault. She tried to teach me that lesson over and over again, but it was not until this time when she made it known that her disappearance this time was different and would be forever. I realized that her actions were a reflection of who she was, not something I may or may not have done. She is a good egg with a big heart, but she can only give of herself as much as she possibly can in ways that she is capable of doing. So we are each other's lessons, I guess," the princess asserted, although she was still a bit on shaky ground regarding this foreign but freeing concept.

"Another excellent assessment! What about the other two princesses?"

"Heck, Alpert, you are challenging my already overtaxed brain and psyche," whined the exhausted Elpee.

Pinch

"Ouch, you big lug! Fine! I will continue, but you will be responsible for any type of emotional or physical breakdown I may suffer due to your incessant nosiness and need for answers. I don't think that either danDayleon or PoliM'aladroit were active performers in this lesson for several reasons. They did not, to my recollection, offer any hints that would make me think that they were aware of what was going on. I think that you, Euterpe, and Hortense kept them in the dark about what was going on and that their motives were entirely pure in aiding your release."

"Why?" countered the wizard.

"Oh, for crying out loud . . . Must you belabor my assertion? danDay is pure kindness and innocence, and I don't think she would pass muster in her ability to comfort me in my suffering while maintaining the secrecy of the intended mission. PoliM'aladroit is too principled and honest to withhold the fact that this was all a ruse – that you were not really being banished and we were supposedly executing your rescue. She would have been consumed with guilt and eventually cracked under the lie. How's that? *Now* I am done, you big dope."

With Elpee's last statement spoken, Alpert removed his Stetson, placed his bent arm at waist level, and bowed to her.

"You have, at last, 'figured it out,' and my hat is literally off to you," declared J. Alpert VII.

"YAY!! Now, let's celebrate. Why don't we go get the others, pack a lunch, and have a picnic with the dragonflies in our wildflower patch?" proposed the Princess of Her Own Life.

And so they did!

And so it would be!

TTFN (TA-TA FOR NOW)

"Oh, hello again. I hope you enjoyed accompanying my cronies and me on our fantastical journey into other worlds. Please know that it was but one chapter in an endless, unwritten story. We (the princesses, Alpert, the gnomes, elves, and furry pet-creatures) can stay here as long or as short a time as we choose to. After all, everything is impermanent, because, what is time? Where is distance? How does one gauge forever? Are destinations endpoints or merely way stations on our travels?

"No bother that this tale will be understood dissimilarly by those who have read it, as all of life is lived by subjective discernment. Perception – ah, now that is the key, which fits every lock in the Universe. Whether we elect to remove it from its fob and how we choose to utilize it is entirely up to us.

"Perhaps, those who are fixed to the fundamental concepts, which they are comfortably acquainted with, will view the adventure and everything contained within it as absolute and real. They will perceive this as a whimsically entertaining tale, which is perfectly perfect. There are times when probing for hidden meanings, messages, or significances is in conflict with the desire to swing on a moonbeam and enjoy a few chuckles.

"Others will wonder if anything at all was authentic or merely the ramblings of a person who had emotionally detached themselves from reality entirely. These people find themselves locked in places or circumstances they do not willingly choose to inhabit, and which will stretch the limits of their sanity. However, soundness is often evaluated by those who are either more educated or less reckless than others of us are. Can it be accurately measured by those who developed the tool to do so?

"*Finally, there are persons, who like me, view life as having the plasticity, in which it is possible to transform circumstances or at least observe them differently. They know that we are free to create our own adventures, alternate realities, and different destinies. They will recognize this as the written voice that whispers to them, 'It is time to peer deeper into your own soul and psyche to find your authentic self.'*"

"*In any event, and in all events, travel your own roads, make your own choices, learn your own lessons. Stay if you wish or leave to begin a new venture, but always look for, and heed, the messages that appear along the way. Build your own castles, read your own tea leaves, travel life with a kaleidoscope in your pocket, return those things to the earth that harm or no longer serve you, and find the flowers born from the seeds you have sown along the way, for then you will know you are home. People will think you odd or insane, and perhaps you are, but weigh your options. Is it better to leave and be deemed crazy or to stay and be driven mad?*"

"*The choice is always ours.*"

"*Thank you for coming along with me on my escapades! Possibly, we may meet again on a star located on the other side of never when never falls on the seventh, and the galaxy, which is as yet unnamed, appears in the western sky.*"

"*Love,*"

"*Elpee*"